"This is a hear[...]
find joy and lo[...]

—[...]

"Benson takes the reality TV world and bends it around in this charming contemporary romance."

—*RT Book Reviews* on *Bet on a Cowboy*

"A great book! A well-written romance, funny and entertaining."

—*Harlequin Junkie* on *Bet on a Cowboy*

Praise for *USA TODAY* bestselling author Angi Morgan

"Morgan pens a lovely comeback story of a hero fighting his inner demons and struggling with PTSD. With equal parts action, romance and compelling characters, she hits all the right notes."

—*RT Book Reviews* on *The Cattleman*, Top Pick, 4.5 stars

"From the echoing shots in a cemetery straight through the hair-raising conclusion, this story of missing memories and murders will rattle readers from the opening pages, as they guess and guess again who the real culprit is."

—*RT Book Reviews* on *Dangerous Memories*

"A great mix of drama, romance, suspense.... Well written, fast paced read... Strong chemistry and connection that leads to some steamy love scenes.... I thoroughly recommend this book to anyone who enjoys romantic suspense."

—*Goodreads* on *Bulletproof Badge*

HOME ON THE RANCH:
FAMILY TIES

———————— ⚒ ————————

JULIE BENSON

USA TODAY Bestselling Author
ANGI MORGAN

⟨H⟩ HARLEQUIN® HOME ON THE RANCH

ISBN-13: 978-1-335-50710-5

First published as Cowboy in the Making by Harlequin Books in 2014 and The Renegade Rancher by Harlequin Books in 2014.

Home on the Ranch: Family Ties
Copyright © 2018 by Harlequin Books S.A.

Recycling programs for this product may not exist in your area.

The publisher acknowledges the copyright holders of the individual works as follows:

Cowboy in the Making
Copyright © 2014 by Julie Benson

The Renegade Rancher
Copyright © 2014 by Angela Platt

This edition published by arrangement with Harlequin Books S.A.

For questions and comments about the quality of this book, please contact us at CustomerService@Harlequin.com.

® and TM are trademarks of Harlequin Enterprises Limited or its corporate affiliates. Trademarks indicated with ® are registered in the United States Patent and Trademark Office, the Canadian Intellectual Property Office and in other countries.

www.Harlequin.com

Printed in U.S.A.

CONTENTS

An avid daydreamer since childhood, **Julie Benson** always loved creating stories. After graduating from the University of Texas at Dallas with a degree in sociology, she worked as a case manager before having her children: three boys. Many years later she started pursuing a writing career to challenge her mind and save her sanity. Now she writes full-time in Dallas, where she lives with her husband, their sons, two lovable black dogs, two guinea pigs, a turtle and a fish. When she finds a little quiet time, which isn't often, she enjoys making jewelry and reading a good book.

Books by Julie Benson

Harlequin American Romance

Big City Cowboy
Bet on a Cowboy
The Rancher and the Vet
Roping the Rancher
Cowboy in the Making

Visit the Author Profile page at Harlequin.com for more titles.

COWBOY IN THE MAKING

JULIE BENSON

For Jennifer Jacobson

Without your support, encouragement and musical expertise this book never would have been written. You are such a shining example of God's love here on Earth, and I'm so blessed to have you in my life.

And thanks to the Starbucks crew at Custer and Renner in Richardson, especially Jason, Angel, Susan, Christine, Ashley (both of them!), Derek and Nate for keeping me caffeinated while I wrote this one. You're the best!

Chapter 1

"I heard the bad news about the Philharmonic letting you go. How're you doing?"

James Westland's hand tightened around his cell phone as he tried to shove aside his growing irritation at his friend Connor's comment. What he wouldn't give for a call from a charity asking for a donation or a wrong number. He'd even be thrilled with an obscene call. Anything but a call from another friend or relative asking how he was holding up.

How the hell did everyone expect him to be when his career was becoming a distant spec in his rearview mirror? Of course he was pissed. At first he'd tried drowning his anger in a bottle of Jameson, but all that did was leave him with a bad hangover. Now he'd reached the not-sure-what-the-hell-to-do stage.

"I'm fine. I'm assessing my options." He almost laughed. *Right. You've got so many of those to choose from.*

Unlike his siblings, Jamie had never excelled in school. He'd studied twice as hard to earn low B's and C's. For their paltry efforts, his sisters had scored straight A's. One now possessed an MBA and the other a degree in engineering. Education that offered them more options, while he'd put all his career eggs into the music basket, leaving him little to fall back on now.

"My sister teaches at a private school in Manhattan," Connor said. "I could see if she knows of anyone who's looking for a music teacher."

"Sure," he said mainly out of ingrained politeness and because he couldn't afford to rule out any ideas at this point.

How could a simple Sunday morning bike ride have ended up turning his life upside down? He still had trouble letting go of the what-ifs.

What if I'd slept in? What if the guy in the parked car had been as concerned about the world around him as his coffee? Would he have opened the door and knocked me to the ground? What if I hadn't tried to break my fall? Would I have hurt my hand so bad?

"I don't know what I'd do if I couldn't play the cello anymore," Connor said, breaking through Jamie's thoughts.

There it was. The barely veiled invitation to spill his guts and say how angry he was or how he was falling apart. If anyone else hinted he was concerned he'd do something stupid like jump off the Brooklyn Bridge, he might throw his phone off said bridge.

His left hand cramped and he switched his phone to his right, staring at the offending appendage as if it should look different. How many people would be thrilled to have the mobility he possessed, and yet for him, it wasn't enough. "It's taking some adjusting to, but I'm managing."

"Maybe you should get away. Take some time to clear your head."

Or at least get away before the well-intentioned people in his life drove him insane. He considered visiting his parents in Philadelphia, but tossed the idea aside. While he loved them, they were planners. They analyzed a situation, determined the risks and probability of success for each option and then acted. That's what they'd want to do with this situation—provide him with a feasibility study. He couldn't take the in-person seminar right now. The phone version had been bad enough.

A picture of his grandfather's small ranch in the Rocky Mountains flashed in Jamie's mind. A simple two-story house straight out of a Norman Rockwell painting with a big old-fashioned porch with rocking chairs perfect for thinking. Going to Colorado was what he needed. There he could clear his head and sort things out.

Mick would understand what he was going through because he'd experienced the same uncertainty when he'd returned from Vietnam after shrapnel from a land mine had torn up his right leg, arm and hand, ending his own musical career. While he'd understand, Mick wouldn't pry. Nor would anyone else in Estes Park, because very few of the town's eight thousand residents knew more about him than that he was Mick's grandson.

Except Emma, but then, last he'd heard she was living in Nashville.

"Jamie, you still there?" Connor asked. "I wish there was something I could do."

Out of patience now that he had a plan, Jamie thanked his friend for checking about the teaching possibilities, ended the conversation and called Mick. When the old man answered, Jamie said, "Mind if I come for a visit?"

"The door's always open to you."

"Great. I'll be on a plane tomorrow."

"You know I'm not one to ask a lot of nosy questions, and tell me if I'm outta line doing it now. It won't hurt my feelings none, but I hear something in your voice so I gotta ask. Is something wrong?"

Unlike when others asked, Mick's question didn't irritate Jamie. "When you got hurt and couldn't perform, did everyone keep asking what you were going to do with your life?"

"Your hand didn't heal right," Mick said in a matter-of-fact voice.

"The doctor says everything looks fine, but when I play my hand doesn't work like it used to. My fingers get knotted up. The dexterity and flexibility just isn't there." Jamie explained how music he'd once played without conscious effort now proved difficult. To the untrained ear he might not sound too bad, but unless things changed, he wouldn't be returning to the Philharmonic anytime soon. "The doctor says there's a chance my hand will get better. He says strengthening may be all it needs."

Keep telling yourself that so you can hang on to the hope that your career isn't over.

"Nothing will do that better than good old-fashioned hard work around the ranch and the restaurant, and I've got plenty to do at both places. In fact, I could use a bartender."

"Making mixed drinks is an art form nowadays. That's out of my league."

Mick laughed. "Maybe in New York City, but most folks that come into my place aren't big on fancy mixed drinks. They order a beer on tap or in a bottle. Other than that it's pouring whiskey or making margaritas for the ladies. I can show you how to do that."

"I think I can handle that."

"Good. I'll see you tomorrow. Let me know when your flight gets in. I'll pick you up at the airport."

Jamie thought about telling Mick he'd rent a car, but right now he'd rather avoid the expense. He had some money in savings, but only enough to last a couple of months. Considering his uncertain future, best to be frugal.

"For what it's worth, I know what you're going through, and I wouldn't wish it on my worst enemy," Mick said. "It really knocked my feet out from under me for a while."

That's right where Jamie was. Flat on his back trying to figure out what to do once he found the energy to stand again.

"People didn't realize playing and singing were a part of me," Mick continued. "When I lost that, it was like a part of me died, and I had to grieve. Until I did, I couldn't move on. Most people didn't get that. They wanted to help, but their concern most times made it worse."

"Concern I can take. It's the pity that's pissing me off."

"Don't let this get you down, son. I know it seems

bad now, but an unexpected blessing can find its way
into situations like this."

Jamie shook his head. If there was something good
in the midst of this mess, fate was doing a damned good
job hiding the fact.

Emma Donovan stared at Molly, the fiddle player in
her band, Maroon Peak Pass, standing in the doorway
of her office at the Estes Park animal shelter.

There's a woman with bad news to deliver.

"I can't do this anymore, Em."

Emma tried not to cringe. This couldn't be happening again. Every time she thought her musical career
would take off and she'd land a record deal, something
happened to snatch defeat out of the jaws of victory.

"I'm in the middle of preparing for a volunteer orientation today. Can we do this later, Molly?"

*As in possibly never, since I don't think I'm going
to like what you have to say. I definitely don't have the
energy to deal with it today.*

"This can't wait," Molly said. The look in her gaze
only confirmed Emma's suspicions of impending doom.

As she tried to quell the unease churning in her stomach, Emma motioned for Molly to have a seat in the
wooden chair on the opposite side of her less-than-im-
pressive desk. Ah, the joys of working for a nonprofit
agency. Rickety, cheap furniture.

"It's Dave, isn't it?" Emma said. Since Molly's mar-
riage six months ago, she'd changed, showing up late
for rehearsals and wanting to leave early. When she was
there, she was distracted and unprepared. "He's pres-
suring you to leave the band, isn't he?"

She knew what that was like. *Emma, you need to*

*grow up. Playing in a band is fine for a hobby, but it's
not a real job.*

"It's not him. He's supportive of my musical career."
Molly picked at the strap of the purse sitting in her lap.
"It's me. I'm tired of putting my life on hold hoping for
a career that's a one-in-a-million shot."

"What're you trying to say?"

"I'm leaving the band."

There was the blow Emma had been expecting, but
even though she'd braced herself, it still left her reeling.
All she could think was thank goodness she'd been sitting. Otherwise the news would have leveled her. Her
mind scrambled to process the chaos Molly's decision
created. No, she couldn't go there, refused to accept bad
news until she knew she couldn't change it. "You can't
quit. We're so close. I feel it. Hold off a little longer. At
least until the state fair contest."

This year the Colorado state fair was having a music
competition with the winner receiving a consultation
with Phillip Brandise, one of the top movers and shakers in country music.

"I want to have kids. My biological clock's ticking
so loud I'm going deaf. I'm afraid if I don't make some
changes now I'll wake up one day and it'll be too late.
I'll have given up everything that really matters, and for
what? Nights spent on the stage in two-bit restaurants
and bars. I've taken a job as an orchestra director at a
private school in Denver, and Dave's requested a trans-
fer. We should be able to buy a house in a few months,
and hopefully soon we'll be pregnant. The movers arrive this weekend to pack everything up."

Emma stared at the other woman, someone she
thought she knew fairly well, as if she'd said she was

going to take up brain surgery. "How can you give up now?"

"I've found something I want more. I'll still have music in my life. It just won't be the center of my universe."

Now that Emma's shock had subsided, her anger kicked in. How dare Molly bail on the rest of the band? People who had counted on her, who thought they'd shared the same goal. "We've got appearances scheduled and the state fair is less than a month away. What're we supposed to do? Do you know how long it will take to find a replacement?"

"I meant to talk to you when I applied for the teaching position, but the time never seemed right."

"Really? I seem to remember a lot of opportunities that would've been perfect. How about when we talked about signing up for the state fair contest, or when we were planning career strategies for next year to increase our visibility and presence on social media? Those would've been pretty good times to mention you were thinking about quitting."

Molly nodded and clasped her hands in her lap. "You're right. The truth is I didn't want to face you. I didn't think you'd understand."

She was right about that. Emma didn't understand how someone could let go of a dream she'd spent years working toward, especially when they were so close.

How could they find another fiddle player, integrate that person into the band and be ready for a performance at a major contest in less than a month?

She'd manage that because she had to. Sure, she enjoyed her job at the shelter, but she didn't want to spend the rest of her life as a volunteer coordinator. Music was her life. Playing the guitar, singing and writing songs wasn't what she did. It was a part of who she was, but playing in local bars and at weddings wasn't enough. She wanted more, and no way would she let this opportunity pass her by. She'd do whatever was necessary to keep her dream alive. Nothing else mattered.

"I won't lie. I don't understand how you can say teaching music to children will be enough for you, but if you think that'll make you happy, then that's what you have to do."

I just wish your decision wasn't throwing my dream into a tailspin, but if you don't want this as much as I do, then it's a good thing you're leaving.

As she watched Molly leave, Emma thought, *six months*. That's all it would take before Molly called to say she'd made a mistake leaving the band. Life could sidetrack people with dreams. Parents got sick. Keeping a roof over their heads or wanting to eat food other than ramen noodles got in the way, but ambitions like theirs never died.

She glanced at her notes for her volunteer orientation and training but couldn't focus. As day jobs went, hers as volunteer coordinator for the Estes Park animal shelter was a pretty good one. It had its perks, the biggest of which being on tough days like today she could hide in the kennels and play with puppies until she could face the world. Yup. A little puppy therapy was the only thing that kept her going today.

Twenty minutes later Emma looked up from her spot on the kennel floor when her best friend and boss, Avery Montgomery, walked in. "You're playing with puppies. What's wrong?"

"Some days it doesn't pay to get out of bed unless you cuddle puppies." Emma pulled the wiggling black bundle closer to her chest as she gave Avery a quick rundown of her conversation with Molly. "Unless we find a new fiddle player, last weekend's performance may have been Maroon Peak Pass's swan song."

"What're the chances you can find a replacement relatively quickly?" Avery asked as she settled onto the floor beside Emma. One fluffy, roly-poly pup crawled off Emma's lap and waddled over to her friend.

"It's harder than you think. Talented musicians who are serious about their craft are already in bands and most aren't looking to change."

"Can you go on without a fiddle if you can't find someone else in time for the state fair contest?"

"It's hard enough to stand out among all the country acts. Adding Molly helped define our sound. Now all of our arrangements and the new music I've written are for a band with a fiddle. I don't want to think about how long it would take to rework everything. We'd definitely have to cancel our upcoming engagements."

"I'm sorry, Em. I know how much the band means to you." Avery scooped up a pup and scratched him behind the ears.

Avery was one of the few people in her life who truly understood how her need for a career in country music drove her. Emma wished her family understood better. They couldn't grasp why she wasn't content with her job at the shelter. It was stable and provided her with a paycheck every two weeks. She could play musician on the weekends. Why did she want more? She couldn't put her need into words. She only knew she couldn't settle for less than giving a music career her best shot.

Not now, when she was older and wiser than when she'd dashed off to Nashville at eighteen all full of hopes and dreams but not much common sense.

"I wish Molly had waited a little longer to quit. Even a day. I could've handled it better. Why did she have to tell me today?" Emma bit her lip and tried to ignore the ache spreading through her. "He turns seven today. Between that and Molly's bombshell, it's too much to take."

Seven years ago she gave birth to a son and watched the nurse walk out of the room to hand him to someone else to raise.

Chapter 2

Emma didn't even know her son's name.

The pain that enveloped her after she'd given him up for adoption had been overwhelming. Looking back she had no idea how she'd gotten through those first few months, but somehow she had. While the sting had lessened over the years, her emotions still flared up at times. Certain days were worse than others—Christmas, Mother's Day and her son's birthday. Each year they became easier to get through, but something was different with his birthday this year.

"I'm sorry, Em. I forgot what today was. I can't imagine how tough this is for you every year."

"I think of him a lot, but I've been doing that more than usual lately. Sometimes I wonder what he looks like and what he's doing. Does he like sports? Is he taking piano lessons?" The list of questions was endless. Did he have her dark coloring and green eyes, or Tucker's golden hair and brown eyes? Had he inherited their musical ability?

The puppy she held snuggled closer to her chest all warm and fuzzy, full of endless energy and unconditional love. While puppy kisses couldn't fix all the world's problems, they definitely helped. "The questions I understand, but it shouldn't hurt this much. It didn't last year. I don't get what's going on."

"Have you contacted—" Avery paused for a minute, lines of concern evident on her beautiful face.

Emma recognized the awkwardness. It showed up whenever anyone considered saying a certain phrase to her.

"It's okay. You can say the word. *Parents.* Have I contacted his parents?"

"Have you? Maybe they've changed their minds about the closed adoption. Could be they'd agree to send you photos or updates on how he's doing. Then you wouldn't have to wonder."

"You know me. I'm an all-or-nothing kind of girl. When I quit dating a guy I can't be friends. How could I be happy with emails and a few pictures?"

"I wish I had an answer for you."

Emma did, too. It would be so much easier if life came with an instruction manual. Then, during the rough spots, she could flip the book open and read the directions. For this type of life problem, do A, then B and everything will turn out great.

"I bet Tucker never thinks about me or our son." He'd barely thought about her when they were living together. The familiar anger welled up inside her—at him for his wandering eye, and other body parts for that

matter, as well as at herself for her schoolgirl foolish-
ness. "His band with that trailer-trash Miranda Lambert
imitation has a top-ten album. They're on a world tour,
performing in front of thousands of people while I'm
playing weddings and anniversary parties."

And working a day job to pay the bills.

She and Tucker had been high school sweethearts
and the star vocalists in the choir. The fall after graduation they'd packed up their belongings and headed for
Nashville. Soon after arriving, Emma had discovered
there were hundreds of other young hopefuls who'd
done the same thing, and breaking into the industry
was tougher than they'd imagined.

Her relationship with Tucker hadn't gone accord-
ing to plan, either. Things grew rocky between them
within a week and got steadily worse. Then, two days
after she'd told him she was pregnant, he'd waltzed
into their dumpy studio apartment and announced he
didn't love her anymore. Just like that. No buildup. No
preparation. No warning. Since by that point she wasn't
all that crazy about him either, it was a horrible relief
when he moved out.

"Hearing about how well his career is going has to
be tough," Avery said.

"I don't begrudge him his success—"

"You may not, but I sure do. He didn't earn it. Not
when the song that got him noticed and led to his recording contract was yours, too."

"I've changed my mind. You're right. He doesn't
deserve it." When Emma had stumbled across a video
of him on YouTube, she'd discovered the ass had taken
one of the songs they'd written, though he swore he
wrote it alone, changed the lyrics slightly—emphasis

on *slightly*—and performed it with his new band. The song's video had received over a million hits and landed him a recording contract.

That blow had broken Emma's spirit. Skinny because her morning sickness lasted all day, broke and depressed, she'd hit rock bottom, packed up her meager belongings and headed home to patch up her wounds. "How could I have fallen in love with such an ass?"

"Cut yourself some slack. You were young, and he was your first love." Avery released her squirming pup, who bounded off and tackled one of his siblings.

Age and lack of experience explained her mistake with Tucker, but what about Clint? She couldn't say the same for him, since she'd made that blunder two years ago. How could she have missed the fact that he was nothing more than Tucker version two-point-oh?

"We need to make a Tucker voodoo doll," Avery said.

"Now, why didn't I think of that? The idea has definite possibilities."

"I wonder if he'd lose his voice if we stuck pins where his vocal chords are."

"Better yet, let's harpoon him in another more private area and hope he loses use of that little piece of equipment." That would serve him right for hooking up with every blonde who could carry a tune—even if she needed a bucket to do it—when they were together.

"That's the spirit. All guys aren't like him, you know."

Avery had always believed in love and happily ever after. Even after her high school sweetheart had left for Stanford and broken up with her via email. Then, a year ago, Reed's brother was deployed to Afghanistan and he returned to Estes Park to stay with his teenage niece. After a bumpy ride, the pair had cleared the air, fallen in love all over again and married soon after that.

"If you want to take the day off, I can handle things around here."

Emma shook her head. "Thanks, but no, thanks. I'd rather be here and stay busy. If I go home all I'll do is throw on sweatpants and crawl on the couch to eat Häagen-Dazs Chocolate Chocolate Chip ice cream while I watched *Thelma and Louise*. That's just a pathetic pity party, and I refuse to do that." Not now. Not when she'd come so far. "But you can help me make that voodoo doll."

Mick Halligan stopped when he walked into his restaurant. For a minute he stood and surveyed what he'd built. With the Formica tables, industrial-style chairs with the plastic padded seats and the country memorabilia, some people would call his place a hick bar, but looks were deceiving. His restaurant was so much more. People came to Halligan's to connect, to celebrate special times with family and friends. Everyone, staff and customers, knew each other and their lives were interconnected. They meant something to each other.

"I've got a plan, but I need your help," Mick said to his friend of almost fifty years and fellow Vietnam War vet, Gene Donovan, when he walked into the kitchen.

"Is it something for the business?" Gene asked as he stood chopping onions for the marinara sauce for the meatball sub sandwiches.

"This has to do with family. Mine and yours."

"You know whatever it is, I'm in."

"I knew you would be, but I thought I'd ask anyway." Mick sometimes wondered how he would've made it through the hell of Vietnam if Gene hadn't been there in the trenches with him. They'd kept each other sane through the madness. Then, when shrapnel had torn Mick apart and he'd lain in a heap bleeding like a stuck pig, Gene had literally saved his life. Risking his own neck under heavy gunfire, Gene had made his way to Mick and dragged him to safety.

"I've been thinking about what matters in my life. It's family, friends, my ranch and this place. What good is having land and a business if I don't have anyone to leave them to?"

"You've got your daughter."

A daughter who'd written him off along with the rest of her past. Having a cowboy, Vietnam-vet father who ran a country-western bar didn't sit well with Kimberly or her hotshot corporate executive husband.

"Fat lot of good that does me." When he'd realized Kimberly wouldn't visit him for fear of her husband learning about her wild-child past and the son she'd given up for adoption, Mick had offered to come to California, but she always had an excuse why that wouldn't work. They were moving or remodeling the house. Her husband was in the middle of a big deal at work. While he wasn't the sharpest tool in the shed, Mick had finally got the message and stopped asking.

"If I leave everything to Kimberly, all she'll do is sell what I've built and pocket the money. I'm not about to spend eternity rolling over in my grave because a developer built condos or a resort on my land, and I don't even want to think about what she'd do to this place."

Gene nodded in agreement. "That would make for an unhappy afterlife. What do you have in mind to do about it?"

"I've been thinking about Jamie. He understands the way I feel about the land and this place." Mick smiled at the memories and the wonder in his grandson's eyes when they'd ridden around the ranch for the first time. The kid had taken to being on a horse like he'd been on one all his life. Some things were just in a man's blood, and Mick knew the land was in Jamie's. "I want to leave everything to him."

"Then do it."

"I intend to, but I miss having family around. I miss Jamie. He's my only grandchild. Hell, my only real family other than you." Since his wife, Carol, had died five years ago, the loneliness had settled into Mick's bones and his soul.

Mick glanced at the clock on the wall. The other staff wouldn't arrive for at least a half hour. Good. He didn't want anyone overhearing what he was about to say to his old friend. "I'm going to tell you something, but you've got to promise not to tell anyone."

"Haven't I kept more than one of your secrets over the years?"

"You sure have, but this one's different. It's not my secret."

Gene glared at him. "Like that makes a difference to me."

"Jamie's hand didn't heal right." Mick explained about his grandson's troubles. "I keep thinking about when I had to give up music. It damn near killed me. This place, your friendship and the love of a good woman saved me."

"Are you getting to the point about the plan and needing my help anytime soon?"

"Hold your horses. I had to tell you all this before I

could get to my idea," Mick said, taking his time despite his friend's good-natured ribbing. "Jamie and your Emma would be perfect for each other. Who knows what would've happened between them if he hadn't gone back to Juilliard at the end of that summer. Hell, they might even be married by now."

"That's a mighty big leap you just took. Sure, they dated, but as I remember, it wasn't anything serious."

"If you ask me, it would've gotten serious if Jamie had been planning on sticking around. You can't tell me there wasn't a spark between our grandkids. I saw it. Could be all they need now is a little nudge to get things restarted. What harm can some matchmaking do? Mothers and grandmothers have been doing it for years."

"And men have been telling them to knock it off."

"Since we can lead the horses to water but can't make them drink, what do we have to lose?"

"They could get so mad they won't speak to us," Gene said as he stirred the simmering barbeque sauce for the pulled pork sandwiches. "That's a real possibility considering how Emma feels about musicians. She rates them between politicians and lawyers."

"This is my grandson we're talking about. Emma won't find a better man than Jamie anywhere."

"That's true, but considering the way Kimberly acted when Jamie contacted her, do you think he can get past the fact that Emma gave up a child for adoption?"

Mick still couldn't believe a child of his and Carol's had acted the way their daughter had when Jamie had contacted her ten years ago. Instead of welcoming the eighteen-year-old, his daughter had told Jamie she wanted nothing to do with him and slammed the door in his face.

Then she'd called Mick, who'd told her to be honest with her husband, insisting a man who'd leave her over getting pregnant at sixteen and giving the child up wasn't worth holding on to. What he'd got for his advice was a lecture about what a wonderful man his son-in-law was and a request that Mick not have any contact with Jamie, either.

He'd told his daughter straight-out that she could do what she wanted with her life, but she couldn't tell him what to do with his, and he'd set out to locate his grandson. When he'd found Jamie a few months later, he'd invited him for a visit, and Jamie had flown to Colorado for spring break.

"I can't tell you why, but I know your granddaughter and my grandson are meant to be together. You're just gonna have to trust me."

Gene shook his head. "I would like to see Emma happy with a man who'll treat her right. What do you have in mind?"

"First, I think I'll be too sick tomorrow to pick Jamie up at the airport, and you'll be too busy handling everything here at the restaurant to go."

"And I'll ask my granddaughter to help out by picking up Jamie."

"That's the first step."

The enticing smell of tomatoes sautéing with garlic wafted through the air as Emma rushed in the kitchen door to Halligan's. Her mouth watered and her stomach growled, making her wish she hadn't punched the snooze button so many times she had to skip breakfast. Now all she could think of was how her grandfather's meatball sub would hit the spot.

After giving Grandpa G a quick kiss on his weathered cheek, she asked, "What's so important that I have to drop everything and come over here?"

While she loved her family, sometimes she wished there weren't so many of them, or that a few of them lived farther away. Both sets of grandparents, her father and three older brothers all living in one town of eight thousand people could be overwhelming. Worse yet, she couldn't catch a cold without her entire family knowing about it within an hour, and half of them calling with advice, and yet, how often had she been at family gatherings and felt completely alone?

"Mick called. He's sick, so I have to handle things around here."

"It's not anything serious, is it?"

Her grandfather shook his head. "It's just a stomach bug, but there's no way he can make the drive to Denver to pick up his grandson at the airport. He wanted me to ask if you'd help him out by picking Jamie up."

She hadn't thought about Jamie Westland in a long time. For two summers when she was in high school they'd worked together at Halligan's. They'd even dated a few times after she'd broken up with Tucker when she'd discovered he'd been two-timing her with Monica Ritz. Had that been a big red flag waving in her face, warning her of what life would be like with Tucker, or what?

But Jamie had been different. When they'd been together he'd made her feel as though she mattered, because he'd focused solely on her. They'd gone out for pizza and caught a couple of movies that summer. Nothing major, because they'd both known he'd be returning to Juilliard in the fall. Well, except for some heavy necking. What would've happened between them if he hadn't been returning to New York? If their plans hadn't been so different? Would she still have gotten back together with Tucker? She shook her head. What good did wondering do? It wasn't as if she could change the past.

"You could have asked me that on the phone, Grandpa. If you had, it would've saved me a trip over here, and I could've had breakfast."

"Why didn't you tell me you hadn't eaten?" Her grandfather strode to the refrigerator and grabbed what she recognized as the ingredients for her favorite breakfast—an omelet with spinach, mushrooms and Roma tomatoes.

"Feeding me won't get you what you want. I can't pick Jamie up at the airport. I've got a volunteer orientation and training all day."

"That's not a problem. His flight doesn't get in until eight tonight," Grandpa G said as he threw together her omelet and poured the egg mixture into a hot pan.

So much for the convenient excuse. "Can't Jamie rent a car?"

"He's from New York City. Who knows if he can drive?"

There were people in the U.S. who couldn't drive? Really? She found that hard to believe. She thought about the summer she and Jamie had dated. "Wait a minute. I remember him driving Mick's truck on a couple of our dates."

"Oh, well. Hmm. I forgot about that." Her grandfather shuffled back and forth, his brows furrowed together in thought as he concentrated on the pan in front of him. Then he plated her omelet and handed the mouthwatering goodness to her along with a fork. "Of course, that was before he spent all those years in the

Big Apple. Who knows if he still has a valid driver's license?"

"You can't be serious." She scooped up a bite of her omelet. The fluffy concoction melted in her mouth. No matter how many times she tried, hers never turned out like Grandpa G's, but she wouldn't let his wonderful cooking sway her.

"All I know is that Mick asked me to ask you to pick up Jamie at the airport, and that's what I'm doing. I don't know why you're being so difficult."

She was being difficult? She didn't know what alien had taken over her grandfather's body, but there was no reasoning with him today. "With as much family as we have in town there has to be someone else who can pick him up."

Grandpa G placed the knife on the cutting board, turned and stared at her. He waved his hand around the kitchen. "Does it look like I have time to call around to find someone else to do this for me?"

Line cooks, dishwashers and everyone else in the kitchen froze, turned and stared with their mouths hanging open in disbelief at her grandfather's sharp tone.

Now she knew something was wrong. Either that or he'd taken cranky pills along with his vitamins this morning. In her entire life she never remembered him raising his voice to anyone. She stepped around the counter and placed her hand on his arm. "What's really going on?"

He rubbed the back of his neck, and when he met her gaze, weariness filled his usually bright eyes. "I'm nervous about handling everything around here with Mick out today."

Things were growing stranger by the minute. Her

grandfather routinely managed the restaurant when Mick was gone without breaking a sweat. He'd once told her that after a tour in Vietnam, he'd handled the worst life had to throw at him and nothing else could ever come close.

"Are you sure that's all that's bothering you?"

"Emma Jean, with a *J,* unlike my name, Gene with a *G,* Donovan. Do this little favor for me. Pick Jamie up at the airport. Then I won't have to worry about it."

How could she say no to that, especially after he'd pulled out the big guns by making her favorite breakfast and using her full name, emphasizing the fact that she'd been named after him? The question was why was this so important? Instinct told her she wasn't getting the whole story.

"I'll make a deal," she conceded. "I'll call around. If I can't find someone else to pick Jamie up, I will."

Her grandfather yanked the towel off his apron and swiped the cloth almost frantically across the counter, clearing away the remnants of mushrooms and spinach he'd chopped for her omelet. "You promise you'll pick Jamie up if no one else can?"

She nodded, and his rigid stance relaxed. "I heard about Molly quitting the band. Are you having any luck finding a replacement?"

The abrupt change in conversation left her a little dizzy. While he supported her musical career more than most of her family, she could count the number of times on one hand her grandfather had asked about the business side of things. "I've got some possibilities, but I've been so busy with my day job I haven't had time to contact anyone."

Luke, her bass player, had offered to make the calls,

but Emma had gently nixed the suggestion. She'd put Maroon Peak Pass together. She managed their engagements, wrote their music and created their arrangements of other artists' songs. No way was anyone being scheduled to audition without her screening him first.

"You know Jamie's a fiddle player," her grandfather said. "What about asking him to play with you?"

"There's a big difference between playing in a country band and performing with a symphony. Asking Jamie to join Maroon Peak Pass would be like asking a soccer player to all of a sudden play football." As if Jamie would be interested anyway. Had her grandfather lost his mind?

"Soccer players often become kickers in football."

Vitamins. Check. Cranky pills. Check. Add taking crazy pills to the list.

"I was just throwing the idea out there."

"That's something to consider." But only if it was between canceling the band's upcoming engagements, asking Jamie or recruiting someone from the high school orchestra.

Later that night Emma arrived at the Denver airport only to discover Jamie's flight had been delayed by bad weather. She'd tried to find someone else to pick him up, but she should've known how that plan would turn out and saved the time she'd wasted. Why was it whenever she needed help everyone in her family had a ready excuse? Brandon had to work at the fire station, but he was the only one with a valid reason. Everyone else either had plans like getting together with friends, or worse, they hadn't bothered to return her call.

At least she'd brought her tablet so she could work

while she waited. As she sat in the unyielding chairs
in the baggage claim area, she put out word on social
media about the band's situation. That done, she contacted the electric fiddle players she'd thought of, managing to coerce two to audition. She called the people
Luke and Grayson, their drummer, had recommended,
screened them and set up auditions for a couple, despite the fact that none of the candidates seemed overly
promising. The kids in the high school orchestra were
looking better all the time. Lord, desperation was ugly.

The grind of the baggage claim broke into her
thoughts, and she gazed at the monitor above the carousel, noting Jamie's flight had arrived.

She scanned the rush of passengers streaming into
the baggage claim area. Picking Jamie out of the crowd
would have been easy even if he hadn't been carrying
the violin case. In the years since she'd seen him, his
resemblance to Mick had become more pronounced.
Same whiskey-colored straight hair, strong jaw, stark
cheekbones and five-o'clock shadow. Normally she
didn't like the scruffy look on men, but on Jamie, it
worked. Very well.

His long, lean build had filled out and his shoulders
were broader now. He'd changed from a teenager to a
man. When he moved toward her, her pulse jumped
and the tiniest warm glow spread through her. For a
city boy, he sure had Mick's Western swagger down.
Who'd have guessed that was genetic?

As she approached, his gaze zeroed in on her with
an intensity that left her almost weak. She didn't know
what had happened in the years since she'd seen him,
but something had because it showed in his eyes. Good
looks she could ignore because a pretty face could dis-

guise a multitude of flaws, but eyes like Jamie's? That was tougher to resist. She'd always been a sucker for soulful eyes.

Too bad he had such a big strike against him—being a musician. Otherwise it might be fun getting reacquainted because he was one fine-looking man. But Emma knew better than to press her luck. For Jamie Westland, as far as she was concerned, one strike and he was out.

Chapter 3

"Emma? Right?" Jamie said, his deep brown eyes filled with curiosity when she reached him. "What're you doing here? Are you meeting someone?"

"Mick didn't tell you I was picking you up? He wasn't feeling well," she said, trying to ignore her bruised feminine ego. While they hadn't seen each other in years, how could he not remember her? They weren't exactly strangers. Not that anyone would know from his reaction to seeing her today.

No woman wanted to realize she'd been so forgettable a guy she'd dated couldn't even remember her name.

"He might have left me a message, but I forgot to turn my phone back on." Jamie reached into his back pocket and pulled out his cell.

"I guess you're not one of those people who are constantly attached to the thing, then, huh?"

"Sometimes it's nice to unplug and really get away." Heaviness tinged his voice and she wondered if something more than a simple vacation brought him to Estes Park. She shoved aside her curiosity. He was a nice guy, but considering what she had going on in her life she needed a man like she needed a two-string guitar that was out of tune.

"Sure enough. I've got a missed call from Mick and have a voice mail," he said once he turned on his phone and glanced at the screen. After he listened to the message he said, "He probably called while I was in the air."

The grumble of the baggage conveyor belt and the conversations of family and friends reuniting swirled around them, making her more aware of the awkwardness between them.

"You didn't have to drive all the way here to pick me up. I could've rented a car."

She laughed. "You should've heard the conversation I had with my grandfather about that. He wondered if you had a valid driver's license. When I reminded him that you knew how to drive, he wondered if you'd forgotten since you live in New York City."

No reaction to her reference to their past relationship. Ouch.

"He said that? Is this the same man who could recall every memory from the time he was three with uncanny clarity? That grandfather?"

"That's the one."

Not sure what else to say, they both turned their attention to the suitcases traveling past them. She wished his bags would hurry up and arrive. The next thing they'd be talking about was the weather.

"I'm sorry my flight was late. Storms rolled in just

before we were scheduled to leave. Lots of lightning and driving rain."

She wanted to groan at his comment. If things between them remained this strained, it was going to be a long ride to Estes Park. Maybe he was tired from the flight and would fall asleep in the car. That would be better than talking about the weather for an hour and a half.

They both stared straight ahead as black bags of various sizes filed past their view, the only distinguishing feature being the luggage tags. Then, out of nowhere, a toddler in denim shorts, a Grandma Loves Me Because I'm Cute T-shirt and light-up tennis shoes zoomed past them, heading for the carousel.

"Hey, little man, where are you going?" Jamie scooped up the boy, who immediately tried to wiggle free as he pointed to the parade of luggage. "I know that looks like fun, but I want you to keep all your fingers. Now, where's your mom?"

While she'd been *thinking* someone should make sure the child didn't get into trouble, Jamie had acted. Emma couldn't help but stare as the exhaustion that had lined his face and filled his voice disappeared. A huge smile lit up his features and his eyes sparkled with affection as he held the toddler.

A memory of a night years ago in Nashville when Tucker had arrived to pick her up after her shift at the diner flashed in her mind. A vacationing family with two unruly young children had been seated in her section. When she'd told him she couldn't leave until they left, Tucker said he'd wait outside and mumbled something about how parents shouldn't take their kids in public if they couldn't control them.

Definitely a different attitude from the man filling

her vision now. Jamie looked so comfortable and at ease. She thought about how he'd stepped in with this child. He'd always been the kind of man who did what needed to be done without a lot of fanfare, without having to be asked. He just took care of things and those around him.

As she watched the pair, the boy grabbed Jamie's nose. Eyes alight with mischief, Jamie said, "Beep." The child's eyes widened at the sound. He released Jamie's nose, only to grab it again. "Beep."

Both males erupted into giggles, and Emma's heart tightened. Her biological clock, the one she'd have sworn possessed a dead battery, kicked into gear, making her ache. First Jamie's soulful eyes and now this. She'd have to watch her step with this guy. He could make a woman forget everything but him and the life they could have together.

"Cayden? Where are you?" A woman's panicked voice cut through Emma's thoughts.

"He's over here," she called out to the slender woman who was frantically scanning the area.

"There's your mom now," Jamie said.

"Momma?" Cayden responded as he squirmed in Jamie's arms.

"I'm hanging on to you. Who knows what trouble you'll get into if I set you free. I'm not sure the world's ready for that."

"He really could've gotten hurt if you hadn't corralled him," Emma said.

"I was a lot like this guy when I was young. Sometimes I had more curiosity than common sense." He peered down at the boy in his arms. "Pal, you're gonna have to work on curbing that before it gets you into major trouble."

"You're right about that," Cayden's mother said when

she reached them. She tucked stray strands of hair that had come loose from her sloppy ponytail behind her ear before she took her son from Jamie and introduced herself. She then hugged the boy so tight he squealed in protest. "I can't thank you enough for snagging him. My friend was supposed to meet us, but she must be running late. We've been in New York visiting my parents. I turned around to grab my suitcase and Cayden was gone. I've never been so scared in my life."

"Glad I could help, Dana," Jamie said.

"Do you need a ride? Are you sure your friend's coming?" Emma asked.

Before Dana could answer, her cell phone pinged. "I bet that's her now." She dug through the diaper bag, located her phone and checked her texts. After discovering her friend was waiting outside the airport, she thanked Jamie again, and then before she left, she leaned over to whisper in Emma's ear. "He's going to make a great father. Don't let him get away. There aren't a lot like him left these days."

Even if Emma was looking for someone to spend the rest of her life with, she wouldn't chose a musician. They were too temperamental and the business was too demanding. Making it and staying anywhere close to the top took everything a person had to give and still the business wanted more. Two people with those kinds of pressures couldn't maintain a relationship.

Too bad because unless he'd changed a lot, Dana was right. Jamie still looked like one of the good guys.

Emma Donovan. Jamie had almost stopped cold when he saw her in the baggage claim at the airport. How he'd managed to act nonchalant, even going so far as to pretend he didn't remember her name, he didn't know. Especially when his heart had been banging against his ribs like cymbals during a John Philip Sousa march.

Slender, yet curvy enough to fill a man's hands, she'd filled out in all the right ways and looked even better than she had in high school. With her long black hair and shining green eyes, Emma sure could get his pulse going. He remembered her all too well...and the fact that he'd been more interested in her than she'd been in him when they'd dated. She'd been seventeen and he nineteen. When he'd heard she'd broken up with her boyfriend, he'd jumped at the chance to ask her out. They'd gone out a few times, and then she'd ended things with him. Emma had taught him a valuable lesson: never be the first guy a woman dates after breaking up with her boyfriend. In this case, being number one was not what a guy wanted.

"When did you move back to town?" he asked in a lame attempt at conversation as they made their way to the parking lot and her car.

"It's been almost two years."

"Mick said you were in Nashville singing with a band, and that things were going well. What brought you back?"

"This and that." She unlocked the doors and got in her car. The door closed with a quiet thud behind her. "How about you? What brings you to Estes Park?"

Her short comment, combined with how she gripped the steering wheel so tightly her fingers whitened, sent a message even a guy with the social skills of a Neanderthal could read. He'd touched on a sore subject.

"Doesn't the Philharmonic have a tour coming up? Mick's been telling anyone who would listen all about it. I'm surprised you could get away."

Now he cringed. Discussions about his career and
its impending doom were exactly what he'd come to
get away from, but what did he expect? When people
hadn't seen each other for years or just met, what did
they ask about? A person's career. What could he say
that was the truth, yet wasn't, and didn't lead to any
further discussion?

"They didn't have a problem with me leaving." He tried
not to wince at what he'd said, since technically it was
true. He was just leaving out the more important details.

He stared out the window as they left the airport
parking lot and turned onto Interstate 270 West. As
the Denver city lights faded into the distance, the sun
turned the rugged Rocky Mountains all orange and yellow. The beauty of the land still amazed Jamie. The
constant strength of the mountains tapped into a part
of him that craved stability and certainty. The Rockies
would always be here. He liked that. They gave him
something to come back to again and again.

"It's been raining a lot in New York lately," he said
when he couldn't stand the silence any longer. "I'm glad
to be getting away from that. Hopefully the weather
will stay nice so I can do some hiking and horseback
riding while I'm here."

"If the weather forecasters are right, you should be
fine."

It was going to be a long hour and a half to Estes
Park. They could only talk about the weather for so long.

When Emma turned onto the drive leading to Mick's
house, Jamie thanked her again for the ride. "I'm sure
I'll see you around."

"In a small town it's hard not to."

Don't sound so excited. More disappointment than he wanted to admit spun through him. *Message received.* He opened the car door, grabbed his suitcase and headed up the walkway to Mick's house as Emma drove away. Too bad, though. They could have had some fun, and he could use a little of that right now.

Mick sat waiting for him, perched in his rocking chair on the front porch. "So life's been a little rough lately."

"It could be better, but then I guess it could be worse." And would be if his hand failed to regain its strength and dexterity.

His grandfather nodded toward the front door. "You know the way to your room. Drop your stuff off and meet me back here. I swear there's no better place to think than this front porch."

As Jamie walked into the house, he smiled at the pictures of Mick when he'd played with his band, ones of his life with his wife and events at Halligan's displayed everywhere. The progression of a life. One that meant something. Like his parents' house, this place was a home filled with memories where love lingered in every corner.

Once upstairs in the spare bedroom, he placed his suitcase in the corner. Nothing about this room had changed since the first night he'd slept here. The antique furniture so like Mick himself—Western in style, strong, sturdy and able to stand the test of time—had belonged to Mick's parents, a tangible link to past ancestors. He ran his hand over the quilt his grandmother had made, wishing he'd had more time to get to know her.

Once back on the porch, he sank into the weathered rocking chair Mick had given his wife when they'd moved into the house as newlyweds, and he stared at the mountains looming around him.

"Emma really helped me out, but then, that's what she does. She's a good girl, that one. She's held her family together over the past two years."

Was that what had stolen the sparkle he used to see in her eyes? She'd seemed different from what he remembered. Subdued. Distant almost.

"She needs to have a life of her own, but every time she tries to, something happens," Mick added, and glanced his way as if expecting him to ask for details.

The words to ask what had happened with Emma sat perched on Jamie's tongue, but he pushed aside the thought. He had enough on his mind without looking for more.

"Now her fiddle player's quit."

"That's too bad," Jamie said, refusing to rise to the bait Mick dangled in front of him. He was here to clear his head and sort out his future. Women had a way of short-circuiting a man's brain. Best to keep from sticking his nose in where it didn't belong. A lot safer, too.

The moon cast a pale glow over the mountains. Gazing over land that had been in Mick's family for generations, Jamie couldn't help but feel a connection to his past. At times he felt like two people compressed into one body. The person created by his DNA that determined his height, the color of his eyes and his musical ability, and the person created by the parents who'd raised him. But what percentage came from which source? He suspected his need for stability, his craving an anchor in his life came from his parents. They'd provided that calm presence, that guiding force in his life, and the older he got the more he wanted that same connection they had with each other. The one he saw flicker in their eyes when they smiled at each other.

He wasn't sure how long he and Mick sat rocking on the porch. The rustling wind through the trees mixed with the creaking of the rockers and their voices as they talked about the restaurant, the ranch and what Jamie could do to keep busy. The conversation soothed his battered nerves. Nothing important or earth-shattering, but the chat was exactly what he needed. Ordinary and uncomplicated.

"I haven't told anyone about your hand, so no one should bother you about that here, but I am going to say one thing about what you're going through. Then I won't bring it up again," Mick said. "Just because you can't play the fiddle like you used to doesn't mean you can't play another instrument. Maybe you could play guitar in a country band. You ever thought about that?"

Jamie shook his head. "I never considered doing anything else." Probably because he hadn't been exposed to other types of music growing up. When his musical ability became apparent, his parents had encouraged him to pursue classical music. That's what they listened to. Math and music went hand in hand. Classical music appealed to them because it possessed a sense of order, precision and structure. Contemporary music seemed so chaotic to them.

"I think you'd be a natural," Mick continued. "After all, you're my grandson, and it's clear you got my musical talent."

As an adult, when he listened to music he chose country or rock. Listening to classical felt too much like work. Popular music let him escape. But playing it? He mulled the idea over. Maybe Mick's suggestion wasn't that crazy. Something new might be just what he needed. For as long as he could remember he'd sung around the house and made up tunes. He smiled recalling how that habit used to drive his sisters crazy. At five he'd started composing his own songs and performing for the family.

"That's something to consider."

Because if he couldn't return to the symphony, he couldn't see his life without performing. Not that teaching wasn't a worthy profession, but there was something about being onstage that gave him a high as addictive as any drug, left him aching for a fix now, but it was more than that. He knew performing was where he was meant to be.

"Which hand do you use on the neck of that fancy fiddle of yours?"

"The left. The one I injured." If he'd injured his bow hand he might have been able to stay with the symphony.

"String instruments have a lot in common," Mick said. "With a guitar you play the chords with your left hand. That doesn't take as much dexterity. You do all the fast picking and strumming with your right hand. The hand that's working just fine."

Mick stood, headed into the house and returned a minute later with a guitar, which he handed to Jamie. "This was my first guitar. When I was a teenager I took any job I could get to save up to buy this. After I got hurt I couldn't bring myself to give it away. I guess part of me never quit hoping I'd be able to play again."

The instrument felt awkward in Jamie's grasp, almost backward as he settled the guitar on his lap. He wrapped his left hand around the neck. He rested his other hand against the smooth wood. His fingers itched to strum across the strings.

Jamie mulled over the idea, not sure how he felt about picking up another instrument. A little voice in his head urged him to think of the guitar as another way to work his hand. Movement was exercise, and that couldn't hurt. Combine playing the guitar with some good old-fashioned hard work and practicing his violin...who knew what could happen? All he wanted was his life back, any way he could get there.

"Can you show me how to play a couple of chords?"

The next afternoon Jamie stood behind the bar at Halligan's unloading the dishwasher and checking stock. The physical work around the restaurant felt good. He'd been in Colorado for less than twenty-four hours, but he already felt different, almost as though he'd left his problems behind in New York. 'Course it helped that no one here was asking him what he was going to do or looking at him as if his life was over and he'd disintegrate before their eyes.

As he iced down bottles of beer for the dinner crowd, his gaze strayed to Emma, who'd shown up with her band a while ago to audition violinists. Her arrival had definitely improved the view and brightened his day. Tall enough that a man wouldn't get a stiff neck having to bend down to look at her, Emma wasn't so tall she looked him in the eye. Her jeans molded to her feminine curves. Her black hair spilled over her shoulders.

While he hadn't spent the past several years mooning over her, he admitted she'd crept into his thoughts more than a time or six, and not just because of her looks, though she could make any man stop and look twice in her direction. Something else pulled him to her. Her openness, the warmth in her shining green eyes and her smile grabbed his attention more than anything else.

When she and the band launched into another song with their current candidate, her voice, belting out the haunting melody, echoed through the room. Angels would be tempted to trade their wings to sing like Emma. Plus she played guitar like a master. The sound she drew out of her instrument could fill a man with joy or make him weep depending on her whim. He stopped dead in his tracks to listen and enjoy. The music swirled around him, working its way inside, seducing him.

While Emma's skills impressed him, he couldn't say the same about the violinists. Noting the slight frown on Emma's face and how her brows knitted together, he suspected she agreed. When this latest candidate sang harmony on the chorus, he wasn't bad, but something was off. The notes were all there, but their voices didn't mesh. Like chocolate and steak. Both good things, but together? No, thanks. But more important, Emma overpowered the man's voice even though Jamie sensed she was backing off.

When the song ended a minute later, she thanked the man and told him they'd let him know when they made a decision. Even from across the room, Jamie could see the guy realized it was a no-go. A person either felt the connection and the music worked in a group or it didn't. This combination clearly didn't. Jamie couldn't blame the guy for being disappointed, though. Who wouldn't wake up raring to race into work if he found Emma waiting for him?

As the musician packed up his instrument, Emma

strolled toward the bar and almost collapsed on a stool. "I always thought auditions were bad from the auditioning point of view. Now I'm realizing they're not so hot from the other side, either." She reached into her jeans pocket and slapped a five onto the bar. "I desperately need a Diet Coke. The ibuprofen didn't work, but maybe the caffeine will keep my headache from going nuclear."

"I'm still in training, but I think I can handle that. Want me to put some rum in it? You look like you could use it." Then he cringed. Slick move. Tell a girl she looks worn out. "That didn't come out right."

"I should be offended at the comment and fire off a snappy comeback to put you in your place, but I'll have to give you a rain check. The auditions have left me brain-dead." She massaged her temples. "Add the rum. After all, it's five o'clock somewhere, and we have two more auditions. I can use the liquid courage."

"Do you always practice here?"

She shook her head. "Normally we use my dad's garage, but the acoustics are better here, and for the auditions I wanted to get a better sense of how someone moves onstage. The garage is a little cramped for that."

"Your band's good. Your voice and guitar skills are phenomenal. What're you doing playing local joints like this?"

When pain flashed in her eyes, he wanted to snatch the question back. Boy, he was on a roll. How could he have forgotten she'd made it clear yesterday that she didn't want to discuss her career or what had brought her back to Estes Park? Now he'd done just that. So much for having better social skills than a Neanderthal.

"I ask myself that daily. Every time I think I've got a shot at making it big, something happens."

"Like someone leaves the band." At her raised eyebrows, he added, "Mick mentioned your violinist quit."

"If it's not something like that, then it's life getting in the way."

The defeat in her voice tugged at him, making him want to ease whatever weighed on her. *Get over it. You've got enough piled on your plate without sneaking a bite off someone else's.*

He reached for a glass on the shelf. When he moved to place it on the plastic mat behind the bar, his hand cramped. The glass slipped from his grasp, hit the cement floor and shattered.

Applause erupted from the staff. After executing an exaggerated bow, he said, "Let me try that again with a little more skill." He tried to ignore the twitches in his left hand as he reached for a glass with his right. After he fixed Emma's drink without mishap and placed it in front of her, he grabbed the small hand broom and dustpan and cleaned up his mess.

"Don't tell Mick you broke a glass. He'll take it out of your pay," she teased.

That was the least of his worries. "Since I'm working for room and board, I'll have to go to bed without dinner and sleep in the barn." Then, wanting to get the conversation on a safer topic, he said, "I hope the last two guys you've got lined up are better. The people you've auditioned so far don't match the rest of the band's ability. The first guy has possibilities. He had a tendency to drag at the beginning, but he resolved the problem quickly. Could be he'd get over that issue once he learned your style."

"Thanks for confirming my opinion, but even if he fixes the tempo issues, I'm not sure he's right for us.

Technically he's fine, but he lacks something. He's almost wooden. There's no spark in his eyes or his voice when he sings."

"I noticed that, too. Could be he was nervous. Is he in a band now?" She nodded. "How's he look when he's onstage with them?"

"Like he's got a broom handle tied to his back."

"Chances are that won't change."

"That's what I'm afraid of." She sipped her drink. "We haven't performed without a fiddle in over a year. If we don't find someone soon we'll have to overhaul our repertoire or cancel appearances."

"That's rough. If my mom were here, she'd say the most complicated problems can bring the most powerful opportunities."

"She sounds like a wise woman. I'll try to remember that."

The front door to the restaurant opened, drawing their attention. A thirtysomething man held the door, his face beaming brighter than the sunshine spilling in behind him as he gazed at his wife and the swaddled baby she cradled in her arms.

"Sorry, folks. We aren't open yet."

"Nonsense. Come on in." Emma turned to Jamie. "Mick won't mind."

Jamie eyed her. "Is that true, or are you saying that because you enjoy contradicting me?"

"There is that, but in this case it's true. Matt and Naomi are regulars."

"You say that like there are people in town who aren't."

"Good comeback." She waved the couple forward. For the first time, the light he remembered twinkled in her eyes, making her face shine. "Don't mind Jamie.

Have a seat so I can see the baby. I was thrilled for you when I heard the news."

"We never thought this day would come," Naomi said as she and her husband walked toward the bar. "We had to wait quite a while, but she was worth it."

Emma peered down at the baby. "She's beautiful. What's her name?"

"Lillian Rose."

"We named her after our grandmothers," Matt added.

Emma asked about all the important statistics like when she was born, her weight and length. As Naomi answered the questions, she rubbed her daughter's smooth cheek. "We were in the delivery room with the birth mother, and got to see Lily come into this world. That was such an incredible moment. Were the adoptive parents there with you when your baby was born?"

Jamie froze. An iron fist clenched his stomach. *Were the adoptive parents there with you when your baby was born?* Emma had given birth to a child and given it up for adoption? When had that happened? He caught sight of her out of the corner of his vision. What did he expect? That he'd somehow be able to tell she'd given birth? Then he stole a look at her face. Was she a little pale? Her even teeth nibbled on her lower lip as if she struggled to keep her emotions under control.

Could seeing this couple's excitement be tough for her? Maybe not all women who gave up a child had a heart of stone like the woman who'd given birth to him.

Chapter 4

Emma saw Jamie's eyes widen and his facial features tighten, revealing tiny lines around his eyes. *He didn't know.*

She was so accustomed to small-town life where everyone knew everything about her, it never occurred to her he might not know she'd given a child up for adoption. She could almost see the gears turning in his head as he struggled to process the information. *He's reevaluating everything he thought he knew about me.* Shutting out his reaction, she turned to the couple beside her.

"The adoptive parents were at the hospital, but not in the delivery room with me. We had a closed adoption."

Naomi nodded in understanding. "It was a wonderful bonding experience. Matt got to cut the umbilical cord. We feel so honored that our birth mother chose us."

Life could be so backward. Teenagers who lacked

the good sense to keep a houseplant alive got pregnant when their boyfriends dropped their pants, but couples like the Sandbergs couldn't conceive. "You two will be wonderful parents."

"We're going to do our best." Naomi reached out and placed her delicate hand on Emma's arm. "I hope seeing us doesn't bring up too many painful memories for you."

None that she couldn't handle. "It's great getting to see how excited you are. I did what was best for my child. He's much better off being raised by two loving parents. Seeing you with Lily only reinforces that." Emma twirled the straw in her drink, swirling the ice, which clinked against the glass. "It's nice seeing the joyful side of adoption. Thanks for giving me that."

Naomi wiped her eyes. "We're here to meet with Mick about the family get-together we're having so everyone can meet Lily. We want him to cater the party."

"I'll find him for you." Jamie glanced at Emma, concern in his warm gaze, as if to ask permission. As if he were worried about her. How odd was that? She flashed him what she hoped passed for an I'm-fine smile and not one that revealed how off balance she felt. After he left for the kitchen, she congratulated Naomi and Matt again and said she needed to rejoin the band for the auditions. As she walked toward the stage on legs she worried would collapse under her, she glanced at her watch, noting she had twenty minutes until the next audition. When she reached her bandmates, she said, "How about we take a break? I need some fresh air to clear my head."

She needed time to fall apart, give in to her pity over what might have been and put herself back together.

Both men nodded. She saw the questions in their eyes, but they said nothing. For a minute, as she walked toward Halligan's back door, the fact that her bandmates failed to comment on how she wasn't quite herself stung. But what did she expect? When she'd formed Maroon Peak Pass they'd discussed keeping their personal lives and their work separate. No getting chummy, going out to dinner or socializing at each other's houses. No sticking their noses into each other's affairs. She'd made the mistake of blurring the lines before with disastrous results. When she'd laid out her expectations she'd explained that, in her experience, all that led to were messy disagreements, hurt feelings and band breakups. Considering what she'd said, she had no right to be disappointed when the guys gave her exactly what she'd asked for, and yet she was.

Once in the alley she collapsed on a wooden crate near the wall, and the tears spilled down her cheeks. She appreciated seeing the happier side of adoption, but the encounter with Naomi and Matt still dredged up memories she'd rather keep buried. More than it should. Her emotions regarding the adoption hadn't been this raw in years. She shouldn't be sitting here falling apart and feeling as if she'd been run over by a truck when she'd made the right decision.

The back door creaked open, and Emma swiped a hand across her eyes. The lie that she'd come out to get fresh air and the wind blew something into her eye perched on her tongue—she turned expecting to see someone bringing out the garbage or sneaking out for a smoke. Instead there stood Jamie, concern radiating from his gaze.

*Those eyes could hypnotize a girl or make her spill
every secret she held close.*

"You okay?" He shoved his hands in his pockets. "I
was concerned when the guys were onstage, but you
weren't."

"I'm fine and dandy." She flashed him her best I'm-
pretending-I'm-on-top-of-the-world smile. "I'm gathering my courage for the next audition."

She stared him down, and suspected he was trying to
decide whether or not to call her bluff. *Come on, fold.*

"Your eyes give you away." He stepped closer. When
he stood in front of her, his hand cupped her face and
his thumb brushed across her skin. "There's a tear on
your cheek."

She closed her eyes, savoring his touch. The simple
comfort of it. It would be so easy to step into his arms,
to find reassurance and strength there, and his concerned gaze told her he was more than willing to offer
those things.

Instead she leaned away from him and crossed her
arms over her chest. She couldn't do this; she refused
to feel anything for him. She had her goals. Her plan
mapped out. Nothing would get in her way. Least of
all, a man.

He nodded toward the door. "That had to be rough
for you. I never knew you gave up a child for adoption."

She nodded. "He turned seven this week."

As Jamie sank onto the wooden crate beside her, she
could tell he was doing the math in his head. "What
were you? Eighteen or nineteen when you had him?"

She nodded, and shoved the memories into the back
of her mind before they bubbled over again. "Deciding to give him up for adoption was the hardest thing

I've ever done. I knew there was happiness and joy, the thrill of the new life ahead of them as a family on the other side, but I never *saw* it until today. It wasn't real."

"Seeing you in there hit home for me how hard the decision could be for the birth mother."

So they'd both learned something. "Rumor around town said when you first contacted Kimberly, it didn't go well."

He chuckled, she sensed more out of nervousness than humor. "That's an understatement. The *Titanic's* voyage went smoother."

"I'm sorry."

"It hurt at first, but finding out she doesn't have much to do with Mick, either, helped. I realize now it's not my problem. It's hers." He leaned toward her. "Despite knowing that, every once in a while something happens, and I get kicked in the teeth. Kind of like you did today."

He understood in a way no one else could. "It's been weird the past couple of weeks. My son's been on my mind more lately. I've got this funny feeling. I can't put it into words, but it's almost like I'm worried something's wrong."

"Contact his parents."

For the first time since she'd given up her child, a person failed to stumble over the phrase.

"Closed adoption, remember?"

"Circumstances change. Deals get renegotiated all the time."

"I agreed to that condition for good reasons, and those haven't changed. Coping with a birth mom as an adult has to be hard enough. You discovered that. But as a seven-year-old? I don't want this being about me and what I need. It has to be about what's best for my son."

"It takes a helluva person to realize that."

She clasped her hands in her lap to keep from picking at her nail polish. "I'm not sure being involved with him is what's best for me, either. Would it be like trying to eat half a cookie? I've never been good at moderation."

"So you'd work on the issue, get better at it."

Life had a way of throwing enough hardships that could land a kid on a therapist's couch without her tossing stuff at her son. That's what worried her most. "How old were you when you found out you were adopted?"

"I was in third grade. We were studying probability in school. I remember Mrs. Little talking about recessive genes and eye color. She said when two brown-eyed people have children there were three possible outcomes. She drew this table on the board to show us." His forearms braced on his thighs, he leaned forward, staring straight ahead, his gaze hooded and distant. "I asked what the probability of two blue-eyed people having a brown-eyed child was. Mrs. Little told me that couldn't happen."

"Your parents both have blue eyes?"

He nodded. "That's why I was so sure she was wrong. When I got home, I found out Mrs. Little had called my mom to tell her what happened. That's when my parents told me I was adopted."

"How would you have felt if you were seven and someone showed up saying she gave birth to you?"

"I don't know what I would've thought. At that age, all I thought was that the person that had me couldn't raise me so I got different parents."

"What about your parents? How would they have felt?"

"That's a tougher question. They were very supportive when I contacted Kimberly and Mick, but I was eighteen."

"And by then your relationship was established."

"Exactly, and I told them searching for my birth mother wouldn't change that."

"What about your birth father?"

"Kimberly isn't even sure who that is."

Now she'd really stepped in it. She tried to think of what to say, but words failed her.

"Don't feel bad about asking. It is what it is."

"I wish I knew what to do. How to shake this odd feeling I've had lately."

"At least call the parents. Explain how you've been feeling. Tell them all you want to know is that your son's okay."

She'd never considered that option. Once she knew her son was fine, that nothing was wrong, her life could return to normal. Reminders of her child would pop up some days to throw her off stride, but then the ache would recede again. "There's one problem. Since it was a closed adoption I don't think the agency will give me any information on the parents."

"If they won't, I can help. I've gone through that kind of search."

"You'd do that?"

"Why's that so hard to believe?"

She thought about his question. Why was it so hard to believe someone would offer to help her? Probably because she wasn't the type of person everyone rushed to assist. Her family assumed she could take care of herself. After all, she'd held her own growing up with three older brothers. She came from strong stock, and that's how everyone treated her. "I appreciate the offer."

She could at least contact the agency to tell them if the adoptive parents expressed interest, she was open to exploring a relationship, as well.

A knock sounded on the door, followed by Luke poking his head outside. "Our next audition's here."

She nodded. "I'll be right there."

When the door closed again, she turned to Jamie, wanting to say something to thank him for his unexpected kindness, but she couldn't find the words. What he'd done by listening and really hearing her had helped her process what she'd been feeling.

When was the last time anyone other than Avery had really listened to her? The past two years it seemed as if when anyone called or stopped by to chat it was because they needed something. Her dad called when he ran out of meals in the freezer. Her grandparents, excluding her Grandpa G, called when they needed a prescription picked up or a ride to a doctor's appointment. Her brothers called, well, never.

But no one other than her best friend called to just talk or to see how she was doing.

Until Jamie.

Before she could change her mind, she jumped up and wrapped her arms around him for a quick hug. "Thanks for everything. For listening."

Then she darted for the door and the safety of the restaurant.

When Jamie walked back inside he watched Emma dash across the restaurant, his body still humming from having hers pressed up against him. His gaze locked on the sway of her hips and he smiled. Who'd have guessed cowboy boots could put the same special something into a woman's walk that high heels did? He was accustomed to women in designer jeans and expensive stilettos, but he was gaining a new appreciation for a simple pair of Wranglers and boots. They made a woman look real, accessible and damn fine.

"You ready?" Mick asked when Jamie joined him behind the bar.

"As ready as I'll ever be." Jamie pulled his gaze away from Emma. "Is there anything else we need to go over before the dinner rush hits?"

"It still gets pretty crazy in here on a weekend night, but don't worry. Usually no one's in a big hurry, especially when we've got a band. They come for dinner and to spend time with family and friends. Then they hang around to listen to music and dance." Mick nodded toward the stage. "I sure hope Emma can find someone to take Molly's place. All that girl's ever wanted to do was sing country music."

"You two gonna stand here jawin' all afternoon, or can one of you deal with the liquor delivery out back?" Gene said as he stormed out of the kitchen.

"I never should have made you day manager. You always were the power-hungry type," Mick joked.

"Fine. It's not my business that'll suffer when we run out of whiskey." Then Gene turned and headed back through the swinging double doors.

"Come on, Jamie. I'll check the order, and you can do the heavy lifting."

The rest of the afternoon went faster than Jamie expected, and then the dinner rush hit. After a couple of hours he felt as though he'd met or gotten reacquainted with all of Estes Park's eight thousand residents while manning the bar. Jamie flexed his hand, stretching out the tight muscles. He'd been amazed how much the repeated motion of picking up glasses had worked his hand, and except for the one dropped glass, he'd done well.

But his hand wasn't the only thought plaguing him tonight. His mind kept wandering back to Emma. Instead of leaving after her auditions, she joined a couple of girlfriends at a table that always managed to stay within his sight no matter how many people crowded around the bar.

As Jamie handed another patron his beer, Mick's cell phone rang. When his grandfather ended the call a few seconds later, his face lined with concern, he turned to Jamie. "That was tonight's band. Their truck broke down. They won't be here for at least an hour." Mick glanced around the crowded restaurant. "The natives are getting restless, which means they could start leaving. Which means their money walks out with them. How about you play something to settle 'em down until the band gets here?"

Jamie stared at his grandfather and thought the man had lost his mind. Had he forgotten about his hand? He leaned closer so the customers clustered around the bar wouldn't hear. "I'm not ready for that. I dropped a glass today because my hand cramped up."

"Hell, that happens to everyone."

"Even if I felt comfortable playing, my music isn't the stuff this crowd wants to hear. There would be a stampede for the door."

"Then don't play your fancy fiddle. Use the karaoke machine. You got a good voice." When Jamie opened his mouth to object, his grandfather continued, "And before you start saying you don't know how to sing any country-western songs, I heard you singing along to the Willie Nelson songs Gene played in the kitchen this afternoon. Sing one of those."

Jamie nodded toward Emma's table. "Ask Emma's band to fill in."

"I could do that, but by the time she gets a hold of everyone, they get back here and then set up, the band I scheduled should be here and half of my customers will be gone. I need someone on that stage right now."

"Hey, Mick, where's the band?" a thirtysomething man dressed in the local uniform of jeans, plaid shirt and cowboy hat asked after he ordered two more beers. "Janet and I are here to listen to some music. We got a sitter tonight and everything. Let's get this party started."

After tossing Jamie a see-I-told-you look, Mick said, "The band's running a little late. They had car trouble."

"How late is a little? If it's much longer, Janet and I may have to go to the new chain place that opened down the street. I promised her we'd go dancing."

"What? The band's not coming?" another man at the bar said.

"Hold on there. The band will be here, and I'm working on fixing the problem of having some music to tide us over." Mick patted Jamie on the back. "My grandson here's a fine musician and has a good voice to boot. He's going to get a karaoke night started. People can dance if they want, and that'll hold everyone until the band gets here."

Jamie cringed. How could he say no to that? He wiped his sweaty palms on the bar rag, tossed the cloth aside and stared at the older man beside him. "I'll do one song, and then I'm done."

Once onstage, his gaze landed on Emma. He'd pretend he was talking to her. Maybe that would help ease his nerves. "Hello, everyone. For those of you I haven't met tonight, I'm Mick's grandson, Jamie. There's been a little detour in tonight's plans. The band's truck broke down so we're going to have a karaoke night until they get here. Thanks to Mick's arm-twisting—"

"Yeah, he's good at that," someone from the crowd tossed out.

Everyone laughed and some of Jamie's tension eased. "Tell me about it. I was tending bar, and the next thing I knew I was promoted to entertainer. Promise you'll be gentle with me."

"I can show you a good time, and I promise to be gentle," a woman shouted from one of the back tables.

Jamie swallowed hard, and laughed along with everyone else. This wasn't like being on the stage at the Philharmonic. Never once had a woman in the audience hollered out that she wanted to show him a good time. What had he gotten himself into?

As Emma sat at a table near the stage with Avery and her friend's sister-in-law Stacy, she stared at Jamie. For someone who spent a good portion of time onstage performing with a symphony, he looked very uncomfortable. His posture was rigid and his voice as he introduced himself lacked his casual assurance. Now there was almost a brittle quality to it. While he joked and smiled at the crowd, his eyes held a look similar to those of a collie brought into the shelter after his owner died—completely confused and overwhelmed.

But then symphony crowds weren't known for shouting out what a good time they'd show a man. Something the rowdy crowd at Halligan's could be known to do at least once an hour. Especially if Carla Timmons was in the crowd and had a few margaritas in her.

"I'm sure you could show me a thing or two, but right now I'm working. I can't let my boss down," Jamie said, a tight smile on his face.

"Better cut Carla off, Mick, before she rushes the stage," someone else called out.

"Poor Jamie. Carla's in rare form tonight," Avery said. "Do you know when Jamie got into town? Have you two talked?"

"He got here yesterday," Emma said. "I picked him up at the airport when Mick wasn't feeling well."

"Why didn't you tell me?"

"There's nothing to tell." *Except Jamie looked so incredible holding this toddler at the airport yesterday my biological clock started ticking again, and then this afternoon he was so sweet when he came to make sure I was okay. A girl could get used to a guy doing stuff like that.*

No way was she sharing that info.

"You two dated for a while, didn't you?"

Emma nodded. "That summer after graduation, but it wasn't any big deal."

She glanced at the stage. Jamie shifted his stance from foot to foot, his movements stiff and awkward. Even dressed in jeans and the hunter-green Halligan's T-shirt, he looked out of place. She shook her head when she noticed his shoes. For goodness sake, the man was wearing tennis shoes. That had to be a first for this stage. How had Mick ever let him out of the house with those on?

"No big deal? That's not what I remember about you

and Jamie. You two went everywhere together. You said he was a good kisser," Avery said, a big know-it-all-best-friend grin on her face.

Good enough to make my toes curl. Thanks for reminding me. That was the last thing she needed to remember right now. Emma rolled her eyes. "I don't remember that conversation, and even if it were true, what does it matter? Jamie and I aren't teenagers anymore. We've changed a lot since then."

"I bet kissing's not the only thing he's good at," Stacy said, her dreamy gaze locked on Jamie.

"Get a grip, you two. You're both married, and the way you're looking at him is embarrassing."

"We're not the only one giving him the eye." Avery nodded toward the crowd around them.

"I know. So is every female in the place."

"Including you," Stacy added.

"Let it go." Emma didn't dare deny the statement, she wasn't that accomplished a liar.

"You're awfully touchy about this subject. Are you sure nothing happened between you two when you picked him up at the airport?"

Something happened between us today, and it left me more scared than I've been in a long time. "What's with the third degree?"

"Have you thought about starting things up with him?" Avery asked, a huge silly grin on her face.

"Now I get it. This is payback for our night here when Reed first got back in town, isn't it?"

"It's not much fun being in the hot seat, is it?" Avery said. "I've got to say an interrogation is more enjoyable from this side."

"Sounds like a good story. Share," Stacy coaxed.

"Just replay this conversation, but change the names to Avery and Reed," Emma said. Hoping her friends would get the message she was done with this particular topic, Emma turned her attention to Jamie.

"Key up one of those songs Gene had on earlier," he said to his grandfather who stood offstage.

"'Always on My Mind' coming up," Mick replied.

How could Mick do this to his grandson? Jamie's awkwardness reached out to Emma. Talk about looking like a broom handle had been tied to his back. The man was a classically trained musician. Someone should rescue him. She pushed back her chair.

Then Jamie cleared his throat and turned to Mick. "Toss me your hat."

The tan cowboy hat spun through the air. Jamie caught it by the brim and put it on. Cheers and whistles sounded from the audience. "That's better."

It certainly was. Now, if he had on a good pair of Ariat boots he'd be close to perfect.

"Now I'm feeling more at home," Jamie said as the music started. He closed his eyes for a minute and started singing.

While he stumbled over the words, the strength of his tenor voice filled the room. His stiffness faded and his features relaxed. Emma sat there as if her butt had been nailed to the chair, unable to do anything but stare, and she wasn't easy to impress. Why wasn't he singing professionally? Not sharing a magnificent singing voice like his was criminal. Even struggling with the words, he possessed an assurance. He commanded the room, but there was also something in the way he moved. A healthy dose of confidence mixed with grace and a whole lot of sensuality.

Be still my heart.

The song ended and the bar erupted in applause, but she still couldn't move.

Someone shook her arm, pulling her out of her haze. "Emma, come back to earth." When she turned, Avery leaned closer, an I-know-what-you've-been-thinking-about smirk on her face. "And you might want to close your mouth. If you don't, you're going to start drooling. Not that I blame you. That man is certainly drool-worthy."

"It has nothing to do with how he looks." Emma ignored the urge to duck under the table in case the Lord sent a lightning bolt to strike her down for her blatant lie. "I couldn't help but admire his voice. It's incredible."

Avery's bright laugh swirled around her. "And you really think I'm going to believe that's all it was?"

"I'm going to ignore that comment."

"Because you can't deny it."

"Now it's your turn," Jamie said to the crowd, thankfully drowning out the brewing second inquisition Avery was gearing up to start. "Who wants to come up and sing next?"

Before he finished the question, Shay Edwards bounced past Emma's table and practically vaulted onto the stage. Quite a feat considering her jeans were so tight they had to be cutting off circulation to her legs. When Jamie tried to hand her the microphone and leave, Shay grabbed his arm and plastered herself against him. If the woman got any closer she'd be on top of him. "Sing a duet with me, Jamie."

When he started to protest Shay struck a pose and pouted. "Please? Come on, cowboy. You were so awesome. I'd love to sing with you. We could make beautiful music together."

Brother. Did the woman think that ridiculous pretty-girl routine actually worked with men? Emma grimaced. Of course Shay did, because usually all the stacked blonde had to do was stick out her double Ds and wet her lips, and men trampled each other to do her bidding.

"Poor Jamie. The night just keeps getting worse. Now Shay's got her sights on him," Avery said.

"Poor us, is more like it. Obviously you don't remember how she sings. A cat screeching because its tail got caught under a rocking chair sounds better than she does." Emma shook her head. "If she gets any closer to him, we'll all get an entirely different kind of show."

The crowd joined in shouting for Jamie to sing again. He tried to wiggle free of Shay's grasp, but instead of letting go she held on like a puppy with a brand-new toy.

"Mick, cue up 'Let's Make Love' by Faith Hill and Tim McGraw." Shay leaned back on her heels, her ample chest practically shoved in Jamie's face as she looked the man up one side and down the other.

Emma nearly choked on her sip of beer. Could the woman be any more obvious? She might as well ask him to get a room.

When Shay and Jamie started singing, Avery leaned closer to Emma. "I thought you were kidding about how bad her voice was. The dogs howling in the shelter are more in tune than she is. Not that the men around here seem to notice."

"Her voice isn't the asset they're concentrating on." Emma winced as Shay hit another clinker. "With the way she's bouncing around up there, it's a wonder she hasn't popped right out of that low-cut sweater."

"She does like to put everything on display, doesn't she? Her bra must be industrial strength."

Unlike most of the men in Halligan's, Jamie looked less than pleased with Shay's display. He kept trying to slide away from her, only to have her follow him.

"Emma, I can't take any more of that caterwauling," Mick said when he appeared beside her. "You've got to go onstage to rescue Jamie before we either go deaf from listening to that harebrained female or she gets us raided."

"Don't tell me *your* grandson can't handle a woman?" she said.

"Come on, Em," Avery added. "I think it would be cool to hear you two sing together. Consider it your good deed for the day."

"That was fun. Let's do another," Shay said the moment the song ended, her voice all bright and airy.

"We need to give someone else a chance. Who else wants to sing?" Jamie pleaded, a look of desperation crossing his features when he glanced in Emma's direction.

How could she ignore that lost-puppy look after what he'd done for her this afternoon?

"Jamie, sing something else," Cathy Hughes, one of Halligan's waitresses, said as she served another round of drinks to a stage-side table.

"I'll sing as long as you sing with me, Jamie," Doreen Stone called out, a dreamy look her husband, Joshua, wouldn't appreciate plastered on her face.

"Help me out, Emma," Mick pleaded, as a heated discussion flared up between Shay and Doreen about who should perform with Jamie. "I'm afraid they're going to go at each other or start tearing at Jamie. I've never seen the women here act like this before. It's downright scary."

"Okay. I'll do it." She turned to Mick. "But you have to get Shay off the stage. I'm not fighting that battle."

"I think you could take her," Avery teased.

"My money would be on you, too, but I'll handle Shay," Mick said. "I don't want any trouble."

Once she and Mick made their way to the stage, Emma picked up a mic and waited nearby while he pried Shay's hand off Jamie's arm. "It's my place, and I want to hear Emma and Jamie sing 'Jackson.' I think they'll do June and Johnny proud." Then he practically dragged Shay off the stage.

When Emma joined Jamie, he smiled. A simple thing. No big deal, and yet her heart fluttered. With his voice, looks and that smile, he would drive women crazy.

Don't let him get to you. You've sworn off musicians, remember?

Jamie put the mic behind his back and leaned toward her. His warm breath fanned against her skin, sending little ripples of delight through her. "Thanks for being part of the rescue posse. The way she was pawing me, I was worried she was going to slip a five in my pants any minute."

His comment made her think of the movie *Magic Mike*. Bad idea. The image of Jamie dressed in Matthew McConaughey's getup of tight jeans, leather vest and cowboy hat in that movie flashed in her mind. Emma swallowed hard and sweat trickled between her breasts.

Jamie Westland would make one fine-looking cowboy.

"You ready?" he asked.

She stared at him and tried to swallow the lump in her throat. She was ready for any number of things, none of which were appropriate for the stage. "Excuse me?"

"Are you ready for Mick to cue up the music?"

All she could do was nod. When the familiar tune filled the room she relaxed. Now in her element, she glanced at the crowd and slipped into performance mode. When she and Jamie started singing, her body moved to the music. Their voices melded. His presence beside her felt comfortable, and yet not. By the time they reached the first chorus, she knew she'd made a big mistake agreeing to sing with Jamie.

Big? More like monumental. Or catastrophic.

Because all Emma could think about was how she hadn't felt this connected to anyone in a long time, and that was not a good thing.

Chapter 5

Mick stared at his grandson on the stage with Emma
and felt as if he was looking at a younger version of
himself. He may not have been a part of Jamie's life
for eighteen years, but no doubt about it, the blood-
line ran true.

Listening to Jamie sing, Mick knew his grandson
could still have a performing career in music. If he
wanted to. Jamie could have the choices he'd never had.
The sparks between his grandson and Emma lit up the
place. If things got any hotter he'd have to turn up the
air-conditioning.

If he hadn't known these two belonged together before, he sure as hell would now. There was a chemistry
between Jamie and Emma that couldn't be manufactured
and everyone in the room knew it. They had that rare
something that some couples just had. Johnny Cash and

June Carter Cash. George Jones and Tammy Wynette. Faith Hill and Tim McGraw.

Out of the corner of his eye, Mick spotted Cody, one of his busboys, and called him over. Whenever the teenager got a break, he was always showing Mick funny videos he found on the internet. "You can take videos on that phone of yours, can't you?"

"I'd never take any videos here at work. Did someone say I did?" the gangly redhead said, fear making his voice crack.

"Don't worry. You're not in trouble," Mick rushed to reassure the teen who'd nearly started shaking in his boots. "I want you to video Emma and Jamie onstage and post it on that video site you're always talking about."

"YouTube?"

"That's the one. You keep that thing running the whole time they're onstage or until your battery runs out."

"You sure? It's crazy busy in here. Cathy will have my head if I don't clear her tables."

"I'll take care of busing the tables."

"Okay, you're the boss." Cody handed Mick his tub of dishes and headed toward the stage, cell phone in hand.

Mick smiled. If he was right about Emma and Jamie, once people saw the video they'd start clamoring to see the pair onstage again. Emma wouldn't be able to resist that. Once he got them working together, then they'd realize they could be good together off the stage, as well. His plan was coming right along.

Jamie wasn't sure he'd ever felt this alive. While things had started out rocky with him stumbling over the words, now that he'd gotten into the song he felt at home onstage. Of course, having Emma beside him helped.

Confident, dynamic and sexy as hell, she made a man come alive just by being in the same room. She was like a lightning bug on a dark summer night—all bright energy, flitting all over the place, shining on everyone and everything and just as hard to contain.

Emma's voice flowed through and around him. Her green eyes sparkled with excitement and drew him in. He glanced at the screen to check the lyrics, then he leaned toward her, smiling as he sang about how he'd teach the women in Jackson a thing or two. Then she took over the song taunting about how she'd be dancing on a pony keg and he'd be a hound with his tail tucked between his legs.

Her eyes flashed with amusement, and he could see her doing just what she said—dancing and sending him on a merry chase. He laughed and wondered when he'd had this much fun. The fact that he couldn't remember left him oddly disturbed.

A minute later when the song ended the thunderous applause and exuberant hoots broke the connection between them. He'd been completely lost in Emma and the song. He stood there staring at the crowd, shocked both at their reaction and his. Definitely not the restrained approval he was accustomed to receiving from symphony patrons.

His chest rose and fell with his heavy breathing. His body hummed in a way it hadn't in years.

Someone in the crowd shouted for him and Emma to sing another song. He turned to the woman beside him. Her smile taunted him. "What do you say? Should we give 'em what they want?"

"Why not?" Her skin glistening from exertion, her eyes twinkled like emeralds when she grinned. Then she slowly looked him up and down from head to toe, and damned if he didn't feel himself blush. "The question is, city boy, can you keep up with this cowgirl?"

"I can take anything you dish out."

The crowd oohed at his challenge. Jamie froze. He'd forgotten about the mic in his hand and that everyone could hear their exchange. This woman could make him forget his own name.

"Then let's see what you've got, city boy. Mick, cue up another song."

More cheers came from the audience.

He and Emma sang five more songs before Mick joined them. "As great as it's been having Jamie and Emma up here, the band's arrived." When some of the crowd started to grumble, Mick added, "I think these two need to come back real soon and sing again. What do you think?"

More cheers and whistles came from the crowd as he and Emma left the stage, and Jamie realized he wasn't ready to let her go. He wanted to hang on to this energy, to how she made him feel, as though he could storm the castle and come away the victor. "Let me buy you a drink."

"I could use a big glass of ice water."

"Wow, you're a cheap date."

The joy he'd seen in her eyes on the stage died, and the bond between them evaporated, leaving her looking at him as if he was the gum stuck to the bottom of her boots. Maybe it was the date comment. That dented his ego. He rushed to salvage his pride. "There's no reason for you to get all out of joint. I'm not hitting on you.

My mom raised me better than that. Let me get you that water. I don't know about you, but I just sweated off five pounds on the stage."

Great way to impress a girl. Tell her you're hot, sweaty and smelly. You're still on that great roll from this afternoon, buddy.

"People don't realize how much water weight performers lose onstage. Lead the way."

They started to make their way to the bar, but only went a few feet before someone stopped them to say how much they enjoyed their singing. Another couple of steps and they repeated the process. When the third group of people waylaid them, Jamie turned to Emma and said, "I say head down and we make a run for the bar. Stop for nothing, or we're going to die of thirst." He grabbed her hand. "Coming through." Someone tried to catch his attention. "Sorry. Join us at the bar if you want to talk. The lady's about to collapse from dehydration." He kept moving forward until they reached the bar.

"That was subtle, and not the least bit overly dramatic." Emma shook her head and sank onto an empty bar stool.

"I got the job done, so quit complaining," Jamie said as he moved behind the bar beside Mick. Once there he plucked a glass off the shelf, filled it with ice and water and placed it in front of Emma. "And now I'm back to bartender."

"Thanks for filling in, you two." Mick patted Jamie on the back.

"The credit goes to Emma. She was the one who knew what to do. I followed her lead."

"You were amazing, Jamie. I haven't heard anybody sound that good in years," one of the women seated at the bar said. Jamie wasn't sure which one, not that he cared. All he noticed was how quiet Emma had become.

"That was because of Emma. Anyone singing with her would sound like a star." Jamie reached for another glass.

"You two were almost as good as June and Johnny," the man sitting next to Emma said.

She smiled at him, but her eyes failed to light up as they had earlier. She sat with her back ramrod-straight, her hand clutching her water glass. Something wasn't right. "That's very sweet of you to say so, Henry. I'm glad you enjoyed it."

"We need to have these two back, boss," Cathy said after she ordered two beers and a whiskey neat for one of her tables. "I bet we'd pack the place, and I could rake in some heavy-duty tips."

"Are you trying to tell us something?" Henry teased.

"You're a good tipper, but let's face it. People open their wallets wider when they're all toe-tapping happy from good music." She patted Emma's arm. "Hearing you and Jamie sing sure makes my night go faster. Say you two will come back again."

"Maroon Peak Pass and the shelter keep me pretty busy, but I'll see what we can do."

Jamie couldn't miss the lack of enthusiasm in Emma's voice. In other words, don't call us, we'll call you. Here he thought they'd shared something special onstage, but apparently he was the only one who thought so.

"Have you had any luck finding a fiddle player to replace Molly? I bet that's weighing on you since the contest at the state fair is coming up quick," Henry said.

Emma shook her head. "I've contacted anyone who might know of someone, and I've spent hours search-

ing the internet. It's downright scary what some people
think passes for music."

"What's this about a contest?" Jamie asked.

"The state fair is having a competition." Emma explained how the winner got a private consultation with
Phillip Brandise, one of the biggest producers in country music. "If we impress him, we have a good shot at
him offering us a recording contract."

"Will not having a violinist hurt your chances?"
Jamie asked as he poured the beers for Cathy.

"Not if I can help it." He wanted to smile at Emma's
grit, clearly evident in the stubborn tilt of her chin and
the determination in her voice. The woman might bend,
but she wouldn't break.

"Maybe you don't have to go without one. How about
Jamie?" Henry nodded in his direction. "You play the
fiddle, don't you?"

"Since I was eight. I was one of those geeky kids
who spent the afternoon inside practicing the violin."

"You should get Jamie to take Molly's place." Henry
took a long draw on his beer and leaned back in his seat,
obviously pleased with himself. "Then you two could
sing together all the time."

He mulled the idea over. Being onstage with Emma
had been the most fun he'd had in a long time. He
could help her out while getting the challenge of learning something new. Granted, learning country music
wouldn't be a huge one—how hard could it be for someone who'd been classically trained?—but it would be
something *different,* and that's what he needed right
now. He'd fill up some of his empty time and get the
added bonus of exercising and strengthening his hand.
As far as he could see it was a win all around.

"You could at least help out until Emma finds some-one." Henry turned to Emma, a big uneven smile on his face. "Isn't that a great idea?"

Jamie glanced at her, about to say they should give Henry's idea a try, but the words stuck in his throat. She'd pressed her lips together so hard they were a thin white line. She clutched her water glass so tight the ten-dons in her hand stood out.

"It's something to consider, but I'll have to think about it since Jamie doesn't have any experience—"

"I've got a degree from Juilliard and played with the New York Philharmonic." His words came out harsher than he intended. Her comment shouldn't have nicked his pride, but it had. "I'd call that experience."

"If you'd let me finish, what I was going to say was you don't have any experience playing with a country band."

She really thought what she'd added would make the insult sting less? "I think I can handle it."

"Just because you possess the skills to play the notes doesn't mean you can make *music*. Everyone thinks country music is easy to play, but it's not. It's filled with heart. It's storytelling set to music. That's what makes it special. If someone doesn't feel the connection, it doesn't work. What you create is just noise."

Wood creaked as people shifted awkwardly on the bar stools.

"I happen to like country music. It has an honesty that resonates with people. Me included."

"Again, that doesn't mean you can play it on a pro-fessional level. The business is very competitive."

He shrugged, but all he could think about was grab-bing her and kissing her long and hard until neither one of them had the energy to carry on this conversation. "Good luck at the state fair."

"Okay, you two," Mick said as he rushed over from the far side of the bar. "I think it's time to change the subject. Jamie, let's get everyone here at the bar another round on me."

Cheers and whoops circled around the bar. The only one besides him who didn't seem happy was Emma as she stalked away to rejoin her friends.

Sunday afternoon Emma sank onto her couch in her living room, a cup of herbal tea beside her as she tried to focus on the sheet music spread out on the coffee table in front of her. Unfortunately all she could think about was how she'd gone off the deep end last night with Jamie.

She'd been so far off her game yesterday she hadn't even been able to see the stadium. That feeling started when she arrived at Halligan's for the auditions and found Jamie there, and the day had continued to spiral out of control. She'd been strung pretty tight by the time she'd sung with him, and hadn't been prepared for her reaction. The excitement, the electricity, the elation. She hadn't had that kind of chemistry onstage in years. Since Tucker. That left her shaking in her favorite boots.

Follow that with how crazy everyone had gone over their performance and half the town jumping on the she-should-let-Jamie-play-with-*her*-band bandwagon, and the perfect storm had formed inside her. And boy, had she let loose on Jamie. The poor guy hadn't deserved that.

As if she didn't have enough distractions to keep her

from getting anything productive done, her cell phone rang. Glancing at the screen revealed Avery's name.

"I wanted to make sure you were okay. What happened at the bar between you and Jamie? You scurried out of there so fast I didn't get to ask," Avery said when Emma answered.

"Scurried? I don't scurry."

"Stomped? Charged? Either of those work? And don't avoid the question."

Emma rubbed the knot in her shoulder, trying to ease the tension there. "I have no idea what happened. I was doing okay."

Okay? You were having more fun, were more alive and happier than you've been in years.

"When Jamie and I were done singing everyone kept saying how great we sounded. Like I sounded lousy before or something. Then Henry Alvarez had the bright idea for Jamie to replace Molly in the band. I said something that Jamie took the wrong way." But what had she expected him to do? Only someone deaf, dumb and blind would've taken a statement that started out with the words *you have no experience* as anything but an insult. "Then it was like we were both possessed, or we lost all common sense and self-control. I don't know. It was crazy. All of a sudden he and I were arguing like two children over who got the bigger piece of cake."

"Having Jamie replace Molly isn't a bad idea."

"Don't start. I can't take it today. I need the I-support-you-in-whatever-decision-you-make speech."

"Then you aren't going to be happy about what's happening on Facebook this morning. You and Jamie have created quite a stir. Someone posted a video of you two singing."

No. Everyone in Halligan's nagging her was one thing, but opening the mess up to the entire free world via the internet? Please, no. Emma booted up her computer and logged on to the social media site. The first thing she noticed was Shay had posted a video of her own performance with Jamie along with a comment about how they had sounded "magical." Really? "I can't believe Shay has the nerve to call her caterwauling with Jamie 'magical.' The woman is either delusional or tone-deaf. Not that anyone's called her on that."

Instead all the comments were from women who went all dreamy over Jamie, his "see into a woman's soul" eyes, his "make me swoon" voice and his "I want to cuddle up with that" body.

"Forget about Shay's post. Have you found the one of your performance with Jamie?"

She located the video. Her stomach dropped when she saw how many likes and shares they had. "I can't believe it. We promoted the heck out of the band's last video, and this thing's gotten more plays in one day than we got in a month."

"If this keeps up you could get some great exposure."

Emma hit Play. As the video started all the excitement she'd felt with Jamie rushed back. She knew it felt right being onstage with him, but she'd had no idea how the energy crackled between them, elevating their performance and their vocals, infusing their singing with a sizzling sensuality. She'd been wrong. She'd never had this kind of chemistry with anyone.

She read the comments. People compared them to some of country's great duos. Her mind rebelled at the thought. She refused to tie her career to one person, especially a man. That's why she'd started Maroon Peak

Pass, and why she was the lead singer. Bass players, drummers and fiddle players could be replaced. Not quickly, as she was learning from Molly's departure. But relying on someone else left her vulnerable, something she refused to do again.

"Promise you won't bite my head off if I ask you a certain question you're not going to like me asking, but I have to ask because it's in the shelter's best interest."

"Avery, it's Sunday afternoon, and my brain's in weekend mode. I have no idea what you just said."

"Don't get mad, but I think we should ask Jamie to sing at the shelter fund-raiser."

"Why would I get upset about that? From the interest he's generated online, I think that's a great idea. He could draw more people to the event." Young, single, man-hungry women, but, hey, their money bought dog food and cat litter as well as anyone else's.

"The thing is, he needs a band to play for him. I was thinking he could sing with Maroon Peak Pass."

Chapter 6

"Just think about it for a minute before you say no," Avery said.

"I don't need to. You want him to sing. That's fine with me, but have him do karaoke again."

"While everyone enjoyed Jamie's singing, they loved you two singing *together* more. Remember the first time Reed and I danced at Halligan's? You told me things were so hot between us you almost ran for a fire extinguisher."

Emma didn't like where the conversation was headed. "Uh-huh."

"I thought the same thing when you and Jamie were onstage."

"That was before our disagreement. I think what we said to each other effectively killed any attraction." *Liar.* At least it hadn't dampened her fascination. "Avery, it was awful. It's not like me to be that thoughtless and hurt someone."

And she had. She'd seen the shock wash over Jamie's features after her "no experience" comment. Then, as she'd continued to lob grenades in his direction, the expression on his face had let her know she'd hit her target. "I wish I could take it all back. We just seemed to push each other's hot buttons."

"That's because there's major sparks between you two."

That's what she was afraid of. She'd always had trouble separating the chemistry she felt with a man onstage from real life. She couldn't afford to make another mistake, not after she'd finally gotten her feet under her and her career back on track.

"You said something else to me that night that fits here."

"I have the funny feeling you're going to throw something I said back in my face."

"You've got that right."

"Your situation with Reed was different. He was an old boyfriend. One you never got over."

"That may be, but I'm going to tell you what you said to me anyway because somewhere along the line you forgot about having a life."

"You're right. After Mom died I should've packed up my Camry and headed back to Nashville." At first she'd been too drained to start over, knowing she'd have to find a new day job, an apartment and, toughest of all, a new band. Instead she'd insisted the smart plan was to take time to grieve and regroup. The next thing she knew another year had gone by. "I may not have the life I envisioned, but I have a life."

"That sounds familiar," Avery said. "Should I tell you what you said to me?"

You forgot about having a love life.

She hated when her words came back to bite her on the ass, and these left teeth marks.

While what Avery said about her love life was true, Emma had consciously made the choice. Women couldn't have it all. That was just a bill of goods the media and big business sold them to keep females from grumbling too much.

For women who wanted to be movers and shakers at the top of their profession, something had to give. Either work or family had to come first. That is, if a woman was lucky enough to find a man who could handle her success, and there weren't many of those around. If she wanted a guy who'd be faithful and didn't have horns and a tail, she narrowed the field even further. But say she won the lottery and found such a man. If she wanted to compete with the big boys in her field, her home life would have to take a back seat. That eventually caused problems. A man might understand for a while, but eventually he'd complain, forcing her to choose between him and her career.

"We've known each other most of our lives, and I've seen you change over the past few years," Avery continued, her voice hesitant but devoid of judgment. "You've shut yourself off from everyone."

"That's not true. I have some close friends. One of whom doesn't know what she's talking about right now."

"It's not just with friends."

"I don't need a man in my life. I've got enough problems."

"You don't let anyone get close to you anymore. I

didn't realize it until I saw you onstage at Halligan's, but you've shut down so much emotionally it's changing your music. When you were singing with Jamie, you let your guard down. You were real. I think that's what made that night so special for everyone watching you two."

Emma's hand tightened around her phone. Avery's words rippled through her like a virus, invading and pervasive, altering everything they touched. Had she changed that much since she'd come back from Nashville this time?

Since returning she hadn't connected with many of her old friends. She hadn't wanted to. In the past she and her bandmates had become friends, but not this time. She rarely socialized, except when Avery cajoled her into going out as only a best friend could. She hadn't gone on a single date, either.

The thought sank in. She hadn't gone out on a date in over two years? That explained a lot of her current problem with Jamie. No wonder seeing him—a guy who, if anything, was hotter than he'd been at nineteen—and remembering how young and hopeful she'd been with him left her reeling. Then add in her memories of how he kissed better than any man had a right to legally, and no wonder her hormones had come out of hibernation.

Avery's words continued to hammer at Emma, breaking through to the truth. She'd been so weary, so beat down from her mother's illness and death, Clint's rejection and having to start over careerwise that she'd gone into survival mode emotionally. She'd quit feeling anything.

Until Jamie.

"Fate sometimes brings people into our lives for a reason," Avery said.

"Don't give me that philosophical bull. My life doesn't need changing. It's fine the way it is."

You're protesting too much. Who are you trying so hard to convince?

"Do you think that's why Jamie pushes your hot buttons so easily? Are you so sure your life doesn't need shaking up?"

La, la, la. I'm not listening. I won't. I can't.

Wasn't it bad enough that Jamie had invaded her weekend, her Facebook news feed and way too many of her thoughts? Now Avery wanted her to let him into her one haven, Maroon Peak Pass.

"With my mom's death and all that's happened over the past two years, I'm not sure I'm strong enough to take my life being shaken up. I couldn't even take it being stirred right now." She chuckled at her lame joke, but the sound came out nervous, almost fragile.

"Then forget about Jamie singing at the fund-raiser. Sure, money's tight at the shelter. When isn't it?" Avery said, executing an abrupt about-face. "But it's not like when we needed to buy the land last year. We'll be fine. You backed me up when I bent the rules about Jess volunteering without an adult because I couldn't face Reed. Now I'm returning the favor."

Tears stung Emma's eyes. She bit the inside of her cheek, trying to regain control as she stumbled into the bathroom for a tissue. "If I were the perfect employee I'd say I'll suck it up, take one for the team and let Jamie play with us because it's best for the shelter."

"So you'll have to settle for being nearly perfect."

"Thanks." She caught sight of herself in the vanity

mirror. Who was that woman staring back at her? The one with the wide, haunted eyes who looked as if she was scared of her own shadow. No one she recognized, that's for sure.

That'd be the day, and no way would she let the shelter lose out on money because she was scared of being attracted to a man.

Sometimes fighting against something was worse than giving in. She'd learned that one year when she'd given up carbs for Lent. The cravings had just about driven her crazy. That's when she learned moderation was the key to almost everything in life. This situation with Jamie wouldn't get the best of her. The key was control and moderate doses. "I've changed my mind about having Jamie sing. If you want him to do a couple of numbers, the band will back him up, but I want it duly noted that my status has changed from nearly perfect to perfect employee."

"Done. I owe you one."

"That's for sure."

After her conversation with Avery, Emma worked on returning emails from prospective volunteers, but messages started popping up on her personal Facebook page. Was Jamie single? Could she introduce them?

She closed her personal page and continued working on shelter business. That worked for five minutes until her phone started dinging with text messages from friends and acquaintances asking the same questions. Lord, you'd think Jamie was the last single man in a four-state area from the feeding frenzy he'd created.

Deciding to put a stop to the nonsense, she pulled up her Facebook page and posted a statement on her wall.

I have two jobs. Running a dating service isn't one of them. If that changes, I'll let everyone know.

She chewed on her lip for a minute thinking about the video of her and Jamie on YouTube, and she started wondering what he was like onstage with the Philharmonic. Out of curiosity she entered his name on Google. When the results popped up she clicked on a link of him playing a solo. A minute later all she could think was that she was an idiot to have scoffed at Henry's suggestion.

Jamie's musical ability made Molly look like a middle schooler who'd picked up the violin a month ago. And she'd had the nerve to tell him just because he had the skill to play the notes didn't mean he could make music. With his talent, merely playing the notes would outshine anyone she'd auditioned. Anyone she could hope to find.

She'd never seriously considered asking Jamie because she'd been too busy running from what she felt for him, but now that she stepped back and analyzed the situation, the idea of him joining the band had merit. She'd been searching for something or someone to grab people's attention and set her band apart. Molly's fiddle playing helped, but not as much as she'd hoped. Between Jamie's charisma and his talent, could he be the answer?

While Emma had struggled to create a presence on social media, Jamie had accomplished more for Maroon Peak Pass in one day than she had with all her efforts, and the more buzz they had going into the state fair, the better their chances that Phillip Brandise would have them on his radar before they played a note.

But working with Jamie? If only he hadn't made her go all weak in the knees and warm and tingly everywhere else. Talk about a job-related hazard.

She opened a new document on her computer and

listed the pros and cons of working with Jamie. The first thing she wrote under the con column was that to get him to even listen to her offer after the way she'd acted would mean letting go of her pride. *Major groveling involved.* She stared at what she'd typed and underlined *major.* Halfway through her list she realized the best thing for the band was to ask Jamie to join them, but maybe Luke and Grayson would feel differently. After all, she hadn't been thinking all that clearly since she'd picked Jamie up at the airport.

Hoping she was wrong about him and the band, she fired off an email with the link to his solo and the pros and cons of her idea—sans the her having to grovel part—to Luke and Grayson for their opinion. Maybe they'd respond saying she'd lost her mind and no way could a classical musician make the transition to country music. Then she could let go of the idea and if anyone brought the subject up again, she could say she and the band had discussed the issue. Case closed.

Five minutes later both Luke and Grayson had responded saying they thought asking Jamie was a great idea.

Now what?

Sunday night when the restlessness hit, Jamie set out for a walk. When the hike through the mountains failed to burn off his agitation, he headed for the barn to muck out a few stalls.

How had he let Emma get under his skin so many ways last night? Lack of self-control. Loneliness. Insanity. Take your pick.

He scooped up a forkful of hay and dumped it into the bin on the far wall of the stall. Bits of straw floated around him, eventually landing on his running shoes. The shoes worked great for jogging through the city, but weren't so hot for ranch work. He should think about investing in a good pair of boots, but he'd held off. He kept telling himself he wouldn't be around that long. Or at least he hoped not. There was something about investing in work boots that made him feel as though he was admitting his situation wouldn't change, that his hand wouldn't improve. Right now he preferred to think of being in Colorado as a vacation, as a distraction from the problems in his life.

And that's what Emma was. One powerful distraction.

He retrieved more hay and scattered it around the stall. He wished he could see in a crystal ball and know if all his hand needed was hard work and time. Until he figured that out, he was in limbo. As if he'd been cut adrift and was floating through life wherever the current took him.

When his cell phone rang, he glanced at his watch, smiled and leaned the pitch fork against the barn wall. Eight on Sunday night. His parents were right on time with their weekly call.

"How are things going in Colorado?" his dad asked.

"Getting away has cleared my head." *Too bad it's now as empty as a ski resort in summer.*

For the next few minutes they discussed his dad's job and how work was going for his mom at the accounting firm. He got the latest news about his sisters, discovering Kate was up for a promotion with 3M.

"I think Wade is going to propose to Rachel soon," his mom said. "Maybe we'll be having a wedding in the spring."

Yup, his sisters had all their ducks in a row. Their

lives neatly falling into place. Yet another way he and his siblings differed.

"So, you've been working around the ranch and at the restaurant?" his mother asked, obviously trolling for information.

He told them about getting roped into singing karaoke when the band was late. "It turned out to be a lot of fun. Emma, that girl I dated a couple of times that one summer, sang with me. We were pretty good together."

In more ways than just onstage.

"I'm glad you're getting out and socializing. It's funny that you mentioned karaoke. You used to love singing," his mother said. "Remember how much you enjoyed singing in the church choir?"

"For a while there we weren't sure whether you'd focus on the violin or singing," his dad added.

He'd forgotten about the children's choir he'd been in when he was in elementary school. He'd wanted to take choir in middle school, but couldn't fit it, orchestra and his core classes into his schedule. He'd been forced to choose, but there'd been no real choice. All his teachers agreed that while his singing was good, he was a gifted violinist.

He hadn't considered singing anywhere but the shower since then. Until last night. First Mick mentioned him playing country music. Then Henry suggested he join Emma's band and now his parents mentioned how much he once loved singing. Maybe fate was trying to tell him something.

"I never understood why schools make kids choose between choir and instruments in middle school," his father said. "Those kids who want to have a career in music should be able to do both."

"I say you should quit worrying about the future so much right now. Have some fun. Life has a way of working out if we give it time." His mother's soothing voice flowed over him. For a pencil-pushing number cruncher, she had a knack for knowing just what to say.

"You'll figure things out. We have faith in you," his father said. "We'll support you no matter what you decide to do. All we want is for you to be happy."

He'd hit the lottery when they'd chosen him, he thought as he ended the call and shoved his cell phone into his back pocket. He was about to head back to the house when he heard Trixie rustling around in her stall. Sensing that something was off, he decided to check on her. When he opened the stall door, the horse swung her head and turned her rear toward him, blocking the entrance. "What's bothering you, girl?"

A couple of Mick's horses leaned toward being high-strung, but not Trixie. The chestnut loved everyone. Of all the horses on the ranch, Trixie was his favorite. Something about her gentle spirit mixed with her curious nature and her calm strength tugged at him. But right now she was definitely out of sorts. Ears back, she moved her head up and down as if nodding. One of the first things Mick had taught him was how to recognize when a horse sent out don't-come-any-closer signals, and Trixie was saying that loud and clear.

Time to tread easy. The most laid-back animals often created the biggest storms when they got upset.

Kind of like a certain woman he'd irritated at Halligan's.

He still couldn't figure out what had happened with Emma. They'd been great together onstage, teasing and joking. Playing off each other, sometimes in such a sen-

sual dance he'd forgotten they were in public. But the
minute the music had ended, things changed. Emma had
almost shut down before his eyes. At least until Henry
had suggested he join her band. That comment sure lit
a fire under her, and if the truth be told, some of what
she'd said stirred him up pretty good, too.

They'd both let their tempers get the best of them.

He was just about to head out of the stall when a
weak, squeaky noise came from the far corner. "What's
over there, girl, and why won't you let me see?" He
managed to peer around the horse at the hay pile. There
he spotted a small bundle of white-and-tan fur. When
the animal wiggled he realized it was a puppy. A very
young one that needed its mother.

"So that's what you're protecting." Not sure what else
to do, he pulled out his cell phone and called Mick. "I
found a pup in Trixie's stall. One too young to be on
its own. Do you know who it might belong to or where
we could find its mother?"

"I don't know of anyone around here that had a pregnant dog or one that had puppies recently. The mom's
probably a stray and the one you found got separated
from her and the rest of the litter."

"We can't just leave it here. From the way it's crying
it's either hungry or hurt."

"Bring the pup to the house. I'll call Emma. She
works at the animal shelter. She'll know what to do."

"Trixie won't let me anywhere near it."

"Then Emma will have to come out here and help
us get the poor thing."

Chapter 7

Standing in his living room, Mick smiled so big he thought he might bust. He couldn't have planned this better.

Most of the day he'd been racking his brain to figure out how to fix things between Emma and Jamie. Now the perfect solution had dropped into his lap, or rather crawled into his barn.

"We don't need to bother Emma," Jamie said. "You and I can get the pup out and drop it off at the shelter."

Sure, they could, but that wouldn't get his match-making plans back on track.

"I don't feel comfortable handling this. Better safe than sorry, I say. Emma deals with stuff like this at the shelter all the time," Mick said with confidence even though he had no idea how many rescue situations Emma dealt with since she was the volunteer coordinator. Hopefully Jamie wouldn't think of that.

"Okay, you're the boss."

Mick smiled again as he ended the conversation with Jamie and called Emma. This would work. When she came to help with the pup he'd make himself scarce, forcing her and Jamie to work together. Taking care of the dog would give them a chance to get to know each other. It would give them something other than music to talk about.

"Jamie and I need some help with a pup we found in the barn," he said when she answered.

"The shelter's closed, but I'll meet you there to accept the puppy."

"The problem is the dog's in Trixie's stall, and she won't let us near it."

"I'll relay the information to Avery and have her call you. She'll know what to do. Since she's the vet, she handles these calls. That way if the animal needs immediate medical attention she can take care of it."

Damn. He should've thought about that problem before he called. He scrambled to think of a reason to get Emma to come out with Avery, but couldn't come up with anything on the fly. "Will you call me back after you talk to her?"

That would at least buy him some time.

Emma sat on her couch and realized she'd actually be glad when her weekend ended and she could return to work. Maybe then she could forget about Jamie Westland.

At least the issue with the puppy would be Avery's problem. Or so she thought, but by the third ring when Avery hadn't picked up, Emma started getting nervous. After the fourth ring, Avery's voice mail kicked in, forcing her to leave a message about the situation. Then she waited.

Where was Avery and why wasn't her phone on? That wasn't like her. After ten minutes when she hadn't heard, Emma started thinking she needed to go out to the ranch. If the puppy was as young as Mick said, it could quickly become dehydrated without nursing. Then if it was flea infested, which was highly likely if it was a stray, it could be anemic and worm-riddled. Combine all those conditions and the situation could turn dire for a young puppy surprisingly fast.

After ten on Sunday night and now she was dealing with an orphaned puppy. That she could handle, but this wasn't a simple drop-off. Unwilling to put the puppy at risk, she snatched her cell phone off the coffee table and called Mick. "I had to leave a message for Avery. Are you sure you can't get to the puppy?"

Please say you've gotten it out of the stall.

"I really think we need another person. That way Jamie and I can deal with Trixie while you get the pup. Otherwise I'm worried the little fella will get hurt. Jamie said it looks like it's just starting to walk and who knows how long it's been since the pup's eaten."

"I'm on my way."

As she drove across town toward Mick's ranch, she told herself she'd stay a few minutes. Tops. That's all this little task should take. After all, Mick had a solid plan. He and Jamie would calm the horse while she scooted around to scoop up the puppy. No problem. Then she'd get back in her car and head for the shelter before they finished thanking her.

Confident that she could handle the situation, Emma's thoughts turned to dealing with seeing Jamie again. She

prided herself on being pretty easygoing. She understood
people, cut them slack and didn't let them get to her. That
was part of what made her a good volunteer coordinator. But she couldn't figure Jamie out. He was such an
odd combination. Distant and formal one minute, and
then—she paused—hot, steamy and sexy as hell the next.

Well, there wouldn't be any of that tonight. As far
as she was concerned he was just another person who
needed help with a stray animal. She dealt with this on a
daily basis, but to make sure nothing went wrong, she'd
avoid the hot-button topics—politics, religion and, in
her case, music. And if he threw her any of those turn-
a-woman-to-warm-goo looks like he had on the stage,
she'd just close her eyes.

By the time she reached Mick's ranch, she had a
smile plastered on her face and an I-can-handle-this
mantra running through her head. She took two calming breaths and tugged open the barn door. The hinges
squeaked, announcing her arrival.

The familiar smells of her childhood—hay, dust
and horses—swirled around her as she followed the
low rumble of male voices until she located Jamie and
Mick. She rounded the corner and froze. All her confidence rushed out of her, along with her breath, when
she spotted Jamie. Nothing made a handsome man look
quite the way a good pair of jeans did, and Jamie was
no exception.

*Remember, he's just another person with an or-
phaned animal. Granted, a better-looking one than
most, but he's just another person who needs help.*

He nodded in her direction. "Thanks for coming."

"We sure do appreciate it," Mick said when she reached

them. Then he patted Jamie on the back. "I'm sure you two can handle this, so I'll head back to the house."

"Wait a minute. Stop right there," Emma said when Mick turned to leave. "You said we needed all three of us to handle this."

"That's right. I did." The older man pushed bits of hay around with the toe of his scuffed boot. Then a second later he snapped his fingers. "We're gonna need a halter. I'll go get one."

"We'll be fine without it."

"Things will be easier if we use one," Mick said as he dashed off.

She turned to Jamie. "Is it just me, or is he acting a little odd?"

"You think?" Jamie shook his head. "I'm sorry Mick bothered you. I told him we could handle this, but he was worried about something happening to the dog." Jamie shoved his hands into the front pockets of his jeans. The movement pulled his dark T-shirt taunt across his broad shoulders.

For a city boy he sure looked comfortable in the barn. Comfortable? No, that wasn't right. He looked as if he belonged on a cowboy-of-the-month calendar. All he needed was a cowboy hat dangling from his long fingers and a good pair of boots. She hadn't expected that. How could a man be at ease on a symphony stage and equally so in a barn?

She tried to focus her thoughts. This would be a lot easier if she cleared the air. "About last night. I need to apologize. My mouth was driving while my brain was asleep at the wheel. Could we just forget the whole thing?"

Relief eased the tension in his face. "That's fine with me. I said some things I'm not real proud of."

Puppy whimpers followed by Trixie's nervous movements drifted out of the stall. "Where's Mick with the halter?" Jamie glanced down the hallway.

The sooner they retrieved the puppy, the sooner she could hightail it out of here. "We can manage without him. Do you want to deal with the horse or get the dog?"

"I'll handle Trixie. She and I are friends, aren't we, girl?"

Emma swallowed hard. *I bet you are. What female wouldn't respond to a good-looking man when he gazed at her with those dreamy brown eyes and whispered her name in that bedroom voice?*

"When you get in the stall, talk to the horse in a calm, soothing voice until you can get close enough to stroke her neck and face. That should keep her relaxed enough for me to get the puppy."

As Jamie turned and walked toward the stall, Emma had to remind herself to breathe. What his butt did for those jeans ought to be registered as an illegal weapon. *Breathe in and out.* Maybe concentrating on that would get her surging hormones under control.

When he tried to step in the stall, the horse swung her rear around, blocking him, and tossed her head. "Now, don't go getting your nose all out of joint, pretty girl. We're going to take this slow."

His smooth, soft voice floated through the still night and wrapped around Emma. *Oh, my.* She'd told him to use a calm, soothing voice. Wasn't working. At least not for her. If she got any more hot and bothered she'd end up a puddle on the barn floor.

"You're worried about that baby, aren't you?" Jamie said as he inched closer. The horse stomped her hind foot.

"Watch out. That means she's—"

"I know. She's giving me a warning, aren't you, Trixie girl? You're telling me you mean business. You want me to leave. I hear you, but we need to see that pup you're so intent on protecting." He moved closer. The horse struck out with her hind leg in a quick stroke.

"Be careful. The next step is for her to make that kick count."

"She won't do that." He slid his hand over the animal's neck. "I won't hurt your little one. I promise."

Emma resisted the urge to sigh. If he promised her the moon in that quiet, make-her-melt voice, Emma would check her mailbox expecting to find it in a box with a bright red bow. She swallowed hard. So much for thinking she could treat him like anyone else they helped at the shelter. Her plan had been solid. Unfortunately, her execution stunk. "For a city boy, you're doing a fair job dealing with that horse."

He glanced over his shoulder at her, his eyebrows knit together, a scowl on his handsome face. "What's with all the city-boy comments?"

Simple self-defense.

It reminds me that you won't be around long, and how that's one more reason I shouldn't get any crazy ideas about you and me.

"That bothers you, huh?"

"As if you didn't know." He laughed and continued stroking the horse. The man had killer eyes when they shimmered from his laughter. Eyes that could get a woman to sell her soul for a wooden nickel. "I've been here a lot over the years, and Mick's taught me a thing or two about horses."

"Apparently you were a good student."

"I'm good at a lot of things."

The earth tilted under her as his steamy gaze locked on her, and she knew. He'd take his time with a woman.

Not what she needed to think about right now, but she couldn't stop the images of them together in all kinds of interesting ways and positions from running through her mind. They'd had some great chemistry when they'd dated as teenagers, and she couldn't help but wonder how he'd matured, what he'd learned and how much fun she could have finding out.

Don't say anything. Take the smart route. Ignore the innuendo.

"No quick comeback to put me in my place?"

No way would she touch that statement with a hazmat suit and a ten-foot pole because even that wouldn't be enough protection.

His gaze moved away from hers and focused on the horse. His large hands moved over the animal, soothing and calming. She glanced at the wall over his shoulder, but couldn't shut out his voice. "How about you let us see that baby? You've kind of adopted him, haven't you? I bet you'd make a fine mama. You've got a lot of love to give. I see that in your eyes."

Jamie's words rippled through Emma. What did he see when he looked into her eyes? No, she didn't want to know.

Boots shuffling against concrete sounded Mick's return and snapped her out of her haze.

Still a little unsettled and trying to regroup, Emma turned to the older man. "What took you so long?"

"What did you have to do, make the halter?" Jamie added.

"I had trouble finding the right one." Mick moved past her and handed Jamie the halter.

As Jamie slipped the leather over the horse's head,

Mick turned to Emma, his voice low. "How a man treats animals and the way they react to him says a lot about his character."

She nodded. Animals possessed more common sense than most people and didn't let things like money, status and looks cloud their judgment. "They see through the pretense to the real person."

"Nope, you can't fool a horse. Be leery of a man that dogs or horses don't like. They can spot a bad one a mile away." Mick nodded toward his grandson. "He's a good man with a strong heart. A cowboy's heart."

Emma chuckled. The phrase sounded as though it should be an article in *Cowboy Monthly*. Does your man have the heart of a cowboy? Take our survey and find out. "What's that supposed to mean?"

"He loves his family, God and his country. He's honest and tough but has a heart of gold."

She laughed. "You sound like an ad for an old John Wayne movie."

"What are you two talking about?" Jamie asked, his brows scrunched together in confusion. "Remember the puppy? The reason we're out here?"

Mick yawned. "It's past my bedtime, and I've got to be at the restaurant early. If I don't get to sleep I won't be worth a thing. You two have this under control." The older man turned to leave.

"We might need some help," Emma said, afraid of losing her last line of defense.

"Once the two of you get in the stall, unless I hang from the ceiling there won't be room for me." Mick took another step. "Jamie, when I see you at the restaurant tomorrow, let me know how things went."

Then, before she or Jamie could say or do anything,

Mick darted for the door. A minute later the barn door creaked open and clanked shut.

"I've never seen him move that fast. It was like someone lit a fire under him," Jamie said, a look of complete confusion plastered on his face.

Wait a minute. Since Mick closed the bar, her grandfather opened in the mornings. Then Mick arrived just before the lunch rush hit. "Something stinks around here and it isn't because the hay needs changing. Mick never opens the restaurant. Why would he say that?"

"I don't know. You want me to go after him?"

"Forget it. You're doing a great job with Trixie. We don't need Mick." The sooner she left, the better, and not just for the pup. She stepped into the stall and stood inside the door as the horse eyed her. "Don't worry, girl. I'm here to help."

Jamie stroked the horse's neck while Emma stepped closer. Impatient to get her hands on the pup, she tried to scoot by the animal. When she did, Trixie swung her rear toward her, knocking Emma off balance. Unable to get her footing and fearing she'd tumble onto the puppy, she grabbed the nearest object to right herself—Jamie. Her hands fisted in his shirt. His arm slid around her waist—warm and strong, offering her support. "Take it easy. There's nothing to worry about."

Was he talking to her or the horse? Not that she cared. Who would when he used that bedroom voice? She tried to focus, but all she could think about was his hand burning her skin through her cotton blouse. That and the fact that he'd been there to catch her.

She'd forgotten how great it felt to have a man's arm around her, but her body remembered. Tingles raced down her spine, bringing heat to places that had been near dead for too long.

Hormone drought. That's what she'd been in, and now that the flow had started again, her body ached. But that's all this was. Her body kicking back into gear. Any man holding her would have brought about the same reaction, the same heat.

Liar.

She'd had relationships since Tucker, probably more than she should have, but hadn't connected with anyone but Clint—but even his touch hadn't lit her up like Jamie's had right now.

This was bad, but being bad could be so good.

"You okay?"

She was fine, all right. Her body was all warm and tingly with happy hormones. A woman could get addicted to feeling like this. All she could do was nod. Her heart beating out a rapid staccato beat, she stepped away.

Trixie shifted nervously and tried to pull away from Jamie. He leaned closer and his soft voice floated over Emma as he started singing. The simple tune, the Beatles' "Blackbird," touched her in a way a song hadn't in years. The man could tame a grizzly when he sang like that. His compassion, his caring wrapped around her. Her heart squeezed.

He's someone special.

No, he's not, and even if he is, I don't care. She had plans. Things she needed to prove to herself and everyone else who'd ever doubted her. A man would only cause problems.

Jamie sang to Trixie to get himself under control as much as to calm the horse. When Emma had pulled away he'd wanted to drag her back against him. Even after the things they'd said to each other at Halligan's, she still sent his pulse racing. Something that shouldn't happen with such a simple touch.

He was crazy to even think about her after she'd given him clear signals that she wasn't interested. Only a fool kept banging his head against a stone wall, and he was no fool.

Too bad his body had tossed out the memo.

While Trixie settled down quickly, he couldn't say the same thing about himself, especially when Emma scooted past him. Her sweet flowery scent swept over him, keeping his body humming at a fever pitch. No woman should smell that good in a barn. The horse shifted beside him, trying to turn toward Emma to keep an eye on her. "It's okay, sweetheart. Take it easy. You can trust her."

But can I?

When Emma reached the corner, she scooped up the bundle and walked back to him.

"See? I'm not going to hurt him." She held out the pup to the larger animal. "He's fine. Will you take him so I can call Avery?" He took the puppy as Emma placed her call.

Jamie peered at the tiny white puff ball with brown fur around his eyes and on his ears. The tiny thing was all ears and legs.

"We've got the puppy I left the message about. He can't be more than a month old." She moved the dog's lips back to expose his teeth and gums. Then she pinched a section of skin and let it go. "His gums are pretty pale and his skin's taking a while to go back into place. He's probably anemic and dehydrated. He may need fluids."

She paused to listen and turned to him after she ended the call. "Avery will meet me at the shelter."

"Is he going to be okay?"

"I'll be honest. Things can go downhill quickly with puppies this young, but Avery's a great vet. We'll do our best."

"Then we'd better get going." He walked out of the horse stall, the puppy cradled in his large hand.

She dashed after him. "I'll take it from here."

Jamie stopped to wait for her and glanced at his watch. "It's after eleven. What kind of man would I be if I let you go out alone at this late hour? I'd never forgive myself if something happened to you. Plus, I'm kind of attached to this guy." He paused and turned the puppy upside down. "Yup. It's a he."

When she opened her mouth to argue, he said, "We can either stand here arguing, and you won't win, by the way, or we can get this puppy the help he needs."

"You're going to be stubborn about this, aren't you?" He stared at her. She sighed. "Let's go."

When Emma and Jamie reached the Estes Park animal shelter parking lot, the glimmer from the lone street light and the crescent moon sprinkled the area.

She unlocked the shelter's front door, entered and turned on the lights. "Follow me. We'll clean him up while we're waiting for Avery. We need to get the fleas off him. They can be deadly for a dog this young."

"This guy's had a tough start." Jamie scratched the pup behind the ear as she led him through the shelter to a back room. "It'll get better from here, buddy."

Emma told him to hold the dog over the tub. Once

he did, she grabbed the spray nozzle, turned on the tap and waited for the water to warm up.

"How does someone with a music degree and a band end up working as the volunteer coordinator for a local animal shelter?"

Such a simple question. Small talk, really. The kind strangers at a party tossed out to each other without even thinking. How could something so supposedly inconsequential pack such a wallop?

"It's a long story."

"I've got plenty of time."

Everyone in town knew her story, but no one ever asked her to talk about what she'd gone through. They just knew, but they didn't understand. She considered fobbing him off with some vague "life happens" flip comment, but something stopped her. His eyes. They could get a woman to reveal her deepest secrets.

He's got a cowboy's heart.

Jamie would understand, and right now she wanted that. Needed it.

"After I graduated from college I moved to Nashville again." She'd packed up her hopes and dreams, tossed them in a 2003 Camry with one hundred and twenty thousand miles on it and swore the second time things would be different. "I was in a band and things were going well. Really well. We'd caught the eye of a promoter and he was on the verge of taking us on. Then my mom was diagnosed with pancreatic cancer."

"Cancer's always bad, but that one's brutal."

She nodded. The odds had been against her mom. Only a little over 20 percent of people diagnosed with the disease were alive after one year, but Emma had hoped her mom would be one of the lucky ones. "Between chemo and the cancer she felt pretty lousy most of the time. She was weak and in so much pain. I came home to help with her care."

Emma held her hand under the spray of water to test the temperature, gently wet the pup's white fluffy fur and squirted soap over him, as memories welled up inside her.

As her mother's health had continued to deteriorate, Emma couldn't leave. She was needed, but more important, she wanted to spend as much time as she could with her mother. While she didn't regret her decision, dealing with the endless appointments and medical issues had drained her emotionally. She'd needed something else to occupy her mind. Something to feed her soul. She'd needed somewhere to regroup. Or to fall apart.

"Once I realized I was going to stay longer than I planned, I told the band I wouldn't be coming back. Turned out they'd already replaced me. They just forgot to tell me."

"Real nice of them. They could've at least had the balls to tell you."

"That's what I said. Anyway, that's when I decided I needed a place of my own. Staying at my parents' house was—" She paused and chewed on her lower lip.

"Too much to take, almost overwhelming."

She nodded, stunned at how he'd understood what she couldn't put into words. "To get an apartment I needed to support myself. I thought about teaching music in a school, but those jobs are hard to come by in a small community. People get one and keep it until they retire."

After she massaged the soap through the puppy's

fur to dislodge as many fleas as possible, she rinsed the
dog. Small dark specks floated among the soap bubbles.
"Those black things are fleas."

Jamie stared into the sink. "Poor fella. It's a wonder
he's got any blood left with those things gnawing at him."

She reached into the cabinet above the sink and
pulled out a fine-tooth comb. "This should get any critters that held on and survived the bath."

"So you couldn't find a teaching position?" Jamie
asked, returning to their previous conversation.

"No. I considered giving private lessons, but that
takes time to find enough students to pay the bills."

"And I suppose you were stubbornly attached to luxuries like hot water, electricity and food."

His comment made her smile. She liked how he made
her do that. "Call me crazy. So when I heard the shelter needed a volunteer coordinator, I thought, I love
animals and this could be a way for me to pay the bills
while I help take care of Mom. It's not what I want to
do forever, but don't get me wrong. I don't regret my
decision. Mom died eight months after her diagnosis."

"Living with no regrets is worth a lot."

Too bad she couldn't say the same for other areas of
her life. At least she was working on her career regrets.

The puppy whimpered when the comb stuck in his
tangled fur. "Hang on, pal," Jamie said as he scratched
it behind the ears. "I know you feel lousy right now, but
things are gonna get better from here."

Good-looking. A voice that could melt the hardest
woman's heart, and he took care of kids and small de-
fenseless animals.

Where was Avery? She could really use the cavalry
showing up. A girl could only hold out for so long.

Chapter 8

"I see you're taking care of the fleas," Avery said when she walked into the room, and Emma almost sighed in relief. Much longer and her self-control would've disintegrated like a child's snowman on an unseasonably warm winter day.

After Avery introduced herself she moved around the room opening drawers and cupboards, collecting the supplies she needed to treat the puppy's issues.

"You're going to need all this for him?" Jamie said as he stared at the materials spread out on the table. "This has to be expensive."

"It's not easy balancing animals' needs with our donations." Avery filled a syringe with saline and delivered the liquid to the puppy under his skin. As she squirted another liquid into the animal's mouth to deal with any internal parasites, she glanced at Emma, her eyebrows raised, and nodded slightly toward Jamie as if to say, *Here's our opening to ask him about the fund-raiser. Go for it.*

Time for her, as the perfect employee, to put her money where her mouth was. "Speaking of donations, we've got our major fund-raiser coming up. Avery and I were talking about a way you could help us."

"We're having a Pet Walk at Stanley Park. Last year we added Emma's band giving a concert to the event," Avery said. "Since you've created such uproar online, we wondered if you'd sing with Emma's band at the event."

He laughed, as if he thought they were joking. When Emma and Avery didn't join in, he froze and stared at them. "Don't tell me you're serious."

They both nodded. The guy really didn't have a clue how amazing his voice was? That seemed hard to believe.

"You think my singing will help the shelter raise money? I can't believe anyone would buy a ticket for that."

"Obviously you haven't seen the online video of you at Halligan's or read any of the comments on Facebook." Or looked in a mirror. Women would come out in droves to watch him stand onstage and read *War and Peace.*

He shook his head. "I've been enjoying being un-plugged since I got to Colorado."

"Then let me fill you in," Emma said. "I swear half of the single women I know who saw the video today contacted me. They wanted to know if you're available and how they can meet you."

"You're kidding." A blush crept up from his neck into his face.

"She's not," Avery said.

"As long as you're sure. Singing with the band sounds like fun."

For one of us, maybe.

"Fantastic. I'll let you two work out the details about the performance while I see to publicity. Now back to this little guy." Avery patted the puppy. "We'll put out the word about our friend tomorrow. Hopefully we can reunite him with his mom, but we need to figure out what to do with him tonight. He'll need to be fed every two hours. I hate to call any of our volunteers this late. Can you take him, Emma?"

"My apartment doesn't take pets, remember?"

Jamie stared at her. "Isn't that like an atheist working at a church?"

"Ha-ha. That's a good one. It was the only affordable place I could find with an opening. What about you, Avery?"

"If I bring home any more animals Reed is going to make me sleep on the couch. We've got Baxter, and we're watching Thor for Jess. In addition we're fostering Molly the Doberman mix and Mumford the ninety-pound Lab. The apartment is overflowing with dogs. I don't dare bring home a puppy that needs feeding every two hours. You sure you can't take him for the night, Em?"

"With Arlene Rogers living next door? That woman has Vulcan hearing, and after the last time I got caught bringing my work home, so to speak, my landlord threatened to evict me."

"I'll take him," Jamie said. He turned to Emma. "That is, if you'll help me get him settled in and show me what to do."

She tried to think of a reason to say no and then

thought, what was the point? The saying "she'd be closing the barn door after the horses had already escaped"
popped into her head. "Since I have to take you back to
the ranch anyway, I might as well stick around to help
with the first feeding." The calm and steady tone of her
voice, despite the knot in her stomach, surprised her.

Something told her she'd be smarter pressing her
luck with the landlord than spending any more time
with Jamie. The things she did for her day job.

Fifteen minutes later, when Jamie and Emma stood
in Mick's small outdated kitchen, Jamie almost smiled
at Emma's determination to stay all business with him.
If he moved closer to her, she backpedaled. She failed to
make eye contact. Her voice remained devoid of emotion. As she explained what he'd need to do to care for
the pup through the night, the harder she tried to remain
detached, the more intrigued he became. She was just
trying too hard to put him in his place, to show him he
couldn't get under her skin. That had to mean something, didn't it?

He dug into a drawer, found a can opener and handed
it to Emma. While she opened the can of puppy milk
replacer and filled the dropper, she explained that every
two hours he'd feed the liquid a little bit at a time to
the pup.

When she went to hand him the dropper, he picked
up the carrier containing the puppy and headed for the
living room instead. He looked at her over his shoulder. "I don't know about you, but I've got to sit down
before I fall down."

"It's been a long night, hasn't it?" she said as she
followed him.

He nodded toward the pictures scattered around the

living room. "I love this house. It's the kind of home that should be filled with family and friends. Looks like it used to be that kind of place."

"Before Mick's wife died they entertained all the time. My grandpa G says Mick's been so lonely since Carol died. You coming into his life has been a blessing."

"It's been that for me, too." A calm port in the storm his life had become. After he and Emma settled onto the worn brown couch, Jamie retrieved the puppy. Wide sleepy eyes peered up at him as he accepted the dropper from Emma. He squeezed some milk into the puppy's mouth. "He's a cute little guy. He won't have any problem getting adopted if we can't find his mom, will he?"

"He shouldn't have any problem finding a home."

"I always wanted a dog."

"How come you never had one?"

For a few days he had. In fourth grade he'd written a persuasive paper on why his parents should let him have a dog. He smiled thinking of his arguments. He'd get more exercise walking the dog and play fewer video games. Having a pet would teach him responsibility. People who had pets were healthier because petting a dog lowered a person's blood pressure. He'd shown his parents his paper. They'd knuckled and had taken him to the local shelter.

He'd been so excited when they'd brought Rocco home. He'd crawled out of bed a half an hour early to walk him before school every day and then walked him again first thing when he got home. They'd been inseparable, the pup even sleeping on the foot of his bed at night.

"My sister had asthma so we couldn't have a dog."

Of course they hadn't known that until his sister had
suffered a severe attack, ending up in the emergency
room the third night they'd had Rocco. The first thing
the E.R. doctor said was having a dog in the house
would make Rachel's condition worse. The next day
they gave Rocco to a couple across town, and Jamie
cried himself to sleep for a week.

When he graduated from college he'd considered getting a dog, but the time never seemed right. He'd been
focused on his career and didn't feel it would be fair to
the animal to bring him into a home where he'd spend
so much time alone.

"You have a sister? Is she older or younger?"

"I have two, actually. My oldest sister is only a year
younger than I am. My parents tried for seven years
to get pregnant and went through all kinds of fertility
treatments before they adopted me. Then, boom. They
got pregnant with my sister. Three years after that they
had my other sister."

"Was that hard, being the only one adopted?"

No one had ever come right out and asked him
that before. People hinted at the subject and hoped
he'd indulge their curiosity, but he'd always ignored
the implied question. For the first time he wanted to
tell someone what it had felt like. No, not someone.
He wanted to share what it had been like with Emma.
"Everyone in my family is very analytical. Very left-
brained. I'm the opposite."

Emma nodded, and understanding flared in her soft
gaze. "I'm the only girl in my family. All my brothers
are outdoor types, and two of them are ranchers like
my father. The farthest any of them has ventured is to
the other side of town when they purchased their own

Julie Benson *119*

spread. You know the Sesame Street song that goes 'one of these things is not like the other'? That was my theme song."

So that's why she understood. He'd never have guessed she was the odd one out in her family, too. She seemed so confident, so at ease in the world, but then people probably said the same about him.

"Noncreative types find people like us hard to understand. Sometimes it was like I was speaking a different language."

He started to deny what she'd said, even though he'd thought it more than once, but stopped himself. Looking into Emma's expressive face, he knew she wouldn't judge him as being disrespectful to the couple who loved him when the woman who gave birth to him refused to. "I know what you mean. My parents were supportive. They went to all my orchestra events. They volunteered at school and in Cub Scouts. They are great parents, but it was weird at times. My sisters would do something that reminded them of someone in the family." He stopped. *And I didn't have that genetic link.*

"And you didn't have that connection," Emma said, summing up his sentiments. "Is that what made you search for your birth family?"

Would he have been so anxious to find where he'd come from if his siblings had been adopted, too, or if he'd been an only child? Would he have been more content? "The genetic link my sisters shared, the fact that people saw bits and pieces of our parents or other relatives in them, made me think about who I was. I wondered what part of me was because of my DNA and what came from the people who raised me."

What it came down to was control. What he had the

ability to change about himself and what was his genetic blueprint. He glanced at the puppy who'd fallen asleep curled up on his lap now that his belly was full. He lifted the animal and placed him inside the carrier on an old towel they'd put inside.

"When I met Mick, so many things made sense. Like where my musical talent and my ability with numbers came from." He smiled thinking of his grandfather. "Mick's amazing with numbers, too. He knows what his costs are for everything, salaries, overhead, utilities, food. What his profit margins are. Once I understood what came from him, I could appreciate everything my parents did for me more. What I am because they raised me."

The dim light of the table lamp bounced off the tears in Emma's eyes. He reached out and placed his hand over hers. "I'm sorry. I shouldn't have said anything. I didn't mean to upset you."

"It's not your fault. I asked you because I wanted to know."

All those years ago, he'd felt an instant connection with Emma, but he hadn't appreciated the fact. Now, after all the women that had come and gone in his life, he knew what a rare thing they shared. The question was now that he was older and wiser, what should he do about it?

Listening to Jamie, Emma wondered if she was getting a glimpse into her son's future. Would some of the same uncertainties and questions that plagued Jamie haunt her son? But unlike Jamie's birth mother, she wouldn't turn her son away if he knocked on her door.

She'd hug the stuffing out of him and get down on her knees to thank God for sending him back into her life.

"What did you decide to do about contacting the people who adopted your son?"

"I called the agency and told them if the parents expressed any interest in talking to me, I'm open to that. Right now I don't think doing more than that is good for anyone."

"Did you ever consider keeping the baby?"

Emma stared at Jamie, trying to decide if she should tell him the truth, something she'd never told anyone. Her chest tightened and she knew. Now was the time, here in the quiet stillness with this man, to let go of some of the pain she'd carried for far too long. Resentment that she thought she'd let go of.

"I did. That was why I came home when the baby's father and I broke up."

"Where had you been living?"

His question caught her off guard. She kept forgetting he didn't know all the details. She explained how she and Tucker had left for Nashville soon after Jamie had returned to Juilliard that summer.

She'd been lonely when Jamie had left and nervous about going to college. Then Tucker had dumped Monica and told her he wanted to get back together. He'd been so apologetic and full of dreams. He'd told her they could have a career together in country music, and she'd been naive enough to believe him.

"When things fell apart, I came home. I needed my parents' guidance and support."

She'd received the advice, that was for sure. She could almost remember her mother's lecture verbatim all these years later. Some words never left a person.

If you decide to keep this baby, you can't live here. Your father and I won't help you financially. You'll have to earn enough to pay for your living expenses and for day care. We're not going to keep your child all day while you work. Think of what life would be like. Is that really what you want for your child?

"Did they help you?"

"They felt my giving the baby up for adoption was the best solution." Who was she kidding? They thought it was the only solution. "They said if I kept my child I'd have to support myself. They wouldn't help with money or day care."

"That seems harsh."

At first his comment surprised her, but then his words worked their way inside her, making her take another look at what had happened. At the time she'd told herself their tough-love approach had helped her grow up and face reality, but had they needed to be so cold? So judgmental? She'd been a good kid, who'd never caused them trouble. She was an honor student who, unlike her brothers, never drank or did drugs in high school. Her parents never had to remind her to do her chores. She'd been the model child.

Until she'd gotten pregnant, and even then, she'd been acting responsibly. She'd been on the pill and had taken it faithfully. She was just one of the unlucky 8 percent.

Her mother's words rang in her ears. *People will think we didn't raise you right. That we were bad parents.* And her father had just sat there.

They'd never really supported her career, and when she'd come home feeling like a failure, they'd reinforced that. *We knew nothing good would come of your going to Nashville.*

"There were options between financially supporting you and not helping at all," Jamie said, pulling her away from her memories.

He was right. There were. Unless you were more concerned with what your neighbors thought than your child. Part of why they'd wanted her to give her child up had been because then they could pretend she was still that perfect child. "I never thought of that before."

Her mother had been so unbending, so unwilling to try to understand, but when she'd gotten sick, who had she called? Her daughter. "I need you to come home. There are things I can't do for myself. I need another woman here to help me."

And what had Emma done? She'd put her life on hold and rushed home to help a woman who'd never supported her dreams.

What did any of that matter now? She couldn't change the past. "They wanted to make sure I considered what raising a child entailed. At nineteen, with nothing but a high school education, what kind of life could I give a child? If they'd bailed me out financially when things got tough or provided day care I might have made a different decision. It would have been so easy to be selfish."

"What about the baby's father?"

"He made it clear he didn't want anything to do with fatherhood." *Or me.* "He didn't have any money then either, so he couldn't help financially. He was living in Nashville, playing small clubs for dinner and drinks." At least until he'd gotten the recording contract with her revamped song, but it had taken years for him to move to easy street.

"You're amazing. What you did couldn't have been easy."

"That's why it was great seeing the other side of the story. The Sandbergs showed me the joy in adoption. You have, too."

Lord, she and Jamie had gotten maudlin tonight. Needing to turn the conversation to a topic lighter than a semitruck, she said, "The band's rehearsing tomorrow night. If you want, you could join us to run through a few songs for the Pet Walk concert." She nibbled on her lower lip for a minute, trying to decide if she should plunge ahead. What the hell. Why not? "I've been thinking about Henry's suggestion that you should replace Molly in the band."

She paused, hoping he'd jump in with a quick "sure, I'd like to do that" and save her from having to ask. When she sneaked a peek at him, he leaned back in the chair and crossed his arms over his chest. Nope, he had no intention of making this easy for her.

"I might have been a little hasty dismissing the idea. At the bar the other night you sounded like you might be open to the possibility." Another quick peek. Nothing. He sat there as stiff and still as the Rocky Mountains. "I've spoken with Luke and Grayson, my bass player and drummer. They think the suggestion has merit. I watched a video of you on YouTube playing with the symphony. You're incredible."

His smile and the light in his eyes disappeared. She didn't know what she'd done, but she'd somehow hurt him.

"Before you go any further, I have to tell you something. I hurt my hand a few months ago. I had surgery to repair the tendon damage, but I've had dexterity problems since then."

"How bad is it?"

"The Philharmonic let me go."

Her vow to remain detached hit the floor and shattered as she gazed into his anguish-filled eyes. She knew all too well what it felt like to be dumped. To see the dreams she'd worked so hard to achieve splinter before her eyes like delicate crystal on cement, and to feel the helplessness of being unable to stop the destruction.

It sucked big-time, no matter what the cause.

"I've been there, for a different reason, but there's nothing I can say that would make you feel better or doesn't sound lame."

"You're the first person that's been honest. Everyone else thinks they can fix it, wants to offer me career counseling or thinks I'm on the verge of suicide."

She nodded. "It gets old."

"You got that right. I came here to get away from all the well-meaning advice. I have a whole new understanding of the phrase 'killing someone with kindness.'" He flashed a weak smile, but what got to her was the trust shining in his eyes. "Mick's the only one who knows."

Until you.

Warning bells clanged in her head, drowning out everything else. She didn't want to share confidences with him.

Too late. Even before now. Don't you remember what you shared earlier in the barn?

Okay, so she didn't want to share any *more* confidences with him. Doing that made it too difficult to keep things light and easy with a guy.

"What are your plans—" She couldn't bring herself to finish her question. *If you can't return to the symphony.*

"You mean if I can't play well enough for the symphony?"

She nodded.

This was scary. They'd started finishing each other's sentences.

"The hell if I know. I was lousy at everything but music and math in school, but doing anything math-wise would mean going back to college and starting over. Who am I kidding? No matter what else I do, I'll be starting over." He rubbed the back of his neck. "The hard work around the ranch and at the bar has strengthened my hand, but I don't know if it'll ever improve enough for me to return to the symphony."

For the first time since she'd picked him up at the airport, weariness lined his face. That and something deeper. Fear? *He's scared because he doesn't know what to do with his life.*

She thought about listing all the options people had mentioned to her when she'd come home the last time. He could teach in the school system and privately. He could write music, but she remembered how all of those suggestions had left her feeling—hollow. And Jamie craved the performing as she did. It was part of him.

"I miss playing music." His words tore at her heart.

She really should tell him to forget about playing with the band. She should say they could rehearse the songs for him to sing at the fund-raiser and leave things there. That was the common-sense decision, but she knew what he was going through, how it felt to try to recover from a setback like this. How overpowering the fear of losing the dream he'd built his life around could be.

But if he couldn't play well enough for the Philharmonic, what were the chances he could handle their music?

Come on, you don't need Charlie Daniels on the fiddle. Give Jamie a chance.

How many guys did she know who would've tossed their pride aside by coming clean even though it was the decent thing to do?

"If you want to try playing with the band and see how things go, I'm willing to give it a shot. Why don't you bring your fiddle tomorrow?"

So much for common sense.

"I'd like that. Now, how about having dinner with me after rehearsal?"

Sirens clanged in her head again. Red lights flashed. "I don't date musicians."

"Any particular reason why?"

"They're self-centered and about as reliable as a fortune-teller."

"That's an awfully broad brush you're using there."

"I'm just going on past experience."

"Some men might see what you said as a challenge to prove you wrong."

Determination darkened his eyes to the color of strong coffee, and she knew he was on the verge of being one of those guys. She froze, unable to catch her breath. For the briefest second she thought about what it would be like to have a man like Jamie want her. A good, solid man. An honest man.

Consuming, but a true give-and-take. That's what it would be like. Jamie could so easily throw her life out of whack.

When he leaned closer, everything else faded away. His presence overwhelmed her more than it had in the barn, but in an oh-so-good, I-feel-like-a-woman way. Heat flashed through her as if she was made of October grass, scorching her, leaving her aching, and he hadn't even touched her.

She stared into his eyes and realized he had the longest eyelashes she'd ever seen. That wasn't fair when he was already so handsome. His eyes had always mesmerized her. Even at nineteen there had been something in his gaze, a look that said he understood things most guys his age failed to.

Sitting here with Jamie in the dim light from the old lamp perched on the scratched end table, she wanted to believe he was different, even though common sense said the odds were lousy. She should move away from him. Say something. Break the spell. She knew what she should do, but she couldn't force her body to move. Truth be told, she didn't want to.

He reached out and cupped her face. His thumb brushed over her lips and she resisted the urge to run her tongue over his skin and taste him.

Then his lips covered hers.

Chapter 9

Emma melted into Jamie, letting his strong presence shut out everything else but the heat racing through her. His lips, warm and inviting, teased hers. Her hands clung to his shoulders, needing his solid strength as awareness rippled through her. She'd missed this. Being held by a man. Connecting with a human being on this intimate level.

Her tongue slipped between his lips to tease his. His strong arms wrapped around her, pulling her even closer. Her hands fisted in his shirt, holding on to him as though he was her only anchor as the emotions, passion and need crashed over her.

"Whoever he was, he must've been a real dick to put that much hurt in your eyes. We're not all cut from the same cloth. Let me prove I'm not like him."

Reality kicked her hard in the teeth. She went to pull

away from him, and realized she was on his lap, practically straddling him. How had that happened? She'd
been so far gone and she hadn't even realized. With as
much dignity as she could muster with the evidence of
his desire pressing against her hip, she slipped off his
lap and slid away from him.

She wanted to give Jamie a chance. Wanted to believe he could be different. That he was someone who'd
put her first. He looked and sounded so sincere, but how
could she trust her instincts when she'd been wrong
before? Dogs and horses were good judges of character, but she couldn't tell a good man from a hole in the
ground.

No more. She'd learned her lesson. She jumped off
the couch, grabbed her purse and clutched it to her chest
like a shield. "You know what to do."

He flashed her a you-bet-I-do smile.

Her heart tripped. Boy, did he know what to do. He'd
demonstrated that emphatically. She cleared her throat.
"You know *what to do for the puppy* tonight. Drop him
off when we open tomorrow morning at ten."

Then she ran for the front door without looking back.

Once in her car, she locked the doors and leaned her
forehead against the steering wheel. Her heart beat out a
staccato tempo while her body coursed with need. Since
coming home she'd worked so hard to control her emotions, to keep from letting anything get to her. She'd decided no more relying on her heart to make decisions.
That's where she'd gone wrong so many times in her
life. A heart that had been broken couldn't be trusted.
She'd rely on her head and her gut instead.

Nothing would sidetrack her this time. Not when she
had her life back on course, a plan in place and her goal

in sight. She'd get the band ready for the state fair competition, win said contest, impress Phillip Brandise in the consultation audition and land a recording contract.

Kissing Jamie was nowhere in her plans.

Fool me once, shame on you. Fool me twice, shame on me. Fool me three times, and I should be locked up for my own protection.

Monday morning Emma walked into the shelter thankful that her weekend was over. Talk about a mess. But now she could focus on work. She intended to forget about Jamie, his soul-searching eyes and his melt-her-panties kisses.

Her plan lasted for all of twenty minutes. Right up until the volunteers and the rest of the shelter staff arrived. After that a constant parade of people tromped through her office to bombard her with questions.

What was Jamie like? How long was he staying in town? Did he have a girlfriend back East? Was he as *wonderful* as he seemed from the way he acted onstage? Could she introduce them? After an hour of endless questions and listening to every female in the place between the age of sixteen and eighty ooh and aah over Jamie, Emma reached the limit of her patience.

"And my nightmare weekend has followed me into the office," Emma said when she sought refuge in Avery's office. After closing the door behind her, she plopped into the chair in front of her friend's desk. "I know this is a small town, but you'd think someone else must have done something over the weekend that people could gossip about. How about I pay you to create a scandal or do something foolish? Nothing major, mind you. Just give everyone something other than Jamie

Westland to talk about. By the way, if our volunteers are any indication, what you've done to publicize him singing at the Pet Walk concert is working. And to make matters worse, Shirley's here today. She's a wonderful volunteer and a generous donor, but she's about to drive me completely insane pumping me for information about Jamie, who she *swears* is the perfect man for Shay because they have singing in common. If you don't do something to get everyone to quit hounding me about him, I won't be responsible for my actions."

Emma paused, realizing she was out of breath. When the silence continued, she glanced at Avery, who sat behind her desk, hands splayed across the smooth wooden surface, a glazed look in her eyes. "Say something, Avery."

"I'm just trying to figure out who you are and what you've done with my calm, levelheaded, never-loses-patience friend."

"Okay. So I've gone off the deep end a little." At Avery's raised eyebrow, Emma said, "Okay, so I've gone off the deep end a lot, but help me out. Let me hide out here until Shirley's shift is over."

"This isn't about what's going on here at the shelter. You can handle everyone's questions and comments about Jamie with a smart quip or a clever change of subject. What's really bothering you? Did something happen last night between you two?"

"What makes you think anything—" Emma rubbed her throbbing temples. "Forget it. Even at my best I couldn't pull off that lie, and I'm not anywhere near my best. He kissed me, but that's not the worst part. I kissed him back."

I nearly crawled into his hip pocket.

"So what's the problem?"

"I liked it. Way too much."

"I'm still waiting for the problem part."

"Now is the worst time for me to get involved with someone, and I'm such a lousy judge of character when it comes to guys. Remember Clint? The guy who replaced me in my previous band two weeks after I came home to take care of Mom, even though he promised he wouldn't?"

Of course that's not what he'd told her. Instead every time she'd talked with him, he'd said he couldn't wait for her to come back. He missed her. The band wasn't the same without her.

He'd told her what she'd wanted to hear.

"Then there's the fact that my relationships have a way of breaking up my bands. Do I really need to go on?"

"As my mother would say, quit borrowing trouble. If you want my advice, I say have some fun and don't worry about the future so much."

"Borrowing trouble? I think trouble has camped out on my front step."

Jamie drove across town to the Estes Park animal shelter, the puppy he'd started calling Trooper curled up asleep in the carrier on the passenger seat. Last night with Emma had been eye-opening in a whole lot of ways.

He'd shared things with her he'd never told anyone. Never really wanted to. When he'd talked about his family, she'd understood how he'd felt both a part of and somehow separate from everyone else.

Then she'd surprised him by asking him to play in the band.

Everything had been perfect until he kissed her.

Damn the guy who'd made her so skittish. When he'd held her and her fingers teased the sensitive spot behind his ear as he kissed her, he'd forgotten everything, his hand and whether or not he'd ever play like he once had. About what he'd do with his life if he couldn't return to the symphony. All he'd thought about was Emma and how she made him feel. As though there was more to life than music and his career. As though he belonged. With her. How he wanted to spend time with her.

Time. How long would he be here? He hadn't given much thought to it. He flexed his hand. In the short time he'd been here, the physical work around the ranch and at the restaurant combined with his exercises seemed to be helping his hand, bolstering his hope that his life could return to normal.

But what about Emma? Was it fair to her to start a relationship when he wouldn't be sticking around? He shook himself mentally. Talk about jumping the gun. All they'd done was share a kiss. Granted, one that had nearly melted his socks, but it was just one.

As he pulled into the shelter parking lot, he told himself he was being silly. How long he intended to stay didn't make any difference, especially since he hadn't made a secret of the fact that he planned on returning to New York. Plus, when did anyone get a guarantee on how much time they had together?

Dating was always a crapshoot.

Confident now that he had sorted things out, he parked Mick's truck, picked up the carrier and headed for the front door. Unlike last night, when he entered the shelter lobby today the place hummed with activity. Meows and barking echoed through the small space. The sound of ringing phones and the buzz of printers floated through the air, mixing with snippets of conversation.

The pretty blonde with big brown eyes behind the desk greeted him with a huge smile. "Hi, Jamie. I'm Callie. You were fantastic at Halligan's Friday night. I was there with some friends. I can't wait to hear you sing again at the shelter benefit. I've already got my ticket. Maybe I'll camp out so I can be in the front row."

"Take a breath, girl, before the man's ear falls off from all that chatter," said an older gray-haired woman dressed in a T-shirt with the phrase Love Me, Love My Cat across her ample bosom. Then she introduced herself as Shirley. "I might have to come hear you sing myself. You've been the big talk around town."

He flashed a smile in Shirley's direction as he placed the pet carrier on the counter. The fact that people were paying good money to hear him sing unsettled him more than he expected. Singing karaoke was one thing, but a paid performance? Despite what Emma and Avery said, he hadn't really believed anyone would buy tickets because of him. Maybe he should've thought the offer through more before he'd said yes. "Thanks for buying a ticket. I'm glad I can help out the shelter."

"Are you taking song requests?" Callie asked, batting her eyes at him. She was pretty enough and curvy in all the right places, but her predatory gleam left him feeling like the mouse just before the cat pounced on him.

"I haven't even thought about it, but that's not a bad idea." Especially considering he didn't have a clue what songs would be good for his voice and something the audience wanted to hear.

"You're the spitting image of Mick when he was younger, except for the hairstyle," Shirley said. "Now I understand why you've been all my granddaughter Shay can talk about. You're one fine-looking fella."

Her comment caught him off guard. He tried not to show it, but knew he'd failed. Lord, he hadn't felt this awkward around women since he was thirteen. "I'm looking for Emma."

"I haven't seen her this morning. Now, about your concert." Callie leaned toward him and wet her lips. "Do you know any Luke Bryan songs? I love the song 'Drunk on You.' You know, if your hair was a bit shorter you could be his twin. Not that I don't like your hair."

"Dial it back, missy. It's unseemly of you to act so forward." Shirley grabbed a scrap of paper and a pencil off the desk, jotted something down and handed the note to him. "If you want to see the town, give my granddaughter a call."

"You thought I was too forward?" Callie said.

Fans of the Philharmonic never acted like this. The most they did was write a polite email extolling his skills and the emotions his playing evoked in words that usually sent him running for the dictionary. "If you tell me where Emma's office is, I'll be on my way."

He wanted to get out of there before they started tugging at him like a turkey wishbone on Thanksgiving Day.

"It's the one to the left at the end of that hallway." Shirley pointed the way. "You think about calling Shay."

Anxious to escape, he thanked the woman, picked up Trooper's carrier and headed for the hallway. After a few steps, Emma's voice drifted toward him. "Forget about having Jamie sing at the fund-raiser. What we should ask him to do is let us raffle off a date with him. That's what'll bring in big bucks. Maybe then everyone will leave me alone and quit asking me to fix them up with him."

He knocked on the door and stepped inside the office. Avery laughed seeing him, while Emma blushed bright pink. He couldn't resist teasing her. "Raffle off a date? That's an interesting idea, but what's in it for me?"

Emma groaned. "Talk about awkward. How do I keep putting my foot in my mouth whenever you're around?"

"I guess I bring out the best in you."

"I was kidding about the raffle. It's been a long morning," she continued.

"Let's not dismiss the idea so quickly. It could make a lot—"

"Not unless you rig it so that one of you two is the winner," he said before Avery could finish. "After the way the women acted when I was onstage the other night and hearing Callie and Shirley go around out there, I'm a little scared of the women in town."

"Callie and Shirley are working the desk together? We never schedule them at the same time."

"I can see why."

Emma covered her eyes with her hands, but peered at him through her fingers. "Do I want to know what happened?"

He gave her and Avery a quick rundown of the gauntlet he'd been forced to run. "For a while there I was worried a fight would break out."

"As the director of the shelter, let me apologize for my volunteers," Avery said in all seriousness.

Emma groaned and reached for a pencil and a Post-it note off the desk. As she started writing, she said, "I'm making a note to discuss that we're not a dating service with the volunteers."

"I don't know," Jamie said. "You might be missing out on a way to up your adoption numbers. Adopt a pet and get a date for Friday night."

Emma laughed. "That's a good one. Thanks. I needed a laugh. It could be our new holiday slogan."

"It's good to see your sense of humor is returning. You had me worried for a while there." Avery nodded toward the carrier in Jamie's hand. "How's our little friend doing?"

"Trooper—that's what I started calling him—is more active and alert this morning. Have you had any luck finding his mother?"

"Not yet, but we're still looking. Have we found someone to foster him?" Emma turned toward Avery, who shook her head.

"If you haven't, I can keep him a while longer."

"I'll let you two talk about that while I give this little guy a look-over since he's here." Avery stood, picked up the carrier and left, shutting the door behind her.

Emma nodded to the chair beside her. "If you're willing to keep him, that would be great. If you give me your phone number I'll call you when we find someone to foster him."

"That's a slick way to ask a guy for his number."

"I don't think there's anything else for us to discuss," Emma said in what he now recognized was her best all-business voice. "You're more than welcome to sit here until Avery's finished examining Trooper. Now, if you'll excuse me, I have to give Callie and Shirley a quick how-to-work-the-front-desk refresher course."

Later that evening when Emma walked into her father's garage, the one he'd been kind enough to clear out when she'd started the band, she still couldn't believe how she'd let Jamie get to her at the shelter. He'd been so determined to push her buttons.

That's a slick way to ask a guy for his number.

And what had she come back with? Pretty much nothing but a lame excuse that she had work duties to see to. His laughter taunting her when she'd left Avery's office told her he'd known she was taking the coward's way out.

Damn right she had. Sometimes retreating was the only way to survive the battle.

"I talked to Jamie," Emma said when Luke and Grayson arrived. "He's bringing his fiddle with him when he comes to work on the songs for the Pet Walk concert."

She'd debated whether or not to tell them about Jamie's hand, but decided it wasn't her place to share the news. Could be that everything would go fine when he played with them and no one would need to know anything about his injury.

But more important, she kept remembering the trust shining in his eyes last night when he'd told her how he'd come to Estes Park to get away. She couldn't betray him.

"I checked out the video of you two singing. Man, women go crazy over that guy. Some of their comments online made me blush."

"Sure, he's got a great voice, but what's he got that we don't have?" Luke nodded toward Grayson.

Seriously? How could men be so clueless? While Luke and Grayson were good-looking and in shape, they weren't...well, Jamie. They lacked his charisma, his charm. That rare "it" so few people possessed.

"He could bring a whole new demographic to the Pet Walk," Luke said.

"Single, man-hungry women?" Emma shuddered at the thought of every woman within a thirty-mile radius showing up at the event. Wouldn't that be a fun audience to perform in front of?

Visions of screaming single women in their audience all vying for Jamie's attention danced in her head. That's what she'd always dreamed of her concerts being—wild events with women tossing their lace thongs onstage. That would get everyone to take them seriously.

What had she done?

"That's my favorite demographic—women between eighteen and twenty-five," Luke said, a big asinine smile on his face.

"This could be way more fun than last year," Grayson added.

Maybe for the rest of the band.

"Jamie's already helping increase our visibility," Luke said. "Because you're in the video with him, people are checking out our stuff, too, and the likes on our videos are way up. We need to capitalize on this."

"I was amazed how good you two sounded."

Here we go. Same song, second verse. The old insecurity welled up inside her, reminding her of the comments she'd heard when she'd returned to Nashville and started singing without Tucker. *Your guitar skills are amazing as always, and your voice sounds great, but you're not at the level you were when you and Tucker sang together. Have you thought about joining another band or finding another singing partner?*

The first time she'd heard that after a show she'd brushed the statement off, but when that became the standard response from industry professionals, she realized a solo career wouldn't get her where she wanted to be.

"The heat you two generated lit up the stage. I've never heard you sound like that," Luke said.

Ouch. Hearing it from half the town had been bad enough, but hearing it from one of her bandmates, who knew her ability probably better than she did and whose judgment she valued, shook her.

"Are you saying I sounded like crap before?"

"Man, you're touchy today. You know that's not what I meant," Luke said.

Forget about it. Don't doubt yourself or doubt what you're meant to do with your life. Instead, think of singing with Jamie as the means to achieving your ends—a recording contract. If he could help her and the band win the state fair contest, did anything else matter?

But then the little nagging, devil's advocate voice in her head decided to chime in. *Say you do win. What then? One major problem with singing with Jamie is he isn't planning on sticking around.*

She wouldn't think about that now. She'd take things one step at a time. The first one being to prepare the band for the contest and give them the best chance of winning.

"It's going to take a lot of work to be ready for

the shelter fund-raiser, but I think we can do it," she
said, trying to regain control of rehearsal. She almost
laughed. Who was she kidding? She hadn't been in control of anything today. "Playing at the Pet Walk will be
a good test run for the state fair."

"You know, the way Jamie sings harmony could add
a new dimension to our sound. We could rework some
of our stuff," Luke added.

And here they were, back on the topic of the day,
Jamie. Had everyone gotten together and plotted to
drive her insane? It was sure starting to feel that way.

"Slow down. We don't know if him playing with us
will work. He might not be able to make the transition
to country music," she said. "If that's the case, he'll just
sing a couple of songs for the shelter benefit. But even
if he does work out, all we've talked about is him helping until we find someone permanent."

Luke smiled. "Who knows. Maybe he'll like playing
with us so much he'll change his religion, so to speak,
and decide to stick around."

The ranch where Emma grew up hadn't changed
much in the years since Jamie had last been here. A
modest house that now needed a coat of paint, a massive red barn that looked as if it was straight out of every
rural painting he'd ever seen, and land guarded by the
Rocky Mountains.

Funny, he thought as he parked by the garage and
headed inside, how some things changed so much while
others stayed the same.

Emma introduced him to the other band members,
Grayson and Luke, and the four of them stood and chatted for a couple of minutes. Just small talk. How long

they'd been playing together. Their backgrounds. All the basic get-to-know-you stuff.

"Now that the meet and greet is over, let's get to work," Emma said and handed Jamie some music. He glanced through the first few pages. So far so good. Nothing he couldn't handle. Then he hit the third page and twinges of apprehension knotted his gut. A couple measures could trip him up. They weren't so difficult he couldn't have played the music when he was in high school, but now? He wasn't sure. Not with his hand less than 100 percent.

He considered saying they should forget the whole thing, but since Emma had asked him to bring his violin he'd felt almost renewed. Definitely energized from the rush of adrenaline at the thought of a new challenge and playing with a group again. He'd checked out various country bands on the internet and found himself getting excited over the possibilities. He'd even found one band that was appearing in Longmont tonight. Maybe he and Emma could check them out.

As much as he'd thought about the performing possibilities this afternoon, he'd thought about Emma more. He'd wondered what it would be like getting up every morning knowing he'd get to see her. Talk about a work incentive program.

No, he wouldn't give up before he even gave this a shot.

"You ready to give it a try?" she asked.

Talk about a loaded question. He was up for trying a lot of things with Emma. He cleared his throat and tried to get his mind off all the things he'd like to do with her and back on the audition.

He placed the music on the stand she had set up and lifted his violin out of the case. "All set."

Emma counted out two measures. He came in on the fifth. The music flowed out of him, filling him with a passion he hadn't experienced since he'd discovered the sound he could produce with an instrument. Confidence surged in his veins. Emma's voice wrapped around him, drawing him in even further. She reached deep inside him, touching him in a way he never imagined possible. He felt connected. Right in a way he couldn't describe.

When they came to the chorus, the violin part dropped out. He switched to singing harmony to Emma's lead vocals. He could spend all day singing with her. All the uncertainty about his future, the fear and anger at possibly starting over in a new career, disappeared. At the second verse he picked up the violin again. They hit the bridge and he held his own for about ten measures. Then his left ring finger cramped. He botched the fingering and hit one hell of a clunker, throwing off his timing. That left him playing catch up with the band, which never quite happened. Figuring there wasn't any point in jumping back in, he gave up.

A minute later when the song ended there was dead silence. Not that he blamed anyone for not knowing what to say. Hell, he didn't even know what to say since the wooden guy from the auditions had sounded better than he just had. That was bad enough, but his performance made him realize how much work he had ahead of him if he hoped to return to the symphony, but would hard work be enough?

"The vocals were fantastic, but, man, I got to ask you, what happened with the fiddle?" Luke said. "You were good through most of it, but there were some spots that were rough. I've heard you play. Your skills are amazing. What's up?"

Before he could say anything, Emma said, "Not everyone can play country music. Remember when Michael Jordan tried to play baseball? He was an incredible athlete. Arguably the best basketball player ever. Despite that, he couldn't make it in major league baseball. That's how it is with music, too. Maybe country music just isn't Jamie's thing."

Obviously, she hadn't told the guys about his injury, and he realized she was giving him an out, a way to keep his secret if he wanted to. He considered brushing off the question with a vague answer about it being a long story that he'd rather not go into, but decided against it. Keeping people from finding out he'd been let go from the Philharmonic took too much energy and the vacation excuse would only work for so long. When he kept hanging around, people would know something was up. Plus, these guys realized something didn't fit and he wouldn't lie.

As he started explaining about his injury he thought he should have a card printed out to hand to people to save time. Former Classical Musician Sidelined Due to Injury. Physical Issues May or May Not Improve. Please Submit Further Questions in Writing and Wait For the Reply That Will Come When Hell Freezes Over.

"Obviously the injury's affecting my playing. My ring finger is the big issue. It's stiff and doesn't move like it should. If it were my bow hand it wouldn't be any problem." He replaced his violin in the case.

"That sucks," Grayson said.

"You got that right. I came out here to get away."

"Your secret's safe with us. As far as I'm concerned,

what's up with your hand isn't anyone else's business," Luke said.

"I appreciate that." The thud as he shut his case sounded like a casket closing and just as final. "Since Avery's started publicizing me singing at the Pet Walk, I'd like to sing with you for that if it's okay with all of you."

"I think you playing fiddle with us could still work."

Jamie stared at Emma, unable to believe what she'd said. *She's either lost her mind or gone tone-deaf.* "You can say that after hearing me play?"

"Understandably you have incredibly high standards, but we could fix the problems you had by tweaking the fiddle parts," she said.

"You mean make them easier?" That hurt. He didn't want a pity job. "No, thanks. I don't need anyone feeling sorry for me."

"If you couldn't cut it on the fiddle I wouldn't make the offer. I don't do pity." Emma stared him straight in the eye, nothing but honesty shining in her gaze. "That ridiculous emotion doesn't do anyone any good. If you discount those couple of measures, you're better than anyone else we've auditioned."

Okay, maybe pity hadn't motivated her offer. He accepted that. A woman with the drive to succeed that Emma possessed wouldn't let anything stand in the way of her goal.

"What you add vocalswise compensates for the little bit we'd have to simplify the fiddle part," Grayson added. "The harmony between you two is amazing. Some of the best stuff I've ever heard."

Luke snapped his fingers. "That gives me an idea. If Jamie sang lead on some numbers it would open up a whole new range of songs for us. We could expand our selections to include more guy-focused stuff and less of this angsty material."

"Yeah, we are a little heavy on the chick songs right now," Grayson agreed.

"Hey, I've written a lot of the material we sing."

"Exactly."

She turned to Jamie. "You've started a mutiny, Fletcher Christian. Thanks."

"Then put a stop to it."

She'd crossed her arms over her chest, her stance stiff and braced. Her brows knit together in thought. He smiled. She was probably weighing the cost of how much jail time she'd get for assaulting Luke and Grayson versus how satisfying it would be to let her anger rip.

Meanwhile, the two knuckleheads rattled on about the songs they could add to the band's repertoire. Jamie cringed. If Grayson and Luke possessed any brains, they'd head for the nearest bomb shelter or, in lieu of that, duck behind the drums for protection from the blast that was heading their way.

"No one is replacing me as the lead singer in this band," Emma said in a low, calm voice, reminding him of the stillness in the eye of a hurricane.

"I'm not saying replace you," Luke backpedaled, uncertainty in his voice. "We'd just change things a little, expand our song choices with Jamie singing the lead every once in a while."

"You saw the comments online. Women love him," Grayson said. "I think Luke's right."

Combined, the two right now didn't have the brains of a scarecrow. Deciding to step in before Emma set

them on fire with her death-ray stare, Jamie said, "I
don't want any part of singing lead." He refused to hurt
Emma like that. When Luke looked as if he might continue pleading his case, Jamie continued, "That's non-
negotiable."

His stern no-nonsense tone left everyone clear that
the discussion had ended. Out of his peripheral vision
he caught Emma's reaction of utter shock. Why did she
find what he'd said so hard to believe? Had she really
thought he'd come in to her band, take over and shove
her aside?

*I don't date musicians. They're self-centered and
about as reliable as a fortune-teller.*

Damn. She'd dated some real winners. Starting with
the guy who'd got her pregnant and bailed on her.

Recovering from her shock, she smiled at him, her
eyes filled with gratitude. "Now that we've settled that,
can we get back to preparing for the concert next weekend?"

"Are you sure you're all okay with changing the violin parts?" he asked, still not sure. Then he almost
smiled. What was he thinking? If she wasn't happy
with something everyone within three counties would
know the fact.

"I thought we'd dealt with that issue, too. We're all
okay with it." She glanced pointedly at Luke and Grayson, who nodded. "I'm not making the offer out of pity.
I truly believe it's the best decision for the band. Now,
are you in or not?"

"I'm in. I can at least help you out until you find
someone permanent."

"If you could agree to stay until the state fair competition that would be great. Our chances of finding someone before that don't look good."

"Deal."

For the next couple of hours they ran through the band's numbers with him marking the measures that gave him trouble. The vocals, the part he would've thought needed work, felt natural and were almost effortless.

When they quit for the day and Luke and Grayson had gone home, Jamie turned to Emma. "I was planning on checking out a band playing at Dick's Tavern in Longmont tonight. How about we get some dinner, talk about those songs that need modification and then listen to the band?"

Before he even finished, she was shaking her head. "That's not a good idea. One of the rules we have is that band members don't socialize. We've found that tends to—" She paused and chewed on her lip.

Jamie braced himself. This ought to be good. When she thought that hard, he'd discovered she was trying to decide between brutal honesty or if she should soften the blow.

"Let's just say having personal relationships complicates things."

"Is this about last night? It was just a kiss."

He wanted to laugh at his ridiculous comment and how he'd managed to deliver the statement with a straight face. Just a kiss? Hardly.

"It doesn't matter because I have plans tonight."

"I grew up with two sisters. I'm fluent in female speak. When a woman uses the vague 'I have plans tonight' comment instead of saying what her plans are, it usually means one of two things. Either she isn't attracted to the guy, but doesn't want to hurt his feelings, or she is attracted to him, but she's afraid of what she feels."

"Then here's the truth. I'm not interested, but I didn't want to hurt your feelings."

This time he did laugh. The little minx thought he wouldn't see through her lie? Wrong. "No way are you selling me that three-legged horse."

She raised her eyebrow at his word choice.

Really? He couldn't use a Western expression? He'd spent enough time in Estes Park over the years that he'd outgrown greenhorn status. Ignoring her expression, he continued. "I know that's not true. There was enough heat between us to make the devil sweat, and it wasn't just on my part, or did I imagine you crawling onto my lap last night?"

"Talk about arrogance."

But he noticed she didn't deny what he'd said. "It's not arrogant if it's the truth." He stepped closer, his gaze zeroing in on her as the memories of kissing her revved his body up all over again. He smiled. She stepped back. Yup, he'd pegged it right. She felt something, but it scared her.

"I'm not going to dignify your comment by responding because there's no way I'm going to change your mind. Wrong though you may be."

"What I want to know," he said as he closed the distance between them again, "is why what you feel for me scares you."

Her eyes darkened and she tilted her chin up at him. He had to bite his lip to keep from smiling as she rose to the bait he'd put in front of her. "That'll be the day, and I'll prove how wrong you are. Seeing a band tonight is a great idea. Not only can we work on the music, we can talk about the band's performance, the pros and cons. It'll help you get ready for our first performance."

"Should I drive or do you want to?"

"I think separate cars. That way we're both free to leave whenever we need to."

He thought about pressing the issue, but a smart man knew when to walk away from the table before he lost everything he'd won. "Fine. Meet you at Dick's Tavern."

Chapter 10

When Emma and Jamie walked into Dick's Tavern, she vowed to prove she wasn't *that* attracted to him—no way could she make either one of them believe there wasn't *any* attraction. She wouldn't touch the rest of what he'd said, that she was scared of what she felt for him, with gloves, a ten-foot pole and a shark cage. Mainly because there was no disproving the truth.

Dick's, while still possessing a down-home feel, was more upscale than Halligan's. There were simple white tablecloths on the tables and less neon over the bar and stage.

Being with Jamie tonight and working together would be a good thing. She'd spend time with him and realize what she felt with him when they sang couldn't survive off the stage. With that gone there'd be nothing of substance left and her vision would be clear.

But what if she didn't find that? So what if she was attracted to him? It was probably nothing more than her body's hormonal cravings from her dating drought. She could keep things between them professional and she could maintain control.

She'd see he was no different than every other musician she'd known. They all craved the spotlight, and if she let him, slowly he'd start taking more of hers.

If that's what he wanted then why had he turned down Luke's suggestion that he sing lead on a few songs?

"I noticed you making notes on the music during rehearsal," Emma said once she and Jamie were seated.

"A few places gave me trouble, but I think I can change the rhythm a little or the notes without changing the integrity of what you wrote."

She nodded and opened her menu. Okay, what should she do now? And she thought first dates were awkward. When was the last time she'd had a first date? That would've been with Clint. What? Almost three years ago?

This wasn't a date, she told herself. A business meeting with food, followed by studying a band. That's what this was.

Simple.

Right. Just like milking a bull.

"I'll work on making the changes tomorrow," Jamie said.

"We'll have to put in a lot of rehearsal time before the state fair, but if you work on the music on your own, I think we can be ready."

"Just let me know the rehearsal times. I'll clear things with Mick."

Awkward silence stretched until the perky waitress dressed in jeans and a two-sizes-too-small Dick's Tavern T-shirt popped up at their table to take their orders. Emma couldn't miss the woman giving Jamie the once-over.

"This band's pretty good," Emma said once they'd placed their order and Miss Perky had bounced off. "Though they don't have a fiddle player, you can still learn a lot from them. Watch for how they move on the stage and how they connect with the audience."

Yeah. Because Jamie needs so much help in those two areas.

"Do you ever think about anything but work?"

"The country music business is very competitive. I need to stay focused." Emma reached for her water glass to give her something to do.

"There's focused, and there's not having a life outside work."

Emma cringed. There was that phrase again. What was it with everyone lately? "Tell me you weren't just as driven when you were with the Philharmonic."

"You got me there. I was, but hurting my hand's given me a new perspective."

When he flexed his hand she regretted bringing up the subject. What would she do if she couldn't play the guitar or sing anymore? What else would she have in her life? Not a whole lot, but wasn't that what she wanted? Sacrifices had to be made for her career, to move forward to the next level.

Wanting to lighten up the conversation, she said, "Growing up with a house full of brothers was noisy, wild and messy. I wanted to hang around with them, but they were always trying to ditch me. What was it like growing up with only sisters?"

"The worst thing was the bathroom. Not only did I have to schedule time to use it, but by the time I got in, the hot water was usually gone."

"That's rough."

"Tell me about it. We lived in Pennsylvania. Do you know how awful a cold shower is in the winter?"

"I bet it gets the blood flowing."

"When it doesn't give a guy a heart attack."

"Come on. Quit whining. It made you tough," Emma said with a grin.

The waitress brought their food, eyed Jamie and asked if there was anything else he needed. Not them, but just him. As though Emma was chopped liver or invisible. Maybe she was invisible chopped liver. Anyway, when Jamie said no, they were good, without even glancing at the woman, the obviously disappointed server flitted off.

Interesting.

"Finally I decided I'd sacrifice sleep for hot water, and set my alarm for oh-dark-thirty to get up before my sisters. What about you? What was the worst part of being the only girl?"

"They used to climb trees to get away from me."

"How long did it take you to learn to climb one, too?"

"How come you're so sure that's what I did? Maybe I gave up and quit trying to keep up with them."

"You? No way. You'd see that as admitting defeat. You're driven and when you set your mind to something there's no stopping you."

The fact that he had her so well pegged both irritated and pleased her. "It took me every day after school for a whole week, and cost me more scraped knees and arms than I could count, but I did it."

After dinner they moved to a smaller table closer to the stage. When the band started playing, Emma relaxed now that she had a comfortable subject to focus on. "See how the lead singer connects visually with the audience? He nods at people and smiles when there's a break in the vocals. He's also good about moving around on the stage."

"The guy's all over the place."

"He doesn't want either side of the audience to feel slighted."

"Since I'm not the lead singer, I won't have to worry about that."

"Oh, yes, you will. I don't want all the women trampling each other because they want to get a better vantage point to ogle you," she teased. "What we need to do is occasionally have you and Luke switch sides. That way no one will feel slighted."

"You really think about stuff like this?"

"Details matter. Those subtleties can make the difference between getting stuck playing local clubs and breaking out. Have you thought about what you're going to wear for the concert?"

"You're kidding, right?"

She shook her head. "There are more options than you'd think. One is the T-shirt and jeans, cowboy style. There's the more plaid Western shirt and jeans look. There's also—"

"You are not going to give me a how-to-dress class. Let's dance."

The word *yes* almost popped out of her mouth. Almost. She loved dancing, and Jamie would be a great partner. The man could move.

How long had it been since she'd gone dancing? Most weekend nights she performed with the band. On weeknights she had her day job to think about. What would it be like to let go of being cautious, of not thinking everything through ten times before acting? Of just living a little?

Too tempting. Too wonderful. Too scary to consider. Business meeting with food and a band. Remember?

"We can't see what the band's doing if we're on the dance floor."

"Come on. For the past twenty minutes you've been analyzing the band's every move and teaching a class. Time for recess."

"I'm trying to prepare you for the concert."

"Don't get me wrong. I appreciate the effort, but I need a break so everything you've said can soak in. Otherwise information is going to leak out my ears."

His comment made her smile. She had given him a lot to process. She glanced at the people on the dance floor doing the "Cotton-Eyed Joe." "You can line dance?"

"I took a class. A friend said it would be a good way for us to meet women."

"That sounds like something my brothers would say."

"Hey, there's always got to be a payoff for the hard work." He pushed his chair back from the table. "You need to lighten up a little and have some fun."

Fun? What is this fun of which you speak? "I have fun. You saw me at Halligan's with Avery and Stacy." She wouldn't mention that before that Friday night it had been more than two months since she'd gone out with friends.

"Fine. I concede. You don't need to have any fun, but take pity on me, because I sure do." When she hesitated, he continued, "Don't turn me into the lonely guy at the bar who has to ask a stranger to dance."

He really thought that line would work? She'd seen most of the women in the place eyeing him since they'd walked in, as they tried to decipher her and Jamie's relationship. Were they out on a date? Friends? Coworkers?

Join the club, girls. I'm still trying to figure that out, too.

"You wouldn't ask someone else to dance and leave me sitting here. That's not your style," she countered.

"Wanna bet?"

Her gaze locked with his as she tried to decide whether or not to call his bluff. Avery's voice popped into Emma's head. *Are you so sure your life doesn't need shaking up?*

Shaking it up would be one thing. Putting it into a blender and turning the machine on frappé was something else. She had a feeling getting involved with Jamie would be the latter.

But what could a couple of dances hurt? Especially line dancing. No touching involved there. "Let's see if you can keep up with me, city boy."

For most of the next set, Jamie didn't keep up with her. He about left her in his dust. Through the "Watermelon Crawl," the "Copperhead Road" and "The Slide." And she'd talked to him about how he should move onstage. She felt more than a bit stupid over having done that.

"Not bad," she said when the band switched to playing a slow song.

"For a city boy?"

"For anybody. You've got some moves."

He leaned toward her. "You have no idea."

Boy, she'd stepped right into that one. The question was how did she get out of this mess?

His gaze locked on hers, hot, steamy and inviting as he moved toward her. When he stood inches in front of her, he slipped his arm around her waist.

A little voice in her head told her to run, not walk, to the nearest exit.

Despite knowing it wasn't the best idea, she stepped into his arms.

Jamie smiled, and thought this was what he'd been waiting for all night—to hold Emma.

Funny thing. The more they'd rehearsed tonight, and the more they connected onstage, the more distant she became when the music stopped. He swore he saw her withdrawing into herself, while he felt the opposite. The time he spent with her left him wanting, and not just physically.

Nothing in his life had ever felt as right as being with Emma. He could be himself. He found a serenity with her that he'd never found with anyone else.

She leaned to the right to see around him. "You should check out the band. They have a completely different presence when they play a slow song like this one."

"Why are you pushing me away?"

Her gaze jerked back to his. When she opened her mouth, he held up a hand. "Don't bother to deny it because I won't believe you."

"You don't beat around an issue, do you?"

"What point is there? All avoiding something does is create confusion, hurt feelings, and it makes us miss out on some great experiences."

"What makes you think I'm pushing you away?"

"Except when we're singing, you're distant at rehearsal. And when we start talking about anything but work, you get nervous."

"It's not you, it's me."

He laughed. "I can't believe you said that. It's got to be the oldest cop-out line in the book. You think too much. This is pretty simple. I enjoy your company, and I thought you enjoyed mine."

"I do." Her voice sounded almost pained. As if she were on the witness stand and the prosecuting attorney had gotten her to admit she'd seen her best friend rob a store clerk at gunpoint.

"Don't sound so thrilled. Is liking me, wanting to spend time with me, such a bad thing?"

"I have to stay focused. I'm so close. I could finally have the success I've waited and worked so long for."

"You know what they say. All work and no play makes—"

"Emma a boring girl?" she finished for him, her gaze hooded.

His hand slid to the spot where her neck and shoulder met. His thumb gently caressed the sensitive area. He felt a shudder ripple through her. "I was going to say 'makes Emma come up empty for new song material.'"

"Right. That's what you were going to say."

"You have a gift, but when we were practicing I realized something. I can tell the newer pieces you've written the minute I start playing. There's not as much of you in those songs."

He resisted the urge to pull her closer. The vein in her neck throbbed at a frantic pace, contradicting the cool image she tried so hard to present to the world, but she couldn't fool him. He knew to back off, though, and handle her with a light touch. The best things were worth the wait.

"I don't know what you mean."

"You're holding back. From me. From life." He leaned closer until he felt her warm breath against his cheek. "We enjoy each other's company. We have fun. No big deal. Is that so bad?"

He saw her shut down. Her gaze grew distant. She stepped out of his arms and crossed her arms over her chest as if drawing herself inward.

So much for his light touch.

"I think it's time I went home."

He nodded and followed her out of the restaurant. When they reached her car, he said, "I'll follow you to make sure you don't have any problems."

"You know what? Before you got here, I managed to get everywhere safe and sound all on my own."

"It has nothing to do with you not being capable. There are a lot of weird people in the world. Don't you listen to the news? It's not smart for a woman to be out alone this time of night."

"This isn't New York City."

"Why does my common courtesy bother you so much?"

"Fine. Follow me home." She yanked open her car door, slid inside and slammed it shut with enough force to rattle the windows across the street.

He smiled as he got in his car and followed Emma

back to Estes Park. She wasted so much energy trying to prove how tough she was. That she didn't need anyone. That she didn't need even small courtesies from him. Was it just him, or did she act that way with everyone?

When they reached her apartment building, he joined her on the walkway. "You followed me home. I'm fine. I made it here in one piece. You've done your gentlemanly duty. You can leave."

The more she pushed him away, the more he wanted to reach the woman behind the wall. The one he'd seen glimpses of and felt so drawn to.

"I had fun tonight."

"I'm not going to ask you to come into my apartment."

"I didn't expect you to." She tilted her head and eyed him as if trying to decide whether he meant what he'd just said. "Remember, I don't beat around the bush. When I say something, I mean it."

He leaned forward and brushed his lips against hers in a light kiss. Then, without another word, he walked back to his car. Yup. Slow and steady. That's what would win the race with Emma.

After the night at Dick's Tavern, Emma changed her game plan. Denying her emotions hadn't worked. Instead she admitted the fact she was attracted to Jamie and that her body came alive anytime he was around. There. The first step to dealing with a problem was openly acknowledging what the problem was.

Now that she'd done that, she developed a two-part solution. Quit fighting her feelings and instead channel all the sexual energy she felt for him into her music.

But the key to success lay in the second part of her plan. Avoid Jamie any other time other than rehearsals.

And that's what she did. She avoided Halligan's during the day since Mick had scheduled Jamie to work then to accommodate their rehearsal schedule. She'd started closing her door when she worked in her office in case he showed up. Yesterday when he'd brought Trooper in for a weigh-in she'd pretended she wasn't there when he'd knocked on her door. While she couldn't say she was happier, she at least felt more under control.

Today when Jamie walked into the garage for rehearsal he marched straight over to her, stopping a few inches in front of her, his dark gaze intent and determined. "How long are you going to avoid me and give me the cold-shoulder treatment during rehearsals?"

"I don't know what you're talking about. With the Pet Walk this weekend it's been crazy at the shelter. I have so many last-minute things to see to, it hasn't left me much time for anything else."

"At least be honest with me. I deserve that."

Direct hit. "All right. I have been avoiding you. My life has been a disaster the past two years. I finally have it back on track. I don't want anything to mess this up."

"And you think I'd do that?"

"I need to stay focused."

He stepped closer. He stood so close she could see the tiny golden flecks in his brown eyes, but she refused to retreat. "Are you saying you can't handle me?"

Her throat grew dry. Then she realized what he was doing. She'd missed the first time he'd manipulated her by saying she couldn't handle something to get her to go to Dick's Tavern, but his ploy wasn't going to work this time.

"I know what you're doing. I don't know how I missed the old challenge ploy after all the times my brothers pulled that scam on me growing up, but I'm on to you now."

He had the nerve to smile.

She stood there, trying to think of the best comeback to wipe that grin off his face, but before she could, the garage door squeaked open. Luke sauntered in, followed by Grayson.

"Everyone's talking about us playing at the Pet Walk." Luke froze and glanced between her and Jamie. "Everything cool between you two? You look like we interrupted something."

"We're fine," Emma said. "I'm so glad everyone's talking about the concert. From what Avery said, ticket sales are up, so we should have an even better turnout than last year. Now we need to get to work and run through the numbers we plan to do this weekend."

Once they started rehearsing, her tension eased. This she could handle. Her world righted as they worked on the music for the concert.

"I thought we'd have to change that section, but you breezed right through it," Emma said when they finished the latest number.

"That surprised me, too." Jamie's face filled with pride.

"You're sounding more like the guy who played with the Philharmonic every day."

At Luke's comment a thought bolted through Emma. Jamie's hand *had* improved. As their rehearsals had progressed, she'd realized that fact, but she hadn't thought about the implications. Somewhere along the line, she'd forgotten about looking for a permanent replacement.

What if they did win the contest, and Jamie decided he wanted to return to classical music? What if a position opened up with the Philharmonic? What if he decided to find another symphony? The thought of him leaving, of not seeing him again, left her shaken.

Hadn't Avery told her to quit borrowing trouble? Now seemed like a good time to put that into practice. If they won, or rather, when they won the contest, she corrected, and if Jamie decided to leave, they'd find someone else. He wasn't the only fiddle player in the country. With Phillip Brandise's interest, she bet some of the musicians who claimed they were happy with their bands wouldn't be quite so content if she contacted them again. The tightness in her chest loosened. A little. Not as much as it should have, though.

"I don't know about the rest of you, but I'm done for the night," Luke said.

"I'd like to run through a few more numbers. With the Pet Walk this weekend and the competition soon after that, I could use the extra practice," Jamie said.

"Trust me, you're ready." The doubt in his eyes surprised Emma, as did her twinge of concern. "Are there any numbers in particular you're nervous about?"

Before he could answer, Emma's phone rang. She mumbled an apology and explained with the Pet Walk she needed to take the call.

"Emma Donovan?" the shaky male voice on the other end asked.

"That's me. What can I do for you?" she said, expecting to hear a question about the Pet Walk or the concert.

"This is Mark Sinclair. The agency gave me your phone number. My wife and I adopted your son. We named him Andrew."

She whispered the name, testing it out. Her son's name was Andrew.

When she'd talked to the agency about being open to communication with the adoptive parents, she wasn't sure she expected this day would ever come. Or if she did, she imagined it way in the future. Now faced with the reality, questions tumbled over each other in her head, creating an indiscernible chaos.

"I've been thinking about your family a lot lately. How is Andrew?"

"That's why I'm calling," Mark's voice broke. "He's sick. Very sick, and we need your help."

Panic, white-hot and blinding, rushed through her. She braced against the pain, forcing it back. Now all the odd feelings she'd been having about her son and why he'd been in her thoughts so much made sense. Somehow she'd known he needed her. "What's wrong and what can I do to help?"

"Andrew had a cancerous brain tumor. The doctor believes they got it all in the surgery, but the chemotherapy damaged his bone marrow. Now he needs a transplant. Carmen and I were tested, but we're not a match. Andrew's doctor says one of his birth parents is his best chance."

She should have been careful what she wished for. She'd wanted to know about her son, possibly even become a part of his life, but not like this. Not because he was sick. What she wouldn't give to be able to trade places with him.

"Of course I'll get tested. Can a doctor's office take care of it or do I need to go to the hospital?"

"Any doctor can take the sample. All he needs to do is swab the inside of your cheek and send it off for typing." Mark said he'd text her the details on the typing she needed to request and where the results should be sent.

She nodded and glanced at her watch. Her vision blurred and she swiped a hand over her eyes, surprised when they came away wet. Four o'clock. Would her doctor's office still be open this late on Saturday afternoon? If not, maybe she could go to one of those doc-in-a-box-type places. "I'll get the test taken care of today."

"I appreciate you doing this," Mark said, and then he sighed. "I'm praying you'll be a match, but in case you aren't, do you know how I can reach the birth father? The agency doesn't have current information on him."

That didn't surprise her. When she'd asked Tucker if he'd wanted to meet with prospective parents, he'd said whoever she chose was fine with him. Then he'd told her to send him whatever he needed to sign in order to relinquish his parental right and said he never wanted to discuss the "issue" again. How could any man refer to his child like that?

He certainly wouldn't be thrilled with anyone contacting him. Too bad. No matter how hard she and Tucker wished otherwise, they were connected and always would be. How could one small moment in time change her life so profoundly and on so many levels? She hadn't realized that when she'd become intimate with Tucker. All she'd thought about was how much she loved him. "I haven't talked to him since we broke up, but his parents still live here part-time."

Thankfully once his career had taken off, Tucker had quit visiting his parents in Estes Park, instead preferring to fly them to Nashville. Then, a couple of years ago, he'd bought a house for them there, as well.

"We'd like him to get tested, too. In case you're not a match."

"I'll text you their phone number, but hopefully we won't have to worry about that. I'm praying I'll be a match." But she couldn't blame Andrew's father for wanting to hedge his bets.

After she ended the call, what she'd learned tumbled over in her mind. Brain tumor. Cancer. Chemo. Her heart bled for the child she'd never known. No seven-year-old should have to deal with those issues. A coldness swept through her.

"What's wrong?"

The concern in Jamie's voice and his warm hand on her icy skin broke through the wall holding her together. Tears stung her eyes and her chest tightened. Her heart banged against her ribs, threatening to break through. "Something's come up. We're done for the day." Then, not wanting anyone to see her fall apart even further, she darted out of the garage.

She ran for the safety of her car. Her brain wouldn't function. All she could think about was the fact that the son she'd never had a chance to know might die. Tears spilled down her cheeks. Her shoulders shook from the pain coursing through her.

The passenger door opened, startling her. She swiped a hand over her face, wiping away the remnants of her tears as Jamie slid into the passenger seat. "Want to tell me what's wrong?"

She tried to speak but she couldn't push the words past her tight throat.

"Take deep breaths." His reassuring voice broke through her fog. Her gaze sought his calm one as she shut out everything but him and matched her breathing with his. "You mentioned a test. Start with that."

"My son's name is Andrew and he's sick. That was his father, Mark, on the phone. He needs a bone marrow transplant. I need to get tested to see if I'm a match."

"What do you need to do? Can a doctor do the test?"

She nodded. "But I don't remember if my family practitioner is open late on Saturdays."

"Call and find out."

She nodded. Her hands shook as she opened her purse and dug around for her phone. After she called the office, she turned to Jamie. "They're open until five. The nurse said they'll work me in when I get there." The fear welled up inside of her again. "Andrew's father said he had a brain tumor. The chemo has damaged his bone marrow so that's why he needs the transplant."

Saying the words out loud made them so much more real. She bit her lip to keep from crying. What if she wasn't a match? Dizziness swamped her.

"Change places with me."

She turned to Jamie. "What? I don't understand."

"You're in no shape to drive. You're pale and you're shaking."

She glanced at her hands. Yup. Shaking like a newborn foal. "I guess the fact that I didn't eat lunch, combined with the stress, is getting to me. I'll be fine. I just need a minute to calm down."

"There's no way in hell I'm letting you drive."

She started to argue but stopped. He had the same stubborn look in his eyes as he'd had that night they'd found Trooper and he hadn't wanted her going out alone. "You're going to be stubborn about this again, aren't you?"

"You got that right."

Okay, then. That settled that. She opened her car door. As she changed places with him, she had to admit she kind of liked him going all caveman and laying down the law because he was concerned about her.

Chapter 11

As Jamie sat waiting for Emma, he couldn't help but admire her strength. When she'd first told him about the phone call in the car he'd seen how pale she was. The pain had been evident in her face and in her voice. Then, right before his eyes, she'd sucked it up, turned all-business and went into get-the-job-done mode. She'd never considered any option but helping her son.

The woman's backbone was made of steel, but her heart was as sweet, soft and gooey as one of his mom's homemade chocolate chip cookies.

What would it be like to have a woman like that in his life? One he could count on when things got tough. Oh, let's say when a guy hurt his hand and had to face the fact that he might need to start over in a new career?

A woman like Emma would give him the strength to tackle the worst life could throw at him, and she wouldn't stand behind him. She'd stand beside him every step of the way.

He thought about rehearsal. Since he'd been playing with the band he'd noticed the dexterity returning to his left hand, but today showed him how far he'd come. Last week he wouldn't have been able to play the song he had today.

Maybe it was time to try playing music he'd performed with the Philharmonic. That would be the true test. He should do that tonight when he got back to Mick's.

He flexed his hand. Funny how it didn't look any different, and yet he knew it was. Maybe he wouldn't be forced to reinvent himself after all. The thought should have him ready to crack open the champagne, but instead he found the idea unsettling. If he returned to his old life, what would he find waiting for him other than his career? Not much more than a few acquaintances who, once he was out of sight, had forgotten he existed.

And what about Emma?

What had he said to her at Dick's Tavern that night? Something like they enjoyed each other's company and had fun. No big deal. He'd been so full of it.

She understood him in a way no one else did. Her enthusiasm, her love of music was infectious. He found himself looking forward to seeing her every day.

The door to the exam rooms opened and she walked out, her face drawn. "All done. They've put a rush on the test because Andrew is so sick." Her voice broke and tears pooled in her eyes. He closed the distance between them and wrapped his arms around her. "Dr. Sampson said I should know in a few days."

"You're doing all you can."

"But what if it's not enough? What if I'm not a match?"

"We'll deal with that if it happens."

His words stunned him. We? When had he and Emma become a we? The thought left him weak.

Needing to lighten the mood for her sake as well as his, he said, "I've been thinking about what to wear to the concert."

She tilted her head and eyed him. "This from the guy who gave me a hard time when I brought up the subject at Dick's Tavern?"

"Yup. I hadn't thought about it then, but now I have. I've got a black T-shirt, but I don't have a cowboy hat or boots." What if the people who purchased tickets pegged him as a smug city boy trying to be something he wasn't?

"Go to Rocky Mountain Outfitters. That's where my brothers shop. That is, when they hit the point where they've either got to wash clothes or buy new ones."

"I could use your opinion," he said as they walked through the office building toward the parking lot.

"Whatever you pick out will be fine."

Was she purposely making this tough? Weren't women supposed to be good at picking up on hints? He shoved his hands in his front pockets and fingered the coins there. "I'm nervous about the concert."

"You've been onstage before. It's no different than the night we sang at Mick's place."

"Oh, yes, it is. People are paying to hear me this time. I don't want to disappoint anyone."

"What do your clothes have to do with that?"

"You really are slow on the uptake today."

"You'd better be nice. It sounds like you're trying to

work up to asking me for a favor, and those who don't
ask nicely get bubkes."

Now he understood. This was payback for him playing dumb when she'd hinted at him joining the band.
"I'm classically trained. Everyone was great at Halligan's when I sang, but that was my grandfather's bar. A
paying audience might not be as forgiving. I live in New
York City. I'm a city boy, as you're so fond of reminding me. I don't want to look like I'm playing dress-up."

"Come on, then. We'll go shopping."

Emma knew Jamie wanted her help the minute he
mentioned he was thinking about what he should wear
for the concert, but couldn't resist giving him a hard
time. Then he'd gone and ruined her fun by telling her
the truth and sharing another confidence. Damn him.

*I'm nervous about the concert. I don't want to look
like I'm playing dress-up.*

His honesty reached inside her, drawing her in like
nothing else could. She thought about what he'd shared
with her in the barn, how he sometimes felt on the outside looking in with his family. That's what this was
about. He wanted to belong.

The man really should take a good long look in the
mirror sometime. With his voice and looks, women
wouldn't notice, much less care, what he wore onstage.
But she hadn't told him that, so instead here she was
shopping with him.

Once they stood inside Rocky Mountain Outfitters,
Jamie picked up a leather belt with rhinestones, sil-
ver studs and a huge shiny buckle. "When we were at
Dick's, you said there were different country singer
styles. You never mentioned country bling. The lights
bouncing off this would be great. It would make me

stand out onstage. Maybe this is the look I should go for."

"I knew you were one of those guys who needed the spotlight to be on him. This only proves it," she teased. But didn't people use joking as a nonthreatening way of telling the truth? "The next thing we know, you'll be asking for a spot dedicated just for you."

"If that's what I wanted, I'd have asked you about this." He shook his head and picked up a belt with an even gaudier buckle. "But since you brought up the lighting issue—"

"I dare you to wear that. To even try it on."

"You sure you want to do that?" His stubborn I'm-not-backing-down gaze drilled through her.

Who knew that he could produce the look on demand when he clearly wasn't annoyed, and only teasing her? She shuddered with exaggerated horror. "Oops. I forgot how stubborn you can be. I take back the dare."

"That's right. You better, woman."

"Can I help either of you find anything or maybe referee?" Emma recognized the voice, and froze.

She'd hoped Harper wouldn't be in. Leave it to the older woman to pop up and spoil all the fun.

Harper, dressed in jeans and the same brown-and-turquoise paisley Western shirt as displayed in the front window, shook her head. "I never knew what my grandmother meant when she said one couple's fighting is another one's dancing until now. You two are having way too much fun trying to get under each other's skin."

"Jamie, this is Harper Stinson, Rocky Mountain Outfitter's owner and board president of the Estes Park animal shelter."

"Pleased to meet you, ma'am. I'm here to find something to wear for the shelter concert. Emma told me she'd help, but all she's doing so far is giving me a hard time."

"Don't blame me when you haven't been taking this seriously. I'm not the one who'll be performing in athletic shoes."

"Don't start any more of that dancing, you two," Harper said. "The boots are this way. I'll help you out because no way am I letting you go onstage for the shelter fund-raiser in tennis shoes, and we'll do something about a shirt while we're at it." She nodded toward Emma. "Between the two of us, we'll take care of things."

After the night spent shopping with Jamie, Emma decided she was done fighting what she felt for him. She was tired of being strong, focused and directed all the time. More important, she was tired of being alone.

Not that she thought she'd found her soul mate or anything crazy like that. She believed the soul mate thing was as real as Bigfoot—but Jamie made her laugh, something she hadn't done enough of since her mother had gotten sick, and for right now, that was enough. No harm. No foul. That became her motto.

From that night on, she and Jamie went out to eat after rehearsals and talked about whatever came to mind. Music, their childhoods. She learned he'd secretly listened to country music in high school. Sometimes they worked on music and had even started writing some songs together. A couple of times they went hiking or horseback riding. Nothing special, and yet their time together fed her soul.

Now today Emma stood in the parking lot at Stanley

Park unloading tables and chairs from the shelter van for the Pet Walk when Jamie pulled up. He'd been such a rock for her when she'd found out about Andrew. It would have been so easy to fall apart, and she probably would have if it hadn't been for Jamie.

He got out of Mick's battered Chevy truck, looking way too good for this early in the morning, wearing one of the shirts he'd bought when they'd gone shopping. As it happened, her favorite, the tan-and-brown plaid that matched his coffee-colored eyes.

Before, when he was dressed in khakis and a polo shirt, he'd looked... She searched for the right word. *Restrained. Reserved.* Almost as if he was apart from everyone and everything around him. Now a relaxed air surrounded him. He appeared at ease. Almost as if she was seeing the inner man for the first time. He looked as though he'd been here his entire life. As though he belonged.

She nodded toward his feet. "Good-looking boots."

"Do I pass muster?"

"You'll do."

Anytime. Anywhere.

The image of him kissing her in Mick's living room flashed in her mind, sending her already racing pulse even higher. What would've happened if she hadn't left? Clothes would have gone flying and they'd have been all over each other, more than likely. Last week the idea had left her shaking in her boots, but this week the idea sounded a whole lot better.

What was she thinking? She needed to snap out of it. Abstinence was rotting her brain. That was the problem.

"It's too bad I'm working today. I bet Trooper would love being out here," Jamie said.

She grinned. "I've seen that look before. Has he found a forever home?"

"I don't know if Mick will want to adopt him or not."

"That wasn't who I was talking about. What about you?"

"My apartment doesn't allow pets."

The boulder came out of nowhere and rolled right over her. How could she have forgotten the fact that Jamie being here was only temporary? Luke's words flashed in her mind. *Maybe he'll like playing with us so much he'll change his religion, so to speak, and decide to stick around.*

See what happens when you have expectations? When you start hoping?

She reached for a stack of chairs, but he brushed her hand aside. "You need all these unloaded?"

"You offering to help?" When he nodded, she pointed toward the tent that had been set up at the park entrance. If nothing else, she'd be grateful for the free labor today, which meant fewer aching muscles tomorrow for her. "They go at the registration desk."

"I'm all yours until nine."

If only that were true.

Where had that thought come from and how could she get rid of it? Lighten things up and focus on work. That would do the trick. "All right, assistant. Let's get these tables and chairs set up."

"You and Emma have been spending a lot of time together," Mick said a couple of hours later when Jamie arrived at the pavilion to help set up the food booth.

"That's about as smooth a move into a conversation as a gravel road." Since she'd found out about her son, their relationship had changed, but the hell if he knew what it had changed into. While most nights they grabbed a bite to eat after rehearsals, he couldn't really say they were dating, and yet, they were more than friends because whenever they were together the air crackled with sexual tension. "With getting ready for today and the state fair coming up, we've been rehearsing a lot."

Mick grinned like a matchmaking momma. "You sure that's all it's been? Rehearsing? The rumor mill says you two have been out almost every night. That sounds like dating to me."

"You're getting as bad as an old woman."

Jamie reached into a box and started unpacking serving utensils and packets of plastic silverware. He thought about what Emma had told him about her baby's father. *He made it clear he wanted nothing to do with fatherhood.* His curiosity ate at him, but he hadn't asked Emma for fear of opening up old wounds. "Since you brought up the dating subject, Emma says she doesn't get involved with musicians. Is that because of her baby's father?"

"That Tucker Mathis always was an ass and never was good enough for Emma."

"Tucker Mathis? As in, part of one of the hottest acts in country music right now?" That's who'd fathered Emma's child?

Mick nodded. "Gene told me he was messin' around on Emma when they were living together in Nashville. She was working two jobs to support them while he was working on making 'industry connections.' Well, he made 'em, all right, with anything in a skirt. Then, when Emma told him she was pregnant, he left her and moved in with that blonde-in-a-bottle he sings with now."

So many things made sense now. Tucker had gone on to live the dream while Emma had gone home to a family embarrassed by her pregnancy and had struggled with the decision of whether or not to give her child up for adoption.

Jamie's thoughts turned to what Emma had said about her last band. *Turned out they'd already replaced me. They just forgot to tell me.*

He'd bet she'd been dating someone in that band when she'd come back to Estes Park to take care of her mother. There had been too much pain in her eyes when she'd told him about that. The betrayal had been deeper. More personal.

"Gene also said the song that got Tucker his first record deal was one he and Emma wrote together. Though, of course, he claims different."

"Why didn't she take him to court?" What a stupid question. Cases like that cost money, were emotionally exhausting and lengthy. After what she'd gone through, how could Emma have dealt with taking Tucker to court? "Never mind. I know the reasons."

No wonder she'd sworn off musicians.

"Hey, Mick, you open for business?" a fortysomething man with a German shepherd on a leash called out from across the walkway.

"Sure are. Come on over, Sam," Mick replied.

"Good, because I'm so hungry those dog biscuits at the Puppy Palace booth are starting to look good. Give me one of your brats instead." Sam dug out his wallet, found a five and handed the bill to Jamie. "It's good to see you here helping Mick. A man his age should have family around."

"I'm glad to do it."

"I got my ticket for the concert," Henry said as he joined the growing line. "When the band makes it big, I expect you and Emma to give me credit since your changing careers and joining Maroon Peak Pass was my idea." The older man scratched his chin. "In fact, I think coming up with the suggestion entitles me to free CDs for life. Don't you?"

Changing careers. Jamie froze. When had he done that? He hadn't as far as he knew. Had he latched on to Emma's dream to fill the void in his life and to avoid having to face deciding about his future?

"I think you're putting the cart in front of the horse there, Henry. All I'm doing is helping the band out. We're just testing the waters." Isn't that what he and Emma had said? "It may not work out. People may not accept a classically trained violinist playing country music."

Or it could be everyone would think he stunk. Could be he'd choke or hate playing more popular music. Great time to remember that he could fall flat on his face. That'll give him confidence to walk onto the stage.

"I love that Darius Rucker. Then I come to learn he was in some Top 40 band years ago," the middle aged woman waiting behind Henry said. "It was some band with a funny fish name. Anyway, country music fans have accepted him. If they can do that, they can accept a classical musician."

"Martha's right," Henry said. "People will sense what's in your heart, and if the music speaks to you, you'll be fine. 'Course you've got to be good, but from what I heard at Halligan's that shouldn't be a problem."

"I can't wait to hear you two sing," Martha said. "I've got my ticket."

Jamie handed Henry his change. "Good, I could use some friendly faces in the crowd."

For the next couple of hours, Jamie served up brats, hot dogs and chips while he chatted with people, most of whom said they planned on attending the concert. He wasn't sure he was ready for half the town to be there. He wondered if it was too late to back out. Then he chuckled. As if Emma would let him do that.

Emma. He'd be fine as long as she was there.

After they finished serving lunch, as they were cleaning and packing up, Mick said, "I've been thinking about the future a lot lately. One day the ranch and the restaurant will be yours."

"Unless there's something you haven't told me, there's no reason to discuss this," Jamie said, trying to keep his voice light despite the tightness in his chest at the thought of losing the grandfather it had taken him so long to find.

"Well, we're gonna talk about it. All I ask is that if you don't want to run the restaurant, you find a reliable manager or sell it to someone who realizes what the place means to this community. Now, the ranch is a different story. If you don't want to live there, at least hang on to it as a place you can come to when you need to get away."

"What about Kimberly?"

"While I love my daughter because she's part of me, we haven't had much of a relationship in quite a few years. I consider myself lucky if she sends me a Christmas card. You're family, Jamie, and to you the ranch and the restaurant won't just be dollar signs. You could have a good life here, you know."

Jamie nodded, not able to trust his voice. He felt a

peace here he'd never found anywhere else, and then there was Emma. She'd become so important to him since he'd arrived in Estes Park, but how could he decide about their relationship when he couldn't figure out what to do with his life? Emma deserved better than a guy who was drifting through life without much purpose.

Since he'd arrived in Colorado he'd settled into a routine working at Halligan's and around the ranch. He did his hand exercises. He rehearsed with the band, spent time with Emma and when he wasn't with her, he was thinking about her. The one thing he hadn't done was consider the future.

Just because he was having fun here and enjoyed the challenge of playing country music didn't mean he could have a career. How could he let go of everything he'd worked for? Choosing to leave the Philharmonic would have been one thing, but now he felt if he didn't give it his best shot to get back there, he would be settling.

But hadn't he been telling Emma there was more to life than a career? There was having someone you connected with on that intimate level, and not just physically. There was being part of a community.

As Jamie set out in search of Emma, he was amazed at the size of Pet Walk and the number of booths with vendors hawking everything from pet toys to pet cemetery plots and headstones. Then there were rescue groups, photographers, big-name grocery stores and insurance agents with booths. He'd known dogs and cats were big business, but not like this.

Someone called his name and he turned to see Avery

and a tall man walking toward him, a scraggly long-haired dog on a leash beside him.

"So you're the new guy everyone's talking about. I've got to say, I feel your pain," Avery's husband said after he introduced himself. "Until you came along I was the favorite target." Then Reed explained how he'd grown up in Estes Park, but went to school at Stanford and lived in California until not too long ago.

"How long will everyone hold the city stuff over my head?"

"I'll tell you a secret. If people didn't like you, they wouldn't give you a hard time. They'd just smile politely and nod your way," Reed said. "We'll have to get together and commiserate over a few beers sometime."

"We've got to keep you in line, and I'll give you a tip." Avery leaned toward her husband, amusement sparkling in her gaze. "People wouldn't tease you if you quit using words like *commiserate* so often."

Jamie laughed at the pair and the genuine love between them. He was ready for that, for something real and lasting with a woman he could hold on to during life's ups and downs. A picture of him and Emma in his grandfather's living room popped into his head. They'd been so comfortable together, but not in a complacent way. In a way that felt right. A man could get used to having a warm woman to snuggle up with at the end of a long day.

"Thanks again for agreeing to sing at the concert," Avery said. "Emma says you've made a huge difference in the band's sound. I can't wait to hear you two. She's so excited about today and the state fair competition. I hate to lose her at the shelter, but I really hope the band wins. She's worked so hard for so long. No one deserves a recording contract more."

"Speaking of Emma, do you know where she is?"

"Right behind you."

He turned at the sound of her voice, and smiled. Her face held a rosy glow from being outside in the sun all morning. Tendrils of her long dark hair curled around her face. Emma walked over to the dog and scratched him on the head. "I'm glad to see you're behaving yourself this year, Baxter."

"Sounds like there's a story there," Jamie said.

"Another reason for us to get together for beers." Reed smiled.

"I hate to break up the male bonding, but duty calls," Emma said. "Avery, a film student wants to interview you for her project. I told her I'd find you and send you to meet her at the registration tent."

"And I'm off." Avery turned to her husband, a wide grin on her face. "Come on, assistant."

When the other couple left, Emma turned to Jamie. "Speaking of assistants. If you've got some free time, I could use your help."

"I don't have anything to do until the concert. By the way, judging from what the lunch crowd at the food booth said, half the town's going to be there this afternoon."

"That doesn't surprise me. We've almost doubled our ticket sales from last year."

His stomach rolled over, churning up the brats he'd wolfed down earlier. "Tell me I won't make a fool of myself."

"You act like someone who's never been onstage before, but if you really need reassurance, I'll play along.

You'll be fine. I wouldn't let you go onstage if you weren't ready. Now, lucky for you, I've got the perfect cure for a bad case of nerves."

"Oh, really?"

"Yup. Some good hard work."

For the rest of the afternoon Emma put Jamie to work. He tagged along with her, lifting and moving tables. He ran simple errands and kept her company. She'd forgotten what simple companionship felt like. Had she ever really had this with any of the other men she'd dated?

"I could get used to having an assistant," she teased as she and Jamie folded up the tables from the various pet contests.

She could get used to having him around, period. Rehearsals had changed over the past couple of weeks. They still worked hard, but there was a balance in her life, and she realized Avery and Jamie had been right. She'd been shutting herself off from everyone and everything. Now that she'd started opening up, she felt a sense of peace and joy again, and her music was better. More personal. More real. More filled with hope.

"Despite you working me like a pack mule, today's been fun. The best-dressed pet contest was amazing. The work some of the contestants put into the outfits was incredible." He shook his head. "The roaring twenties get-up must have taken days to make."

"Avery's going to have to give Mrs. Russell and Chandra a lifetime achievement award or something. It's the fourth year they've won. This year the number of contestants in that contest was way down. I think people are afraid of competing against her."

"That sweet little old lady is scaring off people?"

"I wouldn't compete against her. She's ruthless." Her phone rang. She sighed as she reached into her back pocket. "I wonder what's gone wrong or who can't find what now."

After she glanced at the screen, her gaze sought Jamie's, needing his strength, his reassurance. "It's the doctor's office."

She reached out to clasp his hand. His warmth seeped into her, keeping the cold from consuming her as she answered the call. *Please let me be a match.*

"I am so sorry, Emma. You're not a match," Dr. Sampson said.

Disappointment, fear and blinding pain crashed over her in waves, threatening to level her. She ended the call and with a shaking hand shoved her phone back into her pocket.

"You're not a match." Jamie's voice cut through her haze.

People flowed in and out of her line of vision. The colors of their clothes created a rainbow of colors. An odd buzzing sound rang in her ears. What would happen to Andrew now?

"Come with me, sweetheart." Jamie wrapped his arm around her shoulder, and when he started to lead her away, she followed, too numb to do anything else. Then the next thing she knew they were in a secluded spot behind the large pavilion and she was in his arms crying. Great heaving sobs wrenched from the depths of her.

"I'm so sorry, darling. I know how much you wanted to help Andrew." He kissed the top of her head. "I wish I could make everything right. What about Tucker? Have they heard if he's a match?"

Red-hot rage exploded inside her, obliterating her pain. She stiffened and pulled away from Jamie. "The ass won't get tested."

"You're kidding. How could he refuse to have a simple test to see if he could save his child's life? Did he say why?"

She gazed at the Rocky Mountains behind Jamie. A strong constant presence. So like the man offering his support now. The anger built inside her, threatening to devour her. She started pacing. "All I had was his parents' phone number. When Mark contacted them, they refused to give him Tucker's number. All they'd do was relay the message. The next day they called back to say because of the tour Tucker couldn't deal with getting tested right now."

"Can't or won't?"

She paused. "Exactly. He can't even go in to a doctor's office for a cheek swab? How tough is that?"

The selfish bastard couldn't spare an hour.

"You were there an hour, tops. The selfish bastard won't spare sixty minutes?"

Her heart skipped a beat. There it was again, him almost reading her mind.

"But if he learned he was a match then he'd have to decide about donating bone marrow. I researched it on the internet. He could be in a little pain and stiff for a couple of weeks, but how bad would that be? Is he really that unwilling to reschedule a few concerts?"

"Maybe that's just his excuse. What if he's like Kimberly? What if he's ashamed that he got you pregnant and you two gave the child up for adoption?"

She froze. That thought had never occurred to her. Images were fragile things in the entertainment industry. If the public got ticked off or disillusioned with a performer, it quickly translated to fewer sales and lower ticket revenues. "You may have hit on something. Tucker's worked hard cultivating his image as the honest, hard-working boy next door. If he has to postpone concerts, he'd have to explain why."

"The last thing he'd want to talk about was how he got his high school sweetheart pregnant and dumped her, leaving her to deal with having his baby alone. Not exactly the responsible thing to do. Not that it matters why he won't get tested. The question is what're you going to do about his refusal?"

She knew what she had to do. She had to face Tucker's parents to get his phone number so she could talk to him. He could be the one to save Andrew and someone had to convince him to get tested.

"Let's see his parents say no to me when I'm standing on their doorstep. You can bet I'll get his phone number."

"Atta girl. My money's on you."

She glanced at her watch. "It's already three. Our concert is at four, and I've got to clean up and double-check the stage setup. There isn't enough time for me to talk to his parents now. I'll have to wait until after the concert." She chewed on her lip and peeked up at Jamie. "Will you go with me?"

"If you want me there, that's where I'll be."

Chapter 12

Emma hadn't been this nervous for a concert in years, but she wasn't worried about her performance. She glanced at Jamie standing rigid and pale beside her. He'd been doing okay until he'd seen the crowd. She just hoped he didn't pass out.

"Isn't it great? We've never had this many women in our audiences before," Luke said as he joined them backstage.

Yippee. She'd been right. Every man-hungry female within a thirty-mile radius had shown up for their concert. "I'm just warning everybody right now. If women start rushing the stage, you men are on your own. No way am I getting in the middle of a catfight."

Grayson grinned. Luke laughed. Jamie's eyes widened, and though she hadn't thought it possible, he grew whiter. "You really think someone would do that?"

"Breathe or you're going to pass out." She placed her hand on his arm. Muscles flexed under her palm. "It's going to be fine."

"Don't worry, Jamie. I'll throw myself in the path of any women who make it to the stage," Grayson said.

"Thanks for the sacrifice." Emma rolled her eyes. "No one's going to rush the stage. Quit trying to jerk Jamie's chain."

Over the loudspeakers, she heard Avery ask, "How's everyone doing today?"

The crowd cheered and Emma mentally ran through the program one last time. Beside her, Jamie stiffened. She slipped her hand in his and squeezed. "Don't be nervous. You'll be great. Pretend we're back in the garage. Just us. Now put on a big smile. It's showtime."

She walked onto the stage and adrenaline flooded her system. This was where she was meant to be. This was where she belonged. With Jamie. Where she felt comfortable. She greeted the crowd and they cheered back at her. She counted out two measures and the band started playing.

Music flowed out of her guitar, swirling around her, soothing her soul. Jamie's fiddle joined in. The cheers and whistles grew deafening for a few seconds. Out of the corner of her eye she caught sight of him. He appeared more relaxed now, more in his element. She drifted toward him. Her gaze locked with his. The words of the first song she'd written about her son poured out of her, how she may never see him again but she'd always love him, and she felt pulled to the man beside her.

I'm standing at the edge of a cliff about to take the last step, but oh, what a way to go.

* * *

As Emma walked off the stage, she realized she'd been smart to wait to talk to Tucker's parents. After a concert she always felt energized, as though she could take on the world. Between that feeling and having Jamie next to her, she could handle facing them. He wouldn't let her fall apart. She almost laughed. That wasn't what she was worried about. Her bigger concern was she'd go postal if they gave her any lip, and then who knows what felony she'd commit. Jamie would help keep her under control. He wouldn't let anything happen to her.

Those thoughts sent a wave of panic through her. When had she started relying on him? Counting on him being there the way he'd been when she'd gotten the phone call about not being a match. She hadn't needed to ask. He'd seen that she needed him and was there for her. Offering his strength, his support.

"That was amazing. Talk about a rush. We've never sounded like that before. Did you hear those women screaming? There was a pretty little blonde in the second row who couldn't keep her eyes off me." Luke hooked his thumbs in his belt loops. "I could get used to this."

"We should go out and celebrate," Grayson said. "I know we agreed not to socialize, but we spend so much time together. Seems silly that we're almost strangers."

Somehow it did.

"I wish I could go out, but there's something I have to do." Emma realized Grayson was right. He and Luke were a huge part of her life and it was time she treated them that way. She explained about Andrew needing a bone marrow transplant, how she wasn't a match and how she hoped to convince Tucker to get tested.

"Give 'em hell, Emma," Luke said.

"They aren't going to know what hit 'em," Grayson added.

Incredibly touched by their support, she thanked them and said she'd see them at rehearsal tomorrow. Once Luke and Grayson left, she turned to Jamie. "You're still willing to go with me to talk to Tucker's family, aren't you?"

He glared at her as if he were insulted by her question. Had she ever had anyone offer her such unconditional support before?

"I'll warn you, this won't be pleasant. I'd put talking to Tucker's parents on my to-do list right behind jumping out of an airplane with a secondhand parachute."

"Walk with me. You need to clear your head before you see them," Jamie said.

She nodded, knowing he was right. Instead of heading toward the parking lot, she turned onto the path to their right. "When I decided to give the baby up for adoption, I needed Tucker to sign the papers. I called his cell but it was disconnected, so I went to his parents to find out how to reach him."

"Talk about history repeating itself."

"Exactly. That's what I'm afraid of. They accused me of trying to trap him. They said if it hadn't been for my 'lack of talent and ambition' he would have landed a recording contract much sooner. They had the nerve to ask me if I was sure the child was his. I told them just because their son was sleeping around didn't mean I was. I came away feeling like I'd been dragged behind a truck for five miles."

"They only have power over you if you give it to them."

"I've never thought of it like that before."

"You are an incredibly talented woman, and you're stronger than anyone I know. You have nothing to be ashamed of."

"You're right, and I'm certainly not the naive girl I was. I refuse to let them intimidate me. I'll do whatever I have to in order to help Andrew."

Grayson was right. They weren't going to know what hit them.

When Jamie parked in the driveway of the large brick house with the immaculately landscaped beds and yard, he shut off the engine and turned to Emma. What a woman. This couldn't be easy for her, not after what she'd told him at the park, and yet here she was. She would go through hell and back for those she loved.

A man couldn't ask for a better woman than that, but what about what she deserved? Forget about that. *Focus on what she needs from you right now.* "Are you sure you want me to come to the door? You're capable of handling this on your own, and my being there could tick them off."

She shook her head before he even finished speaking. "I need you there to keep me from doing anything foolish. I hear stories about people snapping in these kinds of situations all the time. I don't want that to happen to me. I'd look awful in one of those shapeless prison jumpsuits."

Her brittle, nervous laugh rattled through the truck.

"Look at me. You're still the girl that spent hours learning to climb a tree. This may leave you with some scrapes and bruises, but you can do it. You're a survivor. No one can take that away from you. Now screw up your courage and get the job done."

He could have chosen softer words, but that wasn't what she needed. She needed a reminder about her strength and the depths of it to bolster her sagging courage.

She stared at him, her eyes wide with shock. "Geez, warn a girl when you're going to take off the kid gloves."

"I have every faith in you. If you set your mind to something, there's no stopping you."

"Thanks. I needed that."

When her gaze met his, a fire blazed in her eyes. One hot enough to wipe out a national forest in record time.

She threw open the car door, climbed out, slammed it shut behind her and stalked up the walkway. When they reached the front door, she inhaled deeply, slowly let her breath go and rang the doorbell. A moment later, when a slender blonde woman opened the door, her eyes widened in shock. Then her lips pursed as though she'd taken a big drink of unsweetened lemonade.

She should be afraid. Hurricane Emma was about to make landfall.

"Go away." When the woman tried to shut the door in Emma's face, Jamie shoved his boot in between the door and the jamb.

"You look just like your grandfather, and I see you have his cocky attitude."

He considered defending Mick, but figured why waste his energy? Someone this angry, he sensed this unhappy with life in general, wasn't worth his effort.

The woman turned to Emma. "I'm not surprised you hooked up with another musician. You always were

looking to slide by on someone else's coattails because
your talent wasn't enough. Now tell him to remove his
foot."

He saw the woman's insult hit the mark as pain
flashed in Emma's gaze before she could hide it, but she
never wavered. "Mary, I want Tucker's phone number."

*'Atta girl. Don't give her the satisfaction of seeing
she hurt you.*

"I can't see as there's any reason for you and my son
to talk, but if you tell me what the issue is, I'll relay the
information to him."

"That's not good enough. I want to talk to him myself."

"This is about him getting tested to help that boy,
isn't it? I told the man who called to get Tucker's number that he couldn't deal with that right now."

Emma stiffened. Her eyes darkened. When she bit
her lip, he knew she was trying to hold back her temper, and he wondered if it would be better if she let it
loose. At least then she'd get the satisfaction of putting
this bitch in her place.

"This isn't just *some boy*." Emma's low, surprisingly
calm voice rippled through him, filling him with admiration and respect. "This is your grandson we're talking about."

"No, it's not. He's someone else's grandchild," Mary
said. "My son signed away his parental rights. We
have no connection with that child. No more than any
stranger we see on the street."

This time Jamie was the one who stiffened. The
woman's words pierced him, nicking a sensitive spot
he hadn't known still existed. This icy detachment, al-

most to the point of cruelty, had been what he'd run into headfirst when he'd contacted his birth mother.

A realization crashed through him. Some people really did lack the capability for human compassion. He caught sight of Emma out of the corner of his eye. Caring, determination and love for the child she'd never known rolled off her in waves.

"You and your son have a genetic connection with this little boy. Tucker is the most likely person to be a match. Are you saying he won't take a simple test to see if he can help save a child's life?"

"If it were any other time, it would be a possibility, but this tour is important to Tucker's career. Maybe after that's over—"

"Andrew doesn't have time to wait. I want Tucker's number. He owes me for dumping me and moving in with another woman when I was pregnant. Let *him* tell me he's unwilling to help the child we created."

"That may be what you want, but it's not what you're going to get." Mary crossed her arms over her chest and sneered at Emma, as if she was the one who was justified in her indignation.

"You relay *this* message to *your* son. He will get the test done. If he refuses I'll tell whoever will listen, starting with the local media, about his refusal to help *that child,* as you referred to him. Then I'll talk about how the song 'My Heart Is Yours' that he's always been so proud of as the hit that launched his career, was actually something we worked on together and how I've never received a dime for my work. Tell him I'm prepared to sell my soul to the devil to pay for a lawyer to take him to court over that fact."

"You can't do that after all these years."

Emma leaned forward, her posture rigid, her eyes hard and unyielding. "I don't know if I can or not, but let him refuse to have the test, and I'll sure check into it. If nothing else, when I'm done with his reputation, Marilyn Manson will look like a choirboy next to Tucker." Then she turned and stormed off.

Disgust welled up inside him for the woman fuming in front of him. Wanting to drive home Emma's threat, he said, "And if you think you can bully her into keeping quiet if your son still refuses to get tested, let me tell you something. If Emma doesn't tell the media about him, I will, and I won't have to start with the local media. I have contacts in New York. It will be your son's worst public-relations nightmare come to life."

Emma sat in the passenger seat as Jamie drove to her apartment, her arms wrapped around her middle as if she could hold herself together.

"Talk about an unpleasant experience. That rated right up there with trying on swimsuits." She chuckled, but instead of a lighthearted sound, it came off almost fragile.

No. I won't let his mother rattle me. I made it through the battle. That's what counts.

"But you survived," Jamie said, echoing her thoughts. How did he do that? In a few short weeks he knew her better than anyone, except maybe Avery. How had she let that happen?

"You're one helluva woman," Jamie continued. "Tucker Mathis may be a star, but he and his mother can't hold a candle to you. None of his money can buy him what he lacks in character and strength. You've got both by the truckload."

I do, don't I? How had she failed to realize that before? She'd had some tough times in her life, but she'd weathered them. She hadn't given up—on herself or her dreams. That took guts and a whole lot of courage.

"But I didn't get his phone number."

"You accomplished what you needed to, which was making sure Tucker gets tested."

"How can you be so sure?"

"I've seen his family's type before. They're all about image. I guarantee she's on the phone with him right now telling him to get tested. She knew you meant business about going to the media. There's no way they want the fact that he refused to get tested to save the child he gave up getting out. He'll do whatever's necessary to keep you quiet."

Jamie had pegged the situation after one encounter with Tucker's family. How had she missed seeing what they were like? Basically selfish, image-conscious people with about as much character as a Pet Rock.

But Tucker and his family always managed to put on a good show. His family, prominent and proper, had appeared so perfect from the outside. They were local business people, community leaders who attended church regularly and supported local charities. She'd been young and had only seen what she'd wanted to see. Now she counted herself lucky for having dodged a bullet. If Tucker hadn't walked out on her who knows how many unhappy years she'd have spent with him before things fell apart.

She glanced at the man in the driver's seat beside her. Even years ago, she'd known what a good man Jamie was and he'd only gotten better. Look at how he'd been there for her since he'd come to Colorado. He'd stepped up to help her with the band. He'd been with her through all of this with Andrew.

When he parked in front of her building she knew should thank him, head for her apartment and lock the door behind her. That would be the smart thing to do, but she couldn't bring herself to tell him goodbye. Right now she was so empty and lonely. So didn't want to be alone. No, that wasn't right. She wanted to be *with* Jamie.

"Do you want to come in? I could make dinner or we could order a pizza."

Emma almost cringed. She sounded as nervous as a teenager asking a boy to a Sadie Hawkins dance for the first time.

"You sure?"

The unspoken question hung between them. She didn't care anymore. All she knew was she wanted to be with Jamie, and to hell with common sense.

"Absolutely."

The minute she closed the front door behind her, the shaking started. Something about stepping into her home, her haven, and in that split second she'd let down her guard, the emotions swamped her. Her feelings for Jamie, though Lord only knew exactly what those were, and her fear for the son she loved but had never known. "What if Tucker doesn't get tested? Or what if he does, but he's not a match? Then what will happen?" She dug into her purse for her phone, found the picture Mark had sent her and held it out for Jamie. "This beautiful little boy could die." The boy with her eyes and dark hair.

Tears stung her eyes and strong arms enveloped her, holding her close. She rested her cheek against Jamie's sturdy chest. His strong and steady heartbeat pounded

in her ear. She'd shut herself off and quit feeling anything, but now, for good or bad, Jamie had changed that.

She pulled back and gazed into his eyes. His soul
lay open, filled with compassion and understanding.

"Hearing what Tucker's mother said had to be hard
on you, too. How she referred to Andrew as 'that child.'"

"I got to admit it stung, but only for a second. Some
people lack the strength to deal with life. Kimberly's
one of those. So is Tucker's mother. For those people
there are only two choices—ignore problems or blame
someone else. Kimberly ignores. Tucker's mom is a
blamer and you're her favorite target." Admiration
shone in his gaze. "You're so much better than they
are. You meet life head-on. You've been through so
much, and yet it hasn't broken your spirit."

"It's come close."

"Close only counts in horseshoes and hand grenades."

She laughed. "I love how you make me laugh."

I love you. The realization rippled through Emma,
starting out small but taking root and growing. She
waited for the uncertainty, the panic, the fear to come,
but instead a calm enveloped her.

Closing herself off from everyone wasn't the way to
live. Sure, she'd been protected, but she'd missed out on
so much happiness and joy, too. She didn't know where
things were going between her and Jamie, but right now
she wanted him. She wanted to feel, to grab on to life
and hold on for however long she could.

Her hands splayed across his chest, discovering his
heart's frantic beating matched her own as she covered
his lips with hers. She wanted this man, to have the most
intimate connection she could have with another person.

He lifted her into his arms. As he carried her the few feet to the couch, she kissed him with all the passion she'd been holding back. He sank onto the soft cushions, and she moved around to straddle him, the evidence of his desire strong and thick against her pelvis.

Her hands quickly worked the buttons of his shirt and she slid the garment off his shoulders. "My, what broad shoulders and great abs you have," she said, sounding a little too much like Little Red Riding Hood. "Who would've guessed?"

"Must be all that cowboy stock in my genes." He grinned at her. "But I do work out."

With excellent results.

She leaned forward and kissed along his collarbone, but it wasn't enough. Their movements grew frantic as they explored each other. Caressing, teasing, exciting. His hand slipped inside her cotton blouse and under her lacy bra to cup her breast. Her moan echoed in the room.

His lips followed the path his hands traveled, and she couldn't think. The pleasure built inside her, threatening to consume her. Not that she cared. All she wanted right now was Jamie. To be alive and with him.

The sound of her zipper lowering echoed through the room. Then his hand, warm and firm, slid down her abdomen and found her sensitive core. Desire welled up inside her as his fingers stroked her. She closed her eyes and leaned back in his arms. His tongue flicked against her nipple and wave after wave rocked through her, leaving her spent.

When Emma's lips moved over Jamie's, he knew he should push her away. She was confused. Her emotions had gotten all stirred up. Fear and love for the child she'd never known. Pain over reliving her past with Tucker, and Lord only knew what else. She didn't know what to do about how she felt and she'd turned to him.

Then she kissed him, and he didn't care about anything but her. Giving her what she needed. Pleasing her.

She stiffened in his arms as her body reached fulfillment and he nearly lost control himself.

"While I'm all worn out and satisfied, the same can't be said for you." She cupped him through his jeans, and he groaned. Pleasure, sharp and overwhelming, shot through him. Her palm rubbed against him. He closed his eyes and for a minute he savored the exquisite joy of her touch. The pressure built inside him, threatening to devour him until he knew he'd reached his limit. He clasped her hands in his.

"What's the problem? Is it that you don't have a condom?"

Common sense warred with his raging need. "I'm not going to make love to you."

"Is it me?"

Rejection and embarrassment flashed in her eyes, making him regret the way he was handling this. "No. It's not. You're perfect." His lips covered hers. His need coursed through him as his mouth mated with hers. At some point he'd released her hands and she slid them over his chest. Her fingers teased his nipples, mimicking his early ministrations. Through his haze he heard his zipper lowering. Then a second later her warm hand covered his heated flesh. His moan echoed through the room, bouncing off the walls, threatening to send him over the edge.

His body throbbed and ached in a way he never imagined possible as he pried her hands away from his pulsing flesh. "I want you. There's no hiding that, sweetheart, but a lot's happened within the past couple of days. Your emotions are all churned up, and you don't know what to do about that."

"Oh, yes, I do. I want you. Inside me."

Her words nearly undid him, but somehow he harnessed his self-control. "No birth control's a hundred percent."

Her eyes widened with shock, and he knew she hadn't thought of that. "You're right. I was on the pill when I got pregnant with Andrew." She leaned down and kissed him. Her tongue slipped between his lips and mated with his. When she pulled away, desire flared in her gaze. Her saucy grin taunted him. "That still leaves us a lot of options."

His mind reeled with the possibilities as she pushed him back on the couch. She tugged at his jeans and he lifted his hips for her to free him. Then she straddled him. Proud and passionate, she stared down at him, her dark hair wild and disheveled from his hands. His heart expanded and he swore she could see inside to his soul. He wondered what he'd missed not having her in his life all these years.

Forget about that. She's here now. With you because this is where she wants to be.

She leaned over him, kissing him lightly as her hands skimmed across his chest. Her calluses from years of playing the guitar created an exquisite friction against his heated skin. Then her lips moved lower. He couldn't breathe. When her tongue licked the tip of his sensitive flesh he couldn't hold back his groan, and he forgot about everything but Emma and how she made him feel. Her mouth continued to do amazing things to him until he gave in to the pleasure and the exquisite release.

A few minutes later, once he could think coherently, Jamie wondered what he'd done. Had the most incredible sex of his life with a woman he cared about more than he wanted to admit. That's what he'd done.

He and Emma needed to talk about what had happened between them, about their relationship and the future, but sprawled here with her all warm and softly snuggled against him, he couldn't bring himself to spoil what they'd shared. Especially when he wasn't sure about anything right now. What to do about his career. His life in general. How he felt about the caring, strong woman beside him. She meant more to him than any other woman he'd ever known, but did he love her? How could he say when he'd never felt that emotion for anyone other than his family?

"I don't know what the future holds, none of us do, really, but can we at least say we're dating, and we'll see where this goes?" he said.

"That's fine with me."

Good. They were both clear on where they were and where they were headed.

Monday Jamie walked into the restaurant for his shift whistling the tune he and Emma had worked on yesterday. They'd spent the day together writing music. Then they'd gone for a mountain hike and talked. About their childhoods, about college and whatever else came to mind. They'd followed that with another round of hot and heavy petting. By far the best weekend he'd had in a long time.

Jamie headed straight for Mick's office. "I need a favor."

His grandfather looked up from the stack of invoices on his desk. "Name it."

"I want to use the restaurant for a couple of hours on Wednesday before we open to have a bone marrow donor registration drive. Dr. Sampson's willing to donate his time. He offered his office, but I'm hoping the turnout will be too big for that space."

"Did Tucker get tested?"

"You're damn right he did." He told Mick how Emma had stood up to Tucker's mother and threatened to go to the media if he refused. "She scared him so much he contacted a local doctor to come to the hotel to take the sample yesterday. It'll be a few days before we get the results, but what will happen if he's not a match is weighing on Emma's mind. I decided to follow her advice of hoping for the best, but preparing for the worst by organizing the drive."

"That's a great idea. I'll be the first one in line to get tested."

"I figured we could open up at nine, and be cleared out in time for lunch."

"Not only can you use the place, I'll give anyone who agrees to get tested a free lunch."

"That should bring people in. Can I use the restaurant's computer and printer to create flyers to put up around town?"

"Use whatever you need to. In fact, work on that now. I'll cover your shift around here. Once you've got the flyers printed, put some up in our window, leave a stack on the bar and take some around town. Now get going. You've got important work to do."

* * *

Around eleven-thirty Emma poked her head into Avery's office. "I didn't have anything to bring for lunch today. How about we go out? I was thinking about heading over to Halligan's. I've got a craving for a burger."

Avery laughed. "Sure. A burger. That's why you want to go there. It doesn't have anything to do with wanting to see a certain bartender."

Heat rushed through Emma, leaving her flushed. *Now he's got me blushing. I'm so far gone, but I'm not sure I care anymore.* "I admit that would be an added benefit."

"With as many hours as we've been putting in lately, we deserve a long lunch." Avery grabbed her purse out of her bottom desk drawer. "You and Jamie looked pretty cozy at the Pet Walk."

You have no idea. "We're kind of dating," Emma said as they headed for the shelter parking lot and Avery's car.

"That sounds like you're not sure."

"We're dating. I'm sure of that. What I don't know is where our relationship will go, but for now it's what I need."

She deserved to have some fun and that's what she was doing, but her eyes were wide open. No rose-colored glasses for her. While she loved him, that she couldn't deny any longer, she wasn't expecting a commitment. She was simply enjoying their time together and the fringe benefits of having him in her life for however long it lasted.

"Has Jamie said anything about when he plans on going back to New York? How long is his vacation? Not that he's really had one with all the hours he's put in at Halligan's and with your band." Avery's forehead wrinkled and Emma knew she was thinking about what she'd just said. "Something doesn't add up here. Who goes on vacation and works nearly full-time?"

"You can't tell anyone, not even Reed, what I'm about to tell you."

Avery glanced at Emma and then back at the road. "The look on your face has me worried. What's Jamie done? Is he on the run from the law? What else could be so awful that you have to swear me to silence?"

"Do you agree to keep this to yourself or not?"

"Of course, now spill the story."

Emma explained about Jamie's hand injury and his being let go from the Philharmonic. "He doesn't know how long he'll be here and he wanted to earn his keep. That's his words, not mine. That's why he's working at Halligan's. He's hoping his hand will improve enough that he can return to the Philharmonic or play with another major symphony."

"What about your band?"

"When I asked him to play, we agreed it would be temporary until we found someone permanent, but I kind of forgot to keep looking for someone else. I was having so much fun, and him being in the band felt so right, I guess I didn't want to. Since then we never seemed to get around to talking about the future."

"Don't you think you should?"

"Let me rephrase that. We touched on the subject." She blushed again at the thought of them together in her bed and looked out the window to hide her reaction. "We decided to enjoy each other's company and not worry about the future."

"Promise me you'll be careful."

"I've gone into this relationship with my eyes open, and anyway, I'm not sure I want a serious relationship right now."

That much was true. After the state fair. When she knew whether or not Maroon Peak Pass was good enough to have a real shot in country music, then she could decide about her personal life. Right now she couldn't handle anything else.

A few minutes later they parked in front of Halligan's. When Emma reached the door, she froze. Staring her in the face was a flyer for a bone marrow donor registration event for Andrew. "Avery, look at this. Do you think this was Jamie's idea?"

"It had to be." Avery splayed her hand across her chest, obviously as touched by Jamie's gesture as Emma was.

If she hadn't been in love with Jamie already, this would've sent her falling head over heels.

"He organized this for Andrew."

Avery swatted her on the arm. "He did this for *you* because he cares for you and knows how worried you are that Tucker won't be a match."

Was Avery right? Of course she was. Emma knew Jamie cared about her, but the question was how much. She shoved the thought aside. She'd been raised on a ranch and knew better than to look a gift horse in the mouth for fear of what she'd learn.

"Could we put a flyer in the shelter window, or would we need to get the board's permission first?" Emma asked as she opened the door and stepped inside the restaurant.

"I think in this case asking for forgiveness rather than permission is the wisest course," Avery said. "I'll take some flyers back with us. We can put a stack on the reception desk."

"Good, that'll save me a trip," a familiar voice said from behind them. Emma's heart tripped. She whirled around and hugged Jamie so tightly her arms ached. "This has to be the best thing anyone's ever done for me."

"For a girl, you sure have strong arms." He grunted. "You mind loosening up a little? It's getting tough to breathe."

She let go and stepped back, still stunned over what he'd done. Without her asking. Just to help her. Because he cared.

"I knew you were worried that Tucker might not be a match," he said. "I figured this way we'd have a backup plan."

We.

The simple word worked its way inside her. She and Tucker had been a couple. She'd dated Clint for almost a year, and yet, she'd never had a man think of them as a *we* before.

Don't go there. Don't start having expectations. Don't count on anything. Hoping for something permanent, wanting more was too dangerous and left her vulnerable.

She knew he hoped to return to the symphony. Mick's words floated through her mind. *He's got a cowboy's heart.* But he'd been raised somewhere else. Why would he want to stay?

Be content with what you have. Enjoy now and say that's enough.

Chapter 13

On the day of the donor drive, when Emma parked in front of Halligan's, she realized she'd been happier the past week than she'd been in years. The state fair competition was this weekend, and Maroon Peak Pass stood a good chance of winning. Her career could really take off, and then there was Jamie. He made life fun again and helped her find the balance she hadn't realized she craved.

If it weren't for Andrew's sickness, life would be perfect. And they were working on that issue. She still had trouble believing Jamie had organized this event. No one ever saw that she needed help and just stepped up to take care of things. Instead, the people in her life expected her to buck up. She was tough. She'd be all right. They didn't need to worry about Emma. She bent, but she never broke.

But having people expect that could be so tiring. Daunting. Like being a superhero without a sidekick to count on.

Until Jamie.

She found him working behind the bar and thought back to when she'd picked him up at the airport. What had the little boy's mother whispered in her ear? *Don't let him get away. There aren't a lot like him left these days.* No, there weren't, but how could she ask him to stay? He had his own dreams, a life in New York. She couldn't ask him to give that up for her. She believed in Maroon Peak Pass, thought they had what it took to make it big, but it wasn't a sure thing. Not like the career Jamie had if he could return to the Philharmonic.

Shoving aside her concerns about their future, she plastered a smile on her face. "What can I do?"

"Nothing. Everything's taken care of."

She strolled around the bar, cupped his face in her hands and kissed him. "You're amazing. Thank you for all you've done."

For Andrew and for me. For shaking up my life.

"We'll find someone who's a match for Andrew today. I know it."

Before she could respond, the front door opened again and Dr. Sampson walked in carrying a large plastic container and wearing a somber look.

Something's wrong.

"What makes you say that?" Jamie asked.

She hadn't known she'd said the words out loud. "Look at his face. That's someone with bad news to deliver. Do you think Andrew's—" She couldn't say the words. Instead she reached out and clasped Jamie's hand, needing his strength and reassurance.

"Can I speak to you alone?" Dr. Sampson said when he reached the bar.

"It's about Andrew, isn't it? He's not d—"

"No, dear. His condition hasn't changed." Dr. Sampson patted her arm. "It's about Tucker."

"He's not a match," she said.

"I'm afraid not. I heard from Andrew's doctor right before I left the office."

Fear washed over her, strong and overwhelming, for the child who might not grow much older and for the parents who would have to watch him die. She bit her lip to keep it from trembling as she sank into the nearest chair. This wasn't over. She refused to dwell on the negative. Instead she'd remain positive. "Then it's a good thing we're having this drive. I'll pray someone here is a match."

"That's what we're all hoping for," Jamie said. She glanced at the man seated at the table beside her and her heart swelled with love. He'd slipped into her life and filled the void. How would she ever cope with him leaving?

"I can't thank you both for all you've done."

"Now let's get this show on the road," Jamie said.

"You can start with me," Mick said as he settled into the fourth chair at the table. The doctor swiped the swab around Mick's mouth, placed the sample into a tube and handed that to Emma. He nodded toward the marker. "Mark Mick's name on this, and place it in that bin."

Happy to be busy, she saw to the task. "Here's to someone being a match for Andrew."

Please, dear Lord. If I can have nothing else in my life, let me have this one wish.

"I hope we get a good turnout. A lot of people who

came into the shelter picked up flyers and talked about coming, but you know how that goes. Everyone says they'll come, but then they forget or something comes up."

Mick patted her hand. "You don't have to worry about that, Emma, girl. We've got a line stretching down the block of folks waiting to get in here."

A line down the block? "I don't know why I'm surprised. This community always has rallied around a cause."

"They're rallying around you. Everywhere I went to put up flyers, people shared stories with me about things you'd done for them over the years. Ways you made them smile or the little things you did for them to help out. They were glad to have a way to repay you."

Beside her Jamie beamed. His hand covered hers and squeezed. "The more people, the better the odds we'll find someone to help Andrew. Now it's my turn."

As the doctor swabbed Jamie, Mick said, "With the line, Doc, I think the smart thing would be for you to take care of any of my staff that wants to get tested before we open the door because I'm gonna need all hands on deck to see to feeding everyone."

Emma smiled at Mick. "Thank you for doing the free lunch deal. I know that has to be costing you a good amount of money."

"It doesn't matter because you're family. You two mean the world to me." He glanced between her and Jamie. Then he cleared his throat and jumped up from the table. "Doc, I'll send the staff out. We don't want to keep anyone waiting too long."

Five minutes later, after Dr. Sampson finished taking samples from the Halligan's crew, Emma opened the front door, Jamie by her side. The first people in line were her father and her brothers.

Since her mother had died, she'd felt a change in her relationship with the men in her family. They didn't know how to deal with her, how to treat her without their mother there. They'd grown distant. Probably because they were guys and it never occurred to them that she might be lonely or need to hear from them. "Thanks for coming."

"We'd have done this sooner if you'd told us about Andrew and that you weren't a match," her father said. "I shouldn't find out something like that from a flyer in the grocery store window. Someone else might be raising him, but blood's blood."

After she dutifully issued an apology, she introduced her family to Jamie. "Good to see you, son. You, Emma and I need to get together sometime. We could go out to dinner or something."

She couldn't remember the last time her father had asked her to dinner. When they got together it was always because she issued an invitation or came to cook for him. Apparently having a man along made things more comfortable for her father.

Tears pooled in her eyes as she stared at the line of people waiting to get tested. The amount of support and love overwhelmed her as she spotted former teachers and classmates, shelter supporters, nearly everyone she knew in town. As she wiped her tears away, she told herself they would find a match for Andrew somewhere here. The odds had to be in their favor.

After the mad lunch rush ended, Emma and Jamie sat at a corner table enjoying their lunch. "I think I need a nap. I'd forgotten how exhausting working in a restaurant could be."

"It's a workout, that's for sure." Jamie's cell phone rang, but he made no move to answer it.

"Aren't you going to at least see who it is?"

"Remember I'm not one of those have-to-be-plugged-in-all-the-time types. I'd rather enjoy our lunch."

A few seconds later his phone pinged indicating he'd received a voice mail. "It was important enough that someone left you a message. Aren't you even curious?"

He chuckled and pulled his cell out of his pocket. "If I check who called and satisfy *your* curiosity, will you let me eat in peace?"

"I won't dignify that comment with a response."

He glanced at his cell phone, then back at her. "It's the conductor from the Philharmonic. Why would Malcolm be calling me?"

A spark of dread went through her. This couldn't lead anywhere she wanted to go. She forced herself to smile and keep her voice light. "Unless you've developed ESP, there's only one way to find out. Listen to the message."

She stared at the fries on her plate. Apprehension gnawed at her. His conductor could only be calling for one reason, to see if Jamie's hand had improved. And the only reason he'd wonder that was because either the Philharmonic or some other symphony had an opening. Great news for Jamie. Lousy for her.

How could she let him go when she got up every morning and counted the hours until she was with him? When he was such a part of her life? But if she loved him, how could she do anything but let him go?

"He wants to talk to me about an opportunity. Would you mind if I called him back?"

Of course she minded. What she wanted was for him to say he loved playing with her and the band. That he wanted to stay. That he wanted to be with her. For the rest of his life. That he loved *her.* But what about what he needed?

"Call him." She pushed her chair away from the table in the now-deserted restaurant, but his hand covered hers, stopping her.

"Stay."

She didn't think she was strong enough to take seeing his excitement if she'd pegged the situation correctly, but nodded anyway. How could she say no after all the times he'd been there for her?

His face tight with apprehension mixed with curiosity, Jamie returned the call. After exchanging a few pleasantries, he said, "I have, but I don't know if my ability is back to what it was."

He might not realize how much his hand had improved, but she did. If he wasn't back to the level of playing he'd been in the YouTube video she'd watched, he was very close.

"Is he okay?" Jamie paused, and then smiled.

Yup, she'd been right. Someone had an open chair. A numbing cold spread through her body. She'd known this day could come and sworn she'd been prepared for it. Wrong.

"I'm in Colorado. I took a vacation to clear my head. I've been playing with a local country band here. We're performing at the state fair this weekend." Another pause. "I understand. Do what you have to. The earliest I can be there is Monday."

Emma knew what she had to do. She wouldn't let him risk his dream for hers. When he ended his call she said, "Does he have a spot for you or is it another symphony?"

"How did you know?" He shook his head. "Never mind. Sometimes you know me so well it's scary."

Ditto.

"One of the other violinists had a stroke. I thought I had it bad, but this guy's only in his fifties and he's got kids still at home. Talk about rough. Malcolm said he'll survive, but it's going to be a long recovery."

"And he wants you to audition."

Jamie nodded.

"Congratulations. I know this is what you've hoped for," she said, trying her best to fill her voice with excitement. "The exile has ended. We should celebrate."

He reached across the table, his hand covering hers, and she nearly lost what little control she had left. "That's not how I've seen being here."

Tell me you love me. That somehow we'll figure out a way to make this work for both of us, because I don't think I can bear you walking out of my life.

She thought about what she'd heard from his end of the conversation. "You can't wait until Monday. You need to get to New York as soon as you can."

"I'll take the first flight I can get after the state fair competition."

Today was Wednesday. That meant the earliest he'd leave was late Sunday night. "Malcolm doesn't have a problem with that?"

"He said it's fine."

"I see a *but* in your eyes."

"He's setting up other auditions starting tomorrow."

Time to cowgirl up and do what was right no matter how much it hurt. "You have to get on the first available flight. I know your hand is healed. You can't risk losing this opportunity." She wouldn't let him. When he flashed her his stubborn glare, she changed tactics. "This is what's best for Maroon Peak Pass, too. I've been meaning to talk to you about that. I just hadn't found the right time, and now here it is."

He leaned back in his chair. "This I've got to hear."

"We agreed your playing with us was only temporary. Say we win the contest with you as our fiddle player. Then I have to explain to Phillip Brandise how you aren't a permanent member of the band. That looks unprofessional and could end up damaging our chances with him. If someone pulled that on me, I'd feel deceived and wouldn't trust them. We need to make it or not as we are."

And that doesn't include you.

She bit her lip to hold her emotions in check. She refused to cry. Not now. Not here in front of him. She'd hold it together if it killed her. Then, when she was home, alone she'd fall apart.

She stared at him and hoped he would say that he wanted this dream, that he wanted her, more than anything else.

"Are you sure this is what you want?"

The heart she'd tried so hard to protect shriveled inside her. "It is."

She stood, walked around the table and kissed him. Her lips moved over his, and she tried to file away the memory of his touch. She pulled away and gazed at the man who'd turned her life upside down, who'd taught her to love again. "I wish you nothing but the best."

Then she turned and walked out of the bar knowing she loved him more than she'd ever imagined possible, and she had to let him go.

The next day back in New York, back on the Philharmonic stage, Jamie placed his violin in its case. The audition couldn't have gone better. Maybe because he'd temporarily lost his talent, he valued his ability more now that it had returned. The complacency he'd felt when he'd been with the Philharmonic before he'd hurt his hand had disappeared. The joy and sense of purpose he'd felt the first time he played with a major symphony had filled him again. He'd experienced the wonder of classical music, its beauty.

"I'd say if your hand isn't one hundred percent, it's as close as it can get," Malcolm said. "Welcome back, Jamie."

He waited for the elation to wash over him, but instead he felt torn. How could he enjoy playing both the classics and country music equally? That made no sense. Shouldn't one tug at his soul more? Shouldn't he know what he was meant to do with his life?

But all he knew was nothing made much sense since Emma had walked away from him at Halligan's. He thought they had something together, the kind of connection that didn't come along every day. But she'd walked away as if he'd been nothing more than a quick fling to pass the time.

That hurt, because to him, she'd been so much more.

He was in love with Emma Donovan.

Talk about a complication. The good news was Malcolm thought he'd improved enough to return to the Philharmonic, the bad news was Jamie no longer had any idea if that was what he wanted. "Can I give you my answer tomorrow?"

"I'll give you until noon, but I can't wait any longer than that."

Jamie thanked Malcolm and promised he'd have his answer first thing in the morning. After he left Avery Fisher Hall, the noise and chaos almost assaulted him. People from the nearby subway stop zoomed past him while he stood there trying to figure out where to go. Taxis honked at everyone and everything. The familiar sites of Juilliard, the Met and the other performing arts buildings reminded him of who he used to be.

Who he used to be? He had changed. Things that had once seemed to suit him so well now didn't. Like his apartment. Instead of being a home, the place felt sterile and empty without Emma and Trooper. Right now that was the last place he wanted to be. He thought about his parents. He hadn't seen them in a while. Now their logical approach to sorting out a problem sounded like exactly what he needed.

Later that evening, when Jamie walked into the living room with his dad, his mother's gaze scanned him from head to toe from her spot on the couch. "What's wrong?"

"What makes you say that?"

"Are you telling me there isn't something bothering you?" She had that mom look on her face, and he knew there wasn't any point in lying. After he sank into the chair next to her, he explained about Malcolm's call, the audition and his uncertainty. "I have what I wanted. My hand's better, and I can return to the symphony. How come I'm not sure that's what I want?"

"If one of your sisters asked that question, I'd tell her to make a list of the pros and cons of each choice, but you're different," his mother said. "That solution won't work for you."

"Has that been hard on you? Me being so different from Kate and Rachel? From you and Dad?"

His dad's brows knit together in confusion. "What makes you ask a question like that? You weren't any tougher to raise than your sisters. Kids are hard work, no matter who they're like."

"Being different isn't a bad thing, Jamie." His mother reached out to him and placed her hand on his arm. "Now, about not knowing what you want. I suspect that's not true. You're just not sure whether to follow your head or your heart."

"I'm glad one of us is sure. Playing for Malcolm again showed me how much classical music still means to me, but there's something about country music and playing with Emma that calls to me, too." He smiled, thinking of their time together. "She's got so much enthusiasm. It's hard not to get caught up in it. When I'm with her, I don't know. I can't describe how I feel."

"I think you answered your own question," his dad said.

Since he'd left Colorado, he'd felt this hole inside him. As though part of him was gone. Because he wasn't with Emma.

How could he give her up? At the end of his life what would matter more, his career or Emma?

Without a doubt, Emma.

"I love Emma, and I want to be with her, but it's complicated. Her life's in Colorado or Nashville because she wants a career in country music."

"What's this really about?" His mother stared at him with an all-knowing gaze.

What could he say? That he was scared to walk away from everything he'd worked for and basically start over. That he worried they'd resent him for tossing away the education they'd scrimped and saved to pay for. That he feared hurting them by choosing to move to where his birth mother was from?

"Are you afraid we won't approve? That we'll think less of you if you sing in a country band rather than play with a symphony?" his dad asked.

I'm more concerned you'll feel like I'm throwing you aside for Mick, and my link with my birth family. Not able to bring himself to say the words and hurt the parents he loved so much, he said, "You worked so hard to put me through Juilliard, and I'd be giving all that up."

"Nothing's ever wasted, especially education or experience." Compassion and love filled his mother's gaze. "This is your life. We get to live ours. We don't get to live yours, too."

He'd once told Emma he didn't beat around the bush on issues because all it did was cause confusion and hurt feelings, but that was exactly what he was doing now. "I don't want you two feeling like I don't appreciate everything you've done for me. That I'm choosing Mick over you."

"So we've finally gotten to the heart of the problem," his dad said.

"This isn't an either-or situation. Do you remember the song about the penny that Mrs. Hall taught you in elementary school?" his mom asked.

Jamie smiled at the memory. He used to drive his sisters nuts singing that song a hundred times a day when he'd first learned it. "I remember something about love being like a penny, and how if a person held it too tight, he'd lose it, but if he spent it, he ended up having more."

"Just because we love your sisters doesn't mean there's less love for you. We've got room in our hearts for the three of you, whoever you marry and any children you have," she continued. "We know you having a relationship with Mick or living in Colorado doesn't mean you love us any less."

Such a simple concept. Why hadn't he realized that? Now he felt kind of stupid.

"All we want is for you to be happy and find someone who loves you. Sounds like you've found both of those things," his dad said from his seat in his favorite worn recliner.

"If I haven't screwed it up by leaving."

"There's only one way to know."

"She didn't seem too upset when I left." He told his parents about the last time he'd talked to Emma.

"Of course she told you to go," his mother said, a look of confusion on her face as if she couldn't see how he'd failed to realize that. "She did that because she cares about you. Think about it. What would you have done if the situation had been reversed?"

He'd have told Emma to go. In fact, he'd have said whatever he had to in order to make her leave. He'd have wanted her to succeed, to follow her dreams. Is that what Emma had done?

Now he really felt like an idiot. Hopefully it wasn't too late to make things right with her.

At the state fair competition, the longer Emma waited backstage the more her nerves kicked in. At least she'd had good news about Andrew. They'd found out earlier today that her brother Brandon was a match. Now all she had to pray for was that once Andrew had the transplant, his body would accept his uncle's bone marrow.

Today's performance wasn't anything compared to that in terms of life events, but she couldn't help but think how things would be so different if Jamie were here sharing this with her. Without him the band seemed flat. He had a way of bringing out the best in all of them, but especially in her and not just musically. She wanted to share every day with him. Life's blessings and trials.

She had to quit thinking about him.

Like that would happen anytime soon.

"I can't let you backstage without a badge," Emma heard a security guard off to her right say.

"It never fails that someone thinks they can con security into letting him sneak in and grab an autograph," Luke said, pulling her away from her pity party.

"Come on, man. Cut me a break."

Emma froze. She recognized that voice. She heard it every night in her dreams. Only then, when they talked about him leaving, he got down on one knee, told her how much he loved her and said he wanted to spend the rest of his life with her. But Jamie couldn't be here. He was in New York. She'd gone from pity party to completely insane and hearing voices in the blink of an eye. That was the only explanation for what she'd just heard.

"Hot dog. Look what the cat dragged in," Luke said, pointing to his left, his voice full of excitement.

Footsteps sounded around her. Through her haze she noticed Grayson and Luke move past her, but she still couldn't bring herself to look.

"He's with us. You can let him through," Grayson said.

What were the odds that all three of them were having a group hallucination?

If they were, she didn't want to come out of it. *Let me imagine Jamie's here a little longer. At least until he takes me in his arms and kisses me. Then I'll come back to reality.*

But she had to know. She turned and there was Jamie. His cowboy boots clicked on the cement as he strode toward her, dressed in that same brown plaid shirt he'd worn at the fund-raiser concert. The one that brought out the color of his eyes.

Her heart swelled. All she could think of was the line from *How the Grinch Stole Christmas!* about how the Grinch's heart grew three sizes one day.

He stopped in front of her. His index finger flicked the brim of his cowboy hat farther off his forehead. She really should say something, but the words wouldn't form in her head. He'd come back.

"I hear you're looking for a fiddle player."

She reached out and poked him in the chest to make sure he really was here.

"That's an odd response."

"I can't believe you're here."

"In the flesh." Then he grinned in that way that made her heart do backflips.

"Not exactly in the *flesh*."

"We'll see about that later. Now, about that job?"

She leaned back on her heels and eyed him critically. "What experience do you have?"

"Not much with a country band. I was with the Philharmonic, but I quit. I took a long hard look at what I want out of life and that isn't it." Jamie placed his fiddle case on the ground at his feet and clasped her hands in his. "I'm sorry I put you through this. For a while I wondered if I'd latched on to your dream because it was easier than sorting out my own. But I want music in my life, and it doesn't matter what kind because I want you more. I love you, Emma Donovan."

He loved her enough to come back. Tears blurred her vision. "I love you, too. So much. I can't believe you're here."

Jamie thought of when he'd first arrived in Estes Park and how his grandfather had suggested he play country music. The old man had been right after all. Jamie couldn't help but laugh now.

"What's so funny?"

"I was thinking about when I first arrived and how Mick suggested I join a country band."

"That's funny because my grandfather suggested I ask you to play with us before you ever got to town. Do you think they planned all this? That they were playing matchmakers?"

"If they were, we're going to be hearing 'I told you so' forever, but I can live with that." He squeezed her hand. "You still haven't said if I've got the job or not."

She smiled, her heart filled with love and hope for the future. "Cowboy, you can have anything you want."

* * * * *

Angi Morgan writes about Texans in Texas. A *USA TODAY* and *Publishers Weekly* bestselling author, her work has been an award finalist several times, including the Booksellers' Best Award, *RT Book Reviews* Reviewers' Choice Award for Best Intrigue Series and the Daphne du Maurier Award. Angi and her husband live in North Texas. They foster Labradors, love to travel, snap pics and fix up their house. Hang out with her on Facebook at Angi Morgan Books. She loves to hear from fans: angimorganauthor.com.

Books by Angi Morgan

Harlequin Intrigue

Texas Brothers of Company B

Ranger Protector
Ranger Defender

Texas Rangers: Elite Troop

Bulletproof Badge
Shotgun Justice
Gunslinger
Hard Core Law

West Texas Watchmen

The Sheriff
The Cattleman
The Ranger

Visit the Author Profile page at
Harlequin.com for more titles.

THE RENEGADE RANCHER

ANGI MORGAN

Many moons ago, I graduated from high school with a small group of kids. Brian and Johnny are fictional characters, but named after two men who won't be returning for our next reunion. I have used the names of people in my hometown, but not their personalities. The characters are fictional, but not my friendships or the respect I have for their namesakes.

Chapter 1

Tall, blonde and deadly gorgeous.

Brian Sloane knew that Lindsey Cook was a looker. One glance would let any male with eyes know that fact. Platinum blond hair that hung to her waist, classic blue eyes that would disappear next to a clear summer sky and a body that should be gracing covers of magazines. A looker, all right.

This was the longest he'd ever been with a woman and he hadn't met her yet.

He knew how old she was, where she'd graduated from college, that her best friend's name was Beth. All that information was on her internet site. He knew she lived in Arlington, drove a sports car, kept two goldfish and was allergic to cats. She'd had five jobs in the past three years and did freelance web design. He also knew why she'd migrated to Texas after burying her cousin.

Jeremy had drowned while they'd been on vacation together about six months ago and she'd stayed after settling his affairs. Her cousin's *female* lawyer had been extrachatty during happy hour.

Unfortunately, accidents happened everywhere, leaving one question he couldn't answer. How long she would live.

Brian entered the sandwich shop and tried not to zoom all his attention on her. Searching the remaining tables, he noticed no one else was alone, so it was probably safe to assume she was his appointment. "Lindsey?"

"You're Brian?" she asked, extending her hand. Her smile could mesmerize him. He'd watched her work that magic on several customers—male and female—over the past couple of weeks.

"That'd be me." He took a slender palm in his own, gave a quick squeeze and sat at the table. A well-chosen table in the middle of the very empty sandwich shop. The red silky blouse clung everywhere and plunged just enough to make his imagination go a little wild.

"So, you said that Jeremy's lawyer recommended me for a job. Your email said something about a ranch website?"

"Yeah, about that. This might sound strange, but I've been doing some research and—" Was that sudden look in her eyes one of surprise? An alert? How had he messed up?

"No website?"

He stared, thinking hard on what his answer should be. It was important she listen to him. Her life depended on it. He couldn't just say that. Could he? He'd avoided the truth long enough. "To be honest—"

"Excuse me just a sec." She looked into her purse.

She brought her keys to the tabletop. Hooked to the ring—now pointed at his face—was a small can of pepper spray. "Who are you and why have you been following me? I saw you in front of the store yesterday and you were in line behind me when I got coffee last week."

"Whoa there." He raised his hands, trying not to jump away from that can. "I really am Brian Sloane. I'm a Fort Worth paramedic, just like I said on the phone. I've got ID."

She shook her head slowly from side to side. Was she thinking about believing him or shooting that pepper spray into his eyes? Okay, so he'd slipped up and not only let her see him a couple of times, but he'd made eye contact at the coffee shop. Who could have resisted? She was smoking hot.

"I'm going to leave," she said, "and you'd better stop following me. Just so you know, I took your picture when you walked in and if I see you again—even by accident—I'll report you to the police as a stalker."

He leaned forward, and she jerked to attention. *Skittish as a newborn colt.* "I know this is a weird way to meet."

"To say the least." She kept the nozzle pointed at his eyes. Extremely close to his eyes.

"But I do have information regarding your family."

"I don't have any family."

"What I mean is… I've been doing research and I think Jeremy was murdered."

"I thought you were an EMT. You sound like a reporter." She brought her finely shaped eyebrows into a straight line, showing her scrutiny and distrust. Not knowing she'd just delivered an insult to highly trained paramedics everywhere by calling him an entry-level EMT.

With a new sister-in-law around his house, he was

picking up on a lot of subtle feminine looks that he'd had no clue about before. This look? Well, it didn't leave any room for interpretation.

He shifted. She jerked.

"Just getting my wallet. Okay?"

"Is there a problem, Lindsey?" The guy behind the sandwich counter stopped wiping the display cases.

"I'm fine. Just dealing with another jerk reporter."

"I'm not a reporter." He shook his head, looked at the big fellow who was very defensive of the woman in front of him and repeated, "I'm *not* a reporter."

"Then why are you following me?"

"It's a long story and I'd rather not have pepper spray aimed at me while I tell it."

Lindsey's long, straight hair gently framed a delicate, expressive, beautiful face that he'd been attracted to since the first picture he'd seen of her online. It sort of took him by surprise when she leaned back in her chair, dropped her hands to her lap and waited, the key ring in plain sight. Her protector returned to cleaning. The shop's patrons went back to business as usual.

"I'd like the short version, please," she said, pushing her hair behind her ear. "You've got five minutes and then I'm leaving."

Short? How did he explain such a complicated story?

"All right. Twelve years ago I thought my brother caused the accidental fire that took the life of one of our former teachers, your second cousin, Gillian Cook. But I was wrong. She was murdered."

"Take it to the police." She pushed back her chair and scooped her keys into her purse, clearly taking off.

"You said I had five minutes."

She stood. Her long hair swayed at her waist, drawing his attention to the fraction of flat belly he could see above her jeans when her shirt rose up as she took a deep breath.

"You have five seconds to remove your hand from my arm or I'll let Craig—" she tipped her head to the sandwich guy, who threw down his bar towel "—deal with you. Four. Three."

Craig dashed to the end of the counter. Brian dropped his hold. Lindsey stared at him as her friend reached for his shirt. He'd been so caught up in her leaving that he hadn't realized he'd grabbed her arm to stop her.

"Sorry. I didn't mean to scare you."

"Wait. Craig, wait." She waved off the man's attempt to lift Brian from the chair—*through* the table. "Look, I'm very tired of people hounding me about my accident-prone family. There have been terrible emails from someone thinking I'm a jinx." She hid her eyes behind slender fingers, then shoved her hair behind her ear again and straightened her back. "I know what happened to my family. I live with it every day, and to have it in the paper or on a blog is disrespectful. It's mean and I've had enough. Just leave me alone."

She tilted her face toward her chest, hiding behind her hair.

"Your family didn't do anything wrong." Brilliant blue eyes opened wide to search him. Why was she ashamed? "Besides, I don't think they were accidents. And I'm fairly certain you're next."

"Seriously? You think someone's out to kill me?" Her long nails were the exact color of one of the flowers on her shirt. It was easy to see with her hand nervously rubbing her collarbone.

"I haven't been stalking you, Miss Cook. Our paths

crossed while I was looking into your cousin's life," he explained. It was true enough. He had been looking into Jeremy Cook.

Craig stood guard at her shoulder, ready to do battle, his arms crossed over a massive chest. It was plain why Lindsey had chosen this location to meet a stranger. "Take it to the cops," Craig said. "You ready for me to throw this jerk out?"

One cross look would have Brian's face pulverized before he could defend himself. Well, Craig could try. Brian had fought with the best around his hometown for a long time. So he shrugged. He'd never convince her while including muscleman in the conversation. She didn't believe him. Hell, he hardly believed himself. His theory was so far out there he hadn't even shared it with his family.

He'd tried, right? That was all he could do. He pressed on the table to push his chair back and long, bright nails tapped quickly near his hand, gaining his attention.

"It's okay, Craig. I'm okay." She looked up at her protector and winked at him, immediately relaxing the big guy and getting her way.

Brian waited until they were alone and lowered his voice, leaning closer across the table. "Look, I'm not a cop or a detective or a reporter. I really am just a horse rancher who pays the bills by working as a paramedic."

"You're wowing me with so many reasons to believe you." She laughed. Her eyes sparkled and were sad at the same time.

He understood that. How an enjoyable moment could catch you off guard and you forget—just for an instant. Then the reason you don't laugh comes rushing back to blur the happy. Yeah, he understood.

"You have every right to wonder about my motives. You should be careful. I should have left this info with your lawyer and never bothered you in person. I'll be on my way."

"Why did you? Come here, that is."

The tap on the tabletop drew his eyes back to her hands, then up her tanned arms, to her shoulders and neck. The slow tap and arch of her eyebrow showed him she knew he'd been taking a long look. He expected a wink any second, and would probably do whatever she asked. He was *that* attracted.

He pushed himself straighter in the chair and caught her doing a little looking of her own.

"I can't convince you to trust me. I'll drop everything off at your lawyer's office after I get out of your hair."

"Wait. I, um… If you're really not a reporter, can you begin again? Take five more minutes?" She brought part of her hair in front of her shoulder and began twisting strands into a tiny braid. "Start with what the police said."

"That I was crazy."

"I can't imagine why." She smiled, sliding back into the chair next to him. "I'm sorry and really trying to understand why you think someone's trying to kill me. You have to admit, it's not news you get every day."

He'd give her that point. He also liked her sassiness. "When you look at each family, the deaths seem to be open-and-shut accidents. But a friend of mine who's big on genealogy did a search. And then there's the regular intervals of the accidents. My brother caught that when—"

"Why do you think I'm next?" she interrupted, eyes worried, her breathing rapid.

"You're the only one left."

Chapter 2

Lindsey wanted to run from the shop and the memories. But the man leaning across the table looking so concerned on her behalf intrigued her. She still had doubts and couldn't possibly believe his theory. It didn't hurt to hear him out. She glanced at the clock behind him. She had plenty of time before she needed to be at work.

His hand covered hers. "I'm really sorry. I shouldn't have said it like that. I'm not used to this kind of conversation."

She could feel the calluses, the warmth, the strength. He looked genuinely worried. A shiver crept up her back. The eerie kind that could make you look under your bed after watching a shark movie. But that was nonsense, just like thinking all her family had been murdered.

"When Jeremy died, I made the mistake of mentioning

to one of his friends that he was my last close relative. He didn't wait until Jeremy had been buried before he blogged about the accidents of those close to me. He ranted about how *lucky* I seemed to escape death while those close to me didn't and insinuated there may be foul play."

"That's why you thought I was a reporter. I don't blame you for grabbing your pepper spray."

Brian Sloane wasn't anything like she'd expected. Honestly, she'd thought the man following her would be a psychopath. Someone following her for a really weird reason like they loved her nails or something. So if this tall cowboy wasn't following her and hadn't been the one asking Craig questions earlier this week, then who was the mystery man and how would she find him?

"Why do *you* think someone wants to kill me, Mr. Sloane?"

"Brian, please. My daddy's still Mr. Sloane and is the only one who deserves that title."

A good-looking cowboy who could charm his way anywhere, she'd bet. It was easy to see the solid, chiseled body just under his T-shirt. Hard not to imagine the strength that came with the square jaw and high cheekbones. *Not so fast, Mr. Sloane.*

"We haven't found a reason."

"We? I thought the police didn't believe you."

"A neighbor and my sister-in-law have been helping me." He leaned his chiseled jaw on his elbow. "Discovering the truth is important to my family. Everybody's chipped in some research time."

"Maybe you should start at the beginning?" And maybe she shouldn't look too much at that million-dollar smile.

"Four months ago, I began trying to find the family

of a neighbor and teacher in Aubrey—the town where
I live. She died just after my high school graduation in
an accident I was blamed for."

"A second cousin who I never met."

He nodded. "I started looking just after Jeremy
drowned in Cozumel. His death made the news in Fort
Worth, so I recognized his name."

"He was snorkeling. His body had lots of small cuts
and scratches. They think he got caught in the coral."
She relived Jeremy's drowning almost every night and
hoped to forgive herself one day. "Over forty people
were in the water and no one saw anything."

His grip on her hand tightened and he nodded as if
he understood.

"Mabel, my dad's friend, researched your family
tree. Every name she gave me passed from an accident." He paused and removed a piece of paper from
his back pocket. "Here. Fourteen names. They're all
related to you and all died in the past twenty years.
Most out of state."

He pushed the paper over to her with a long finger,
then leaned back in his chair, lacing those fingers together behind his neck. His brows arched high, waiting
for her to acknowledge his assumptions.

"The police are right. A list doesn't prove anything."

"Don't you see?" He jumped forward, his hand landing a little too loudly on the tabletop.

Lindsey automatically reached for the mace again,
stopping herself when she saw the concern in Brian's
puppy-brown eyes. Wouldn't it be the perfect ploy for a
serial killer to pose as the person trying to stop himself?

Don't be a ninny.

"I can't see anything with the exception that there are several people on that list I loved very much."

"I'm sorry. I know how hard that must be."

"I don't see how. Your father's still alive." Remembering brought a very fresh pain of responsibility for Jeremy's accident. *Accident.* Not murder. She was the one who had taken off instead of snorkeling with him. "I'm sorry, Brian, that was rude."

"It's all right. This information is out of the blue from a complete stranger."

"You aren't the first to come to me with this type of conspiracy story. One of Jeremy's friends spread it across FriendshipConnect. But just like all the others, you can't offer a reason why anyone would want us dead. Nor do you have proof. So... I'm leaving now and I'd appreciate it if you didn't contact me again."

Lindsey threw her bag over her shoulder and left before the sympathetic cowboy could talk her into staying. Her hand found the pepper spray—just in case. Good-looking or not, he had a look in his eyes that promised he wouldn't let this story go. What he'd gain from it... what any of them gained from it, she had no idea and would never understand.

She used her shoulder to push through the door. The afternoon heat wasn't too bad for mid-October. But she was used to much cooler temperatures. Nothing even close to the record-breaking heat wave they'd experienced through the summer in the Dallas–Fort Worth area.

She searched her bottomless pit of a purse until she felt the familiar shape of thick-rimmed sunglasses and pushed them onto her face to block the UV rays. At the next doorway, she ducked under the awning, close to the window, to get out of sight in case Mr. Sloane followed her again.

Someone wanted to murder her? *Ridiculous. Right?*

It didn't make sense. Jeremy had drowned. There were forty other people snorkeling on that reef from his boat. Another twenty-seven from a second tour. They'd all been interviewed and no one had seen anything unusual. Nothing except people snorkeling.

They assumed Jeremy went too deep. From the scratches around his ankle, it looked as though he'd gotten caught on the coral. Nothing foul or sinister. Just tragic.

If I'd been there... I could have prevented his death.

The stinging sensation that preluded tears was just behind her eyelids. They were seconds away from shedding, just like most days. She watched a couple walk by, shopping bags looped over their shoulders, hands clasped together, no determination in their stride. Perhaps a fun day off?

Maybe she needed a manicure or a sweater since it was beginning to cool down in the evenings?

No. That was the old Lindsey. The one who would take off, not caring if her supervisor got upset, not caring about the job. There was always another job. Not this time. Now she worked regular hours, at a regular job, with the possibility of advancement. There would always be a demand for cell phones, and she was due to start her shift in an hour.

What was here that didn't require spending money? Nothing. It was an outdoor strip mall next to the only real shopping for miles. In fact, her store was just around the corner. She'd have to avoid that section or just be early. She could do that—be early for once. Turn over a new leaf. Take that new start Jeremy wanted for her.

"Okay, then." She left her car parked by Craig's sandwich shop and walked to her boring job.

Seven boring hours later, she rounded the building to empty storefront parking. The lone exception—her car. Jeremy's car, really. The other employees had parked closer and all these shops had closed about an hour before. It was a busy street corner. Lots of traffic, well lit, and she still got a creepy feeling crawling up her spine. She couldn't see anyone. No tall paramedic-psycho-cowboy nearby. She jumped out of her skin when her cell buzzed in her pocket.

Beth.

"Just wanted to make sure you were all right, Lindsey. It seemed like you had a rough day. We all miss him, you know."

"I know. I'm sorry I'm on the verge of crying all the time. There's no mystery why. I live in his apartment. I drive his car. I'm working in the store he managed. I don't just have survivor's guilt because I didn't drown, I'm living his life." She stopped and dug the keys from her purse. "Oh, gosh, I'm sorry to dump on you like that."

"I wouldn't have asked if it wasn't okay. You at your car now?"

Keys in hand, she was close enough to click a button to unlock, she answered, "Yes, I'll see you in a couple of days."

She'd become very used to the little luxuries that had filled her cousin's life. Having a dependable car with hands-free capability was a must from this point forward.

Relaxation would be hers soon. In twenty minutes,

she'd be soaking in a hot bath, bubbles up to her chin and lots of candles on the windowsill. There was little traffic on her route home, but a flashing light and detour sign had her turning on an unfamiliar street. Then again. Where was the button for GPS?

The route between apartment and store was easy, but if she got turned around, she could easily get lost on the south side of Arlington. She hadn't been in the area very long and she'd never had a good sense of direction. Another mile and she was so turned around it was silly to try to get back without directions.

No signs at the intersection. She stopped on the right shoulder far enough from the corner to let traffic pass by, then put the car in Park and tapped the screen. The GPS switched on and she looked up in time to see a car approaching behind her. The road was narrow, but with no other cars around, she powered the window down and waved the car to pass her.

The car didn't slow. Was it swerving? Still on a collision course with her. She jammed her foot on the gas. The lights blinded her in the mirror as she sped through the red light.

The impact at the rear of the car was an ear-piercing sound. The jolting crash hurt almost as much as the abrupt stop at the fence post across the street. She closed her eyes and choked when the air bag exploded in her face, feeling the burns shoot across her skin like skidding hard on cement.

By the time she could look up, the only lights around her were from the dashboard. She heard the engine rattling and cut off the ignition. Then nothing. She half expected an evil car to be sitting on the road, racing its engine. But nothing.

All alone.

Sore with every move, she searched for her purse and cell phone, then dialed 911 and explained what had happened.

"Rescue assistance is on the way. Do you want me to stay on the line with you?"

"I'm shook up but I think I'm okay." She reached to disconnect with shaking hands, and that creepy sensation returned. It had sure seemed as if that driver had meant to hit her car. "On second thought, do you mind talking? There aren't any cars around and I..."

"I'd be glad to stay on the line until the police arrive. The squad car is only a couple of minutes out."

Her narrow escape had been close.

Too close?

"Did you see the vehicle that hit you?"

"Not really. No." But it had deliberately swerved onto the shoulder. She was sure of that. "I think there was a black car following me earlier."

What were the odds of a hit-and-run accident on the very day someone claimed she would be a murder victim?

Should she tell the police about her meeting? What if he actually was the crazy psycho who'd followed? Would they laugh at her like they had Brian? Or was it time to find her own answers? Would anyone believe her except Brian?

"Ma'am? Do you see the police?"

"Yes. Thank you."

She should take charge of her destiny. Take charge. That sounded a lot better than becoming another "accident."

Chapter 3

"Who wants him?" Brian gave the vitals as they came through the emergency room doors. They pushed the gurney to a room where the victim was quickly assessed as stable and blood drawn for an alcohol level. He was the only victim after running a stop sign and causing a multicar pileup in downtown Fort Worth.

"Don't go anywhere, Sloane," his favorite nurse, Meeks, instructed. "After you hand him off, wait for a doctor to stitch up that forehead."

"You know that's not going to happen." He touched the cut and looked at a bloody finger. "Thirty years without stitches and I'm not starting now."

Cam, his rig partner, had laughed when their patient had lashed out, taken him by surprise and knocked him to the floor. Distracted by a pair of sky-blue eyes and convincing himself there was no way to see them again, the drunk John Doe's flaying had sent Brian's forehead into the defibrillator. He hadn't shared the real reason he'd been caught off guard—just complained about the bumps in the road.

He swiped at a drop of blood, keeping it from falling into his eyes.

Meeks ripped open a package and handed him a sterile dressing. "Sit."

"I'm fine."

"You have to wait for the doctor anyway." Meeks pointed to the chair in the corner and Brian sat, applying the dressing to his gash. "You're staying. Wow, he reeks of liquor. It's one of those nights. Someone said it was quiet around here and now we don't have enough doctors."

"Meeks! He's coding," a voice shouted from across the hall.

He could use the E.R. staff owing him a favor. So he waited with his patient while they were called away. Drunk Driver Doe was still out cold and snoring.

"I'm going to clean some of your blood out of the rig. Back in a few."

"I really don't need stitches." He jumped up and spoke to an empty room. At least empty of anyone who could get him out of here.

The gauze quickly soaked with blood. He hadn't taken a good look at it and there weren't any mirrors in the room. So he mentally agreed to wait with Drunk Doe. He looked at the man's vitals again and leaned on the counter. The chair looked more inviting with every throb in his skull. So he sat again.

Closing his eyes, he was immediately immersed in memories of the night of the fire. He hadn't thought about it for twelve years and now that was all he could see. Or hear. Or smell. He and his brother, John, had gone over their movements of the night that had changed their lives so often in the past four months that it played in his head like a movie.

"Sorry I took so long, took me a while to get some coffee. Hey, partner, you okay?" Cam asked, his arms full of their gear. "You're um…dripping."

"You've got to be kidding." Brian was on his feet. The bloody gauze was on the floor next to him instead of in his hand. "I must have slept a couple of minutes in spite of all the noise around here."

"Passed out's more likely," Meeks added behind Cam.

"Yeah, man. I was gone close to twenty-five minutes. Dispatch is calling, I have to take this." Cam left, answering his cell, his voice fading so fast Brian couldn't hear what he was asked or reporting.

"Sit back down." Meeks donned gloves and assessed his wound, took his BP and asked him standard memory-loss questions. "I'm finding a doctor for those sutures. You're most likely concussed and need a scan."

There was nothing wrong with him except a growing headache—more from all the fuss than injury. But he took it all in stride. If it had been Cam sitting here, he'd have done the same thing. His best efforts to think of another subject led him straight back to his gorgeous bundle of trouble and how to convince her that her life was in danger.

After their first meet, Lindsey Cook thought he was a stalker. He needed to move forward and put the past behind him. Without her. Hadn't he done everything he could do?

So why did he have a bad feeling in the pit of his gut? Why was he trying so hard to convince himself he'd done everything possible? Memories of the town uproar after he'd claimed the fire had been his fault came pressing back to weigh him down. He'd thought he'd done all he could do then, too.

Claiming responsibility for an accident so his brother could continue in the Navy had been the optimal option at the time. But if they'd just talked about that night instead of being so hardheaded, they wouldn't have lost twelve years. Hard years neither of them would get back. Years that had set a chain of events into motion. Not only for him and his twin, but for his family, the ranch, the town and all of Lindsey's family.

If they'd stopped this maniac by forcing the police to discover the truth twelve years ago, how many deaths could have been avoided?

Now he was grateful he'd waited on a doctor. He never wanted to fight with Nurse Meeks. An ironic name for Cindy's demanding personality. Old enough to be his mom, ornery enough to be a prison guard and still loved by everyone who came through her E.R.

A new intern entered pushing a tray. "Are you Sloane?"

"About time. The patient's been unconscious since transport—"

"Wait. I'm not here for him. Meeks said you needed some, um, sutures."

I trust a shaky EMT rookie more than a green first-year med student. "Does Meeks hate me?" If this kid did a terrible job of it, he'd walk out. "Why'd they send you?"

"Everyone else is tied up and they said it would be

good practice." He filled a syringe and got the needle
ready to deaden Brian's skin.

"Dispatch is ordering you home, buddy," Cam said.

"Ow. Take it easy."

Cam laughed. "Call when you're ready to leave and
I'll see if we can swing by and take you back to your
truck."

"Come on, Cam. Get one of the real doctors." He
kept still while his partner shook his head and covered
his laughing hyena mouth. "On second thought, get out.
I'll get my own ride back and convince the old man to
let me finish my tour."

"Paid leave, man. Take it." Cam patted him on the
shoulder and started to leave. "You need to be cleared
by a…" He looked the intern over and snickered again.
"A real doctor before showing up tomorrow."

Brian was stuck in more ways than one. The strong
odor of booze mixed with antiseptic as the intern irri-
gated the wound, and kind of made him woozy. The kid
spun on the little stool and picked up the needle and su-
ture. Then he spun back with shaking hands, seemingly
eager to jab the thing into Brian's forehead.

"Hoover Dam, kid!" Brian swatted the intern's fingers away from his head. "Wait for me to deaden up or
hand that needle over to me."

"Sorry. We're sort of busy, so I was in a hurry. I forgot."

"Well, go check on a patient or something and come
back in a few."

As soon as the kid left, Brian grabbed the needle and
planted himself in front of the counter. *Cell phone, flip
the camera, instant mirror.* He took a look at the deep

gash, couldn't feel anything above his brow and put a couple of clean stitches in the middle.

"Not half-bad," he said to Drunk Doe. He added some tape and was washing his hands when the door opened. "You can tend to your other patients, Doc. I took care of it. You ready to take this patient off my hands?"

He spun around, expecting the intern, but found those sad blue eyes that had haunted him for weeks.

"Hi. I bet this seems strange to track you down in the middle of the night," Lindsey Cook said, as if she hadn't threatened a restraining order that afternoon.

"A little. I didn't think I'd see you again after this afternoon." The abrasions on her face screamed for him to ask, but she'd sought him out for some reason. Maybe he should wait to ask, but her face was ashen. If he wasn't mistaken, she was in a great deal of pain.

"They said you'd been injured and might need a ride home." She sounded less confident. Almost afraid.

"Don't take this the wrong way, but you don't look so hot yourself."

"I'm fine." She sat on the rolling stool he'd just vacated. "So you really are an EMT."

He didn't want to correct her on the difference between an EMT and paramedic. "Yeah, I am. How'd you find me?" *More important, why did you want to?*

"I called a Fort Worth fire station and asked for you. One fireman was kind enough to explain that the ambulance service is a different company. I found the number and they assumed I was your sister-in-law for some odd reason. I didn't bother to correct them."

The shy smile she shot his direction didn't hide that she'd lied to find him. She reached to push her hair behind her ear and winced. Even an untrained person could figure out she was hurt.

"I guess it didn't dawn on my colleagues that my sister-in-law would just call my cell." He tapped his phone still on the counter.

"Not if she had a surprise. But they assumed you were getting a CT scan or something and couldn't answer your phone."

He pointed to his head. "No scan for me. So why didn't you just call me? You had the number."

"Well, I wanted to have this conversation face-to-face."

So she'd done her own amateur detective work, found him and had something to say. The room was a little small, throwing them within touching distance. Something he'd wanted more of since shaking her hand that afternoon.

"I'm sorry for frightening you today. I just thought you'd want to know," he said to start the conversation again. The intern would be returning soon and it would be even more awkward.

She seized his hand, clinging to it with a sense of desperation he knew all too well. The desperate need for someone to care and make you feel like you weren't alone. He'd been there four months ago when his father had suffered a major stroke.

"I think someone tried to kill me tonight," she whispered, her eyes darting to the drunk on the bed.

"What happened?" He moved to lean on the counter. Nothing jerky, but it shifted her arm.

She released a sharp hiss between her teeth. "I got lost on the way to Jeremy's house and—"

"Hey, first things first. Did you see a doctor? Where are you injured?"

"My shoulder's hurting. It's just bruised from the seat belt."

"Mind if I have a look?" His fingers were already heading toward her.

"Do you really know what you're doing?"

He had to laugh. "Yeah, I've been doing this over eight years now. More if you count all the horses on the ranch I've nursed back to health." When she turned those baby blues on him he had trouble focusing. "You didn't answer me. Did anyone look at your shoulder, and how long ago did it happen?"

"The EMT checked it around ten. And another doctor at the E.R. I'll be fine."

Seat belt injury equaled car wreck. He gently probed her left shoulder through her shirt where the strap would have bruised. "So you got lost and had an accident?"

"I don't think it was an accident," she whispered again. She didn't jerk away, just looked at Drunk Doe. "Is it safe to talk here?"

"He's unconscious. We have plenty of time to go over what happened while I get one of the doctors to examine you."

"No. Please. I've already been to the emergency room. It's okay, really." She caught his hand again. "Does that mean you'll help me? You're the only one who might believe me."

"What can I do? I'm a paramedic, not a bodyguard."

Brian wanted the truth, but attempted murder was out of his league. He had other problems to think about anyway. His twin brother was home for good and married with a kid. His family's ranch was getting closer to foreclosure. And he wanted to say yes so badly to this woman his mouth was forming the word.

"If someone tried to kill you, then the police are working your case. I should probably stay out of it."

The relief rushed his body like a warm shower. He could focus on finding the money to take over the ranch payments. Maybe stop working as a paramedic and focus on breeding champion quarter horses again. Maybe see a little more of the world. Maybe watch some Sunday football. Buy a boat and get some fishing in. Lots of boring choices instead of working every minute.

Nothing like his brother's life as a Navy SEAL. And none of which involved spending time with a beautiful blonde.

"I hate saying this, Brian, but I'm afraid to go home alone. I need your help. You're my only hope."

"I'm not a hero in some movie. I'm a nobody." He pushed on her shoulder to make sure it was in place. "I think it's just bruised. Did they get an X-ray? I'll call a nurse."

"Wait." She latched on to his biceps. "You're the only reason my car didn't shoot into a telephone poll. Your warning made me extracautious and I kept watching the car behind me. If you hadn't spoken to me this afternoon, I wouldn't need your help now. I'd be dead."

He was dang tired of being anyone's *only* hope. His brother twelve years ago. The ranch. His dad. He'd warned her. That was all he could do. "This is a job for the police, not an amateur with some friends who did some digging for him."

"But they won't. The police officer called it an accident and blamed me for not pulling farther off the road." Those picture-perfect eyes filled to their full mark and one tear escaped down her tanned, freckled cheek. She swiped at it with the back of her free hand.

"God-d...bless America." He couldn't say yes. "This is such a bad idea. I'm not the guy you need to help you."

"But you're the one who told me—"

"I'm going to have a doctor look at your shoulder." Brian gently cupped her injury, gave it a soft you'll-be-all-right pat and grabbed the door with every intention to march into the hall, shout for Meeks and continue his life. But that nagging gut feeling wouldn't let him. "What is it you want me to do?"

"Tell me how to convince the authorities someone's after me."

"I haven't had much luck with that."

Was this the same woman he'd met earlier, so full of confidence protecting herself at the sandwich shop? Injured, sitting with her shoulders slumped, waiting on answers he didn't have. If he hadn't put the idea of murder into her life, she wouldn't be afraid to go home. It would have been just another car accident.

Another accident.

"How do you know it was deliberate? You're certain the car swerved off the road? Were there any witnesses?"

"I can tell when a car swerves directly toward me." She sat straight with confidence. "How did you get that cut on your forehead?"

Leave. Forget Miss Blue Eyes and your curiosity. You can't do anything to help.

"I fell." His hand was still on the door handle. "Why?"

"Any witnesses?" She rubbed her shoulder. "I'm sure

the police will believe you. It shouldn't be a problem, but you could have been in a fight. Or drunk. Lord knows you smell like you bathed in alcohol."

"Got me. You didn't mention to the cop at the scene about your family history? Or that I think the family accidents might actually be murders?"

She pressed her lips together, shook her head and nervously raised a finger to twist her hair. "I sort of told them, but they wouldn't believe me when I said I didn't know who you were."

"You had my number and I could have confirmed your details. Why wouldn't you? Oh, I get it. You think if you tell the cops that I'll be in trouble?"

"Hey," she said, standing and putting a hand on a hip. "I don't know what to believe. Right now, I'm exhausted but there's no way I can go home alone. No, no, no, you get that look out of your eyes, mister. I'm not asking you to come home with me. Shoot. I sort of thought you might have been the guy who hit me. I don't think you are, since the other firemen confirmed your shift began at seven. But honestly, I don't know you."

"Did you hit your head?"

"No. At least, I don't think I did. The air bag scraped me."

He watched the realization of his words wash over her in an embarrassing shade of pink.

"Oh, no. I'm sorry. When I get nervous, I tend to babble. I think you misunderstood what I meant earlier."

"What part? When you asked for help? Or when you thought I might have tried to murder you?"

"All I want is a cup of coffee and some pancakes." She cradled her arm closer to her side.

Pancakes? He could go for some pancakes. "Cafeteria's closed. Will Pan-Hop do?" Maybe she could fill in some blanks in his research?

She nodded. "Great. I love their double-stack special. What about him?"

"I almost forgot about Drunk Driver Doe." He pressed the nurse call button. "Meeks. I've gotta leave."

"I'll be right there, Sloane."

"For the record," Lindsey said with the confidence he'd seen when they'd first met, "I don't know why I started looking for you, but this seemed like my only option. I don't intend to have any more *accidents*."

"The folder's in my truck back at the lot. My captain's already told me to head home." He pointed to his bandage. "Get me pancakes and I'll tell you everything."

"My moment of feeling sorry for myself is over. I want all the details. Everything you've learned about my family."

He could pass along what he'd discovered. Maybe not everything. He couldn't admit that he'd been admiring her gorgeous body since seeing her picture on her website four months ago. Probably better to keep that information to himself. At least for a while.

And why today? If this guy waits years, planning his murders to disguise them as accidents, then why attempt a hit and run? Had he brought Lindsey to the murderer's attention? Or worse, sped up his timetable?

How could he walk away if he was responsible?

Chapter 4

Lindsey restrained herself through the short drive, asking only how Brian had received the cut. He'd laughed as he'd said to avoid an inexperienced intern with over-eager fingers, he'd stitched it himself. But the story had left her queasy after dropping him off at the ambulance company's home base. The Pan-Hop was right around the corner.

While she waited, the memory of the car lights blinded her again. The awful thought that her life had been about to end replayed over and over. Because of Brian's visit earlier that day, she was still alive. She'd only been alone waiting for him to arrive about five minutes before a tap on the window made her jump out of her skin.

"You ready to go inside?" Brian asked.

She grabbed her purse and locked the car. He'd

changed into the street clothes he'd worn when they'd met that afternoon. A lifetime ago. She hadn't noticed his scuffed boots until he'd held the door and she'd looked to the ground. The only boots she'd noticed before were on men shopping for a new phone. She hadn't been in Texas too long and hadn't made an effort to get to know anyone or discover any real cowboys.

Now one had found her.

He waited, holding the restaurant door open while she looked past him through the windows. Any of those people could have been driving the car that rammed her off the road. It could be anyone...anywhere.

A creepy feeling crawled up her spine. He was out there. She could feel him staring from his hiding place. Pure panic drove her. She spun and searched the dark.

"We going to eat?"

"I can't." Darting under his arm, she began clicking the rental's key, trying to unlock the door. The car alarm set the horn blaring and she looked closer to see which button was which, but her eyes were full of embarrassing tears.

Tears? Now? She'd remained calm throughout the accident and police. But couldn't handle pancakes in a public place.

Brian clasped his hands over hers, tilted her chin toward him and took the keys. The alarm stopped, then she heard the horn beep that it was reset. He hadn't looked away. His dark eyes reassured something deep inside. More than basic attraction, sort of as though he shared part of her no one else could—or would—ever understand.

Even with his eyes comforting her, the panic bubbled. She looked into the dark corners of the building, right at the edge of the light. He was there, watching.

"What's wrong?"

"I can't go in there, it's…it's too crowded." Her mind acknowledged that the restaurant was more than half-empty, but it just didn't matter. She couldn't force her feet to move through the entrance.

Brian seemed to understand. He led her by the elbow to his truck, opened the door and removed a bag from the floor. "Want me to help you inside?"

It was an older model and it took a little doing one-handed, but she managed to climb in on her own.

"Mind if I hook you up? This thing can be sort of stubborn." He pulled and held the seat belt forward.

She nodded and he leaned across the seat. She would never have been able to lift her arm to lock herself in and he'd helped without her asking. He smelled of a mixture of hay and man. Attractive. Musky. Like a guy who did honest work or who'd driven with the top down on a bright sunny day.

His hair was short, but didn't look like his normal style since he kept tossing his head as though there were longer locks there. She recognized that toss of his head and the nervous running of his fingers across his scalp. She did it herself to get short wisps away from her face. It looked as if it was growing out from a military cut close to his head, curling at the base of his neck.

He hadn't been exaggerating when he'd said the seat belt was stubborn. It wasn't just a play to get closer. His hands touched her hip more than once and as hard as he tried not to, his arm grazed her stomach and thigh.

The urge to twist those curls around her finger was a little heady. She'd acted on impulse before. It would

be so easy to reach out and use her nail to trace the lean
tendon leading down to his shoulder.

She watched her hand sort of float down, getting
closer to that musky skin.

"There." He stood straight, brushing her hand to the
side with his shoulder, smiling from ear to ear as though
he'd accomplished something much harder than snapping a seat belt. "Dang thing had an animal cracker
stuck in it."

"Great." She didn't feel great. Maybe she had hit
her head because she was definitely a little dizzy. He
seemed perfectly fine and totally unaffected by all the
touching.

"Your shoulder okay?" he asked, adjusting the strap
to make it a little looser while holding an animal cracker
tight in his palm. He was thinking of his niece, not her.
He just wanted her to be safe while in his truck.

Shoot, he was a paramedic. He probably got hit on
all the time. Girls probably fell at his feet. Well, that
was the old Lindsey. The new Lindsey didn't fall at
anyone's feet. She used her own. The tenseness she felt
had nothing to do with the physical and everything to
do with the potential threat on her life.

Anyone would feel like this.

"Great, thanks. Your mother must be very proud of
raising such a gentleman."

The smile faded from his eyes and his lips twisted
tightly into a thin line. He quickly shut the door. "Mom
died of cancer a long time ago," he said softly through
the open window.

He walked around the back of the truck, pausing
to drop the bag in the back and again at the door. His

face was out of sight, but she heard the deep inhale and slow release.

Trying to pay him a compliment, she'd brought up a terrible pain. She knew all about the death of a parent and felt two inches tall for the remark she'd made about him still having his father when they'd first met.

He got in and pulled from the parking lot. "Don't feel bad, Lindsey. You didn't know."

"I meant it as a compliment."

"And that's how I took it. She's been gone a long time."

"My parents' accident was six years ago. When I remember that day...all the horrible feelings make me hurt all over. I can't imagine it ever gets easier."

"It does and it doesn't. Hang on to the good stuff." He shifted gears and stopped at a red light.

The streets were practically empty. She looked around for a black car, trying not to but paranoid. Each time they stopped, she searched.

"I doubt he's going to do anything when you're with me. This guy makes it look like an accident. That's why no one's caught on. So where do you live?"

"You must already know, since you're headed there. It's really okay. I looked up a couple of things about you, too. The fire did more than kill my cousin. It destroyed all your plans and your family's. I think it's cool that you're an identical twin. You might have told me what happened this summer. Your story made the news. And your poor little niece."

"You didn't seem too receptive to more talking this afternoon. Were the articles and pictures helpful?"

"Yes. You can't blame me for checking out your story. You could have been driving the car that ran me off the road for all I knew."

"And yet, you didn't tell the cops my name."

"How did you know?"

"I don't seem to be in police custody on suspicion of murder."

"Right. The police already thought I was drunk or high or just crazy. Then there was the mess when they thought I'd stolen Jeremy's car. *That* took forever to clear up. So I let them take me home and used the internet."

"Wait, go back. They thought you stole a car?"

"That's beside the point, but if you must know, Jeremy left me his car. I've been making the payments. The bank wouldn't put it in my name. When I told the cop at the accident that the owner was dead..." She rubbed the scratches she'd gotten from the handcuffs they used while escorting her to the police station to sort things out. "Part of the reason it was so late when I found you was that it took a long time to find Jeremy's lawyer and verify everything."

"Is this your place?"

"Jeremy's, really."

"If it's got a lock on the door, you'll be fine. Want me to walk you to the door?"

"Yes. I mean, aren't we going to talk? You can tell me what your plans are. How do you plan to catch this guy? Oh, wait, we should talk inside. But what if it's bugged or something?"

"Lindsey." He lifted a hand as a universal stop sign. "Lindsey, slow down. I'm not that guy."

He reached forward and gently popped her seat belt loose. At some point he'd already undone his and twisted on the old vinyl. Draping his arm over the back of the seat, he rested his head in his hand.

He arched his brows, waiting, but she didn't know how to respond. She didn't completely understand the question, so what did he want?

"Look, kid—"

"Stop right there. I'm not a kid. You can't be more than three or four years older than me. Remember, I did research on you, too. So I'm not your kid, sweetheart, baby, doll or whatever nickname you can create. My name's Lindsey."

"Yes ma'am. Like I was saying, I'm not the guy you want defending you. I have no resources, no knowledge, no experience or desire to protect you. You need someone who knows what they're doing."

"But who else is going to believe me, Brian?"

"You've got me there. I had a helluva time just getting myself to believe me. Then Mabel did some research and all those accidents didn't seem so accidental."

"You'll help?" She focused on his eyes, the slight tilt of his mouth that was much more comforting than those tight, strained lips.

"I don't know what I can do, *Lindsey,* but I'll tell you what I know. Stay there and I'll help you out before you hurt that shoulder again. The muscles are probably stiffening up about now."

He scooped the folder from the seat and she waited while he walked around the truck. If he wanted to be gallant, she'd let him. Allowing him to open the door for her wasn't being a pushover—especially if he wasn't doing any pushing.

She creaked to the edge and stepped down. Brian was right. She ached all over.

"Aw, I told you."

The wince had probably given her away. She would have stumbled to the ground if he hadn't been there helping. "I can't believe how sore I am all of a sudden."

"The adrenaline's wearing off and I bet you'll be out as soon as your head hits the pillow."

"No way. We have things to discuss. I want to know everything you know."

"And I'll be here in the morning. Does that perplexed look indicate you don't know if it's a good idea or not?"

"I just... I mean, just because I tracked you down doesn't mean I invited you to spend the night." *Remember, someone's trying to kill you.* A little voice in her head, sounding so much like Jeremy, kept reminding her to look around. The paranoia had her doubting Brian's motives.

"I thought we were past all that. I didn't try to kill you. You can trust me."

Fear made her anxious. She could feel it trying to take over again. Then Jeremy's voice prodded her, *You need his help. What about your mother and father's accident? You may have been murdered. You need to find the truth and this guy's already found a great deal. Don't stop until you get the psycho who's been destroying our family.*

She scraped her scalp with the metal key ring still in her palm as she shoved her hand through her hair. She'd been doing so well on her own. She shook her head, wanting the answer to be different than what was obvious. She couldn't do this on her own. Good or bad, she needed him.

"I'm sorry. This situation is just a little overwhelming." She stretched her neck back to get a look at the most comforting eyes she'd ever fallen into. They made her next words much easier to say, "Would you mind staying awhile? I'd feel safer."

He held out his hand for her keys. She'd promised herself never to ask for help again. Did this count?

The keys dropped into Brian's palm and they moved inside with no more debate. Lindsey was obviously on her last ounce of energy, stumbling out of her shoes and falling onto the leather couch.

"Why don't you head to bed?" He flipped on lights, set the file on the coffee table and wanted to remove his boots. If he could just close his eyes for a few... The exhaustion from his shift was intensifying the pounding behind his eyes from the slight concussion.

"I'm so wound up, I really don't think I can go to sle..." She stopped, staring at the goldfish tank on the corner of the desk.

"What's the matter?"

She moved next to him, no longer wilting. "Someone's been here," she whispered. "Could they still be in the house?"

"How can you tell?" He pulled her close under his arm, as if that would actually protect her if someone attacked.

"The fish-food container was on top of Jeremy's papers. Not next to the bowl. Feeding them was one of the last things I did before I left this morning." Her whispering voice shook with fright as much as her body shook under his hand.

"You're certain?"

"Yes."

"We're leaving."

"But—"

"Now, Lindsey. Out."

She turned and ran. He didn't linger. He wanted to check things out. Might have if he'd been alone. But he wasn't. For whatever it was worth, Lindsey had chosen him as her protector and he'd do his best. That did not include a fool idea that he should seek out trouble.

Trouble had a way of finding him all on its own.

When he pulled away from her home, Lindsey explored her purse until she removed her cell. "Shoot, my battery's nearly dead. Can I use your phone?"

"I don't think calling anyone is a good idea. Let's talk first and come up with a game plan. Sound good?"

"But what about prints or stuff like that?"

"I don't think this guy left any sign he's been in your house. He's been pretty darn good about covering his tracks."

"Okay, we'll play it your way right now. Just know that this is my life and if *I* decide to make a call, I will." She hugged her sore shoulder close to her chest.

"Absolutely." He pulled to a stop and snapped her belt. "It's over an hour to my place. You can use my jacket for a pillow. One of us should get some sleep."

He drove the truck, trying not to be distracted as she shifted and got comfortable without another word. Hell, he'd shut down for months when he'd thought John had accidentally started a fire that had killed Mrs. Cook. He couldn't really fathom what it would be like to have someone try to kill him.

"Thank you, Brian."

"You're welcome. Now try to get some shut-eye."

He should force her to go back to the police or hire someone who could help. Taking her to the ranch seemed the easiest choice he'd made recently. Since he and John had cleared the air and actually talked about the night that had changed their lives forever, decisions he'd made on his own for years about the ranch were suddenly up for a group discussion.

For four months he'd craved catching the murdering son of a bitch who had destroyed his future. Now it was more important than ever. He couldn't leave Lindsey to handle this on her own.

The hour zoomed by—even in the old Ford his grandfather had bought and used for fifteen years. Brian tinkered with the engine, keeping it running smoothly. It might not have AC, but it was his. The bank couldn't repossess it like they were trying to foreclose on the ranch.

One trouble at a time.

Keeping Lindsey alive was more important than finding a way to buy the ranch. He turned down the drive, cut the lights and parked next to the barn. Lindsey was still out. She mumbled a little when he shifted her to open the door.

The wind had blown her hair across her face. He leaned close, gently blowing the small strands to the side. He couldn't resist. His lips grazed her forehead so softly he wasn't certain he'd connected with her flesh until his lips cooled again. He scooped her up in his arms, cradling her head in the crook of his shoulder.

He was behaving like a sentimental and romantic idiot. He knew all there was about Lindsey Cook. More than he wanted or needed to know. No way would she go for a cowboy like him. He wasn't anywhere near her league of resort-hopping rich and didn't know how to get there. Didn't want to get there.

Dawn was just around the corner. Time for the morning chores, and no extra hands to do any part of them. What would this beach bunny think of his family's ranch?

The old house needed a coat of paint. The barn needed a new roof. The stock tank needed to be dredged. And there were hardly enough horses left to be considered a farm anymore. It wasn't anything to show off, but it was his.

Or could be. He'd done a lot of thinking since John had come home. Since he turned fifteen, the one thing he'd been talking about doing was leaving this small piece of real estate. Now he couldn't figure out a way to keep from being kicked off the place.

Brian got through the door without the screen slamming shut, a sleeping beauty still in his arms.

"I thought your shifts were for three days?" His brother yawned and scratched his head coming into the kitchen. "Want coffee?"

John finally looked up from the pot that had automatically kicked on and brewed. He pointed and raised an eyebrow, recognition at Lindsey's identity twisting his face into shock, then anger.

Brian was tired and didn't want to wake his new responsibility with loud voices or explanations.

"Don't ask, bro. Just don't ask."

Chapter 5

Serendipity at its best. He could do nothing except admire how the universe worked to bring him back to the only man to have received acclaim for one of his masterpieces.

The Sloane brothers had been the perfect pawns. He'd switched on the voice-activated microphone he'd installed years ago to record his work. There would come a day when someone would transcribe his dictation and print his book, *Details of a Successful Serial Killer.*

"Will Brian Sloane's primitive investigation cause problems for your last plan?" He asked himself the question as if a reporter sat in the room. "The paramedic is a growing pain in the ass and will be eliminated as soon as the opportunity arises."

After he was gone, someone should know what he'd

accomplished. There shouldn't be any supposition regarding each case. When the world discovered his lifelong achievements, it should be in his own words.

The idea came to him after the second successful death. Each plan was chronicled and stored in a fireproof safe once completed, but there was nothing like hearing about the conceptualization or nuances that made each one different to execute.

"But that wasn't the question, sir." The reporter in his mind continued to dig. "Will he present a problem?"

For several years, he'd been using the recording device like an audible journal. At first, it had been to document his work. Basically, he was so good at creating *accidents* that no one knew he'd done anything.

"Keeping track of the Sloane brothers for twelve years hasn't been difficult. They lead uneventful lives with the exception of John's return home. He set off a chain of very unfortunate events. That has only forced me to accelerate my plans for the last Cook family member. With Lindsey's death, there are no claims on what's been mine for many years now."

He pushed away from his desk, preferring the supple leather of his couch for what amounted to a debate with himself to logically reason his way through a new challenge.

"If those laughable amateurs who kidnapped Lauren Adams hadn't gotten greedy, the Sloanes would never have discovered my craftsmanship with the Cook deaths. Hiding Gillian's murder within the barn fire was convenient, but also brilliant. I was so close to perfection."

He opened and poured a shot of his favorite vodka.

He needlessly swirled it in the cut glass, waiting for the right moment to consume.

"To recap, Gillian checked on the fire pit each time those high school children left her property. One swing of a board and she was unconscious as the barn burned around her. Convenient, yet brilliant. No one has ever discovered the truth of her murder."

There was a right moment for everything. People had forgotten the art of patience. Waiting made the win worth savoring.

"I'll need to get rid of them both. Soon, and without a lot of fuss." He downed the clear shot. One was his limit. He enjoyed the burning sensation as it traveled through his body, immediately craving more of the fiery liquid.

"No, there isn't a problem. But I am conflicted. Arranging a major accident would get the entire ranch out of my way for good, yet forcing an accident on their ranch is irrational. There would be too many witnesses. The pertinent question is, how do I get Brian and Lindsey to leave the ranch?"

He brushed the back of his finger under his mustache, verifying no drops of liquid moistened his upper lip. Reaching for the bottle, he realized the cool glass was in his hand and shouldn't be. He slammed it on the table, shooting drops in the air that landed on the polished wood.

"How can I overcome this setback? Strike that. I consider this puzzle a welcome challenge. I haven't had any in many years." He leaned into the leather, resting his head, focusing on the microphone in the ceiling tiles. Closing his eyes, he pictured the horse ranch where Sloane had taken Lindsey. It was the only logical place he could go. He envisioned the buildings and the distances, places to hide, the horses and where they wandered.

"I have to admit, this challenge is the first time I've desired to meet my opponent face-to-face. If the opportunity presents itself, I might consider doing so. But that's part of the beauty of this operation. No one knows. Not even my victims knew I controlled whether they lived or died."

He'd given his word to himself and anyone listening to these tapes that they'd always be completely truthful. The last murder had been slightly different than the rest.

"Addendum. Pathetic Jeremy Cook most likely saw a distorted image through his snorkeling face mask. That was the closest I've ever gotten to any of my victims. When I was within striking distance, he was still completely at ease. My sheer strength kept him underwater. Fear never showed in his eyes until the last bubble of air escaped from his lungs. Then he knew. He knew there was no escape."

Reliving the experience made his heart race and made him need more of the same exhilarating excitement. He wouldn't put that on the tapes. Doctors or the media would twist the pleasure he took from a well-executed plan. They'd distort it and turn his excellence into something sick that needed analysis.

"Back to the problem at hand. How to eliminate the Cook line and take care of the Sloanes with the same deed." The map of the property was firmly in his mind even after twelve years. As were the images of each building, the road, the fields, the pond...all there, creating a secret thrill he couldn't share. He ran the idea from start to finish.

Excitement. Anticipation. Reward.

"Brilliant. Yes, a tip to the press connecting Brian to a possible hit-and-run accident will work nicely. A photographer should spook them sufficiently to where they are alone and vulnerable. I'll record the details upon completion. There's no need to repeat myself in dictation."

Some men were thrilled by the hunt. Some by the kill. He poured another shot. It was time to celebrate. He held the glass in the air.

"A toast. To twenty years of excellence in murder."

The vodka did its job, and he rose to switch off the recorder. There was one part of himself that he refused to share with the world. They'd label him perverted if they discovered his need to hear the moans of torture. He hid his tendency, only allowing himself to indulge as a reward for his greatness.

Fate had stepped in and brought him an opponent for his last plan. His own intelligence would be Lindsey's downfall, and deserved to be fed and stroked. Seeing the report of another assumed overdosed prostitute in the news would meet his growing need for acknowledgment. It would also satisfy him in other pleasurable areas while she or he died.

The perfect subject for his reward had already been chosen and would fit into his plans nicely. But not a random death on the street. He had the perfect place to carry out his deed.

The celebration after his Cozumel success had been near Jeremy's home. With Lindsey secure with the Sloanes, it might be risky to return there. But Jeremy's bed would make the satisfaction all the sweeter.

Chapter 6

Brian's head throbbed. He was tired. Not just from hitting his temple earlier. He needed sleep and a couple of days off. It seemed like years since he'd sat down and wasn't on the clock, looking at ranch records or researching murders. Recently, the spare hours he'd had between shifts were spent following Lindsey's every move. His bed looked very inviting. His father's bed even more so with Miss Blue Eyes curled under the sheets now.

If he was lucky, he'd be under some sheets with her fairly soon. She had to be feeling the chemical reaction every time they were in the same room. Right? Hitting the hay with her could happen once they knew each other better, but not here. Not with a houseful of his family around.

The rooster crowed at the first peek of dawn. He might as well help with the morning feeding for once since he was up. It beat balancing the ranch books. Changed and gulping down a cup of coffee, he caught up with John halfway through feeding the stabled horses.

"Ready to tell me what's going on?" his brother asked.

"There was an accident."

"You didn't do anything stupid, did you? We talked about this." John sounded like an older brother or more like a former Naval officer used to getting answers.

"I didn't do a damn thing, John. Lay off." He pushed his hat to the back of his head. "And stop lecturing me every time we have a conversation. I've been taking care of this place for twelve years."

"What the hell happened to your head?" John's hands framed Brian's face, turning it so he could get a closer look. His thumbs stretched the laceration, tugging at the bandage. "You're bleeding."

"Blast it, John. Stop treating me like I'm ten." Brian shook free and swiped at his forehead. "I've got a father and don't need you to baby me."

Sometime during the past four months they'd switched their traditional roles. Identical in every visible way, Brian had always been the responsible one, older by minutes but by light-years in responsibility. The complete opposite of John's jokester personality. His little brother had finally grown up while in the Navy. Or maybe it was coming home, making amends with his high school sweetheart and planning to adopt her daughter.

"Whoever stitched you up did a crappy job, bro. That's going to leave a scar. And don't think *I'm* slicing my forehead so we can switch places again."

"Seems as though every time we've switched it was your idea and I was getting *you* out of trouble."

"Don't change the subject. What happened?" John stepped back, stiffening, as if he was at attention, commanding his men. It was obvious he wasn't continuing with scooping oats until he got an answer. "After you went to the cops and they laughed in your face, I thought we agreed that it was over."

"Stand down. This ain't the Navy, man. Nothing major happened to me. This is from a drunk in my rig." He straightened his hat. "Lindsey's the one who had an accident. She's a little freaked to be alone, that's all. I brought her here. That's it. No big deal. Now, I'm awful tired, so why don't we get through the chores and I'll explain after breakfast. Once. To everyone. Alicia will be home and Dad can pretend that he's been home all night. Right, Dad?"

His father popped his head around the open double doors leading to the paddock. "I didn't want to interrupt."

"You're not interrupting. Maybe Blue Eyes will be awake for your interrogation. That work for everybody?"

"Blue Eyes?" John and his dad questioned together, sounding so much alike it was creepy.

"Yeah, Lindsey."

"You agreed to leave this alone. What happened twelve years ago doesn't matter." John picked up the scoop and measured oats for the horses.

"It matters to me. And I never agreed. You ordered and I reminded you that I don't take orders from you."

Brian left each bucket in a different stall, feeding the trained quarter horses he'd been trying to sell for months. He was ready to move to the next chore when John began laughing. "What's so dang funny?"

"It just occurred to me, you put those stitches in yourself. Right?" He slapped his thighs, stumbling back a couple of steps, laughing hard at his own joke. "I knew it."

"What stitches?" his dad asked, leaning on his cane. Not bad for a man recovering from a major stroke four months ago. He walked a good two miles every day just coming home from Mabel's across the street.

"John's losing his mind. Glad you're here to take care of him if he starts convulsing." Brian lengthened his stride to leave faster. "I'm going to make breakfast."

"We need to talk about the ranch, boy-o," his father said loudly. "The bank called again."

"Can't right now, Dad. I have a date with the griddle." Brian left as John expounded on the crooked sutures. If his brother noticed, it was probably a good idea to let his sister-in-law, the professional nurse in the family, redo his sutures.

Right now, he was starved and needed to get his mind off some sky-blue eyes and corn-silk hair spread over a pillow in the front bedroom.

"Yum. Pancakes."

The distinct smell of a hot griddle and syrup wafted into Lindsey's nose, encouraging her to breathe deeply and enjoy. She stretched her arms above her head. No surfing today, her shoulder was a little sore. She rubbed it as she sank back into the pillows, surrounded by the comforting feeling of her favorite place in Florida. The sun streamed through the windows every morning and she'd breathe in the soft, fresh smell of sun-dried sheets. There was a plus side to not owning a dryer.

Snuggling the quilt closer to her chest, she wanted to spend the rest of the morning asleep. But there was work or something she was supposed to do. And pancakes. Her eyes fluttered open to an unfamiliar room.

Wide-awake in an instant. Panic. Aches.

Where am I?

Then her memory kicked in with Brian's words that he was taking her to his home. Darn. She was on a ranch, not back at the beach. She'd be inside the storefront cage where she worked by three that afternoon. Stuck inside. It couldn't compare to working in the sun, walking in the sand or having the surf as part of every conversation.

She missed the sun. But she was responsible now, with a real job and possible advancement. A permanent roof over her head instead of crashing with relatives during the winter season when she was broke. Responsibility was a good thing.

The room didn't look like Brian at all. Pictures in old frames were placed on a dresser around a handmade doily and jewelry box. Grandparents, baby photos of two identical boys and a stunning woman in a wedding dress from the 70s. Either the loner she'd met wasn't much of a loner or it wasn't Brian's room after all.

She was still completely dressed except for her shoes—a good thing, no awkward moments. She made the bed like a good guest—she'd been one often enough. Hit the bathroom, then not wanting to disturb anyone, she tiptoed through the hallway leading to the living area. She followed the heavenly smell of pancakes, hoping to find her cowboy rescuer.

A man was crashed on the couch. His face was pressed into the back cushions, but she knew it was Brian. His boots were at one end with his hat resting on top. She wasn't surprised he was still asleep. He'd worked all night, then stayed up with her. What she couldn't believe was that he'd carried her to bed and she hadn't woken up.

"Shh. You'll get in trouble if you wake up Uncle Brian," a little girl tried to whisper from the kitchen entrance, placing her first finger across her lips but speaking loud enough to be heard across the room.

Lindsey followed the little girl into the kitchen, hesitating before interrupting the woman cleaning up, uncertain how to explain why she was in her home. These two had to be the new additions to the family. She recognized their pictures from the articles she'd found involving Brian and the little girl's kidnapping last summer.

"Mommy," Brian's niece said, sending her pigtails bouncing over her shoulders.

"Lauren, you know you have to eat before you can go outside. Get back in your seat and leave Uncle Brian alone." She didn't look away from the dishes in the sink.

"Brian's lady is up," she announced, and her mom turned. Lauren laced her fingers through Lindsey's and tugged her across the kitchen. Mother and daughter looked alike; both had rich, dark brown hair and the same arch to their brows.

"Hi, I'm Alicia. Brian said y'all got here at dawn. I didn't expect you up this soon." Alicia wiped her hands on a dish towel. There had been a moment of hesitation with her smile, but it looked genuine now that it was in place. Then she knelt by her daughter. "Lauren, you didn't go and wake Miss Lindsey up, did you?"

Another surprise, Alicia Sloane knew her name. "Oh, no, I had a great sleep," Lindsey rushed to explain. "I met Lauren in the living room. Oh, and I'm not Brian's lady. We just met yesterday and he brought me here because I had no place to go. Great, that sort of sounds horrible. I mean, the story's a little complicated. A lot complicated, actually."

Alicia smiled bigger, stood and tapped Lauren on the bottom, scooting her toward her booster seat at the table. "Thank you for minding me, sweetie. Now get up there and finish eating. Don't worry, Lindsey. Brian explained everything over breakfast. Are you hungry? I was instructed to give you hotcakes as soon as you were ready."

"They smell delicious. Can I help?"

"Guests don't cook, silly." One of the cutest giggles she'd ever heard came from tiny lips and a mouth full of pancakes.

"Lauren, that was rude. You don't call grown-ups silly." Brian's sister-in-law retrieved the batter from the refrigerator and slid it onto the mixer stand. "And you don't talk with your mouth full."

"But you do. You said Uncle Brian bringing a guest to Pawpaw's very full house was silly." She folded another half of a small pancake and stuffed it in her mouth, smiling with a drip of syrup on her chin as she chewed.

"Oh, gosh." Alicia's hand covered her cheeks. "I'm so sorry."

"It's okay. You're right, me being here is quite silly. Um…" Lindsey understood. Staying here wasn't only awkward for the Sloanes. She had a bit of background, but what did she really know about Brian? "I guess I should go. If you know where my purse is, I'll call a cab to take me home."

"Don't be silly," Alicia said. "Oh, my, there I go again. What I meant to say is you're more than welcome to stay here as long as you want. This is Brian's house more than mine, and I shouldn't have spouted off about a lack of space. Lauren, we'll talk about this later, young lady."

"I really think I should go." She backed up, trying to leave gracefully. Maybe she'd missed her purse in Brian's room. Two strong hands cupped her shoulders, steadying her as she tripped into a rock-solid body.

"You've got nowhere to go. Remember?" Brian's voice said just above her head.

"Are you in trouble, Mommy? Uncle Brian looks mad."

"I'm tired, baby girl. Just tired." His warm breath tickled her spine. "I get ornery when I only get a half hour of shut-eye."

"I told you to sleep in our room," Alicia said.

"That will never happen." He laughed. "Don't worry about it. I function on naps all the time. Besides, the smell of that griddle made me hungry again." He patted Lindsey's shoulders and guided her to a chair at the old-fashioned table. "How's the shoulder?"

"A little sore, but fine."

The strange part of the scene around her was that she didn't feel unwanted or a burden or even more than slightly awkward. When Brian was in the room, she felt at home. Her hand skimmed the table top as he pushed her chair closer to the table.

Metal legs, green Formica, scuffs, a few crayon

marks—old and newish—made her feel as if the table had been there a very long time. The extension was in the middle and six quaint matching chairs were in place.

"How long is your lady friend going to be here, Uncle Brian?"

"I have to be at work this afternoon, so I should be heading home," she explained to Lauren, but looked at Brian, who raised an eyebrow and rested his head on his hand.

"After some pancakes, right?" Alicia set a stack in front of her. Big and fluffy with a dab of butter melting over the top.

"Go ahead. This is second breakfast for me," Brian said, or encouraged, or ordered. It was hard to tell. The man spoke with such authority, she was compelled to listen and wanted to follow his instructions. He was like a lifeguard even without water around.

"She likes 'em, Uncle Brian."

"I think you're right, baby girl. Her eyes just rolled back in her head for a second."

Lindsey completely understood why Lauren had spoken with her mouth full. The pancakes were wonderful and she wanted to let Alicia know as soon as they touched her taste buds. And the coffee was simple and excellent. She'd thought she was spoiled with Jeremy's one-cup flavored machine or the corner coffee shop at work. But there was something about the rustic flavor of black coffee that went with the pancakes and pure maple syrup.

"These really are great, Alicia. Thanks for going to the trouble." Lindsey stuffed another big bite between her lips. Totally in heaven.

"All I did was flip 'em. That paramedic sitting beside you learned some secret ingredient and won't give it up." Alicia pointed the spatula toward Brian. "He mixed up the batter and cooked breakfast before he caught some shut-eye."

If the screen door hadn't shut behind two men and startled her into silence, Lindsey probably would have blurted her astonishment at how kind this man had been to her. The men were close in size to Brian, but one was on a cane.

The other, once he removed his hat and wasn't back-lit, she could tell was John, Brian's duplicate. "Woman of the house, two starving men need some lunch."

Alicia set the pancakes on the table in front of Brian. "As if one of them in the room wasn't enough."

"I was thinking that exact same thing." Lindsey watched John kiss and twirl his bride right back to the sink. The older man joined them at the table and a cup of coffee appeared at his fingertips. He had to be their father—they looked just like him. All three men took turns adding the same dollop of milk to their cups.

"Lindsey Cook, that jerk pawing my sister-in-law is my younger brother and this old man is my dad." Brian patted his dad's shoulder.

"Younger by twenty-three minutes but older by necessity, Scarface," John said.

"Let me see these stitches." His dad pulled Brian's face closer. "Alicia, I think you need to take a look at this mess."

"I'm done, Mommy," Lauren informed everyone, dropping her fork on an empty plate.

Alicia and John whispered softly behind her.

You're the only one left. You're the only one left.

The family voices teasing each other in playful exchanges swirled in her head. As everyone grew closer to the table the walls began closing in behind them. *Someone tried to kill me last night*. The pancakes turned to cardboard. She couldn't untangle what happened around her; it all mixed together just like when they brought Jeremy's body to shore. She could hear them, but she couldn't actually hear anything except a buzz in her ears.

"Lindsey, you okay?"

She whipped around and had to think twice about who had a hand on her shoulder. *Brian...murder you*. "I need out of here."

She shook off the help, the questioning concerns and just ran. The screen slammed behind her as she got her bearings and headed down the gravel drive. The second slam of the door let her know that someone was following her, but she didn't stop. She had to get free of everything.

Jeremy, his life, his dreams... If she disappeared, whoever was after her couldn't kill her. She could go back to her life on the beach, not worrying about responsibility.

"Lindsey! Where are you going?" Brian shouted.

"I can't stay here." She turned to face him but kept walking backward. Her shoes would be ruined from the gravel but she didn't care. She wouldn't need them on the Gulf beaches. Or maybe she'd try her hand up the East Coast. Get a job on a yacht or something. She had experience and knew some people.

"You can't walk back to Fort Worth, especially in those things."

"I'll call a cab."

He laughed. "Sweetheart, Aubrey doesn't have any cabs. Let's go back to the house."

"I can take care of myself. I don't know why I tracked you down last night." She must have been out of her mind. "And how do those people know who I am? Not one of them was curious about a strange woman in your bed. Do you pull this *danger* routine regularly?"

"For the record, the only female who's ever slept in my room happens to be five years old. Lauren took it over and I sleep on the couch when I'm home. That was Dad's room and I didn't know you'd get so upset—"

"I'm not upset. Why would I be upset? You claim someone's trying to kill me. What's to get upset about?"

"You're right. It's more like you're hysterical. I know a lot's happened to you since yesterday—"

He dashed forward and grabbed her arm before she could turn and run.

"Let me go." She twisted, flaying her arms.

"Ow, damn, that was my ear." His arms wrapped tighter, bringing her closer to his chest. "I'll let you go when you calm down."

Upset or desperate, she didn't know which, she just knew she needed to get free. She kept twisting. His arms tightened their hold. Soon her cheek was flattened against his cotton T-shirt. Grass and sunshine. His scent from working that morning should have put her off, but instead it attracted her like crazy. She tipped her head back, taking a long look.

He seemed relaxed. His jaw wasn't clenched, just sprinkled with a five-o'clock shadow. His chest expanded with normal breaths, as though the effort of chasing her hadn't been an effort at all. And he had the kindest brown eyes. Eyes that were easy to get lost in and forget exactly why she wanted him to release her. Eyes that cut through to her soul.

This man wouldn't have brought her to his family if he'd intended to harm her. Brian Sloane wasn't responsible for Jeremy's death or the car accident. He was helping her find the man trying to kill her. It was just that simple. Her overactive imagination screamed to a halt. Even if her racing attraction didn't.

Chapter 7

If Brian didn't watch himself, he would be kissing the blonde in his arms and damn the consequences. Once he did, there'd be no turning back. He'd fall. Fast and hard and completely. Alicia waved from the kitchen door, verifying everything was all right. Last thing he needed was another lecture about getting involved with Lindsey Cook.

"Let. Me. Go."

"God…bless America. I'm too dang tired for this." He released his grip and the woman he'd like to devour fell into the tall Johnson grass between the fence and gravel.

Sitting on her backside, she drew her knees to the breasts that had so recently pressed against him. The urge to swing her back into his arms, jump in the truck and drive away from the pressures of job, ranch and family was right there. Obtainable, just a few steps away.

He couldn't leave. He was stuck here. His hands were hot resting on his thighs, itching to soothe Lindsey's back. It was the weirdest feeling ever, knowing so much about a person you didn't know at all.

"We're just trying to help." He finally forced words out. They weren't the words he wanted to say to her. Nothing close.

"I know. I'm..." she said with her forehead resting on her kneecaps. "I'm sorry about the meltdown. I don't know what's happening to me."

"I'd normally say it doesn't matter, but I think it does." His ear was still ringing from the accidental slap he'd received on the side of his head. "What happened back there? Are you afraid of us?"

"No," she emphatically replied. "You wouldn't have brought me to your family if you intended to hurt me. And you aren't responsible for the accident last night or Jeremy's death. But the talking...the closeness of the kitchen...so many people. It just sort of all caved in on me and didn't make sense. I couldn't think or catch my breath."

He knelt beside her. "Are you thinking now? Breathing now?"

She looked at him, defiance and determination turning her eyes a deep, rich blue. The leaves from the oak trees lining their drive created a soft pattern of light and dark across her blond hair.

The sutures itched from the sweat popping out on his forehead. Desire pounded through his blood. The swiftness knocked the air from his lungs. He felt sucker-punched crazy. "What the hell's the matter with me?"

"What? I don't understand." The confusion brought her delicate eyebrows together.

"Nothing." He stood and extended a hand to help her to her feet, this time dreading the touch of her silky skin against his rough palms. He'd never given a second thought about blue eyes or corn-silk hair. Never. Thirty years old and he'd never had a notion to take a woman on a third date, let alone home to his family.

He could answer his own question, knowing what was the matter, even if he never admitted it to himself or to John. Especially John. The infatuated fool would be in hog heaven knowing he was riding the same lovesick bronco.

He released her hand as soon as she was on her feet. "You okay now? I don't have to worry about you trying to walk home, do I?"

"No. Not in these shoes. But for the record, you'll never catch me in a pair of those." She pointed to his scuffed-up, broken-in boots.

"Great. Let's go to the barn for some privacy." He shoved his hands into his pockets to keep from guiding her with a touch. He couldn't risk it, not until he got himself under control. "We're going to sit and talk like we should have last night at the Pan-Hop."

She walked next to him, silent, watching the ground.

"Do you have panic attacks often?"

Her head snapped around, her face full of question. "Never."

"You've had two in twelve hours." He propped the door open for ventilation. He was already hotter than blazes.

"How do you know they're panic attacks?"

"First off, I've seen a few professionally. And you have plenty of logical reasons to be upset."

"Is there any way to make them go away?" She sat on a bale of hay, legs and arms crossed.

He shook his head. "But you'll be okay. Promise." Stupid promise that he had no way of knowing how to keep.

"Why are you doing this, Brian?"

"You know why. I need to find out who framed my brother and me for murder."

"I get that part. I meant, why bring me here and involve your family? Why were none of them surprised I was here? And why do I get the feeling they aren't too happy about me showing up?"

He picked up and straightened tack someone had left on the rail. Delaying, but knowing he had to admit everything. She needed to know what was driving him and he needed to tell her.

"Finding information about your family has been a Sloane project for a couple of months now. I tried to tell you yesterday how we pieced everything together. And I guess they aren't too happy about more trouble on their doorstep."

"Because of Lauren's kidnapping and the court case deciding the future of her trust fund?" Lindsey scooted back and leaned on the post behind her, smiling. "I have a smartphone, too."

"Yeah, things are kind of up in the air about that. Any calls to the police or trouble around here, well, it might cause a judge to look unfavorably on my brother. He's trying to adopt Lauren."

"They want you on your best behavior and yet you contacted me anyway." Her lips tilted upward. "So you *have* been following me."

"Yes."

Lindsey's reaction wasn't what he expected. She tilted her head back, looked into the rafters and let out a long breath. The action eased his guilty conscience, but did nothing to ease his attraction. With her body arched backward, her breasts thrust upward. She did a little kick thingy with her feet slightly off the ground, and then she laughed.

Hoover Dam! He searched the barn entrance for work. Tack, salt, saddle, something heavy to lift and force his body into submission. Fifty-pound feed bags were ready to put in the storeroom. He hefted one on his shoulder and dragged another with his free hand.

There was something between him and Lindsey Cook. Somehow, he knew it would be very good if he just gave it some time. That possible relationship—if he understood the use of that word—would go nowhere fast if he gave in to desire and crushed her body to his. What he wanted versus what he needed were fighting a battle, and he really didn't know which would win.

"Can I help?" Their hands collided on the edge of a feed bag.

"No." He hefted the bag to his shoulder and forced another under his arm. Work. Good, honest sweat would keep him on track. Head down, one foot in front of the other. Nothing to watch except his boots. "You should head back to the house."

"Not so fast, mister. I want some answers."

"I have work to do before I take you back to your rental." He stacked the feed and turned for the last bags.

"You agreed to tell me everything." She placed a searing hand on his chest.

"That's not a good idea right now." He looked at her

hand, but it didn't move. Such a small thing that had him stuck in his tracks.

"We aren't leaving until you start spilling what you know."

"Drop it." He meant her hand. He'd tell her what he'd discovered. He just needed sleep and some space between them. Preferably an entire room, maybe filled with his family.

"I will not."

She pushed at his chest a little, nothing he couldn't have withstood, just enough to get closer and make him need to back up. But soon there was nothing behind him other than a stack of horse feed. She kept pushing and he sat, the bag he was carrying falling to his side. He went from looking at the part in her silky hair to staring up at her heaving breasts in a blouse that had no business in a barn.

Especially *his* barn.

"Okay, okay. You win." He threw his hands in the air, closing his eyes to block the view. Praying she'd back away with his surrender.

Silence blasted through him. The point of entry was her hand. No longer just a finger forcing his retreat. Her palm had weight behind it. He could hear her breathing hard, smell the maple-coffee scent of her warm puffs across his cheek. If he opened his eyes, he'd see her closer than she'd been since he'd carried her to bed this morning... *If* he did that, there'd be no stopping his body from doing exactly what it wanted.

"Open your eyes," she whispered.

"Not a good idea." His body was about to betray his resolve and if she took a closer look...

"But you need to see this thing." Her breathy whisper was having an irrational affect on his senses.

"I don't think so."

No way they were talking about the same *thing*. But when she shook his shoulder, he opened one lid and then the other. Her look of iceberg fright was the complete opposite of his volcanic heat. He tilted his head, but his hat got in the way.

"Don't move. It'll get you."

By the look on her face it had to be a barn critter. "Is it a snake or a mouse?"

"Just be still and maybe it will slither away."

"Sometimes those things hang in the rafters until a mouse creeps by. You don't have to be afraid of—"

Lindsey's hand cut him off. Her stare moved behind his right shoulder and her body slowly inched on top of his. Within seconds she'd shifted and pulled herself onto his lap, and the simple rat snake disappeared under something in the corner.

"You can stand up now." And she should hurry up before he forgot what he wasn't doing in this small space with a gorgeous woman on his lap.

"But it's…"

"Hell's bells." He scooped her into his arms and marched into the sun before setting her on the ground.

When he let go, her arms were still locked around his neck and his arms steadied her at a tiny waist. Satiny red shirt to sweaty T-shirt. Slacks to jeans. Designer belt to rodeo buckle. City high heels stood on top of his country Western boots.

Lindsey was completely aware of standing on Brian's toes and pressing against every part of him. She didn't want to move. Safe from the snake and other horrible four-legged crawly things, she kept her arms where they were for a much simpler reason.

She liked Brian's hands where they were. Maybe it was the whole knight-in-shining-armor thing—even though she hadn't seen him near a white horse. But if her lips began moving, she'd babble nonsense and he'd never kiss her.

And, man alive, she wanted to know how he kissed. Bad, bad, bad idea.

Either way, she couldn't get higher or closer to him. He'd have to bring his chiseled chin down on his own. The smolder in his eyes she'd seen earlier when she'd run down the driveway returned and she knew what was next. His head tilted to his right ever so slightly, he bent his neck and then...

Tsunami tidal wave.

Brian Sloane was a skilled kisser. He had controlling firm lips, just the right amount of curiosity mixed with pure desire. He applied the right amount of pressure on her back to tow her tighter against him without trapping her. She parted her lips and encouraged more exploration, doing a bit on her own.

He wrapped his arms tighter and raised her to his height. Her fingers had been itching to play with that hair growing at the back of his neck. His cowboy hat toppled to the ground.

Go for it. Encouraged by her body, she shifted and wrapped her legs securely around Brian's waist. He did some shifting of his own, including a move with his hands cupping her bottom.

"Uncle Brian?"

Lindsey's feet hit the hard dirt faster than she could

blink her eyes open. Lauren stood holding Brian's hat, smiling and looking as though she knew something they didn't.

"Whatcha need, baby girl?"

Even though her heart was surfing faster than she'd ever surfed before, the little girl's cute giggle brought another type of smile to Lindsey's lips.

"Pawpaw said to give you back your hat 'cause... 'cause your head was getting too hot."

"Thanks." He kissed his niece's cheek, shoved his hat on his head. "Now skedaddle back to your pawpaw."

Brian grabbed Lindsey's hand, forcing the rest of her to follow him back into the darkness of the barn, shutting the door behind them.

Desire skirted her like champagne bubbles popping up the side of a glass. More kisses? No. They couldn't. Brian dropped her hand and headed straight to the pile of leather, turned his back and untangled more rope.

"I think it was a very wise decision for your dad to send Lauren outside. Don't you? I mean, your family's here and I've got a nut job trying to kill me."

"You're right. We're too different for this to work out."

"Oh, I wouldn't say that. My old self would be all over you for a beach romance." But they weren't at the beach. They were on a ranch. And someone wanted her dead.

"Old self? Beach romance?" He quirked one of those wing-tipped eyebrows.

He didn't need any more information about her. She was the one in the dark when it came to him and his reasons for helping her. She shimmied onto the bale of hay, just so no little creatures would crawl across her shoes. "Forget about me. Spill it. Where do we start looking for this monster who's been killing my family?"

"I've explained before that I'm a paramedic, not a bodyguard. Do I really have to tell you how I am not trained or skilled enough to investigate twenty-year-old murders?"

"You keep denying you're capable of looking for this guy. Yet you've discovered more than anyone else. I knew about my immediate family, but twenty years...? I don't understand how he hasn't been caught." She brushed aside a piece of hay that poked her backside and pulled her legs back tightly against her chest, keeping them far from the barn floor. "And by the way, I can hold my own."

"Right. That's why your feet have barely touched the ground since we've been inside." He waved toward her sitting position.

"Don't deviate from the question."

"Deviate? Son of a biscuit eater." He yanked a bridle or something to the dirt and the rest tumbled after. The tall man shifted his hat, blocking his eyes from her view. He wasn't pleased. He mumbled a couple more disguised expletives, scooped up the tangled mess and started over.

"I can explain something I bet you don't even know."

"Is that right?" He looped a rope, finally free from the rest, into a coil and hung it on a post.

"I know all those 'sons of biscuit eaters' and 'Hoover Dams' are your attempt at not cursing in front of a five-year-old."

He acknowledged her with a *hmph* and a finger pushing the brim of his hat a little higher on his forehead.

"And I know why you brought me here."

"Why's that?" He looped a second rope over one palm, making it all nice and tidy.

"You hoped that if I met your family, I'd trust you and your information."

"Or it could have been I was tired, my head hurt and you were asleep in my truck."

"I don't think so. You wanted me to trust you and I think it worked." She could see the truth of her words reflected in his eyes. He had a hard glare when he was hiding emotion, but it was very easy to spot if you knew the signs. And she did.

"Got me all figured out?"

"You think you know me because you've done all that research and followed me around." She searched the shadows along the wall to verify they weren't moving, then she stood and leaped to the door. "There are so many things in my life that can't possibly appear on paper, Mr. Sloane. Aren't you just a wee bit curious?"

She backed out of the barn door, almost tripping on the way. She turned and squinted into the bright sunshine, raised her hand to shade her eyes and found herself face-to-chest with duplicate Brian.

"Back inside before they see you out here." John spun her around and through the door. "We've got a visitor taking a close look at the property from the south."

"Why were you watching the road? Did you think we were followed?" Brian asked, moving quickly. He pulled keys from his pocket and went to a newish-looking locked cabinet. "How many and where?"

"Old habits are hard to break." John shrugged. "Same van parked across from Mabel's place now was in town three hours ago when I went to get the buttermilk. Binoculars or a camera lens reflected in the sun while I was trying to get a better look from the stock tank."

"Someone want to fill me in?" she asked. "I'm completely lost even though I hear English being spoken."

Brian and John removed weapons from the cabinet. They were a wonder to watch as they moved as one, without instructions, each anticipating where the other was reaching. They handed each other ammo and they both pocketed it, but left the guns empty.

"Whoever's after you found you." Brian connected a scope to a rifle on the edge of a stall.

"That's plain enough. What do I do?" Surprisingly, her voice hadn't quivered like her insides currently were.

"Sit tight," John and Brian answered together.

She swallowed the panic. Now that Brian had put a name to the overwhelming apprehension, it made it a little easier to handle.

"Just wait. Let us take a look," John continued as Brian slung the rifle across his back and climbed the ladder to the loft.

The horses, silent before except for a few shakes and tail flicks, whinnied or neighed—whatever the noise was that sounded so nervous. She could feel it, too. The tension from the two brothers radiated off them like sun reflecting on the white sand.

"I was hoping to avoid this for a while when I mustered out," John said, pushing the gun in the waistband of his jeans. "But someone insisted on sticking their nose into places—"

"Give it a rest, bro."

"See anything?" It wasn't the time for a sibling squabble. She didn't have a brother or sister, but she recognized the signs of an *I told you so* starting a fight. She'd had them often enough with Jeremy.

Now that her eyes had adjusted, she could see the tension in John's face and body movements. He was worried. His wife and daughter, along with his and Brian's father, were inside the house. All at risk because of her.

"I didn't mean to put your family in danger." She hoped she spoke softly enough that Brian couldn't hear her from the rafters.

John had been watching his brother but looked at her, quirking that identical brow in the same way that she adored on her cowboy knight. It didn't work. No magic tingling shot up her spine.

"But Brian did put them in danger, whether he meant to or not," he answered in a strong voice. Brian apparently overheard and responded with another *hmph*.

"Was that the reason you were upset this morning? I get it. Brian went against you guys and you think he chose me over his family."

"Are you through summarizing things you know nothing about?" He shook his head and looked away like she was entirely off base. Gone was the feeling of playfulness she'd had with Brian. With John, his intimidating looks made her feel inferior.

"Sorry."

For all the ways these two men were exactly the same on the outside, they couldn't be more different at their cores. Where John came across as commanding, Brian seemed helpful. Navy versus paramedic? Had their careers changed their basic personalities so much?

"You're part right, part wrong. It's more complicated than a two-minute conversation." John clapped a strong hand on her shoulder. "I'd feel better if you were in the tack room."

He'd pointed to the tiny closet with the snake. "There? No way."

He mumbled real curse words and stomped to the bottom of the ladder. "Got anything?"

"Plate's blocked. One guy. Camera. Don't see a gun." Brian stuck his head over the edge. "Lindsey confused me with a reporter yesterday. Any chance this could be one?"

"Give me your shirt and hat. Then you can find out." John loaded his handgun while Brian practically jumped from the loft.

Both men tugged their T-shirts over their heads. John's sunglasses slipped to the ground, Brian picked them up. Identical muscles rippled as they pulled the borrowed shirt over their heads, changing identities. Brian tucked his in like John had looked before undressing. His brother left his out, hiding the weapon at his waist.

An untrained man shouldn't confront a potential killer. "You can't send him out there. Aren't you the Navy SEAL?"

"Was. Now I'm a rancher, just like him." He jerked his thumb toward Brian.

"I can handle myself."

"You keep saying you're just a paramedic," she argued. Brian handed his brother his hat and she saw the teasing smile. "What's so funny?"

"Nothing. I'm just glad you finally believe me. Don't worry. I'll be fine."

"I don't believe you're doing this. Why not call the police?" Lindsey wanted to kick off her shoes in spite of the creepy crawlies and run with him.

"John." Brian ripped the white bandage off his forehead and stuck out his hand. "Keys?"

The twin now dressed like Brian dangled his car keys above his brother's palm. "Don't do anything stupid like follow him and wreck my car."

"Alicia's car."

"Community property state." John flipped the handgun, handle to Brian. "Be careful."

Brian checked the weapon, nodded and stuck it in his waistband.

"Will someone tell me why we don't call the police and report a trespasser?" If something happened to Brian, it would be her fault for convincing him to help her. "I get the feeling this is more complicated than Lauren's adoption."

"That's a long story, Lindsey. John can explain while I'm gone. Don't forget…he may look like me, but John's a married man." He kissed her lips in a brief flyby and headed out the door.

She stared after him in a stupor, not really knowing how to feel. She'd been so confident she was breaking through that tough exterior just a few moments ago. And their kiss—whew. The heat of it still had her insides all gooey.

Chapter 8

"Come on, Lindsey." John spoke in a calm voice, but those tense lines were still straining his good looks. "Let's take a look out in the paddock and give our paparazzi a show. Remember to stay between me and the house. If he does have a gun, he'll never get a clean shot."

"What? Do you think he's going to shoot at us?"

"I don't think that's his M.O. From what I've seen, he seems like a guy who likes to plan things with a little more control of the outcome."

The roar of a muscle car coming to life and driving too fast up the gravel made John cringe and shake his head. He seemed so much older than his brother. Older and more experienced.

The duplicate of the hand she loved curved around her waist, touched her back and guided her around the metal fence. John was just as handsome as his brother but strangely, she felt nothing. No pings or tingles of excitement. Only frightened worry about Brian.

The Sloane house was far enough off the road, you could barely hear a car drive by. Even a muscle car with a muffler as load as Manhattan.

Screeching tires. Then a shove to her knees kept her from turning to see the cars on the road.

"Damn it, Brian. I told you not to go after him," John shouted, slapping his thigh as he stood straight.

"I take it he didn't listen to you?"

"Never does." He stepped a little farther away from her now that he wasn't playing Brian for the man in the van. "Let's head inside."

"Aren't you going after him?"

"In what? Brian's truck? That thing belonged to our granddad. There's no way I'd ever catch them."

"Then you should call the police."

"Yeah, about that. The police won't be stopping Brian Slone, they'll be stopping John Sloane, who will probably say I'm running off more reporters."

"You'll explain that in a slightly less cryptic way once we're inside?" She was totally lost. They had a problem with reporters, too? The questions about why the police wouldn't help spun her around harder than a wipeout in Malibu.

"Sure."

They sat at the table again and Alicia joined them. The plastic wrap was removed from Lindsey's pancakes and they were popped in the old microwave, which took up a third of the kitchen counter.

"Mrs. Cook was the coolest teacher in school," John began. "She let our class hang out on her property. We had plenty of fires there in a pit her husband had used at one time. Nothing ever happened until the night she died."

Alicia laced her fingers through her husband's. "My guy here," she patted his hand, "was about to leave for the Navy and we were arguing about what would happen. He was upset, fought with Brian and they both stormed off. They didn't speak for twelve years."

"Back then we shared the truck and always left the keys in it. I needed some time so I spent the night alone. Brian came back to the Cooks' place in the morning. But witnesses saw our truck leaving the actual fire."

"It wasn't stolen?" she asked. "And neither of you left in it?"

"That's right. For twelve years I thought Brian drove it home and he thought it was me. You see, it was our responsibility to put the fire out that night. It spread to the barn where they found Mrs. Cook—"

"My second cousin."

"Everyone thought she tried to put the fire out and the barn collapsed on her. She had massive head injuries." Alicia continued the story. "Brian took the blame for the accident. He didn't want anything to stop John from getting into the Navy."

"He said he did it, even though he thought you were responsible for it spreading?" This morning, the brothers had moved together as though they'd never been apart. What must it have been like back then when they hadn't been separated for twelve years? "Wait, that still doesn't explain why the police won't help him."

"This town blamed Brian for Mrs. Cook's death and treated him like a convicted felon even though it was ruled an accident," Alicia explained, while John's knuckles turned white in a death grip. "He lost a full scholarship to college and each time something goes wrong in town, the cops blame him."

"Like for Lauren's kidnapping? I did some research of my own."

"They arrested him, then tried to beat a confession out of him before he made it to the jail." John's look turned to steel. He might say he was a rancher, but the man in that chair was every inch a Navy SEAL. "He still hasn't told me how many times it happened over the years."

"Too many," Alicia whispered.

"But he's a paramedic, he helps save lives."

"No one knew that except Alicia and Dad. Everyone else thought he was a drug dealer."

"You aren't serious?" She couldn't believe it. That shy cowboy/paramedic? "How could anyone get that impression from that teasing smile of his? I've known one or two— Sorry, but he's definitely not into drugs."

"We know that, but he never cared what the town thought and wouldn't let us set them straight," Alicia said.

"Why does he want to find the murderer so badly?" A shiver shot up her spine. "It's still hard for me to believe someone really wants me to die."

"He's been obsessed with clearing our name since we cleared the air."

Alicia jabbed his shoulder. "Since I threatened you both if you didn't speak to each other."

"I was wondering why he'd go to all the trouble to help me, especially after the police didn't give his theory any merit." She toed off her shoes, dreading having to walk on gravel in them again. "So what now? Will he come back soon?"

"Those shoes are a disaster waiting to happen," Brian said behind her, then pulled the door open. "I go chasing bad guys and you can't keep a sharp eye on things? I've been standing out there for five minutes. Some Navy SEAL."

"Give me some credit. I heard the car pull in. Maybe you needed to hear how ridiculous it is for you to continue this investigation."

"I caught up with the photographer in the van. He said he got a tip there might be a story. He snapped a few pictures." He looked at his brother. "You know what that means."

"What does it mean?" Lindsey asked, looking around the room.

"We should go." Brian latched on to her upper arm.

"Don't be silly," Alicia said. "The way the sheriff watches the ranch, this is probably the safest place for you both."

"Yeah, it's better if you take off before more show up. Or someone we don't spot gets too close." John was really talking about the murderer.

"I can't believe you're agreeing with him, John." Alicia was clearly upset.

"It's okay, everybody. I need to head to work at three." She gently removed her arm from Brian's grip.

"You aren't going to work. Too much exposure. My family's at risk now and I'm sticking to you until we figure this thing out."

"But I—"

It was useless to defend her point of view. He'd made up his mind, and left the room.

"John, you can't let him just take off," Alicia pleaded with her husband.

Lindsey could see that they needed privacy. There wasn't much space to give them in the tiny house, but she went into the living room.

An older man raised a finger to his lips. Lauren was asleep on his lap.

"I'm JW and you must be Lindsey. You'll be safe with him," he said in a low voice. "He's got reason to be broody, but don't let him be. I think you'll be good for him."

"I beg your pardon?"

He grinned. It was a window to the future on how his two sons would look at his age. Still handsome and charming. "I'm the one who sent Lauren out earlier."

The heat of embarrassment spread up the back of her neck. First, Brian's father had seen that hot kiss, and second, he already had them as a couple. "It was just the intensity of the moment."

"You might call me a dirty old man for spying on you. But I'm not and wasn't. I just happened to look. And you two were kissing where anyone could see. Including the man in the van." He lifted his chin toward the hall bedrooms. "He knows that. The man who's after you. He'll assume you're with Brian now."

"So I really have put everyone in danger. I'm so sorry."

"Not your fault, Lindsey. That madman started the feud with my family twelve years ago. I just wish I was strong enough to come with you."

Brian filled one doorway with a bag over his shoulder. John filled the other with Alicia ducking under his arm and snuggling against his side.

"We'll keep looking into the records, trying to make sense of the deaths," JW said.

"Ready?" Brian asked.

"You should get a cheap phone. Same as during the kidnapping, we talk through Mabel. Don't underestimate this guy. He's got a lot of practice and he's patient."

JW moved Lauren to the couch and stood. The little girl was in a deep sleep. Brian hugged his dad with one arm, very manly, then bent to kiss his niece, very sweetly. Alicia hugged him and opened her arms, hugging Lindsey before she could react. John just tapped her shoulder, pressed his lips into a straight line and nodded.

"Got plenty of ammo? Any idea where you're headed?" John asked. "Never mind, we don't need to know."

"You take care of each other. And don't forget to eat. I think we forgot to eat for three days. Hiding out isn't easy, but sometimes it's necessary." Alicia looked up at her husband, who winked.

"You'd better take the car," John mumbled, but his reluctance was evident.

If she wasn't mistaken, there was a story behind that car. She envied the family dynamic between these people. Their courage through Lauren's kidnapping was unmistakable. There might be strain between the brothers, but they were trying to make it work.

"It'll be at the airport when we pick up a rental," Brian said, making an executive decision.

"I should call Beth and let her know I won't be at work." Alicia handed her a cell and she dialed.

"Keep your head down, boy-o."

"You don't have to tell me twice, sir."

Brian gathered a few things while she lied and left Beth a message that she wasn't feeling well.

No one followed them out. She slipped her feet into the heels, following Brian to the trunk of the cherry-red

Camaro. He threw his bag inside along with the rifle she'd seen him with earlier. She watched him retrieve her purse from his truck. He gallantly opened the muscle car door to let her in.

"You okay?" he asked, tossing his hat in the back.

She wasn't sure she could answer him clearly.

"Are you certain about leaving with me? I'm far from certain you're doing the right thing. In fact, I'm not sure I understand what it is we're actually doing."

He kissed her over the window. Crisp, clean, on the lips as if he'd been doing it for years. And she kissed him back the same way. Wanting more, knowing there would be more.

"Are you going to tell me what we're doing?"

"We're going to catch this son of a bitch."

Chapter 9

Entering his office, he turned on the recorder before he talked himself out of documenting his mistake the night before with the car and again when Lindsey had run to Brian for help. He'd already gone through the pros and cons of admitting he'd underestimated his opponent. And now he had a new one—Brian. It seemed the twin cowboys were slightly more complex than he'd given them credit for.

"What made you expose yourself to— Strike that. Expose is the wrong word. I became too inquisitive and forgot the key to my success—patience. The real question is how Brian Sloane could make me forget my protocol."

That answer needed pondering. The leather of the couch creaked under him as he stretched out.

"Side note. Brian Sloane is certainly good-looking. Many would say he's handsome, especially in his work jeans and T-shirt, but he would never succumb to my... indulgences. He'd never beg for his life. Perhaps that's why he's higher on my radar than Lindsey."

He sat straight, realizing he'd recorded the wild, uncontrolled side of his personality. The half he rewarded, not the disciplined planner he wanted the world to have firsthand knowledge about. He could rerecord that particular segment—just run it backward and tape over it again. It was almost cheating.

"And I hate cheaters."

The selected words he left here were for history. He didn't need to *cheat* by deleting the tape. Just clarify.

"That's what's so frustratingly brilliant about the Sloane brothers. Facing two of them is almost like they're cheating. I watched Brian while he was with my next victim. He's very attached to her. Even through the camera I could see his attachment growing."

He smiled at his play on words. Then eyed his decanter, longing for the sharp sting of the liquor washing down his throat.

"Brian's feelings for the Cook girl will eventually work against him." The vodka decanter caught his eye again and he swung his legs off the couch, sitting closer to the clear ambrosia.

"When John turned from their drive, I knew he would pursue me. Very predictable, since I would have done the same thing. And that's what I'll enjoy most about this last campaign. Those brothers will force me to be more creative in my thinking. I must also be careful and not misjudge them again. This game is different. They think they know something about me."

He picked up the vodka decanter and tipped two fingers' worth into his glass.

"They think I'm patient and predictable, waiting for an opportunity to strike. No one understands me, nor will they. The best time for me to strike is soon and unexpectedly. Catch her off guard and blame the Sloanes, just like I did twelve years ago."

He turned the recorder off, then swirled his drink and saluted the hidden microphone in the ceiling. Knowing he had to finish his reward sooner than he'd wanted.

"They'll never see me coming."

Chapter 10

Brian drove the speed limit, not taking any chances about being pulled over. This wasn't the time to push his luck with law enforcement. His one saving grace through the past eight years had been his boss at the ambulance company. He'd looked at him as a person and given him a chance when no one else would after a background check.

Playing the part of a supposed criminal had been rebellious for a while, but when he needed money to supplement the ranch, there'd been nowhere to go. An EMT course at a junior college and the trust of one man willing to hire him showed him a different path. He'd advanced as a paramedic in Fort Worth but had never cleared up that bad-boy image his hometown had accepted.

"I really hope you know what you're doing," Lindsey

mumbled again. She'd been doubting him from the moment he'd pulled out of his drive and stated they were headed to her house.

It was clear as a hot summer's day that he didn't know what he was doing. When would she catch on? How was he supposed to find a man who had orchestrated fatal accidents for fourteen people and never been caught?

"You know, Lindsey, I'm a rancher or a paramedic, depending on what day you choose. I can track a bobcat or keep you alive with a rig full of equipment. But keeping you safe from a murdering madman? I think that needs some special training."

"As in police?"

"You got it."

"Then why are we headed to Jeremy's?" she asked, maybe picking up on his hesitation to pull into the driveway. "What are you looking for?"

"We'll take a quick look at your cousin's papers and hopefully find a place for the police to begin an investigation. If the cops have evidence, they'll have to get involved and offer you protection."

"Are you certain you want to go back there?"

He shook his head. "We need your cousin's papers and you need clothes. And sensible shoes."

"I have hiking boots and running shoes."

"Get them." He backed into the driveway. "Can I park in the garage?"

"Sure, the opener's in my purse. Give me just a sec."

What was he doing? Was she in danger here? Was he so desperate to find a clue that he hadn't thought about her safety? He was out of his depth and needed to convince her. He couldn't protect her. He shouldn't be trying to. He'd been forced to get Lindsey away from his family and that was as far as he'd thought about it.

What if the rat bastard chasing her took his vengeance out on Lauren? That couldn't happen. They'd been through enough with the little girl's kidnapping and Alicia's crazy stepfamily.

"Here it is." She pointed and clicked before he could say wait.

Garage was empty, not even a lawnmower. And there probably wasn't anyone in the house, but he needed to make certain.

"Why don't you get behind the wheel and I'll go inside to check things out. Alone. Just in case, be ready to get out of here in a hurry."

"Sorry to disappoint, but I'm not staying anywhere by myself. That'll be my scared-to-death hand hanging on to your back belt loop as you search the creepy dark rooms." She got out of the car. "My door is staying open for a fast getaway. You should leave yours open, too."

He began to shut the Camaro's door, but left it open after a cute, manicured finger pointed directions to do so. He'd laugh if she weren't so serious. Then again, being cautious couldn't hurt. He unlocked the trunk and retrieved his SIG. Gun in one hand and keys in the other, he unlocked the dead bolt.

A gentle tug on his pants assured him Lindsey was just behind, hanging on tight. He cracked the door open, listened, slid through the opening and flipped on the lights. Total silence in the house with the exception of the gurgling fish tank. They made a thorough search, room by room. They flattened curtains to the wall, opened closets filled with her cousin's things.

It was midafternoon. The curtains and blinds were

closed in the main bedroom, making the room darker, but nothing was blacked out. But even if it had been, he recognized the smell of death. In his line of work he experienced it often. The distinct smell of blood hit his nose as soon as he cracked open the door.

"Go wait in the kitchen."

"Why?" she whispered, death grip still on his jeans.

"I don't think you should see this."

"I stay with you. Period."

"Shut your eyes and cover your mouth. Whatever's in there...don't scream and have the whole neighborhood calling 911."

She did as he instructed. One glance at the body on the bed and he knew the person was dead. Between the smell and the amount of blood on the white sheets, there wasn't any doubt. It was recent; most of the blood hadn't dried.

Lindsey moved to his side, released his jeans, and he knew what was next. He wanted to scream along with her. Or shout and curse the animal who had done this. The sound began behind him, but he was able to shut it down by blocking her view and placing his hand over her open mouth.

The light from the master bath was a beacon in the dimness. He shoved Lindsey through the door and she immediately knelt by the toilet, heaving. He left her there.

There was even less afternoon light with the door pulled closed. He used the back of his hand to flip the light switch. Eight years as a paramedic and he'd never seen anything that turned his stomach. This did. He hadn't noticed it in the dim light, but now that his eyes were adjusting, the blood was everywhere.

Some of the blood spatters on the wall were dry. Could the murderer have done part of this after they'd left? Had he been here waiting for Lindsey to come home after the accident?

If he had dropped her off at the curb last night, that would have been Lindsey.

The woman was bound to the headboard, her blistered hands limp. It looked as if she'd been forced to hold a searing iron. Brutally tortured. There were dozens of slashes and burns on her body. She'd been in a lot of pain for hours.

Checking for a pulse would be useless, but the paramedic in him had to be certain. There was no way to get near the body without stepping in her blood. He reached the head of the bed and raised the blood-soaked throw pillow by its corner.

The fright in the woman's eyes—he'd never seen anything like it. Patches of her face had been skinned. He couldn't imagine what type of psycho would do something like this. He touched her carotid artery.

Dead, but not yet cold.

The victim had pale blond hair, sky-blue eyes—she could easily have been mistaken for Lindsey. But the man chasing the last of the Cook family knew her. Had studied her. Wouldn't make the mistake of killing someone in error.

No, he'd done this deliberately to make it look like Lindsey was dead.

"Oh. My. God. Oh, my God." Lindsey stood in the bath doorway. "Brian, how could anyone do this? She doesn't have— There's nothing left— Didn't anyone hear her scream? Didn't she scream? There's so much blood. How could someone do this to another human being?"

Dropping the pillow, he leaped away from the bed, spinning Lindsey away from the horrific scene and slamming the thin door behind him. Lindsey's breathing became erratic. She shook, her hands flailing and hitting his shoulders.

"Look at *me,* Lindsey. You are not having an attack. Not now. Do you hear me? We don't have time for you to fall apart. Get control. You're hyperventilating and we need to slow your breathing."

Her panicked eyes locked with his as he slipped his hand over her mouth, allowing her to draw air through his fingers. He slowly laced his fingers of his free hand with hers while her breathing slowed. He needed her to hold it together.

"You okay?" he whispered, swallowing down the bile gathering in his throat and wanting to forget everything he'd seen in the bedroom. "Do you know her?"

She shook her head, eyes still wide with disbelief.

"You said you had a pair of hiking boots?"

She nodded.

"Grab 'em, along with some jeans, T-shirts, a coat. Anything you might need. You aren't coming back here."

She drew a deep breath. "We should— What about the police? We can't just leave without—"

"Yes, we can. I've been picked up too many times over the past twelve years. They're going to lock me up *now* and clear me *later.*" He looked at the blood he'd tracked onto the tile. "If I'm lucky."

"That's ridiculous. We can prove you had nothing to

do with her death. The…the photographer. He knows you were at the ranch this morning."

"I didn't get the guy's name. There's a bunch of circumstantial evidence pointing toward me." He'd researched her family, tailed her, confronted her at the sandwich shop. Then the accident and witnesses who saw them leaving the hospital together. "Damn, how could I be so stupid? The man trying to kill you is smart. He's been following you, yet you haven't seen him. Hell, *I* followed you and didn't see him."

"What are you talking about?"

"The van. Seeing the van parked so obviously on the road directly in front of the barn. He wanted us to see him, to feel threatened and leave the ranch. That was his plan. This girl hasn't been dead long. It's a setup to get me out of his hair. While I'm in jail, he'll eliminate the last Cook."

Lindsey's face went pale under her golden tan. "That's despicable. I can't imagine anyone going to that much trouble to kill someone. You can't know that for certain."

"Right or wrong, we don't have much time." He gently walked her back a couple of steps to crack the door open behind him. "I have a feeling the killer will phone in an anonymous tip, bringing the police here shortly."

"That's ridiculous. I've been with you the whole time. Or your family was right there."

"And during the time you're proving all that, who's going to be protecting you?"

"The police, for one."

"They won't. You'll be alone. Vulnerable to attack."

"What if I'm with someone? You can take me to Beth's house or Craig's. I can hide there with his wife."

She shoved her hair back from her face. "No, that would put his family at risk and Beth lives alone. They'd all be in danger."

"That's why we leave. Together."

"All right. But I'm not going back into that room to get my stuff."

"I'll take care of it. Did Jeremy have a laptop?"

"It's in his study, mine's in the living room."

"I'll get you a couple of days of clothes. Where's a suitcase?"

"In the hall closet. Brian..." Her soft touch down his bare arm stopped him. "I'm sorry for getting you involved."

He pulled her to his chest, speaking into her hair. "You aren't to blame. The psychopath targeting your family is the only person responsible."

"But what about your job, your family? I can disappear and not worry about this guy again." She tilted her head back. Her soft blue eyes were filled with fright and questions. "You don't have to do this."

The idea of her walking out of his life forever made his brain scream no. If she really wanted to leave, he'd go with her. But would this guy walk away, too?

"Whoever's trying to kill you has been at this for almost twenty years. Do you think he'll give up? Ever? After seeing what he did in that room, I don't think he's going to stop with you. He likes it." Saying the words left a disgusting taste in his mouth, but he knew they were true. "We have to stop this guy."

"You're right." She dropped her forehead against his chest again.

Keeping his arm around her, he placed a towel across the counter, very aware of every minute they delayed.

"Put what you need on the towel. And grab stuff for a first-aid kit."

She slipped from his arm and was done in seconds.

"Trust me, Lindsey." She nodded and he placed a second towel loosely around her face to block the view and smell, then walked her back to the living room. "Did your cousin have any legal papers? Anything that might help us figure out what this guy is after?"

"I'll find them."

"We're out of here in five. If—"

"No ifs. I'll get everything from his office and be ready."

He left her and went back to the murdered woman, hating to disturb the scene even more, but he had to. He couldn't wipe this place clean just in case the killer had left evidence. But the police would find out who Brian was fast enough. His prints were in the system, not only because of his job. The police in Aubrey had booked him when he'd confessed the night of Gillian Cook's death.

He typed a detailed text to his brother and took a minute waiting for the reply, deleting the phone history afterward. Then he composed a message to an officer he knew in Fort Worth and left it on the screen, leaving his phone on the dresser in plain sight. He hoped the cops would find the man in the message and he'd give a word in Brian's favor.

The phone was useless since the GPS could ping their location as soon as he turned it on. His brother knew where to meet him. That message would be retrieved, but the police would be delayed ordering the phone records. He didn't need much time at the apartment. A couple of hours of rest and a plan. That was all.

They wouldn't be able to show their faces in public, so he grabbed the things on top of the towel and shoved clothes from her dresser inside the carry-on and turned off the lights.

Lindsey was scrubbing her hands at the kitchen sink, a laptop bag next to her feet. There was something wrong with her actions. The rubbing got faster, almost frantic. She was in shock.

Lindsey was certain blood was on her hands. How it got there, she didn't know. She hadn't touched the dead woman, but it was there. The afternoon sun was bright coming through the kitchen window, and her hands were covered in soap as she used the scrubber to claw at her fingers. But she could feel the cold blood sticking to her skin.

Brian's warm exhale skimmed her neck, and his fingers wrapped around hers under the scalding water before he reached around her and cut the faucet off. "It's okay, Lindsey. We should leave now."

He put the strap of the bag over his shoulder and nudged her toward the garage door.

"Wait. We'll need food." She pulled cans and frozen dinners and health bars and dropped them into grocery sacks.

"We should go—"

"Stop. We need this." She dropped everything that wouldn't spoil into a sack.

Brian backed away and carried the bags to the back of the car without another word of protest. There was a small ice chest in the bottom of the pantry and she dumped ice inside for the milk and orange juice along with the six-pack of beer and bottle of wine that had sat in the back of the fridge since Jeremy's death. The freezer door shut and she was eye to eye with a picture of her and her cousin. She jerked it from under the magnet and shoved it in her bra.

Brian lifted the cooler and guided her to the car.

"Wait! There's bottled water still here from Jeremy's funeral. It's behind the door."

"I'll get it."

Lindsey buckled up and looked at the picture of her cousin. The weight of the water being added to the trunk shifted the car a little, but all she could do was stare at Jeremy's image. *Now what?*

"One more thing." Brian sat in the driver's seat. "Take the battery out of your phone and put it in the glove box."

She did as he asked. "How are we supposed to run from a man capable of the butchery inside the house?"

"First thing we're going to do is head to my place and get some sleep."

"Sleep? There's no way. How can we go back to the ranch?"

"I share an apartment in Fort Worth with several of the other paramedics. They switched us to twelve hours on and twelve off, so my partner, me and four others from the firehouse went in on a place to sleep—and only sleep. It's cheap and my name's not on the lease. My partner's taking the day off since I'm on mandatory leave and it's the beginning of the others' shifts. We'll have the place to ourselves."

"You've got this all figured out, then."

"Hardly."

"Wait!" She stopped his hand before turning the ignition. "Jeremy had a fire safe for important papers in his bedroom."

"Stay put and I'll get it."

Lindsey tried to wait once Brian was back inside the house. She hadn't told him the safe was on the shelf and hadn't given him the combination.

He could find it. She could handle five minutes by herself.

Five minutes crept by. Then six. She entered the kitchen, expecting him to laugh at her silliness.

The house was empty. Still...it felt as if the walls were shaking. Impossible. It must be her insides.

Brian had been right. Now that she knew about the panic attacks, she could recognize the signs and try to prevent them. She peeked around the door. A creepy feeling hit her, like watching a scary movie where you knew someone was about to die. Creepier still...the shaking couldn't be her imagination. Impossible. It must be her insides. She took a deep, deep breath and let it out slowly.

No shaking. No panic.

Entering the hallway, she ran her fingers along the wall to guide her. Something hit the other side...in her bedroom. "Brian?"

"Lindsey! Run!"

Chapter 11

The body slams, crashes and sounds of a fight grew louder as Lindsey ran straight to Brian's voice. The dresser overturned, the mirror smashed in front of her at the door. She flipped the lights on. Glass and small objects had been knocked from the dresser and mixed with the blood on the bed.

Worrying about the dead woman's body struck her as a bit bizarre. She watched a man dressed in a black jumpsuit wait for Brian's attack near the closet. Brian swung, connected with the man's ribs, spinning him sideways. But the man in black countered by slamming the back of Brian's thigh, forcing his knee to the carpet.

Then the man in black lifted something shiny from the floor.

"He has a knife!"

"Get out of here, Lindsey!" Brian shouted between defensive grunts. "Now!"

Trying to help Brian didn't make a lot of sense. She should run, but couldn't. If no one heard the woman scream, they wouldn't hear her either. He needed professional help—the police. Her phone was in the car. Frightened for them both, she released her grip on the door frame and turned. The bedsprings creaked and time slowed.

It was as though each second was recorded in her mind with an exclamation point. The creak made her look behind her.

The man leaped across the bed, stepping on the poor woman's legs. His arm stretched toward her.

Two more steps and her body lurched in reverse, back into the bedroom. He jerked her hair, yanking while she screamed. She lost her footing, slamming to the floor. He was over her, the knife raised.

Even his eyes were distorted with thick, shaded glasses. The knife descended, she threw her hand up to deflect. Pain. Her own hiss and scream blocked out all the other sound. Where was Brian?

A deep shout, more of rage than warning, and the man in black disappeared from her view.

She rolled to her stomach and blinked away the automatic wetness in her eyes. The knife shot against the door, bouncing past her into the hall. The man kicked the side of Brian's knee sending him to the floor. He jumped over her, scooped up his knife and ran.

"You okay?" Brian asked, pursuing him through the door.

"Catch him," she gritted through her teeth.

Brian's running steps vibrated the wood floor where she rested her cheek and sucked a few painful breaths through her teeth. She crawled to her feet, staggered to the hall bath, got a hand towel for her arm and locked the door.

If Brian didn't return… *He will.*

The door shook with the pounding. "Lindsey!"

She trembled so badly it was hard to turn the knob to let him inside. Should she? Was he alone? Was there a knife to his throat forcing him to call out to her?

"He's gone, honey. I saw him drive away. You all right?"

"I'm… I'm fine." She twisted the knob and lurched backward as Brian stumbled into her. She tried to get past him. "Let's get out of here."

"That bastard cut you?"

"Let's look at it later." She turned her injured arm away from him, trying to shove the rock in front of her aside. "Did he hurt you?"

Brian used his calming gaze and gently prodded her to the sink. Looking into his face and feeling his soothing touch made her think everything would be okay.

"You're going to need sutures. I'll get the wound cleaned a bit, then get you to an E.R." He turned the water on, ready to clean her cut. "This is going to hurt."

"Later." She jerked her arm to her side, blood oozing from the gash. He reached for her arm again and she turned from him, reapplying the towel. She moved away from his comforting arms. "No doctors. Please, just get me out of here."

"We do this now, Lindsey, or I drive you straight to the hospital."

Didn't he know he was covered in blood? Was it his or the dead woman's? She was beginning to gag at the thought.

"Please take that shirt off. Jeremy's clothes are still in his room. I'll rinse my arm while you get rid of it."

From the corner of her eye she watched him in the mirror as he shoved away from the counter and jerked the T-shirt over his head. "I need to take care of this now."

She closed her eyes. "Please change."

She heard the running stride of his boots, then they disappeared on carpet.

Before she lost her courage, she quickly forced her arm under the running water, gritting her teeth in agony as the sink turned red below her. Queasy and surprised she hadn't pulled out all her hair, she got a clean towel and put it on her arm.

Brian reappeared in a tight-fitting T-shirt Jeremy had worn all the time. "Got first-aid tape?"

"Maybe in the cabinet behind me."

He looked at the wound, pulled the sides together and replaced the towel. "The closest hospital is on I-20. I can get us there in eight or nine minutes. They'll take good care of you."

"I'm staying with you."

"That gash is deep enough to need sutures," he said as he dropped the tape on the counter.

"You did your own."

"But—"

"You said this killer won't stop until I'm dead. All the reasons we weren't going to the police still apply." She tapped her finger against his chest. She knew he agreed with her when his brows drew into as straight a line as his lips. "I'm sticking with you until we catch this son of a bitch."

Chapter 12

"Choose a bed, Goldilocks." Brian set her suitcase down next to the bathroom and tugged her cousin's shirt over his head.

Wicked-tight jeans drew her attention to his bare lower back and then up to his sculpted shoulder blades. He put water on to boil. She was either completely woozy from the cut and car ride or the attraction was growing so strong she couldn't stop thinking of running her fingers over his strong shoulders again.

Then he faced her and she noticed the tint of his skin was pink from the blood-soaked shirt he'd left at Jeremy's.

"I'll get my sewing kit." His long stride took him into the bedroom faster than she had time to react.

She knew what the water and kit were for. Cleaning her arm and his scrapes. There would be no complaints

from her. Complaints would land her dropped off at an
emergency room. The last thing she wanted was to be
separated from this man she'd come to trust so quickly.

Convincing the authorities she was in danger would
be very difficult without evidence. This murderer
couldn't be infallible. Somewhere, at some time, he had
to have made a mistake. And she was going to find it.

"You weren't kidding about beds and nothing else,"
she said, loud enough he could hear her in the bedroom.
With a stiff upper lip, she peeled off the packing tape
Brian had used to hold the towel in place. She tried not
to dislodge the towel, afraid it would start bleeding. If
it hadn't stopped, Brian swore they'd be on their way
to the hospital.

"Kick your high heels off and get comfy," he said
from behind the closed door.

The place was tiny but open. There was a futon on
one wall folded as a couch, with the sheets folded on
the end. She sat facing the television, leaning back to
get rid of the wooziness in her stomach.

"This place is surprisingly clean. Are you sure it's
six men sharing? I expected a lot worse."

"Yeah. Six males, but I'll admit that one of the guys
pays Debbi—she lives down the hall—to pick up, do
the dishes and the laundry."

"Now the cleanliness makes sense." She had the tape
off by the time Brian returned without the pink-stained
chest.

"I pick up after myself," he said, swiping his chest
dry. "I do let her wash my towels and sheets since we
all share them."

She closed her eyes, unable to watch as he peeled back

the makeshift bandage. He wore gloves, and had gauze pads ready to replace the dish towel on her forearm.

"You ready?" he asked with a steady voice.

She nodded, her mouth suddenly dry, silently praying it wasn't as deep as he'd thought. But behind her closed lids, she fell onto a carpeted hallway, a man with bottle glasses and a large knife headed for her. She jumped when Brian touched her arm.

"You drifted a minute. I'm ready to give this a shot. Are you certain?"

"It was just the gloves. They reminded me of the attack."

Brian's finger touched her chin, coaxing her to look into his rich brown eyes. "This is really going to hurt, Lindsey."

"Is this normal practice for paramedics? To scare their patients before beginning?" His eyes soothed her as much as the gentle touch he had through his gloved fingers. "Did you learn how to stitch people up in paramedic school?"

"Taught myself for the horses. Cheaper than a vet coming out when one of 'em got sliced." He went into the kitchen.

"You mean—"

"Drink this." He set a tea glass full of her favorite deep, dark merlot onto the side table.

"If I consume all that on an empty, woozy stomach, I'll be drunk. I may even throw up."

"Something important for me to remember—the lady can't hold her liquor." He sat on a chair he'd brought from the card table in the kitchen. "I'm serious. I need you relaxed. I can't deaden it and it'll hurt worse if you're jerking your arm."

When he picked up the needle and wet thread, she picked up the wine, squeezed her eyes shut and guzzled. She concentrated on a picture of his jeans and tapered waist. The muscles in his back. The picture of him was so vibrant there was actually a catch in her breathing.

"Don't worry. I know what I'm doing," he soothed.

Her imagination didn't prepare her for the level of pain that a tiny needle created when punched under her skin. But his voice assured her through everything he did, every step of the way, no surprises. Once he was done, she saw six neat stitches before he covered her entire upper arm with a bandage.

"Think you have enough tape?" she asked remembering some of the images she'd concentrated on of him in those tight-fitting jeans. She'd drunk the wine much too fast and was definitely tipsy.

"If you won't let me take you to the hospital for antibiotics or… Yeah, you're keeping the bandage. First sign of infection and there won't be any talking me out of a real doctor. Got it?"

"I agree. No arguing." She carefully formed her words so they wouldn't slur. "Thanks for doing…well, for everything, Brian."

She'd been a flirt since the second grade and Ronnie Willhite had told her she was pretty and wanted to kiss her. She wanted to crawl onto Brian's lap, wrap her arms around his neck and kiss him until his vision was as blurred as hers. But she slumped back against the cushion instead.

One short nod and he put away his equipment. "Showers and then some shut-eye, unless you feel like eating."

The thought of food made her head swim. "I don't

know how you expect to sleep while that murdering serial killer is still out there."

"I plan on relaxing and closing my eyes."

"But—" He handed her a second glass of wine.

"I can't drink that. The room's already spinning."

"Good. You need some shut-eye." He set the glass
on the table next to her.

When he smiled, she wanted to forget everything except the kiss they'd shared that morning. She wanted to
be back in front of the barn with her legs wrapped tight
around his waist. Or maybe sitting on his lap again,
even with a snake slithering in the corner. It beat having a serial killer slither free outside their door.

"We can't stay here. It can't possibly be safe."

"We weren't followed, and a former Navy SEAL
and former Marine will be outside watching the place
very shortly."

"You forgot to explain."

"I sent a message to my brother. He got in touch with
one of his buddies. We'll get some rest, and as soon as
the cops show up at the ranch, he'll take the Camaro
home, leaving us Mabel's sedan. For the moment, we're
safe enough for you to get some rest. You're going to
need it."

She lifted the glass and he clanked it, following a
salute with his beer bottle. He walked to the window
covered in thick black curtains, lifting the edge to take
a look at the street below.

"A Marine and a SEAL?"

"That's right. John's calling a buddy. One'll be out
front and the other 'round back. That should make you
feel safer than a police squad car. Mac's already here."
He disappeared into the bedroom, continuing his expla-

nation. "He'll have a phone for us. If you want on the Net, codes are taped to the side of the TV. Bolt this thing behind me. Or you could fall asleep. I've got a key."

He ran out the door, pulling a T-shirt on, hiding the handgun stuffed in his pants, and she was alone. She should be upset that he'd made the arrangements without telling her. Or maybe she wasn't because she was relaxed enough not to care. Either way, she would not be falling asleep anytime soon.

Not even with guards to protect her and being slightly drunk. But she could begin searching Jeremy's laptop and powered it up. Most everything she did on the internet for the past four months had been on her phone. She'd lost most of her web clients after her cousin's death because she'd been dealing with his affairs and getting into the habit of working somewhere every day again.

Now she was glad she hadn't given away any of her cousin's things. Even his clothes hung in his closet. It was time to give it all to charity. The idea of being so alone no one else would want anything you left behind made her so sad. But there wasn't anyone left.

She was alone.

All because of a horrible man targeting their entire family. "Why? Why us?" The laptop didn't power up correctly. It was trying to open nonexistent files on a memory stick Jeremy had left plugged in. She removed it and dropped it back in the bag. When everything was booted and signed on, she skimmed one file, then another. Brian walked in, moved the merlot closer to her fingertips and she sipped.

"Should I tell someone I won't be coming into work tomorrow?" She sipped again, the merlot warming her shakes away. "Beth will probably stop by Jeremy's after work tonight to see if I'm okay."

"They might get a call before they close. Homicide arrived at your house shortly after we left."

"How would they know where I work?"

"Paystubs? Did you ever sell a phone to a neighbor? Anybody around there know where you work?" He walked to the window again.

"Oh, I guess they do. It's more likely that they remember Jeremy managed that store."

"That's good." Then back to the kitchen, where he put some of the food she'd taken from the house into the refrigerator.

"Oh, my gosh. You want the police to think that dead woman is me?"

"For a couple of days. Long enough to find out why this guy wants you dead. He's obsessed with your family. There has to be a reason."

She set the laptop on the futon and quickly stood. She probably would have fallen straight off her high heels she'd been wearing all day. She was shaky even on bare feet. "Brian, did that woman look a lot like me?"

He encircled her within his arms and she knew the answer before he said, "Yes."

"That's the reason he did those things to her face?"

He nodded, holding her tighter. "He also burned her fingerprints away."

"That's horrible. She died because of me. How can I live with that? No one else can die, Brian." Her fingers curled into a ball around his shirt. "Who's to say my life was worth more than hers?"

"Me, for one. Not more, but just as important. And

I think your cousin would want you to live." He kissed her forehead, keeping her safe in his embrace.

"You don't know me." She tilted her face to look at him.

"Then that's something we'll have to change."

Brian delivered a trail of hot kisses down the side of her face. His short, practical fingernails gently gathered her hair as his lips continued a path back up to her forehead. Lindsey turned her mouth into his path, and the fireworks were as explosive as the kiss earlier that morning.

Their tongues danced and explored. His fingers barely grazed her waist and then she felt a tug on both sides of her shirt. Brian backed away, leaving her lips cold and desperate for more of him.

"As much as I'd like to keep on with this—" he dropped another kiss on her cheek "—I'm dead on my feet and heading to bed." He stood and stretched his arms high, raising his shirt to expose an inch of his flat belly. "And no, that's not an invitation, unless you want to curl up in my arms. Our first time is not going to be when we could be interrupted at any moment by my brother."

She stood there with her mouth open at the audacity of his words. *Our first time?* If she didn't agree with him, she'd be insulted at his assumption. But she was super attracted to him and wanted to explore more of those abs she'd caught a glimpse of.

There was something about the way he took everything in stride. She'd seen the horror on his face at finding the dead woman. He couldn't hide it as much as he tried. But he didn't allow it to override his ability to think on his feet and come up with a safe place for them to go.

"A Marine and a SEAL. Sounds like the title of a book."

Books!

Jeremy had been reading a book in Cozumel. She opened the link to his electronic library. There were lots of mysteries, thrillers and action books. Then she found the one that had stuck out—*Texas Real Estate and Land Titles*. Why would her cousin be reading this heavy material on vacation? It had to be connected.

But how? She reached for another sip of merlot and realized the glass was empty. She should get some water before she was seriously tipsy. The apartment spun as she stood to fill her glass. She barely made it back to the futon and definitely couldn't do anything with the clean sheets. She'd laugh and giggle but was too busy yawning.

Laptop closed, sheets used as a pillow, she curled on the mattress with her back secure against the cushion. She drifted off thinking of how well Brian's hands fit around her bottom.

If they'd only met before all this...

Somebody had tied one on before coming to the apartment to sleep. Brian banged on the wall between his bed and the front room. "Come on, guys. I'll remember this the next time I come in and you're getting some shut-eye."

A few seconds was all it took to remember he was here only with Lindsey. The thrashing continued. SIG palmed, he was barefoot and shirtless at the door to the other room. He stuck his head around the frame, staying low like his brother had reminded him.

A nightmare. Lindsey was alone and fighting only someone in her dream. The loose sheets were in knots at her feet. Her red silk shirt was tangled high under her breasts, showing him a flat, tanned stomach. He returned his weapon under his mattress and noted that he'd been asleep a couple of hours.

Lifting his blue-eyed dream into his arms, he cradled her, shushing her nightmare like he would have Lauren. He placed her in his bed, then gathered her stuff, bringing it all to his room and locking the door. If any of his roommates did venture past Mac in the hallway, they wouldn't barge into his room.

The vent blew right on his bed. That was the way he liked it. But Lindsey was already shivering. He pulled the covers around her and had every intention of being a gentleman. He'd stay on his side of the bed, not touching or exploring or…anything.

He did manage to lie on his back and not move. Completely prepared to hit the hay again. Yep, that was his intention. He could do it.

Right until Lindsey curled tighter, sidling up to him. He lifted his arm and she molded herself to his chest. Shifting to his side was more comfortable, then they were spooning. He couldn't very well keep his arm above his head and get any sleep. Was it his fault if it wrapped around her middle?

Sleeping—really sleeping—with a woman wasn't something he was used to, because he never did it. There was no reason to. He didn't bring women here and certainly didn't bring them home to the room next to his father's.

Sleeping at the moment wasn't happening either. He was too aware of the soft breasts pressing on his arm.

Enjoying the rise and fall of her chest, the silkiness of her hair against his chest. Everything about her made him want her and yet made him want to wait until the time was perfect.

Finding a murder victim in your house—not to mention in your bed—was repulsive enough. Running from the murderer probably didn't make you very amorous either.

Yet, he was wide-awake and only thinking of making love to the woman in his arms. He should be thinking about a plan. Since he wasn't sleeping, he should go down and talk with his brother.

That was the last thing he wanted to do, but he eased away. By the time he sat on the second bed to pull on his boots, Lindsey was tossing as though she was in another bad dream.

Making sure Lindsey got some rest was as important as figuring out a plan of action. He didn't want her to fall apart or have more panic attacks. His boots were soundless falling back onto the carpet. He slipped in beside Lindsey before he could change his mind.

Resting on his elbow, he traced her troubled brows, smoothing them like his mother had after his nightmares. A rhythmic motion that he'd always thought hypnotic. Her jerking slowed, then stopped, and she relaxed into his side.

John had already outlined a plan and could tell him details later. Differences aside, he'd be the good, inexperienced brother and salute when told what to do in order to save Lindsey and his family.

It would be the only time John would get that level of cooperation from him. To keep the woman in his arms sleeping soundly, he slipped an arm under her head and the other around her tiny waist. Even with his eyes closed, he could see her sky-blue eyes sparkling like diamonds in the sunlight.

Diamonds in the sunlight? What the heck? He wasn't a poet and had never thought like this about any woman. Hell, he'd never thought like that before, period.

Chapter 13

"I'm in blessed shape and health for a man of my age. I will, however, admit that fighting a younger paramedic proved tiring."

The wall panel hiding his souvenirs and recording equipment slid open. He placed the bag with the clothes he'd worn during the fight with Brian Sloane along with the rest. All neatly labeled and vacuum sealed to preserve the DNA.

"I should remind curious minds that I have no desire to be blamed for crimes I did not commit, nor will I be denied the accomplishment of one either. It will be hard for authorities to believe my flawless record. I have kept the necessary proof of each and it is properly organized." He pushed the button, closing the panel behind his wall safe, then shut the doors to the actual safe and replaced the heavy books on the shelf, hiding the catch.

"What an exhilarating day. The police believe Lindsey has been killed, and now Sloane is wanted for her murder. Yes, quite an accomplishment. I will have to work late into the night making up for what landed on my desk today, but it is well worth the time I spent."

Time for his vodka. Then the work that paid his bills.

"Sloane acted exactly as predicted. Until the time that the police place him in jail, it will give me the necessary interval to plan the next stage of my Cook finale. I daresay I hate to postpone the preparations for the hunt." He toasted himself, letting the vodka heat his throat. "And the kill."

Chapter 14

"She doesn't deserve nightmares." Brian had tried to explain to his brother several times about his fascination with Lindsey. He barely understood it himself, so the words he'd stubbornly uttered over the past month sounded like a lovesick cow speaking a foreign language. Today was no different.

"I'm sure there are other people who can handle that problem." John pushed a piece of notebook paper across the card table. "My plan is the only way to be safe. I've written everything down for you. I'd like your word that you'll follow my instructions."

John, the man with all the answers, casually tipped his chair back against the wall and linked his fingers behind his head, waiting. Brian knew that look. He'd had one himself years ago when he was confident and certain his way was the only way. Before life got complicated with possibilities.

Walking away from the ranch or from years of paramedic training. Losing his heritage or starting a new life. His dad and John thought they knew his answer. Hell, he didn't even know his answer, so how could they? He reread the list.

Number one in big red caps: Brian surrenders to police. Two: Lindsey secretly travels to a friend's house—alone. He glanced through the ways to avoid getting noticed. And the last thing on his brother's instructions: let the police find the murderer.

"You want me to sit around and do nothing? Did that work for you?" With a flip of his wrist, Brian sent the list back across the table. "I've already given my word and I won't go back on it. You might as well understand that I'm not going to salute you like one of your soldiers. You can't order me to retreat into a jail cell and wait for this all to blow over."

The Naval Lieutenant inside his brother didn't get it. Brian wasn't leaving Lindsey's side. Not voluntarily. Not until she was safe and had choices for her safety.

John ignored the paper as it floated to the floor. "You can't be serious."

"As serious as you when you were wanted for murder a couple of months ago and kidnapped Lauren to keep her safe."

"That was different, Brian. You don't know the first thing about this woman."

"You didn't know Alicia after being gone for twelve years, yet you jumped in when she was in trouble." He scrubbed his face with his hands, trying to think, and ended up irritating the sutures on his forehead. His brother's look hadn't changed. If anything, he was more irritated with the mention of his wife. "Come on, John. I need you to back me up here."

"I've trained for rescue missions. We had a plan and were lucky it worked."

"You know your instructions are a death sentence for Lindsey. We have to find this guy. If we run now, he'll disappear again and kill her later."

"There's no choice here, bro. We can't do anything with your name and our mug shot on every television screen in the state."

"That didn't stop you from helping Alicia."

John stood, knocking his folding chair to the floor. "Damn it, why won't you listen to me? Every cop in Dallas–Fort Worth is out for your blood. The P.D.'s catching all sorts of flak for not taking her reported threat seriously."

"Good."

"Not good. They don't want explanations, they want your head on a media-frenzied platter. And she's not even dead."

Brian tapped the table, trying to think. He wanted to understand and accept his brother's advice. But shouldn't his brother understand why he wanted to help Lindsey? John hadn't ever been supportive of him finding the truth behind Mrs. Cook's death. Saying things like "what good would come of it" and that "they all knew the truth so why did finding whoever was responsible matter?"

Well, it mattered to Brian. He was the one who had been blamed for her death. Not John. Not his father. And not the murderer.

"Even if I did follow your suggestion, Lindsey won't leave town. Not without me."

"You don't know that. You haven't asked her." John stood at parade rest.

The way he thought he knew everything they should do now, and how they should act, ticked Brian off. It was his breaking point. He slapped the table, prepared to brawl to win this argument. "This dictator role you've taken on needs to stop. Just accept the fact that we're not running. It's done. Now, explain what you would be looking for on the laptop and we'll do it. Lindsey used to run a website company. I bet she could—"

"Finding hidden files has nothing to do with design. You're over your head trying to rescue your new girl-friend and can't see that you're both drowning." John kicked at the cheap chair. "I told Alicia you'd be an idiot about this."

He put a lid on the feeling of self-pity and screwed the lid on tight. He was the one who chose to take the blame for the accidental fire. Not John. Not anybody. If he'd trusted his brother back then, twelve silent years could have been avoided. He wasn't going to cause a rift between them again.

"Hey, stop shouting. I hear fine and Lindsey's still in there sleeping. I know we'll need to find a safe place to lay low until the police eliminate me as a suspect. What I don't know is why you're so reluctant to help."

"The news is reporting her murder and you're the primary suspect. Unless the police talk to her, know that she's alive, how are they going to eliminate you other than with a bullet between your eyes? They will find you, Brian. Then what?" John asked. Genuine concern or authority oozed out his military straightness.

He hadn't answered Brian's question of what was holding him back.

"It'll be okay. I have a solid alibi."

"That's right, he does," Lindsey said from the bedroom door behind him. "Don't you need to be at home talking with the cops, John? I mean, you're part of his alibi, too. Can't you tell them that poor woman isn't me?"

"Right. Like they'll believe me."

"You doing okay, Lindsey?" Brian watched his brother's spine straighten even more with Lindsey's presence. She looked as if she'd been dragged through the wringer. Her hair was prettily tangled from the tossing and turning she'd done even while she'd been safe in his arms. Her eyes were slightly puffy with smudges of mascara. He wondered if she'd taken a look in the mirror or avoided it, afraid of what she'd see.

"Just peachy." She grimaced as she folded her arms across her chest. "I found a memory stick last night. It might mean something."

Brian remained at the table, willing his brother to leave. He didn't want to argue any longer, just wrap his arms around Lindsey and maybe take off to hide in the mountains.

"What happened to your arm?" John asked. His brother was calm enough on the surface, but Brian could see his tolerance chipping away.

Right then, he didn't feel like the older, responsible twin at all. He tried to catch Lindsey's eye before she filled John in on the details he'd left out about their encounter with the murderer. Luck wasn't on his side.

"A maniac sliced it with a knife after he murdered

an innocent woman in Jeremy's house. A woman who looked just like me, apparently."

Apparently she didn't like him holding back information either. It was Brian's turn to stand suddenly and let his chair collapse with a clang to the floor. The noise didn't slow John or Lindsey's discussion.

"You heard the authorities think you're dead?" She nodded and John's eyes narrowed. "My brother neglected to mention you'd been wounded. Did you see a doctor?"

"It was a minor altercation." Brian tried to play it down. An identical set of jaws clenched, and fingers formed fists. Maybe they'd get that brawl in after all.

"Brian stitched it up last night." Lindsey lightly stroked the overkill bandage he'd wrapped over the sutures. "I will never doubt the power of a deadener again."

"Are you nuts, man? She needs a real doctor, a hospital, antibiotics."

Lindsey shook her head and compressed her gorgeous lips into a straight line. "Let's get past this, John. You've argued too long and need to admit that you've lost this battle. I'm following Brian's lead regarding this matter. If you can't help, then you should go."

As tall as his blonde beauty was, she still had to tilt her chin to meet his eyes. But there was nothing weak or confused about her glare at his brother. She wasn't bluffing. She'd made a decision and that was the end of the discussion.

John placed his chair back at the table and mumbled about stubborn women and idiot brothers as he sat. There was a new energy and assuredness to Lindsey's step as she crossed the room, scooped up John's list and opened her cousin's laptop. Brian watched, leaning on the kitchen wall, completely confused as to why he suddenly felt proud.

"How long before we need to leave?" Lindsey's nails gently clicked keys while she raised one blond brow in question.

"Soon," he said, along with his brother.

"Did either of you hear me when I said there was a memory stick with Jeremy's laptop? I should show you what I found last night before Brian got me drunk."

"Drunk?"

Brian pointed to his upper arm and mouthed *stitches* to his brother.

"I remembered something strange from my last trip with Jeremy." Lindsey ignored his brother. "I teased him because he was reading a Texas real estate manual, even highlighting passages. Who reads that sort of book *after* you buy a house? Anyway, it's still on here."

"It's a start. Is there any other file that might be unusual?" he asked, not needing his twin's challenging glare. He knew nothing about computers. He rode horses or in an ambulance. Neither allowed a lot of time for gaining computer skills.

"I'm not sure, but the drive indicates there's a lot of data there. I can't find a file list. It looks as though Jeremy just used a hidden file program. You can get them off the internet. The trick will be thinking of his password."

"I have friends who can take care of that." John had a shoulder against the wall, listening, a hand rubbing the stubble on his chin.

"I can figure it out. Jeremy was like my brother. I knew him pretty well."

Brian looked up to see the same "yeah, right" look on his brother's face. Lindsey harrumphed.

"The concept might be foreign to the two of you, but I did know Jeremy. Thanks for the offer, but these are my files now and I'm keeping them." She shook her head looking back at her keyboard. "The protection program he used was just a GUI."

"Did you say gooey?" John asked.

"Yes, a Graphical User Interface that's easy to install and use."

"I think Lindsey speaks your lingo, bro." Brian crossed his arms and leaned back in his chair, striking the same pose his brother had earlier.

"Can I see you for a moment?" John asked.

He stood, and the first thought that raced through his head was what would break when they came to blows in the bedroom. Nothing important or nothing at all. He'd successfully controlled his temper for twelve years. He even avoided the teens around Aubrey who didn't know why their parents were angry at him. They just liked to pit their fighting ability against the town's bad boy. John was the only person who got under his skin far enough to get a rise.

His brother turned, and they were face-to-face. Once again, it was like looking in a mirror. Gritted jaws. Clenched fists. Narrowed eyes. John moved and instinctively Brian brought up his hands to defend himself.

"Damn it, Brian. I don't want to fight you." John clapped a hand on his shoulder. "After I leave, I can't help you. You won't be able to come home. It'll be more than the local police camped out on our doorstep and it won't be safe."

Brian jerked away from his brother, feeling more

alone than he had in the twelve years they were apart. "Don't worry. I wouldn't put you guys in danger. I'll keep my distance and keep you out of this mess."

"You're taking this all wrong. I didn't mean it like that." John scrubbed his face, then his head, the worry apparent in his eyes. "I was thinking it might be easier if we switched. You stay at the ranch and I'll protect Lindsey."

"I thought that wasn't possible with my new scar?"

"Don't be too hasty and hear me out. I have special skills and training that might come in handy."

"I think I can hold my own. We're not much different."

"With most things, sure." Both of John's hands went to the top of Brian's shoulders. It was the closest they'd gotten to a brotherly hug since they'd graduated from high school. "You know this guy's not going to stop. What are you going to do when you find him?"

Be more prepared than the last time. His hand went to the gun at his waist.

"Are you prepared to pull that trigger and kill someone?"

"If it comes to that." He didn't have to debate it. The answer was clear in his head and heart. He'd defend Lindsey without question.

"You could both die." His brother sounded more like his father for a minute.

He understood wanting to protect his twin. It was exactly the reason he'd stepped forward and taken the blame all those years ago. "It means a lot that you want to take my place, but this is something I have to do."

His brother clapped him on the shoulder, squeezed his fingers. "I figured. I've seen the way you look at

her. I didn't think you'd do anything different, so I got
Mac to let you use his place for a few days so you could
lie low."

After the Sloane men headed to the bedroom, Lindsey had been tempted to follow them and eavesdrop at
the door. But only for a second. If the thin walls didn't
allow her to overhear an argument, just like it had earlier, she'd ask Brian what John had to say later.

The brothers were identical in so many ways, and
yet different in so many, too. John acted so confident,
but she had a sneaky suspicion he was just worried
about losing his brother. Brian had appeared so withdrawn at first. It was much easier to like him when he
was around his family. Whether he realized it or not, he
smiled more on the ranch. Maybe it was the youthful
playfulness even when he argued with his brother about
serious subjects. Or maybe he was just cute. Period.

Right now she needed to find a lead. Some tiny bit
of information to begin a search. There had to be something.

The slash on her arm ached. If she rubbed it or complained, Brian would insist she go to the hospital. He'd
be arrested and she'd have no one to help her find this
madman or a connection to her family. If the police
hadn't found a reason to investigate any of their deaths
before, why would they now?

"Lindsey have you seen my folder with your family information?" Brian began thumbing through Jeremy's papers.

"Hmm?"

"I had the folder last night at your place when you
noticed the fish food had moved," he said, looking at

her. "Then I— Son of a biscuit eater, I left it on the coffee table."

She went through the picture of her living room in her head. "It wasn't there this afternoon when we went through the house."

"He knows exactly what we know." John walked to the window, taking a quick look through the blinds.

"How can he use that against us?" she asked. "Isn't it more important to concentrate on why he's killing my family?"

"What if he doesn't need a reason and he's just a nut job? How are you going to stop him then?" John asked.

John was right. The murderer was patient and had outsmarted them twice already. All he had to do was wait until the police stopped investigating him. Then one day when she was alone, he'd resurface and finish the job, crossing her off whatever insane death list he had stuffed somewhere.

"You okay? You look woozy and didn't answer."

"Maybe she needs the hospital after all. Mac will take her."

"I'm fine, and I'll decide if I need to see a doctor." The nausea she felt had nothing to do with her arm. It was from being scared down to her bone marrow at the idea of being hunted for the rest of her life. Hunted and never knowing why.

"You sure you're okay?" Brian asked. "The police wanted a motive. If we find the reason why the murderer has a feud with your family, we'll find him."

John looked at his watch. "I need to hit the road and would feel better if you got going."

"He's right, Lindsey. We need to head out. Mac gave

us the keys to his place for a couple of days while we come up with a plan."

"There's got to be something to this book and memory stick. It's just going to take me time to piece it together." She shut the laptop, then held her hand out to John. "I'm so sorry I've brought more chaos into your family, but I'm so grateful I'm not facing it alone."

"It's more as though we brought a killer to your doorstep." John pulled her into a bear hug. "Don't let him do anything foolish," he whispered.

"I'll try not to."

John nodded toward his brother. They both paused, and he left.

"Are you absolutely certain that we're doing the right thing? Your brother seems very upset at the idea of us trying to catch the killer." She shoved the laptop in its case and slung the strap over her shoulder. "Shoot, I'm upset about finding a murderer."

"Sometimes he forgets who's saved his hide more than once. But if you have any doubts about my abilities—"

"No. It's nothing like that." Maybe she trusted too easily, but she did trust him. He'd put everything on the line for her, a virtual stranger.

With her bag of clothes over his shoulder, his hands warmed her inside and out when he slid them along her back to draw her closer. He smoothed her hair behind her ear and trailed his fingers across her now-flushed cheek.

"I'll do my best to keep this guy away from you, Lindsey. I promise."

"I believe you." She thought she spoke, maybe a broken, breathy sentence. But it didn't matter.

Brian tilted his head and leaned close. Her hand felt the wild cadence of his heart under the thin cotton of his T-shirt, along with the strong muscle tone. He oozed protection and sexiness. As his lips claimed hers, she remembered the feel of her legs wrapping around him, how he'd lifted her with ease and how she wanted to repeat the wild forgetfulness from earlier that morning.

Gentle, firm, in control. He was all those things. She wanted more, wanted to drop their bags, kick off their shoes and head back to his room. Who was she kidding? She wanted his arms tight around her and didn't care if they moved another inch.

His lips gently pulled away, replaced by his finger smoothing the fire-parched surface.

"It's a good thing my brother was in here for the past hour. Otherwise—" he touched his lips to her ear "—I might have kissed you when you woke up and taken you straight back to bed."

She gulped, wishing they'd met last week when she'd first noticed him in the coffee shop. She dragged her nail across his lips, avoiding his teeth when he tried to snag it. "That's pretty presumptuous, considering we just met yesterday and you haven't even bought me dinner yet."

"We'll get that taken care of as soon as the police aren't trying to arrest me for your murder."

"Absolutely, cowboy. It's a date."

Chapter 15

They were in another unremarkable four-door car that belonged to the woman across the street from Brian's family. The car couldn't be traced back to them, but she still turned her face away from drivers pulling along-side. Lindsey had picked up enough at the ranch to understand that JW Sloane was spending his nights at Mabel's and she was practically family.

It had been a long while since her family had consisted of more than Jeremy. And she was ashamed to admit that she'd put him off several times before begging him to come to Cozumel with her. He'd gotten his life together and she'd kept "bumming around," as he'd put it.

"You sounded pretty knowledgeable with all that computer lingo back there. I guess I should hire you to get a website together for the ranch."

"I let all that go when I moved here."

"Aren't you good at it?"

Brian's question seemed like ordinary conversation and probably was. She was half mad at herself for walking away from that dream. She'd been getting new sites and had loyal customers. It was hard to explain to an outsider that one of the last conversations she'd had with Jeremy was about keeping her word and responsibility.

"I hold my own."

"Then why'd you give it up to sell mobile phones?"

She'd promised Jeremy that Cozumel would be her last "fling." She hadn't meant it at the time, knowing full well that she'd talk him into another spur-of-the-moment vacation later. But when he'd died, it all rushed her as though she'd been hit by the lip of a wave and totally wiped out. She hadn't surfed since.

"Why are you riding around in an ambulance instead of on a horse?"

"Touché. So you know how to surf?"

"I practically lived on the water. I surfed every day I could." The rush and power of doing something well hit her as strong as the desire to run back to the ocean. Leave searching for the serial killer to someone else trained to find a sicko like that. Leave and disappear on the beaches with some waves and a good board.

"Wow. Not sure I'd like it out there with sharks under my toes."

"I loved it at the time."

"Is there any money in web design?" Brian drove, seeming as though nothing was wrong. Not as if they'd seen the killer or were running from the cops. He was so laid-back she could easily imagine him as a surfer. No bumps in a wave for him.

The conversation was such that two people might have on their first date. She knew so little about him other than he was a rancher who supplemented his income by working as a paramedic.

"I suppose there's money in it for those who try. I mainly did it for friends. I couldn't spend much time on it while at work. There wasn't good internet access at the beach huts."

He rubbed his forehead, scratching the stitches on his wrinkled, confused brow.

"Most of my jobs revolved around renting boogie boards to tourists. I'd follow the coast, working in different cities, crashing with different friends—or a friend of a friend. Sunup to sundown. Barefoot with sand between my toes. Spring break until it was too cold to open the rental huts. I made enough helping with websites to pay my share of the rent when the beaches were closed. That's all I cared about."

"You sound like you miss it."

"I shouldn't. There was no stability in that line of work. And I'd never get ahead, as Jeremy constantly reminded me. Wouldn't you know that as soon as I have my act together, a serial killer smashes my car trying to murder me." A cracked laugh escaped from high in her throat, making her sound a bit frazzled. Or a little loony.

Brian cleared his throat, creating a nervous silence that she didn't know how to get herself out of. There was nothing to comment on except the darkness. In the middle of nowhere, on the edge of civilization, but far enough away to remind her just how much light streetlamps provided. Brian slowed for a stop sign and her heart jumped into her throat.

It had only been twenty-four hours since her car had

been hit. There weren't any other headlights, but her hands gripped the edge of her seat, bracing herself. A warm hand covered hers. His strength shot a different type of adrenaline through her system.

"It's okay."

His deep baritone voice whispered a complex comfort in its simplicity. Something her body understood more than her mind. His callused fingertips rubbed her cold hand back to life. She no longer concentrated on the crash. The excitement of his kiss washed over her and she wanted to recapture all the exhilaration she'd felt moments before leaving his apartment.

The dashboard lights softened the sharp angles of his face and smile. He waggled his eyebrows before he looked both ways along the deserted road and stepped on the gas again. Bringing her hand to the side of his thigh, he laced his fingers through hers and held tight. So did she.

"Mac's place should be around one or two more curves," he said after a couple of minutes.

"Have you been there before?"

"I never heard of the guy until my brother texted me. I am, however, great with directions. I never got lost when I drove the ambulance."

It was on the tip of her tongue to ask if they should trust a man they didn't know, but it wasn't necessary. Mac had already proved his friendship to them both by guarding the door while they slept. She also wanted to avoid speaking of the reason they needed to hide. She was enjoying the silence and holding Brian's hand.

Two days ago, if Beth had told her those two things would be appealing, she would have fallen over laughing. Now having this man's thumb tenderly caress her hand was sweet and sexy at the same time.

The stress of the past day had kept her adrenaline at extreme levels. There was a strong desire to forget all of it for the rest of the night. Just being on an even, relaxed keel was appealing. But not as appealing as being safe enough to explore every inch of the man beside her.

The thought of how they could fill some downtime had her blood bubbling with excitement and tingling so much, her body shivered.

"I know you want to plan out our next move. So do I. Let's find Mac's place and then we can work our way through Jeremy's paperwork."

"Sure." She didn't want to think about papers or trails or clues. But most of all, she didn't want Brian to let go. And she didn't want to think about why.

How could she consider an interlude—to put it nicely—with a guy she just met yesterday?

Impossible. No way. That was the old Lindsey. The Lindsey who tossed her sleeping bag on a beach chair half the summer. She was responsible now and couldn't do things like that. She wouldn't sleep with Brian Sloane, no matter how much she wanted to. No matter how tempting or how safe she felt with the man trying to save her life. She would not break her promise to Jeremy.

"Here we go." Brian used both hands to turn the big car onto a dirt road overgrown with tree limbs in spite of the drought they'd seen all summer. "Mabel's going to have a cow if these sticks scratch her paint job."

"Uh-huh." She stuck her hands under her legs to keep them from wandering back to Brian's.

Less than a minute of driving and the tree limbs

stopped creeping near the car and then were gone. Camouflage for the Marine's home that was at the end of the short road. What had seemed like a dark trail actually opened onto a large open field surrounding the small house.

"You okay?"

"I'm fine, and you can stop asking me that."

He parked the car in back, off the driveway and close to the back door. He twisted in his seat, no longer looking casual, but very calculated as if he was thinking about how each word would sound before they crossed his lips. "If you're upset about what I said earlier, I can apologize."

"I don't need an apology." And hated that he thought she did. "I need something to let me know that I'll eventually wake up from this nightmare."

Just his luck. Hold a girl's hand and she calls it a nightmare.

Brian knew it wasn't him and could admit he had no business telling her earlier he'd rather take her to bed. Crass. Rude. Ungentlemanly. And a couple of other things if his daddy found out. Being nearly thirty years old wouldn't stop the old man from giving him a good earful on how to treat a lady.

"One day the nightmare will be over." He hoped. "Remember, we're going to catch—"

"This creep." She laughed, finishing his sentence. She dropped the partial braid she'd been nervously plaiting and slapped her jean-covered thighs. "I think that must be our mantra for this adventure."

"And a damn good one to remember until we do." Brian laughed. Easy, pleasant and infectious. "Adventure, huh? Ready to find out if Mac has running water and electricity?"

"Where are we?" she asked as they unloaded and unlocked the door.

"A little north of Fort Worth. Not too far out in the boonies."

"It feels like the boonies. I'm horrible at directions, but it doesn't seem possible that we're still near Fort Worth."

"We're not far. Straight highway and we can be back at your place in half an hour. Good, he has lights."

"You were just joking about the running water, right? I never did get that shower."

"Try that door." He pointed to one next to the small kitchen.

She cracked the door enough for him to see a sink, gave him a thumbs-up and disappeared behind the closed—and locked—door.

Mac's house was totally off anyone's radar if they were looking for someplace Lindsey would be hiding. She'd be safe here, which was Brian's primary objective. He heard the shower and a long, relieved sigh through the thin wall. He finished unloading the food from Mabel's car, breaking a sweat and making the skin under his bandage itch.

But that wasn't all that was itching. His skin was irritated by the T-shirt as he put away the last of the beer and wine. He was irritated at himself when he realized he was looking for an excuse to take it off. The idea of meeting Lindsey bare chested prompted him to open the new stainless-steel fridge and pop the top on a beer.

He took care of the basics, securing the doors and windows, getting the bed ready, putting a pillow and blanket on the leather couch. All the while having no trouble picturing Lindsey's sun-kissed skin lathered in soap. And no problem imagining the small bubbles being rinsed away. Or how he wished he was in that shower with her.

"Damn it. Get a grip."

The water stopped and he reached for another beer.

"You look as if you've gone for a run," she said, stepping from the bathroom in a short, skimpy T-shirt and shorts cut up to her hips. Her hair was wrapped inside a stark-white towel that made her skin all the more appealing.

He gulped down the cool liquid, swallowing the desire building low in his belly. Any sweat on his upper lip was purely from his heavy breathing, not any labor he'd done while she was cooling off.

She crossed the small area rug in her bare feet, making him glad he was still in his boots. Maybe checking the perimeter one more time was a good idea. It would get him out of the house and out of arm's reach.

"How do we start looking for someone we know nothing about?"

"We know something about him." He tipped the end of his second beer between his lips and crushed the empty can before setting it on the table. "He can't fight worth a Hoover Dam."

"Well, neither can I." Lindsey unwrapped the towel and shook her hair down her back, finger combing and fluffing the damp wheat-colored strands. She dropped the towel over the chair next to him. "Seriously, where do we start?"

He had himself under control. Right up to when she

batted those long lashes in his direction and those baby blues taunted him with their brilliance.

She took a step back and he caught her hand. With a little tug and footwork he remembered from the couple of times he'd danced in public, he had Lindsey securely wrapped in his arms. It might be very ungentlemanly, but he had every intention of kissing her until she admitted she wanted to see if the bed was as new as the kitchen appliances.

"How 'bout where we left off?" he whispered, almost afraid to ask. He had to ask, of course. Because as much as he wanted to show her she couldn't resist him, the decision had to be hers.

She didn't move, but she was far from frozen. With his free hand, he traced the outline of her mouth. She sighed as her lips parted and her eyes closed. Her head tilted to the perfect angle for him to enjoy his prize.

He expected something to happen. An interruption. Someone handing him his hat or waving from the porch. But no one was there. They were alone. Far from his family or danger. No one would be stopping them but them.

He hesitated too long and she opened her soft, sexually charged eyes. Then she followed the path his finger had taken and moistened her lips. He was a goner. Had been the moment he'd sat at that table and finally spoken to her at the sandwich shop. His dad had told him more than once that when he fell, it would be hard, and there'd be no coming back.

He leaned closer, breathing the same breath she didn't seem able to catch. His hand skimmed her silky skin and continued down her back. Her curves met his chest with little resistance, just as her lips crushed into his. She might not realize that he'd fallen and couldn't come back. It might not be the time to tell her, but it was definitely the time to show her.

If he did it well enough, maybe she'd fall just as hard.

Chapter 16

Staring at Brian's lips made Lindsey want to devour him like fresh water after hours in the surf. Tasting him? Wow. Just wow.

He sipped her like hot chocolate on the beach in front of a bonfire. She could hear the surf pounding between her ears, building. The crescendo had never felt so welcome or right.

Making love to Brian here, in a strange house owned by a man she'd never met, was a little more than crazy. But she kissed him back. Long and hard and enthusiastically.

They only made it a few steps away from the table. Her arms risked a journey to his back, pulling his work-hardened body closer. Anticipation pulsed through her with every gulping breath. She wanted to get the feel of cotton from under her fingers and leave nothing between them.

Kissing Brian took her to the top of the highest wave she'd ever ridden. She should rethink, slow them down. But just like being at the top of that magical crest, it was too late to turn back. The hard ridge against his zipper left no doubt where he thought they were headed.

He ran his tongue down her throat, nipping sensitive places along the way—places she had no idea existed. It was as if they'd never been discovered before. She clamped her eyes shut as all the blood rushed from her brain and her knees.

Lindsey hadn't thought about the way she'd dressed until Brian's hands slipped higher under her shirt, brushing skin and nothing else. Her hands rose and slowed his advancing fingers. When she'd left the shower, she hadn't allowed herself to imagine being this close to Brian. She'd been ready to get started on their manhunt, not curl up next to him. When she lifted the pressure from his hands he'd find out just how ready she'd become. But he knew that. She could see it in the smoldering embers of his eyes.

Lindsey tugged the soft, worn shirt over her head and her damp hair swished against her blistering skin. Her arms came down on top of his shoulders. Before she could discover the sinewy lines of his muscles, his mouth captured one nipple while his fingers circled the other.

The instant his callused palm brushed her, she wanted to scream for more. There was no way to stop the reaction building inside. She wanted to torture him by running her nails across his tanned muscles and teasing him into mindless oblivion.

Somewhere in her brain, some neurons fired a warning. Where they were exploring was dangerous waters. She'd never been the type to venture too deep without her surfboard. Even though she knew it could only end in disaster, she wanted him beyond reason.

A relationship with Brian would be like a tourist on a bodyboard preventing real surfers from enjoying the waves. Or worse, pearl diving off the front of her board on takeoff. Why would she set herself up for failure? She knew nothing about family, roots, ranches or animals. Her life had been waves, sand and sunsets.

Unfamiliar thoughts floated through her mind, mixing with the sexy essence of who Brian was. Someone she'd been attracted to from the first time she'd noticed him. It was one of the reasons she'd remembered him so clearly from the coffee shop. There was something familiar, something comfortable and something so sexy she couldn't think straight half the time she looked at him.

Her fingers reached for his belt buckle, big and all cowboyish. His mouth nipped her breast, causing a hitch in her breathing. She was used to drawstring swim trunks and baggy jeans, but she'd noticed Brian's tight jeans once or twice. Maybe three or four times if she was forced to admit the truth.

The way they hugged his thighs and backside. Just thinking about him made a shiver travel the length of her body. She had her fingers on his zipper when he twirled her around and wrapped his arms tight—one covered her breasts, the other kept her waist close to his rigid body.

"Are you sure you want to go there?" he whispered in her ear. His breath shot all sorts of tingles down her spine. "Once we reach the bedroom, I'm not sure I can turn back."

"Yes and yes again." The words were spoken without a thought to any of the concerns she'd had seconds ago. Her body was already humming for release. "Don't you want—"

"Definitely." His voice was deep, husky, sexy. He nipped on her neck to the soft flesh of her shoulder. The evidence of just how much he wanted to continue pressed against her as she squirmed in delight. His hands wandered over her aching flesh. "Walk."

"How can I when you're... Oh, my."

His fingertips dipped under the elastic of her shorts. Teasing her before pulling back. He swung her into his arms and carried her to the bedroom, dropping her on the bed.

"If we don't get naked fast, I'm going to make love to you with my boots on."

They laughed together, kissing and tugging at his clothes. He ripped his shirt off over his head, baring his strong shoulders, revealing a smattering of chest hair that made him even more sexy.

As much as she adored her cowboy/paramedic, she wanted to see all of him. She tugged at his jeans, lifting one leg into the air, reaching for his boot. He lost his balance and toppled next to her on the bed.

Brian smiled the most genuine grin she'd seen, lying nose to nose next to her. One of those moments she'd dreamed about imitating from a book or movie. A moment where grins and laughter turn into a monumental life-changing instant. Maybe the thought changed her expression, but in an instant, Brian's changed.

He reached out and cupped her cheek, turning to his

side, close enough and suddenly so serious she wanted to remember every detail. This time was different. She felt it. Knew it.

At this exact moment in time...this was exactly where she was supposed to be. With this man who looked at her as though she was the only woman who could ever make him smile like that.

Later, she may get mad at herself for being irresponsible. But she had such a strong desire to be the only woman who would be in this position with him again. And that scared the daylights out of her.

Brian watched the laughter leave Lindsey's beautiful face. He almost jumped off the bed to save her the embarrassing trouble of talking her way out of his arms and back into her clothes. Then her lips parted, waiting for his kiss.

There was no mistaking the longing. He felt it in the depths of his soul.

Playfulness was replaced with frenzied touching and heavy caresses. They rolled, scooted, shifted to the middle of the king-size bed. Overkill for the room, but he didn't care and wasn't analyzing why Mac didn't want more than a bed in the bedroom.

He cupped a set of perfect breasts, dragging his thumbs across each, causing the perfect rose-colored peaks to tease him more. Lindsey tugged at his belt, not realizing the tip of her tongue was squeezed between her lips and driving him insane. She unbuttoned the top of his fly and he couldn't resist. He devoured every inch of her skin, shoving the short shorts down her hips as he discovered all her contours and secrets. He still couldn't believe she was his.

For one night or a single moment.

"You still have your boots on." She sighed, arching her back as his hand continued exploring.

Fortunately, he could toe his boots off and did so without much difficulty. His jeans were a different story. He might get them off if he stood, but there was no way he'd stop the passion that was building inside of Lindsey. And then there was the problem of pre-paredness. He hadn't exactly been thinking of casual sex, since he'd spent all his free time following Lindsey during the past two months.

So his pants would stay zipped and they'd be safe. But there was no reason Lindsey couldn't have some fun. He could see her getting closer and closer to fulfillment. She tipped her head back, surrounded by a halo of hair. Her body arched into his hand and relaxed, finally opening the eyes he loved to look into.

"I don't think this is at all fair." She paused, gesturing to his jeans. "You still have clothes on."

"And they're staying there." No condom. No sex.

"What?" Realization washed over her face. "Oh. I saw..." She shivered under his hand again and drew in a deep breath. "He has them on his...in his bathroom."

"Lindsey, we can't do—"

She sprung from the bed. "Get out of those jeans. No socks either." She ran from the room.

He didn't waste any time. He stood, stripped his jeans, boxers and socks and by the time he'd stopped dancing on one foot, she was waltzing back into the room, tearing a small package.

One look at him and she stopped in her tracks, taking a long stare at his splendid physique. A lesser man might have been intimidated. Hell, he might have been if she'd stayed in the doorway too much longer. When she leaped on him, he fell backward onto a soft mattress and he stopped wondering about everything.

With a hand on either side of his shoulders, Lindsey lifted herself open for a fun attack. He dropped light kisses across her clavicle, finding her pulse strong and rapid at the base of her throat. He skimmed his chin stubble across her smooth flesh, causing her to sit up.

She lightly raked her nails from his shoulder to his hip. He sucked air through his teeth as she shifted on his lap and rolled the condom into place. Brian ran his hands around her thighs to her bottom. He pulled her hips closer, using himself to excite her until she dropped her chest to his, catching her breath.

Panting, she took his face in her hands and kissed him deep and long. Her hair dropped around them and he splayed his fingers through the golden mass. It fell around their kiss, forming a small cocoon.

Shutting out the world.

He searched her sky-blue eyes, close enough to see the darker flecks and count the freckles adorning the tip of her nose. He wanted to believe he had an emotional handle on this ride.

If he was honest, he was barely hanging on to the words he wanted to say. He knew what type of person Lindsey was on paper. He knew what he thought she was like from what he'd seen in the past twenty-four hours. He just needed time.

Time to discover if she could feel the same way. Even if she couldn't, he'd fallen long and hard. He really hoped Lindsey wouldn't mind keeping a piece of his heart tucked somewhere safe.

Stopping his teasing, he flipped her onto her back and slid inside. They moved together, their bodies hitting a rhythm age-old but unique only to them. Sweet, tender, hard and sexy until she cried out and it echoed through the house. He followed with a sweet release he wanted to repeat. They kissed, sated and smiling. He rolled to lie by Lindsey's side, the breeze from the ceiling fan cooling the fine sheen of sweat making love to her had created.

Simply dragging her nails lightly back and forth across his abs created another burn that wouldn't be doused easily.

No more debate why Mac had gone with the large bed.

Chapter 17

Lindsey was totally and completely exhausted. Brian was a marathon champion lover. Their schedule was completely off. She hadn't had four hours of straight sleep since leaving his ranch. They'd drift off, touch in the middle of the ginormous bed and wouldn't be able to stop the nuclear blast until they were both on their backs breathing hard to recover.

Exhausting, but wonderful. She'd never imagined spending every waking—and sleeping—moment with a man would be this rewarding.

"You know, we're going to have to trek back into the real world sometime soon." She pointed to the empty box of condoms that needed to be replaced. "The last two are on the nightstand."

"We've spent two days in bed. Searching, talking and—" he kissed her shoulder "—other things. It's time to make some decisions, Lindsey. We're even out of frozen food."

"I could always make a run to the store. I doubt anyone would recognize me and I hardly think you want to give delivery boys directions, as if anyone would deliver out here in the middle of nowhere to begin with." She popped the laptop open and read Jeremy's notes on the real estate book. It was what she'd been doing when Brian had awakened and a simple kiss had led to a delectable round of lovemaking. But she was determined to find the reason Jeremy had been looking into the sale of mineral rights. It had to be a clue.

"You've been at that memory stick for two days. Making any headway?" He quirked his brows together, causing his crooked stiches to wrinkle. He was propped against the headboard, finishing off the orange juice they'd mixed up from frozen concentrate. "Mac's going to need his place back soon. We should probably think about our next move."

"I think we're close." She focused on the screen, hiding Brian's rippling muscles behind the lid. His simple movements made her want to close the laptop and continue hiding with him here in the cabin. No. They had to finish at least one conversation and make progress.

"You said that yesterday," Brian said from his side of the bed, swinging his legs over the edge and sitting.

"Well, it's true." She closed the lid and set the laptop aside, trying not to let her frustration show. "If we don't come up with something, then where do we stand? What do we do then?"

"Leave?" He stretched as he stood.

"The murderer is still out there and determined to kill me, Brian. Or kill the both of us now. You're the one who convinced me that running wasn't an option." She tossed the large pillows against the wall, then flipped the silky sheet aside. "Who'll run the ranch if you leave?"

This particular conversation would chase him from the room and she was going to follow him this time.

"Same people Dad sells it to next month."

They'd talked every minute they weren't making love or sleeping. She knew all about the ranch's financial problems and a little about how the town had treated him over the past twelve years. "Stop being a jerk. You told me you don't want him to sell."

She admired him for sticking it out, continuing to live there and help his dad. She even knew how Alicia had finally made him fight his twin so they'd start talking again. What he wouldn't admit was how much he loved working with horses. But she could tell. It was his life, his passion.

When he spoke about training a spirited animal, his face lit up. And she'd learned quickly if she wanted him excited to ask about how he'd improve or how to get a stronger breed. Then she'd watch the disappointment drain his energy when he remembered it was just a pipe dream.

"The bank will never give me a loan."

She rounded the bed and wrapped her arms around him, burying her face in his shoulder. "You don't know that, Brian. You haven't applied."

"I asked you to drop this subject the last time you brought it up, Lindsey." With the tip of his finger he drew a design on her skin, down her back, then back up, getting closer to her breast with each pass.

"Don't change the subject this time. This is important to you. Running away isn't a possibility."

"It may be necessary for you to stay alive. Are you saying you'd rather do it alone?"

"I'm not admitting defeat yet. I still want to find this guy." She lifted her face toward his, seeking a kiss.

He kissed her into silence and she let him. She was still tingling in all the right places from waking up in his arms. The desire to change his plan of attack and avoid this conversation just wasn't strong enough.

Making love to Brian Sloane was a pleasure she didn't want to give up.

Brian stood naked, drinking directly out of the carton of milk. The only light slicing through the darkness was from the open fridge door. It was a small pleasure, but one he'd enjoyed many times over the past two days.

"Tell me again why standing there like that makes you happy?" Lindsey had slipped into one of his T-shirts. The shirttail hit her low enough to make his wandering eye curious to see more—even when he'd seen more many times.

"It's simple. Because I can." He tipped the remainder of milk into his mouth, then wiped his mouth with the back of his hand. "I never get to do this. I live with too many people to walk around 'nekid as a jaybird.'"

Her arm circled his waist as she leaned past him for a bottle of water. Her soft breasts molded to him before she eased back to stand next to the counter. She crossed her arms and could barely drink through her smile.

"What's going on?"

"I think I've found it."

"A connection? Are you kidding?" He wanted to grab her around the waist and twirl her in celebration before she said anything else. Before they could discuss it further and realize there wasn't a connection at all.

But if he touched her, they'd end up back in bed. Two days of making love to her hadn't quieted the need even a little. So he stood here with a hand on his hip and an empty milk jug in the other.

"I wanted to know when Jeremy got curious about real estate, so I checked the actual downloads on his laptop. And that stupid memory stick that didn't have anything listed, but said it was full? I finally thought of the password to open the hidden files, and there are a ton of them. Copies of research and references to emails. An email that occurred after a string of conversations regarding mineral rights that weren't transferred with the sale of property about twenty years ago. The current property owner wanted to know if Jeremy would be interested in selling."

"Was he?"

"Jeremy didn't own them. They thought he was part of the corporation that does."

"How does this connect to a man trying to kill your family?" Brian searched the fridge for something to take his mind off the long and very sexy legs in front of him. If he attacked her right now in the middle of her discovery, he might not hear the end of it.

"The rights are worth a lot of money now. Jeremy was trying to determine which family member sold them to the corporation. He couldn't find any records."

"So you think the guy he was emailing decided to kill him?" He leaned an elbow on the top of the door.

"We could go see."

"Right. Just ring the doorbell and ask if this guy is trying to exterminate the Cook family?"

"Of course not. I haven't thought of everything." She smiled, taunting him by crossing her arms under her braless breasts and showing him the bottom half of her derriere as she spun around. "But I did think of something to pass the time until we have to leave."

It hit him. Just like that, he didn't want to leave. Didn't want her in danger. He tried to hold his finger off the panic button, but it wasn't working. He wanted her safe, wanted to turn the evidence over to the police and keep her hidden somewhere. He wanted to tell her he loved her.

Just like that. In an instant, he knew.

"Lindsey?" He took a step, spun her into his arms and let the fridge door shut. His eyes adjusted as he stared into hers, wanting to tell her. He couldn't wrap his mind around saying the three little words aloud. He'd never done it. Never expected that he ever would.

"What's the matter? You said we needed a game plan. The lady lives straight up Interstate 35."

"I wanted to…" After. He should tell her later. Somewhere romantic. Not naked as the day he was born in a kitchen. "Never mind. You said a woman?"

"I searched the map for her address. One of her emails said she divorced a second cousin of ours years ago. But his name is on your list of accidents."

"We should probably talk to her."

"You don't sound very excited."

Should he be? "I guess I didn't expect you to find anything."

"I would have found it sooner if I hadn't been so distracted by other things." She smiled, hiding a glance at his body.

"So there wasn't anything wrong with the...um... memory stick."

"Nothing that I found. Oh." The double entendre hit her and she blushed from head to toe.

"You surprised me, Lindsey." He reached out, trying to bring her into his arms.

"Wait. I thought you believed I could do this all along. If you didn't, then why did you take up for me in front of your brother? Was it just to score points or to get him out of the way?" She jerked her injured arm free from his hand. "Why did you bring me here?"

"There's a guy trying to kill you and—"

"And I was your alibi in case you couldn't avoid the police."

"No. I've been trying to help you."

"Right. And now that I have a real lead you don't want to." Lindsey tiptoed backward, facing him like a cornered she-cat, claws extended and ready to pounce to protect herself.

"A lead to what? Jeremy might have been helping a friend. Have you read all his emails?"

"I think you're wrong." She shook her head back and forth. "You have to be wrong. Doris Davis was married to one of our cousins and had nothing to do with Jeremy."

"Then why isn't she dead, too?"

Lindsey ran into the bathroom, slammed the door and turned the lock. He leaned against the door, wondering if he needed to coax his way inside. He heard a few words he assumed were surfer slang. Words like *feeling maytagged* and *launched from the nose of her board*. Stuff from a different world that he didn't un-

382   *The Renegade Rancher*

derstand. The shower started and then he heard tears. What did he know about those?

How could he apologize for making her cry? He didn't know what to apologize for, let alone understand half of the conversation that had just taken place in the kitchen.

He could be a jerk and ignore it. Pretend he didn't hear her crying. Repeating the conversation in his head, he could see that Lindsey might have been excited about her clue. It had just taken him by surprise. *So tell her!*

He knocked.

"Lindsey?"

"Go away. I don't need your help."

"Come on, now. Whatever you think you heard, I didn't mean it."

"Think I heard?"

The door flew open. His blue-eyed beauty was covered in soap bubbles—not far from what he'd imagined the first night here. The fire in her blood turned her eyes a deep sea blue. He hadn't seen them close to that color before.

One hand was on her perfect hip and the other on the door until she started wagging a finger at him. "What do you mean, think I heard? Because I know what tone I heard in your voice and I know what we've done for the past two days."

"I didn't bring you here to stay in bed."

"But we did. You didn't do anything to try to find the family connection to the murderer." She pushed his chest with her finger, slipping a little on the tiled floor.

He reached to steady her. She was as slippery as a newborn colt that didn't want to be handled. "You took me by surprise. That's all."

He'd been prepared for another round in bed, not a revelation that she'd found a connection that would put her in the murderer's path again.

"I think you wanted me to fail so you wouldn't have to help me. We could wait it out here until your brother's friends figured everything out and the police caught the guy."

"What's wrong with laying low and allowing someone with experience to help? It's better than spending the time in jail."

"You want to know what else I think? I think you *want* to run away from home. Away from all the problems you've been facing. Maybe someplace where you can be *nekid as a jaybird*." She impersonated his heavy Southern accent perfectly.

"If I'm such a jerk, maybe you shouldn't have anything to do with me." He released her and she skidded across the floor, catching herself before she fell.

"I don't think—"

"Wait. You got your turn to talk. Now it's mine." He didn't really want to say anything at all. But he didn't want to hear an explanation from her either. He'd claimed it was his turn and she was waiting on him. "I knocked on this door to apologize. For what, I didn't know, but I was going to do it. We just met and I get that. I understand where you might get the impression I wasn't enthusiastic about tracking a murderer. Go figure. I'm not thrilled about being a murder suspect—in your murder, no less. But you should probably rein it in a little before assuming you know what makes me tick. You don't have a damn clue."

He left her near the side of the tub, her eyebrows drawn together in confusion, but he didn't care. He didn't really know Lindsey Cook. He knew the woman he'd created in his head.

He was used to people assuming they knew what type of person he was. Used to people assuming the worst. Used to— He swallowed hard, pulling on his jeans. He was used to being alone.

Chapter 18

"Where is she? Where can that little bitch be hiding?"

Pacing the length of his couch, he chided himself to hold his chatter to a minimum. And promptly reminded himself he hadn't switched on the recorder this evening. He'd decided against rambling and would record a summary of this segment of the chase after he was done.

Talking to himself had become a habit. Especially in his office. Frustration would make him look bad and he was never going to let anyone see him in this panicky state.

He'd been checking various places for two days. After the police had finished with an apartment in Fort Worth, he'd taken a visit to see if any clue as to their destination had been overlooked. But to his consternation, nothing. No one had returned to the apartment. Even the paramedics hadn't returned. Neither Brian

Sloane nor Lindsey Cook had called or been to the ranch since he'd encountered them at Jeremy's home.

One delight, which shouldn't have surprised him, was the amount of information Brian had collected on the demise of the Cook family. Sloane had managed to discover all the victims, putting together cities and time-lines. There were a lot of question marks in the margins of the murder articles. And someone had put together a family tree, including carefully printed death dates.

He'd placed the rendering safely with his other keep-sakes.

He poured himself yet another vodka. He'd lost count how many he'd had since sending his secretary home for the night. The decanter was nearly empty. Frustration did that to him. It made him break his rules.

If the couple would run, there would be hours of searching and traveling. He had looked forward to this segment being over. It would take him a while to devise a new plan, find new victims, new rewards.

If they had run...

"*If* they had run. But that's just it, I don't believe they have."

The police, however, no longer thought Brian had murdered the prostitute. After assurances from John Sloane and his Marine Corps friend that Lindsey was very much alive, Brian was only wanted for questioning.

"That's it! How could I have forgotten the Marine? He provided them a place to stay hidden. A home or piece of property the police don't know about."

Staying in the area meant they'd be surfacing soon. He didn't have to look for their hiding place; they'd reveal themselves soon enough. Did they really think they could match wits with someone of his intellect?

"The thing about those who hide…they always come out to see if someone's still after them."

There was nothing pressing on his desk, just a bit of paperwork that he didn't need to file until the end of the month. Other than the day he'd closed for his trip to Cozumel, he hadn't taken a vacation in years. Closing again wouldn't draw special attention. Perhaps it was time to finish this game.

He filled his glass with the last of the fiery liquid from the decanter. "A toast. May the best hunter win."

Chapter 19

Brian unfolded his tall frame, grabbed his hat and shut the door. He stood at the corner of the car, waiting on Lindsey to follow. The car would be hot and she already had a layer of itchy sweat accumulating on her skin. She opened the door and swung her legs to the gravel.

"You coming?" Brian asked, not hiding the impatience in his voice. He looked at his watch as if he had an appointment to keep.

Behind the wheel, he hadn't been relaxed. He'd rarely smiled. Shoot, he'd been more relaxed after being in a knife fight with a murderer. And as many times as they'd ridden in a car together, this was the first time he'd rudely listened to the radio instead of talking with her. Going so far as to turn it up when she tried to mention the emails.

Mrs. Doris Davis lived about an hour north of Mac's

secluded house. A house that hadn't been as far out in the middle of nowhere as Lindsey had originally thought. The drive seemed to take five times longer since Brian wasn't communicating with her. He was polite enough, speaking when necessary. But things had changed between them.

It was as if he had no vested interest in her situation any longer. More like he was treating it as an obligation.

It had only been two days with an amateur—her—searching, but this was their only lead. Maybe not even that. Jeremy might have been curious about something he found while researching his family heritage. There was no way to be certain other than actually talking to this woman.

As excited as Lindsey was to be at Mrs. Davis's home, she was more devastated that things might be over with Brian. If she could just explain… Maybe tell him how much she was scared the connection wouldn't pan out. How frightened she was of facing a lifetime of running.

She'd messed up. He was right. She shouldn't have assumed anything about Brian's motives. With her limited people skills, it was easier to move to the next beach instead of working through problems with people she liked. And she really liked this man. In fact, she could just be falling in love for the first time in her life.

"Lindsey?" Brian stood in front of her, hand outstretched to help. His fingers clasped around hers and, simply put, she felt safe.

Two hours without him on her side and she wanted to cry. How could she figure all this mess out alone? *Stop!* She couldn't assume anything else. Right now, she was about to verify what type of clue she'd uncovered—useful or useless.

"I feel stupid because I never realized someone was killing off my family," she blurted, staring at the ground. "If you hadn't done the research and tried to warn me... What if we never find out who he is?"

Brian pulled her into his arms, burying her face in his shirt. "There's nothing you could have done to prevent any of it. No one caught on, Lindsey. People with a lot more experience than us labeled the deaths as accidents. Hell, I hardly believed it myself until we found that poor girl."

"If I had paid more attention, Jeremy might still be alive."

"Or you could be dead, too." He tipped her chin so she'd look at him. "You were right about me wanting to stay at Mac's. But you got the reason wrong. I don't want you to risk getting hurt or worse."

"We can go back. Let your brother's friends take care of the investigating."

The front door opened. "You two coming in or what?"

Doris was thrilled to receive guests. They arrived for morning tea, just as scheduled, and she had the service all set. A full English tea along with a variety of cookies. It seemed very out of place, but so did the frilly yellow house surrounded by prairie grass and cattle.

Tea wasn't really Lindsey's thing. It was something you ordered cold, with lots of ice at dinner. Hot, flavored with lemon or milk? She didn't know which would be better with the vanilla macaroons she'd fallen in love with.

Brian sat next to her on a tiny settee, leaning forward across his knees, sipping out of a delicate china cup. His tight jeans hugged the thigh muscles she'd run her hands along such a short time ago. And honestly, he looked very uncomfortable. As if he were sitting in on a tea party for a child.

Doris, a petite woman less than five feet tall, refused to talk about her ex-husband during tea. Brian sipped away, and with every question popped another cookie into his mouth, then gestured back to Lindsey.

"So how long have you two been a couple?" Doris asked from her window seat.

"Us?" Brian shook his head and waved in Lindsey's direction.

Leaning forward like he was, she couldn't give him a stern look to stop evading conversation. If she was going to do all the talking, he could just live with her version of the story. "Brian followed me around like a puppy for months before he gathered the courage to ask me out."

The cowboy almost spit out his latest bite of cookie. He stuttered over the word *no* for several seconds before giving up. Good. He could choke a little more.

"Yes, the poor thing is so shy," Lindsey continued, gently patting him on the back. "You'll have to forgive him. Even now, you can see he's barely talking to you."

The man finally turned his head, wrinkled the new scar on his forehead and growled a little at her. Doris didn't catch it. The silver-haired matron seemed to be a little hard of hearing.

Doris put her cup on the rolling service tray. "That's okay, dear, my third husband was just like that. I love the strong, silent type. At least for a while."

Lindsey laughed along with her hostess. Brian choked a little more, quickly swallowing more of his tea.

"Now, you wanted to know about your distant cousin, which would have been my second husband, Joel. Quiet man and terribly boring. I was so surprised to hear about his sudden death. When was it? Almost twenty years ago?"

"Yes ma'am," Brian answered, then shot Lindsey another look.

"Horrid little man, really. He didn't leave me a thing in his will. Now, if you wanted to know about my side of the family, if they were related to me, they were wonderful people."

"Can you tell me—us—why Jeremy was so interested in Joel's will?" Lindsey asked.

"We only got into that a little. I had no idea your cousin had died, Lindsey. The emails and phone calls stopped and I thought he must have been one of those scammer people out fishing for information. That's why I insisted on meeting you in person. You just can't be too careful nowadays."

"Right," Lindsey agreed. "You never know if someone's going to lead a serial killer to your door or not."

On that-below-the-belt jab, Brian set his delicate teacup aside and stood. She knew he hadn't meant to speed up the killer's timetable. And she also knew that Brian was the reason she was alive. But she was a bit miffed at him and he deserved to feel a little uncomfortable.

"Do you need the facilities, dear?"

"No ma'am. I just…have a cramp." He halfheartedly rubbed at his thigh. "So what did Jeremy ask about?"

"Joel sold his family home when we married and moved in here. The house wasn't worth much, just an old building that the next owner was going to tear down. Thank goodness his mother wasn't alive to see that happen. Anyway, your cousin Jeremy wanted to know if I might have a copy of the deed. He mentioned something about a trust that was looking for heirs. He was particularly interested in the mineral rights."

Lindsey was ecstatic that she'd been right. So happy that she had a hard time concentrating on what Doris actually said next.

"I don't think your cousin could obtain copies of the sales if they were available. It gets a little confusing."

"That's a shame. Sorry we bothered you," Brian said quickly.

"Hold on, Mr. Sloane." Doris motioned for Brian to sit back down, which he did. "That's what started our conversations, but it's not what really caught Jeremy's interest."

Lindsey sat forward, almost even with Brian. She wanted to jump up and down. Detective work was fun if you could forget about the murder portion. She wanted to hold Brian's hand again. Good news or bad, it would be better with him along for the ride.

"You might have noticed all the cattle wandering around here when I am far—" she waved at all her frills in the room "—from being a rancher. I lease my land. Lots of people do."

Lindsey was trying to be patient, but she didn't want a lesson about ranching. Brian's hand reached out to cover hers. Maybe she was showing a little more angst than she had thought. She laced her fingers through the strength he shared and stopped her toes from the rapid, nervous *tap tap tap*.

"I not only lease my grazing land, I lease my mineral rights. Did you know you can sell your mineral rights?"

Brian nodded yes but Lindsey was trying to string the information together. Joel. Property sales. Murders. Mineral rights. "This doesn't make sense. Why would anyone want to kill Jeremy over his house?"

"Jeremy was killed? The internet said he drowned in Cozumel."

"We should go." Brian stood and drew her to her feet. His eyes told her not to say anything else. She pushed him to the side; he hit the tea cart, scooting it inches but rattling the china.

"Doris, why is it interesting? I don't understand."

"Remember I told you Joel sold his mother's house? Well, there's no record of the mineral rights being sold prior. So who owns them now?"

"Let me guess, the house is right in the middle of the Barnett Shale."

"You'd be guessing correctly," Doris confirmed.

"I don't understand."

"Natural gas that's being extracted by fracking, dear."

"There's our motive," Brian cursed.

Something significant had just been revealed, and Lindsey was still confused.

"Thanks for your time. It was nice meeting you."

"You'll need the address." Doris handed him an envelope.

Brian ushered her outside and hustled her into the car.

"Why are we leaving? I had a ton of questions."

"We don't need to involve Doris. She's been safe so far. She needs to stay that way."

"Why wouldn't she be? And where are we going?"

"We need some answers."

"You're confusing me, because I thought we were getting answers back there with Doris."

"We need more information than Doris can provide."

"So we should have let Mac search Jeremy's computer to begin with."

He slowed at a four-way stop and instead of moving forward, he draped his arm over the backseat and got two bottles of water from the cooler, handing one to her.

"We don't need a hacker, at least not yet. Property owners are listed at the county tax office. We just need to fill out some forms. I went through that looking for the owner of Mrs. Cook's property. That's how I found the rest of your family."

"Won't the police arrest you if you show up at the county clerk's office?"

"Maybe. That's a risk I need to take. But just in case, I still have John's military ID." His smile was back.

Her confidence was returning by the minute. Brian would help her put an end to this madman's killing spree. Maybe somewhere along the way she'd find the courage to tell him how much she appreciated him saving her life.

Chapter 20

"Is this still a risk you're willing to take? Should we tell that to the judge?"

Lindsey laughed, smiled, seemed relieved and sort of drooped in her chair. She was handcuffed to the desk across the aisle from him and acting as if she was as care-free as a wild mustang. If Brian was jealous—there was no way he actually was—he might get the impression she was flirting with the officer assigned to wait with her.

It was almost an unnatural kind of fun drunk. Unnatural because he knew she hadn't been drinking. Yet her flushed cheeks and behavior suggested that she had been.

They were waiting to see if his fingerprints were in the system as John or Brian Sloane. They didn't believe he was John. They shouldn't believe he was John, but he wished they had.

Three hours had passed while they took their statements and waited for confirmation he wasn't John. He'd been very stupid about taking her to the county clerk's office, thinking no one would recognize him. The first person at the counter was very helpful and said she'd start looking for their request. Half an hour later he was under arrest.

What would happen to Lindsey when they put him in a cell? All he had was a working theory of why this serial killer wanted Lindsey dead. They had no hard proof. Who would believe them? Especially with Lindsey acting almost drunk.

"I can't believe they're arresting you for abducting me—a completely bogus charge," she directed at the officer sitting next to her. "Don't *I* have to press charges or something?"

She turned back to face him. He could tell her eyes were dilated and her speech was slurring a little. "I mean, I insisted on coming with you. And you weren't obstructing justice or fleeing a crime scene. You were protecting me. So how can they, you know, claim that you had anything to do with that girl's murder?"

Brian shot a stern look at Lindsey, attempting to communicate that she needed to be quiet. It didn't work.

"I can promise you—" she switched her attention back to the officer, but dropped her head toward Brian "—*he* didn't do it. He was with me the entire time. I mean, Brian was, 'cause that's John over there that you're trying to arrest."

She giggled and grabbed the officer's sleeve.

"Keep your hands to yourself, ma'am," the officer stated and pried her fingers free, allowing her hand to drop to the top of his desk. "Did this man give you any-thing? Have you been drinking?"

"Me? Just tea. Awful tea. Who puts milk in tea?" She tipped a water bottle upside down. "Empty."

Brian had heard that silly laughter before. When he'd gotten her half drunk before suturing her arm. He caught the officer's eye. "I think she needs more water or maybe coffee."

The officer shook his head, gave a disapproving look and walked into the hallway.

"What the hell happened?" he asked Lindsey, whose head was sort of wobbling. She stared, her eyelids look-ing heavy and staying closed longer with each blink. He kicked the desk with his boot, causing a loud noise and drawing the attention of the officers in the hallway. "Come on, man. Can't you see something's wrong with her? Somebody slipped her something."

"Not here they didn't. Now shut up," the officer shouted as he left. "Your lawyer's here to pick her up."

Lindsey cradled her head in her arm, resting on the cop's desk. "I'm okay, Brian—I mean, J-John. Jus' re-ally tire…"

"She's out. And you're headed to holding, Brian Sloane," a different officer said as he came over and began unlocking his cuffs from the desk.

"Seriously, man. There's something wrong with her. She has a cut on her arm. I haven't checked her today, but maybe she needs a doctor. Can you get her to a doctor?"

"There's something wrong, all right. You. Maybe when she sobers up she'll be pressing charges, too."

"You've got to believe me that she hasn't been drink-ing. There's something wrong and she needs your help."

Brian got to his feet and had the overwhelming urge to use his elbow to knock the officer away from him. He'd been angry, but never over a woman.

"Nothing's going to happen to her in the middle of the squad room. I guarantee that."

Brian wanted to jerk away, wanted to run back to Lindsey. He watched her as far as he could strain his neck to see her. Once in the hall, he turned straight, catching the eye of a man who quickly looked down at his expensive shoes.

"You'll get your turn in a minute, counselor," the officer said as they passed him.

They rounded a corner. "Counselor?"

"Right. Your attorney saw the report that you'd been arrested and he's been hanging around waiting his turn."

It was on the tip of his tongue to state he hadn't asked for an attorney, but there was something about the guy. He couldn't remember ever seeing him before, but he'd helped a lot of people as a paramedic. Yeah, there was something about the way he'd avoided eye contact that set Brian's teeth on edge.

Brian was led to another small room. No one-way mirrors. Just a camera in the corner near the ceiling. He tugged at the cuffs out of frustration. It wasn't his first time in a police station. He'd fought hard to keep his job with as many times as he'd been hauled needlessly into jail.

There wasn't a way to shrug this arrest off. He'd be booked for dang certain. If that guy was a real lawyer, he had to make the cops understand just how much Lindsey was in danger.

He rested his head in his chained hands. The sense of

utter failure hadn't hit him like this since the first time
he'd been in jail for another crime he hadn't committed.

They'd been so close to finding this bastard. Twelve
years of wondering why Mrs. Cook had tried to put out
the fire and died. Twelve years of being isolated, never
allowing anyone close because he didn't want to explain why his life was a mess. The first time he cared
about a woman and he might lose her because of his
stupid pride.

The door opened and the man from the hallway entered, carrying a briefcase that he set on the edge of the
metal table. He took a step back into the corner. And if
Brian hadn't already seen the camera pointed directly
toward him, he might not have noticed that the man
kept the top of his head available for the recording and
nothing else.

The man shoved his hands into his pockets instead
of introducing himself. Odd, but each thing built on the
next and that fuzzy memory gnawed at him. Something
about his body language. The way he stood, ready to
pounce. And his eyes had a gleam as if daring him to...

It's the son of a bitch responsible for everything!

"Why are you here?" He knew he was right. Everything about the man told him he was.

The stranger's brows raised, inventorying Brian's position like a hunter ready to raise his bow. "So you've
connected the dots. You are my most worthy opponent.
I say that in all honesty."

"You don't have the right to say the word *honest*.
You're a serial killer. A butcher. You slaughtered that
woman for no other reason than she looked like Lindsey."

"You're slightly wrong there. I might have selected

her because of your girlfriend, but I had such delightful fun. So there was definitely more than one reason."

Brian swallowed the rage building in him. Nothing good would come of him losing his ability to think. This murderer was baiting him. That was all. He had to see this through, get the man to reveal himself to the police.

"Guard?" Brian looked at the camera. Was anyone watching? Did anyone realize a serial killer was here impersonating a lawyer?

"Ah, yes. I realize you want me gone. I soon will be, I'm afraid. But not as soon as you'd hope. This isn't recorded." He pointed to the camera. "Privileged information and all that."

"What do you want?" he asked between gritted teeth. The muscles were tensing in his arms. He wanted his hands around this man's neck. It was the first time in his life he had considered seriously harming another human being.

"Why, Brian, I'm here to drop my gauntlet for a private battle."

"If I agreed, you'd have me at a disadvantage." Brian shook the metal, letting it make noise against the table. "Why the hell would I *battle* you anyway? You ran from our last fight."

"You did take me by surprise at Jeremy's. That won't happen again."

"Quit talking riddles and just say what you came to say." Brian laced his fingers. The small room was much hotter than where he'd left Lindsey. His skin seemed almost sunburned, a red haze almost. He was hot and mad at himself.

"I can see the wheels turning in your head, Brian Sloane. Don't be stupid. You can't cry out. No one will believe you anyway. I'm a respected lawyer who felt sorry for the way you've been treated throughout this terrible ordeal."

"It may take time, but the police can discover the truth. I know about your mineral rights trust."

He finally pulled a hand from his pocket, swiping at the corner of his eye as if he was laughing so hard he cried. "Oh, Brian. That's so funny. You've been accused of murder. Your DNA is at the scene and will match their samples. And of course, they'll find the knife you used on the prostitute in your barn."

Brian's hands were fisted; the metal rings pinched and scratched his wrists as he tugged and then tugged again. He knew he couldn't break them, but the gesture kept him from losing it completely.

"Not to mention the testimony of your lawyer when I attempted to get you to surrender after being interrupted at your prisoner's home." He laughed in a tenor old lady voice. "You're making this too easy. I thought you seemed the sort to fight. Are you, Brian? Are you willing to fight me and save the damsel in distress?"

Brian swallowed hard, keeping it together because of Lindsey. Wanting to tear this guy apart with every word from his mouth. "You know an awful lot about me. Aren't you going to introduce yourself?"

"In due time." He slipped his thumbnail in the small space between his two front teeth. "In due time."

"What's your definition of battle?" *You raving lunatic!* "And if you want to fight me again, you're going to have to get these charges dropped. Hey, you could do that, couldn't you? Confess to the murders and they'll let me go."

He nodded. "Right. And on a more realistic note, you

know that the only leverage I have over your behavior is Lindsey? She's resting, by the way. I slipped a little mickey into her soda. So easy, no challenge at all. But you'd already guessed that, hadn't you?"

"Why are you telling me all this?" Brian could feel his chest rising and falling rapidly. His hands shook from the adrenaline. His eyes were slits because of the anger. He deliberately took a deep breath, trying to calm down. It wasn't working.

Nothing riled him and made him lose control, especially when he was aware of the situation and was debating with himself. He'd taken too many hits over the years and never swung back.

Teenagers, cops, drunks. They'd all hit him and he'd never taken a swing at anyone except his brother. It couldn't be the thought of Lindsey. In fact, his thoughts were different than the physical reaction his body was having.

"You drugged me."

"Yes, as a matter of fact. I gave you a natural something or other. Of course, I gave you much more than the vitamin store suggested. Are you feeling a little anxious? Is your chest getting tight?"

"You really are a freaking...madman." Hyperventilating. He closed his mouth, breathing through his nose, attempting to slow down the racing in his body. "Why are you...you trying to..."

"Trying to kill you? Why would you think that? You're the most fun I've had in two decades." He leaned forward to pop his briefcase open and pulled out a card. "You might go into cardiac arrest and these oafs might not be able to revive you. I would hate that. Such a disappointment since I'm looking forward to the climax of our story."

Even telling himself not to, Brian strained at his handcuffs without getting any closer to his target. At this rate he might break his wrists. His pulse pounded in his head, the veins in his arms popped to the surface, he felt his head rocking and couldn't stop.

The lawyer, murderer, serial killer leaned forward and slid the card down his shirt. The four corners made his skin itch on the way down.

"Don't disappoint me. You might have been clumsy enough to get caught, but I'm smart enough to get you free." He shut the briefcase. "That is, if you really want to end this venture and you're willing to do whatever it takes to save your little Lindsey."

Brian tried to call for help. It was a weak attempt. He swallowed air, not spit. Mouth too dry. Whatever this maniac had given him, it was fast and hitting all his senses. He finally croaked out, "Guard."

"We're finished for now. We should be able to tidy up loose ends soon. I'm ready to be done with this cat-and-mouse game and move on to something new."

The tightness this brute mentioned felt like a stampede on his torso. His jaw clenched tighter with each breath. The amount of restraint it took to keep from reaching up, grasping this killer's neck and snapping it…was only surpassed by the pain growing across his chest.

"You need to remember this, Brian. Do you think you can? Your car's waiting for you at the E.R. Clever of you to drive Mabel's. I'm going to collect Lindsey. I just happen to have a document assuring the court I'm her lawyer. I'll convince them I should take her to her doctor. I can be very persuasive. We'll be waiting. The card shows you where. Can you remember?" He tapped on the door. "Guard!"

Brian used his last bit of remaining strength to push forward, his hands jerking him to a stop inches above the table, he threw his shoulders from side to side, feeling as though he was about to explode. "You son of a… If you touch her…"

"Oh, I plan to, Brian. Many, many times."

Chapter 21

Every inch of him hurt. Brian had been thrown from plenty of horses. Had the breath knocked from his lungs more times than he could remember. Broken his collarbone and his tailbone, but he'd never hurt like this before. He ached all the way through and his fingers were crossed it wouldn't last long.

"Lindsey." He had work to do.

He was in the Denton Regional Medical Center emergency room. He recognized the sounds and the room even through his blurred vision. He'd dropped off his sister-in-law plenty of times. Why was he—? He lifted his arm...handcuffed and in a hospital gown. His foggy memory mixed bits and pieces of scenes flashing between shards of pain.

Lindsey. Jail. Drugged. Serial killer. Pain. Nothing. Either all those jumbled memories had actually happened or he'd been kicked in the head by one of his horses and was having a very realistic dream. Yeah, it had all happened. He could remember the taste of Lindsey's skin, the face she'd made at the bitterness of Doris's tea. His days and nights with her were very vivid.

Alicia walked into the room, her finger across her lips to caution him from speaking. He caught a glimpse of a uniform at his door. "We came as soon as your story broke on the news. They said you began having seizures while at the jail. And we're both very lucky they haven't changed my ID yet. I doubt the police would let your sister-in-law check on you."

"God, please tell me you haven't seen me naked. And if you have, lie."

"Get a grip, brother-in-law. I see that exact body every day on John. But no, I just came on shift so I didn't see anything. John's in the parking lot." She pumped up the pressure cuff already on his arm, looking over her shoulder toward the door.

"Have you heard from Lindsey? That bastard's got her. I've got to get out of here. Fast." He tried to sit up, but his head swam, turning the rest of the room to a blur. The metal handcuffs banged. His sister-in-law shushed him.

"Hold on, buster, you aren't going anywhere. You're a very sick puppy."

"He drugged me."

"Are you stating or asking?" She flipped his chart to where he should have been able to read it. "They pumped your stomach. Juanita was on duty and called us when you were brought in. She said it was a little touch and go. Your heart nearly stopped, Brian."

The writing was blurry. He couldn't make out why

they'd pumped him, but it explained why his voice sounded scratchy. "Alicia, get John in here. He's going to kill Lindsey."

"Are you still feverish? John's not killing anyone," she whispered, stuck a thermometer into his mouth and then wrote down his vitals.

"I'm dead serious, Alicia," he mumbled around the stick under his tongue. "I need John. The freak didn't tell me his name. He's a lawyer or faking at being a lawyer. But we found out he's working some kind of scam stealing mineral rights when properties are sold. He drugged our drinks in the middle of the freakin' squad room."

She removed the thermometer and disposed of the covering. "Calm down. You aren't making sense."

"Just call John. I need him to wait this one out for me."

"What are you suggesting? You know he's better trained to find this lawyer. Did you consider just telling him? You want him to go to jail for you?"

He tried not to be angry. He wanted to say the words that hung between them. *How many times had he gone to jail because John left and their small town blamed him for Mrs. Cook's death?* He didn't. They hung there until she pulled her cell, talked, hung up and then took his IV out.

"You're going to have a horrible headache. Can you even see straight?"

"Straight enough." He'd be lucky to see a hundred feet in front of the car, but he had no choice.

"I suppose you'll need my keys."

"Mabel's car is out there."

"How do you know? Oh, gosh, I don't want to know

that answer, do I? How are you even going to find this killer if you don't know his name?"

Remember this, Brian. Can you remember? He'd put something scratchy down his shirt.

"Where's my stuff? I think he dropped a business card in my clothes." She shook his clothes. The T-shirt was ripped in half, his jeans looked just as bad. His Ropers were fine. He would take John's clothes, but he preferred his boots that molded to his feet instead of John's Justins.

Alicia tipped the second boot upside down and out fell a card.

"Victor D. Simmons, attorney at law. You didn't imagine him, but it doesn't mean he's a lunatic who poisoned you. It could have been that woman with the tea." She must have seen his confusion. "You called after leaving her house. John and I both tried to talk you out of going to the county clerk, but no, you had to rush in. You're as bad as your brother."

She straightened the room, putting his clothes back in a bag, stowing them, swiping at a tear and trying to hide a sniff from the tears.

"Hey." He bent his finger, gesturing for her to come back. "Sorry."

"Lauren misses you and your dad sends his love even though he's a stubborn Sloane man and just squeezed my shoulder." She smiled and her phone buzzed. "That's John. Pretend to be asleep when I leave. I'll get the officer to help me and John can get in here while he's away from the door."

She waved nervously and backed up, wheeling a crash cart behind her. She deliberately hit both sides of the cart on the frame. Brian closed his eyes when the uniform moved to hold the door open. "Thank you, Officer. Could I borrow you just a sec? The wheels on this thing… Don't worry about him. He's sound asleep, will be for hours. We had to sedate him."

The door swung gently shut. Behind his closed eyes, Brian saw his world spinning out of control. Alicia had been friends with him and John for a long time. She'd married his brother. He could forgive her for thinking he was crazy. The thing was, the jumbles in his brain had *him* thinking he was nuts.

"You were waiting outside?"

"You have to ask? Alicia filled me in. Why would a murderer risk walking into a police station and drug two people?" John asked, already working on picking the lock on the second handcuff. "It doesn't make sense, man. Then hand you his card? It has to be a fake card."

"Look him up. The cops seemed to think he was legit. He said he was my lawyer and waited until they verified who I was. I don't know how he convinced them to talk to me. Or how he could just walk out of there with Lindsey. It was as if he was waiting on us at the courthouse. He even told me Mabel's car had been moved here for my getaway."

"He drugged you so you'd be delivered to the E.R. instead of transferred to Arlington for questioning. Pretty smart."

"Smart or not, he's got Lindsey and I need out of here so I can find her."

"You going to be able to handle this? You were so out of it you didn't know I'd come into the room or hear Alicia fill me in." He finished and pulled his shirt over his head. "Are you even certain he has Lindsey?"

"If she's not at the ranch, then yes, I'm sure."

"Then find him before they lock me up, will ya?" John handed him his service weapon.

They switched clothes and John got on the gurney. "I hate to say this, but you're going to have to put a needle in my arm."

Brian found a clean IV needle in the drawer and stuck his brother's vein on the first try. He adjusted the IV to the slowest drip possible.

"You're pretty good at that. Ever think about becoming a doctor?" his brother asked.

"Not ever. I want to raise quarter horses." The response was instinctive, not thought about, not debated. He wanted the ranch.

"We have a lot to talk about when this is all over."

"Right. Now I need to concentrate on finding my girl."

"You know I'd go for you," he said, clapping a hand around his shoulder, smiling.

"I have to do this."

"That's what I thought. Do you know where to start?"

With a bandage over his forehead to cover the missing scar, the IV tape in exactly the same spot and handcuffed to the rail on either side of the bed, John looked exactly like Brian, with one exception—

"We forgot about the blasted hair. You cut yours."

"You should have cut yours. Hell, Brian, they won't notice with me just lying here. Alicia's going to check on me. The shift changed from when you were admitted. She'll cover. Just don't leave me hanging, bro. So again, do you have a clue where to find this guy?"

"The bastard said to remember. I can start with his flippin' business card." He looked on the reverse side. "Or follow the map he conveniently left with me."

* * *

Lindsey had been groggy for a long while. Sort of aware that she was moving and unable to react. Her eyes hadn't opened fully since giving her statement to the police in Denton. She remembered that. Remembered Brian and…confusion.

She'd lost control, feeling more like a lump of flesh being directed, molded and fixed in place. She couldn't see, barely could feel, but the fog was lifting.

How she'd gotten out of police custody wasn't clear. Neither was what happened to Brian. She didn't think he was with her. It didn't seem as if he was with her.

Blindfolded. That was why she couldn't see.

Someone was there; she'd heard the unidentified person breathing. The madman snickered a few feet in front of her. It had to be the man wanting to kill her. She didn't know how she'd ended up in the paws of the monster. But she was there.

A flapping noise—maybe startled birds flying away.

Wrists tied with plastic rings, she could feel the edges biting into her skin. Her arms were stretched forward, bent but not high above her head. Her feet seemed to be free. A smooth surface was at her left hip, something like a wall.

No one was coming to her rescue except her.

She slid her hands a little and a rope rubbed against her fingers. That was how her hands were extended in the air. A rope tied around the plastic. She took a small step. Could she shift enough to remove the blindfold? Maybe there was enough slack if she moved forward.

She screamed as her right foot stepped into nothingness and she fell. The rope jerked the plastic into the flesh of her wrists, halting her descent a split second later. Dangling like a fish on a line, she stopped kicking her legs and lifted her feet back to the beam where she'd stood before. At least she wasn't flaying around in midair.

A man's laughter. The monster was watching.

"What do you want? My hands are cut and tied. You can't possibly think this is going to look like an accident."

Was he having fun?

When he didn't answer, she strained, lifting her body weight until she could get both feet back on whatever she'd stood on before. Then she pulled on the taut rope, tugging until she was back where she started.

If there were birds... A beam, perhaps. An image of a high-rise under construction, workers walking on beams and steadying themselves on the beam above.

Was that where she was? High in the sky with no safety net? She didn't hear traffic. She heard nothing except her blood rushing, frightened, through her veins. Then the snickering of the murderer laughing at her.

She couldn't hang like this indefinitely.

With both her feet on the support—whatever it was—she held on for dear life and stretched her left toes until they pointed down. She had about six inches to stand on. What was at her hip? She gently kicked out, hitting something metal, a hollow sound like a chute of some sort.

"What do you want from me? Or from my family all these years?"

Even if she knew where she was or how to leave or any other small detail that may save her life, how could she get free? No, she was staying put, hands tied

and already aching from pulling on the rope to keep
her balance.

"Your Prince Charming will be here soon enough.
That is, if he survived at all. Shame if he didn't, I was
looking forward to our battle."

What was he talking about? Brian was in jail. She
didn't remember leaving the police station. Didn't remember much after the initial interview at all. But
they'd been in custody, she remembered that.

She also remembered the fright she'd felt at Jeremy's
house. Face-to-face with the creature who had carved
that woman's face off her. Then when she'd seen the
knife coming toward her neck but slicing her arm.

The knowledge that she was on her own shot the
same panic up her spine. She couldn't depend on anyone but herself. No one else knew she was here or knew
she was even missing. She wasn't ready to die. She'd
just found Brian and wasn't about to give up on him.
Or her own abilities.

Her arms and legs shook, partly from the stress but
also from the drugs. She was already weak, but had to
get herself free. But how could she, with that maniac
watching and laughing at her efforts?

She turned her head toward the creaking of old wood
on metal. She hadn't heard him in a while, but she knew
she wasn't alone.

Sunshine reflected off something. She could see it
around the edges of the cloth tied over her eyes. She
held tighter, scooted forward until she could lift her
shoulders one at a time and inch the blindfold to hang
around her neck.

Her first look made her dizzy, and not just because
her eyes had been closed for so long. She was a heck

of a long way up in the rafters of an abandoned building. Three long flights of stairs. Rusted beams, ducts and pipes crisscrossed around her. If she fell, she'd die from blunt-force trauma from everything she'd hit on the way down.

Heights normally didn't bother her. She'd been on waves taller than this. It must be the drugs still in her system, slowing her down and messing with her equilibrium.

With her arms in this position, it tugged at the stitches Brian had put in her arm. The strain from balancing and easing the pressure on her shoulders had started a definite trickle of sweat down her back. It felt like bugs crawling on her, which started her imagining all of the creatures that holed up in barns.

Including snakes. Hadn't Brian talked about barn snakes in the rafters? *Please, please, please...no snakes in these rafters.*

"It's very entertaining watching you discover your surroundings and trying to compensate. Good job, Lindsey."

"Is this some kind of test?"

"Oh, no. We're just having a little fun until Brian arrives." He returned to a post just above her where the stairs turned.

Logically, if this man killed her, he'd finish an objective and get away with it. No one knew who he was and wouldn't know as long as he kept his mouth shut.

"Brian was arrested. So unless you mixed up his fingerprints, you're wrong."

"My dear, I've gone to great lengths to assure he'd be here. So he'll be here. If he lives up to half my expectations, it'll be a worthy fight."

Had the other people he'd killed felt this way? Had he ignored them as insignificant? He'd been targeting her family members for at least twenty years. Why was Brian so important now?

"Did you kill Jeremy? Or my parents? Why? Why do you want the Cook family dead?"

"You want to alleviate your conscience? Make yourself feel better? Tell yourself that your cousin's death wasn't your fault?" He paced along a short wooden platform—it was the creaking she'd heard earlier. "That information isn't ready for public knowledge yet. Unfortunately, you won't be alive when it is."

"Can't you at least tell me why you want my family dead? Or even who you are? What did we ever do to you? And what does Brian have to do with it?" The sun was sinking, the shadows were getting longer. But she saw bright light from a porch or window. Someone was nearby, if only she could scream…

"Don't think about it, Lindsey." He leaned over the rail with a finger over his lips. "If—and I mean that in the slimmest way possible—*if* you manage to get their attention and they venture here to see why we're on the premises, I will be delighted to kill them, too. No thought or debate needed."

Dear God, what if a child wandered in here?

For all she knew, they were in a populated area and this man didn't look worried about being caught. Maybe he wasn't the one responsible for all the deaths after all? Maybe he worked with someone else and couldn't make the decisions on his own.

There had to be someone else involved. Someone had been following her. She couldn't recall ever having seen this man. Was he the butcher in black clothes who had tortured that poor girl? This well-spoken egomaniac was the same man who had nearly sliced her throat?

"Since I'm not the public and you assume I'll be dead when your statement's ready, it won't matter if I hear the imperfect version. Would it? I don't think you're the beast responsible for killing my family. You lack…authority."

He didn't like that at all. He ran down a flight of stairs until he was even with her, until he could look her in the eye and point his finger at her face.

"I am Victor D. Simmons. How did your arm heal after our encounter at your home? Or should I refer to it as Jeremy's home, since that's how you refer to it?"

"That proves nothing. The real murderer could have told you lots of details."

"You aren't going to goad me into admitting I'm the mastermind. I have nothing to prove to you."

"So you did kill him. You're the monster. A horrible little man who never fights face-to-face."

That got his attention. "What makes you assume that?"

"You cut me loose and I'll show you what happens when you give one of us a fighting chance."

He threw his head back in laughter, slowly clapping his hands. "Brava, Lindsey Cook. It's going to be thrilling to describe how you die."

Chapter 22

There was only one place in Aubrey Victor D. Simmons could be referring to on his map. Brian knew the small town like the back of his hand. He'd avoided the main roads for several years when he'd been the focus of every questionable action that happened. Many years ago he'd learned the habits of the police and the sheriff—when they liked to eat, what streets they liked to drive looking for troublemakers and especially the speed traps on 377 where weekenders heading for the lake would forget to slow down.

That was exactly where he hoped both cops were tonight. Those heading up to the bigger lake, Texoma, would be heading home now. He took a slightly longer route, Sherman Drive from the hospital instead of the more traveled road. Speeding with blurred vision and taking risks he didn't ever consider while driving the ambulance, he actually made fairly good time.

Lindsey had to be in the abandoned peanut-drying plant that still sat on either side of the railroad. Rusty from top to bottom, it had been officially off-limits but just sitting there for a couple of decades. But every kid in town had played there sometime in their life. It was one of the few places he still remembered with fondness.

It was in the middle of town, across a gravel parking lot from the fire department, which was next door to the police station. Brian couldn't just drive up to the front door and ask him to hand Lindsey over.

He also knew he couldn't involve the police if he wanted to keep the woman he'd fallen in love with alive. As his head cleared, he deciphered more of the jumbled visit with Victor D. Simmons.

The beautiful body he'd explored extensively meshed with the image of the woman slain in Jeremy's home. The words in that small room just before he'd passed out— *If you touch her... Oh, I plan to, Brian. Many, many times.*

She was alive.

She had to be alive. He wouldn't think of her vibrant personality any other way. Rage coursed through him with any thought of the lawyer's hands on her. Leftover effects from the drug that had been pumped from his stomach. He had to get himself under control and think clearly.

Running would clear his head. He parked the car two blocks from the building and ran, pushing through the aches and clearing the throbbing in his head. He avoided the police station, noting that no squad cars were there so that meant both were out on patrol, but Polly's car was in the lot so someone was manning the dispatch.

He stopped at the corner where the city kept the fire truck, catching his breath.

Two peanut buildings—both were on his map. If he held someone captive, where would he do it? Hell, he didn't know and there was no way he could think the same way as this guy. He'd never have broken his opponent out of jail or been as bold as to face him in a police station.

Trying to understand a murder was not solving the problem. The only thing different about *this* Cook murder was him. It wasn't because he'd tried to think like a killer for the past couple of months. It was because he'd thought like himself. He was the difference.

He pulled the magazine from John's gun. Full, but that was it.

An all-volunteer squad meant the fire station was empty. He twisted the knob. Locked. He pushed up on a window and hit the jackpot. It was unlocked and he could get inside. He needed another weapon. A plan.

The way the adrenaline was still pumping through his system, it was hard not to rush in shooting and ask questions later. That was what John would do. He and his brother hadn't ever had the twin connection that people talk about. He'd accepted responsibility when he screwed up and John had sweet-talked his way out of more than one problem. Neither would work this time.

What he really needed was his brother and some of those SEALs he worked with. They'd have a lot of gadgets to locate Lindsey and extract her from a hostile environment. He should have swallowed his pride and just told John to take care of the rescue. But he hadn't, and he wasn't his brother.

Then why was he deliberating what his brother

would do? The knowledge to save lives worked both ways. It was his grit that would find the way to get both him and Lindsey out of this alive.

And stop Victor D. Simmons forever.

Lindsey was tired and drained. If she weren't perched on a six-inch beam three stories above the ground, she'd make fun of herself for being totally out of shape. It had been hours and several attempts to get herself untied, always resulting with a slip and jerking her arms from their sockets when she fell.

At the moment, exhaustion was her most immediate enemy. If she fell again, she wouldn't be able to lift herself back to the beam. She'd be useless if help arrived. *If help arrived.* At the moment she had her doubts.

Without any explanations or reason why he thought Brian would be arriving to honor him by "doing battle," her captor had stopped talking and disappeared. As if there was any honor in murder or abductions. Almost dozing, she wobbled on her perch.

Catching her balance, she looked again for a way to reach the knot. Her fingers were numb and raw from gripping the rope to stop the plastic from cutting her skin. She startled herself awake again, her hip hitting the chute next to her.

This time when she'd almost fallen, there hadn't been a snicker from some odd location in the building. Could she hope that he'd left her alone? Maybe she could get someone's attention if they passed by. But for as long as she'd been trapped in the rafters, she'd only heard a couple of children's voices, and that had been before night had fallen.

Groggy as she'd been, she had no idea how he'd got-

ten her onto this beam. And as weak as she was, she had
no idea how she'd hold on to anything to get down if
she could get free. The stitches pulled, her arms shook,
everything ached, especially her neck.

A train whistle sounded in the distance. She heard
the birds rustle. Then the familiar creak of wood. Her
captor was on the platform. Somewhere to her right.
Moving up or down or across, she didn't know.

"How long are you going to keep me here?"

"Long enough."

"Why haven't you just killed me?" her parched throat
hoarsely whispered, and didn't expect an answer. She'd
asked before. "This is senseless."

"Nothing I do is without purpose."

Now she could see his outline in the dim light. The
sound of the train grew louder.

"Ha. It's very easy for you to claim whatever you
want since you refuse to explain."

"You're trying to taunt me, Lindsey? How very predictable."

"Oh, I'm not taunting. I think you're an idiot. There's
no way that Brian Sloane is coming anywhere near this
place. He's in jail by now. I'm just wondering how long
I have to endure your threats."

"I think you understand that I don't threaten. I succeed."

"But at what?" She pushed the words out through her
parched throat, loud enough to be heard over the train
passing next to the building. A bit of dust falling from
the ceiling caused her to shut her eyes.

Her captor appeared close to her at the rail, just to
her left. Close, and yet not close enough to kick out
and do damage.

"I set things in motion to make it impossible to say no. As predictable as human nature is, I'm confident he cares too much for you not to handle it himself."

"Flaw number one. Brian's smarter than that. His brother has kick-ass Marine and Navy SEAL buds. Why in the world wouldn't he let them tear this place apart and you along with it?"

The train passed the building, doing weird things with the light coming through the side panels that had broken free over the years. She tilted her head up. The monster looked even more frightening. Dressed in black again, his eyes loomed large in his shadowed face.

His fist pounded the metal pipe used as a rail. "He has to come."

"Flaw number two. I barely know this guy and our relationship hasn't been a piece of cake. Assuming he wants anything to do with me any longer is a huge assumption."

She didn't have to see his fist hit the panel of the chute that hung over his head. It shook next to her. Perhaps it was stable with birds resting on it, but along with the slam of his fist came loud creaking and a trail of dust from overhead.

"Flaw three. If—and that's a big if—someone decided to rescue me, why in the world would they meet you face-to-face for this 'battle,' as you put it? Even if you're honorable—" she tried not to choke using that word "—why do you think they are?"

"Shut up! I've planned this. My plans always work."

She'd finally gotten to him. Or maybe the wait had. Maybe he had his own doubts about whether anyone was coming. Whatever the reason, he raced up the stairs. Loose particles rained from the ceiling. She closed her eyes and dropped her chin to her chest.

When the train had passed and was somewhere in the distance, she could hear every creak and moan from the building. Including every wing flutter and scurry of small animals' nails clicking on the metal beams and pipes. The metal staircase and wooden platform creaked as they had every time the savage had approached.

She didn't want to look up, petrified she'd goaded him into action. Action might mean he finished her off. She ignored him, tired beyond reason and with no thought left other than keeping her balance.

More debris fell on her neck, sticking to the sweat, begging to be brushed aside. *Concentrate on your grip. One thing. Keep your head down and don't fall.*

A larger sting. More creaking. She didn't listen to herself, she opened her eyes, letting them adjust to the low light. In seconds she could see someone...

"Br—" *Brian,* she finished in her head, immediately stopping when she saw his finger across his lips.

How had he gotten free from the police? Why had he come for her? What difference did it make? He was there. She was free.

He held up a finger, then a palm. *One stop?* She shrugged, not understanding.

He moved two fingers pointing to the ground. *Walking?*

Pointed to his chest. *Him.*

Patted his back. *No!* She shook her head, silently screaming no. He couldn't leave her here. He just couldn't.

He held up four fingers and then pointed at her. He was coming back for her? She lost her footing with all the movement, one foot sliding off the side, and she wobbled. Brian was half over the pipe rail. She locked eyes with him, hoping that her fierce glare told him she was okay.

Her arms ached from the strain, but she managed to nod her head in the direction of the stairs. He stopped, one leg over the rail, ready to come to her rescue. She shook her head, this time agreeing he needed to take care of their tormentor first.

There was only one quick way down, and that wouldn't happen as long as the rope held. Freeing her was much more complicated than it looked. She was stabilized, and yet Brian wasn't moving away. She pulled herself upright, wanting to cry out, biting her lip so she wouldn't. Hoping beyond all reason the madman wasn't watching and ready to push her rescuer over the side.

She'd tapped into a strength she'd never realized she had and got her feet under her again. Brian waved, used his broken sign language to indicate he was coming for her now. She shook her head, mouthed "no," then, "I'm okay."

Tears of pain washed her eyes clean, but she was able to see the last sign he made for her. He stood with the rail between them again, put both hands together in the shape of a heart.

It was enough to make her lose it as she watched him climb the stairs. A heart. His? Hers? She waited, knowing this time she'd torn a muscle in her shoulder. The raw pain wasn't easing like it had before. She clung with her left hand to the rope and balanced on her right foot—her left ankle now caught between the beam and the metal chute.

She couldn't move and was completely helpless if the monster returned victorious.

Chapter 23

Brian turned his back and climbed the stairs. He left her, obviously needing to be cut down and gotten to safety, one of the hardest things he'd ever done.

The noise of the train had covered his entry through the door. Overhearing the exchange between Simmons and Lindsey caused him to take the bottom three steps to intervene when the murderer lost it. But the knife had disappeared and Lindsey was no longer threatened, allowing Brian to press against the wall and hide. Simmons had returned to the roof where Brian had seen him keeping watch.

Leaving Lindsey now, dangerously hanging there, was tearing his guts out. It put another burr under his saddle as he took the steps two at a time.

It had been a long time since he'd climbed to the eagle's nest—what they'd called the east peanut elevator as kids. He rushed through to the outside, remembering that the stairs turned back over the roof. He could see Simmons ahead of him, dressed in black, but showing up against the rusted tin roof as plain as day.

Hang on, Lindsey.

Since Simmons was running, he probably knew Brian was chasing him. They both pulled on the hand-rail, taking the stairs. The place had been structurally sound sixteen years ago when he'd gotten caught exploring. Now he could feel the joints giving way, wondering if the rusted bolts would pop with the weight of two grown men.

He took the last step to the metal grating, did a one-eighty, grabbed the ladder rungs to the top. Just as he raised his eyes, his opponent stopped, and Victor's work boot caught him in the chin. He lost his grip, falling a couple of feet until he hooked his arm in the circular safety cage on the outside of the ladder.

Simmons couldn't come down the ladder with Brian blocking it. It was the only way down. If he descended on the outside, Brian could still grab him. He heard Simmons scrambling around the far side of the catwalk.

The blurred vision from knocking his head cleared a bit. Once he knew Simmons was headed across the chute to the roof, Brian bent and twisted to get upright again. He grabbed a rung, then a second until he pulled himself free to follow.

As Simmons jumped the rail to descend to the roof, Brian twisted through the safety rail and slid to the warm tin in time to grab the man's foot. Simmons kicked out. Brian avoided being hit by rolling to his side. He stopped and began racing up the steep slick metal. Brian caught the older man just as he straddled the building's ridge to head down the other side.

Simmons lifted his leg to strike out again, but Brian kept hold. Victor D. Simmons may have been older, but he gave as good as a weakened Brian. They rolled, and Simmons threw himself to the west side of the roof. Brian didn't let go and couldn't stop the headfirst slide.

Brian couldn't slow the three-story downward tumble on his own, but the hackberry branches helped.

"Grab hold!" He released Simmons and the man did as directed. Brian grabbed a second branch before plummeting over the edge.

Why had he told the man what to do to save his hide? Simmons was able to sit, and began kicking at Brian's grip. Then he rolled to the roof joint, crawling over the edge before dropping to the lower side.

Brian caught his breath before following the maniac to the west-side ladder. Simmons was three or four seconds ahead of Brian, dropping to another peanut chute and running along the metal grate. Going up was the only way to get down. Brian didn't trust his swimming head or shaky hands to climb the pipe on the side of the ladder.

As he took the first step onto the grate, Brian remembered the gun tucked inside his waistband. He pulled and released the safety, but Simmons made it over the edge before he could fire. He dropped to the grate, looking for a shot, pulled the trigger, nothing. Pulled again, but he still couldn't hit Simmons mixed in with the crisscrossed metal supports.

Again, Brian was just slightly behind. He followed Simmons to the ground and ran as if he was racing from an explosion. Across the uneven dirt, back into the old building, swinging around the bottom of the stairs and each zigzag landing back up to Lindsey. He was within five feet of Simmons.

But seconds behind was all the bastard needed to lean over the rail, tug and then slice the rope.

"Lindsey!"

Lindsey had prepared herself. If she fell, it meant her death. When the monster cut the rope, there was a moment of unadulterated panic. It was going to hurt. Her foot was caught and she'd be lucky if her ankle didn't snap.

There had been moments like that on a wave. She'd known she was about to wipe out and the eternity clock began ticking. It only took thirty seconds to fall, but you can't scream underwater. Maybe that was why she was coherent enough to fall and stretch for something to grab with her good arm.

Her fingers grabbed the bottom of the platform where the monster now rolled in a struggle with Brian. She shifted, latching her hand in place where a board was missing. Then she became conscious of the pain in her ankle and screamed.

Hanging and watching the fight as if the men were defying gravity, Lindsey saw them roll and exchange punches. She clung tightly with one hand as the arm of her injured shoulder was useless. Still zip tied together, she couldn't get a better grip or reposition her good hand.

The psychopath scurried up the stairs, kicking at Brian, who followed. Then Brian fell hard onto the platform. The jolt caused Lindsey's grip to shake.

"Brian, the gun," she tried to warn. The weapon that

had been tucked at the small of his back fell through the wooden slats. It clanged again and again as it hit metal on its journey to the floor she'd been staring at all afternoon.

Lindsey tried her best not to scream and distract her rescuer. But her foot was working free from her shoe. Once it was, all her weight would be hanging thanks to the loose grip she had on the edge of wood that was already cutting into her hand.

"Brian, I'm slipping."

The monster laughed as he stood on a step out of Brian's reach. Attached to his leg was a handgun. He unstrapped it and pointed it at Brian.

"Don't move, Brian," the lunatic commanded.

Her heel slid farther from her shoe. "Oh, God, please."

Brian turned on his side, his hand on hers. "Go ahead and shoot me, Simmons. I'm not going to let her fall."

"Uh, uh, uh. Not until I say go."

"If you wanted her dead, you would have killed her when you got here," Brian spat at him, but his fingers moved closer to her wrists and to the plastic tie.

"All right, hold on to her and pull her up."

Brian locked his hand on her wrist, her foot moved and she swung side to side in the air. Maybe the pain shooting throughout her body had short-circuited the neurons that needed to fire to scream. Or maybe it was the simple confidence that Brian wouldn't let her fall.

"You wanted to save her, so save her," Simmons demanded. "I'll watch you from here. I would like to inform you that I can officially declare myself the winner of our battle. It's time to finish this project."

"He's a monster."

"Forget him, Lindsey. Focus on me. Are you okay?"

"Just…peachy," she said through gritted teeth. "But I might…pass out."

"Come on, Lindsey. Stay with me."

Brute strength saved her. She could do nothing other than keep her eyes from completely shutting and passing out. She hung there as Brian lifted her like a free weight and saved her.

Maybe she did pass out for part of it as he pulled and tugged to get her through the rail. Lying on their backs, Brian clasped both her hands in his, bringing them to his chest. She didn't care how awkward or how much it tugged at the torn shoulder muscles, she needed his touch. Needed to know he was really next to her and she wasn't facing the rest of this night alone.

"Time to get up, lovebirds."

"I need a minute," Brian said, still breathing hard.

"It took you much longer to get here from the hospital, Brian. I'm afraid you got us off schedule."

"Schedule? You have a schedule to kill us?" she asked. She was too injured to stand and walk anywhere. Brian squeezed her hand.

"I didn't give you the impression that I'm a planner? Get up." His voice changed with the last command.

Brian stood, using the rail to help himself, then he helped her sit up.

"I said we're leaving. Get up, Lindsey." He kicked her thigh.

Brian turned on the monster, who acted more as though he welcomed another fight. He looked disappointed when Brian backed down.

"She can't walk on that ankle." He pulled his T-shirt off. "She has a dislocated shoulder that I'm going to stabilize. Unless you want her screaming in pain walking across Aubrey."

She'd had no idea they were back in Brian's hometown. All of the fighting and noise the two men had made and no one had called the police. They were still at the mercy of this madman.

"Cut her cuffs. I can't stabilize the shoulder with her wrists pressed together."

"Back up and hook your leg through the rail. I want to make certain you don't come at me."

Brian did what he said. The man pulled his knife and cut the plastic between her wrists. He put the knife away and Brian returned to her side.

Brian worked quickly. He didn't try to put her shoulder back in place. He angled her arm around her waist, ripped his shirt and tied her arm to her torso. He lifted her and took off down the stairs before Simmons realized he needed to keep up.

"Where are we going?" she asked, trying to use her good arm to hold around his neck and not doing a very good job. She rested her head on his shoulder. She was past any level of exhaustion she'd ever faced.

"Trust me, Lindsey," he whispered, then brushed her lips with his. He turned his head to speak to the monster. "Good question. Simmons, what now?"

"We need your car. Your story needs to come full circle for this town. Their hatred with you began during another *accident*. This one will validate all their fears."

She wanted to sleep, rest, not move. Every step jostled a part of her that ached.

"My ride's inside the firehouse."

"Convenient."

Brian had already been heading straight across the

parking lot to the fire station. *Trust me, Lindsey.* He had a plan and he knew who this murderer was. Simmons. There were so many questions she wanted to ask. Brian's jaw muscles tightened along with all the muscles in his neck. He was either angry or very determined. Probably both.

Whatever Brian had planned, he didn't seem to like it.

"You're setting me up to take the fall for the Cook family killings?" Brian asked.

Where was everyone? It was just after dark and they were in the middle of town. She could see shadows of people from the lights behind the drawn curtains. Cars in the driveways. Flowers on the porch.

If she could see all that, what was stopping these neighbors from noticing a fight on a roof or the noise from the shouting? She raised her head, looking at the man Brian called Simmons.

Just a man. Not a monster or devil. A man who could be defeated. She did trust Brian. They would find a way to escape.

"You really are an egotistical psychopath, holding me in a building down the street from the police station and a playground."

"And if you had called out to any of them, they'd all be dead. Keep that in mind, Lindsey. Just like now." He pointed the gun at Brian's head. "You call out. Someone gets curious. Someone else dies."

"Trust me," Brian whispered so softly she wondered if she actually heard him speak or if the words were echoing in her head. "Why come here, to town? Why risk being seen instead of going directly to where you're going to stage this last accident? Why the fight?"

"After our fight in Jeremy's home, you piqued my curious nature."

Brian spun to face the madman. "Curious about what?"

"Well, who was the better man, of course."

"I'm curious. Who are you?" she asked, looking over Brian's shoulder. She watched his eyes. Wild. Dark. Insane. There was no other explanation for his rash, odd behavior. Then again, was there ever a rational explanation for someone planning multiple murders?

"He didn't introduce himself? This is Victor D. Simmons, attorney at law."

"A lawyer who I bet works with people selling property and steals their mineral rights."

"I was right to assume that the two of you together would be my toughest challenge."

"My car's inside the fire station bay."

"Then we should get inside before we're seen."

"You'll have to open it, my hands are full." Brian stepped to the side, revealing the door.

Lindsey paid close attention to his brown eyes, wondering if he'd set some sort of trap inside. Simmons must have wondered the same thing. He tipped the gun back and forth like a wagging finger.

"Why don't you empty your hands and go through first, Brian."

"Okay." Brian kept one hand around her waist, letting her slide down his side a little, keeping her high enough that her feet didn't thump to the ground. He turned the knob and let the door swing open. "Nothing there…except maybe some field mice."

"Get inside." Simmons pulled the door shut behind him. "Where's your vehicle? I thought you said it was here."

Brian walked across the open floor toward the office, set her on her feet close to the wall and flipped a switch that turned on a row of lights with a high-pitched whine. "I lied."

"Stop," Simmons cried out, losing his composure. "We've already fought and I proved myself the better man."

The portion of the man who had screamed at her from the stairwell came into full focus. The man who totally lost it when someone said he was wrong. Brian was using it against him. But that man still had a gun and Brian had nothing but his hands.

Hands that saved lives.

"You see, I don't agree. You're not the better man at all, Victor 'D is for dumbass' Simmons. I think you're a coward. You can't call the peanut-dryer chase a real fight. I've had better fights with one of my horses."

Even in the dim light, she could see Simmons turning red. He was about to explode. Brian kept inching forward. His thumbs were hooked in his jeans and he didn't look as if he was about to fight with anyone. That casual, withdrawn voice was calming—no matter what antagonizing words were coming from his mouth.

Lindsey held her tongue, but while Simmons's focus was on Brian, she searched for a weapon. She quickly found the source of the whine.

They weren't weaponless after all. Brian had turned on the defibrillator.

Chapter 24

When John had asked Brian if he could pull the trigger, he'd said yes. In his head and heart he knew if it came down to it, he could. But he'd had a crazy, wild thought while sitting in the police station—he didn't particularly like explaining himself over and over to the cops.

The empty firehouse reminded him it would be a lot easier to take Simmons alive and let him explain himself. So he'd gone into the abandoned peanut-dryer warehouse thinking he could capture a serial killer who had been at it for half of Brian's life.

Stupid. He'd stepped right in the middle of it. At least he'd had a backup plan.

Brian might not know a lot about how to extract a target, which was his brother's world. He did know a lot about what would take a man down without a weapon. And a defibrillator was perfect.

Now all he had to do was get Simmons near the paddles that had begun charging when he'd flipped the lights on. And he had to do it before he realized what the beeping noise behind them indicated.

"Are you a coward, Simmons?" He needed the gun put away, not fired.

"How dare you talk to me that way." Simmons looked as if he was going to pop a gasket. He was agitated and his gun hand shook. "I have nothing else to prove."

"Don't you?" Lindsey asked. "You don't think I need to know why you were killing my family, but I'm the only one who can judge the real victor of the fight on the staircase. If you hadn't cut the rope, Brian would have won. So I think you cheated."

Victor Simmons laughed. His gun wrist went limp when he crossed his arms and relaxed. Brian hadn't expected that. A different man stood before them.

"Such a valiant effort deserves my appreciation, not my rage. I heard the defibrillator charging next to Lindsey. Did you really think you could manipulate me and shock me?"

Brian saw his chances of disarming Simmons waning. He began to charge when Simmons came to attention, pointing the gun at his chest.

"Far enough, boy. Don't you think I'm accomplished at the art of killing yet? It's been twenty years." He faced Lindsey. "You don't deserve to know anything. You're barely a footnote in my manuscript."

"Manuscript? You've written down how you killed my family? You really are a monster." Lindsey shuddered.

"Nothing personal, my dear. It must have been fate that brought your relative to my office. It began with a mistake. You see, mineral rights automatically sell with a property unless excluded in the contract. I made sure of that, but I didn't assign them to anyone. Joel Cook thought I was trying to cheat him and wanted my head. We exchanged words. Then blows. Unfortunately, he died. Purely an accident."

"There was nothing accidental in the other thirteen family members you killed."

"Oh, there have been more than thirteen."

One side of his mouth tilted in such a smirk, Brian itched to knock it from his face.

"I can see your anger building. You want to kill me for all the harm I've done."

Brian stretched his hands open, not allowing himself to keep his fingers balled into fists. He opened his palms, as if he was calling a stubborn horse. "That's not my decision, man."

"Where's your car?"

Keeping his back to Simmons, he walked to Lindsey's side. He didn't want to lose Lindsey before their relationship really began. This man would kill them both. He stood just in front of the defibrillator. It was charged and ready to go. All it needed was a patient.

In front of his chest, he motioned for Lindsey to grab the paddles and shock him. Simple. His heart would either go into AFib or stop. Either way, it would give her a chance to run. A chance to live.

She shook her head. He gave her a thumbs-up.

"Don't be stubborn, Brian. It's time to go," Simmons said.

Brian ignored him, counting down with his fingers: three, two, one.

He turned, screamed like a Highland warrior and

leaped the last six feet before Simmons could pull the trigger. The gun flew from his hand. They both fell to the cement floor and rolled, only stopping because of the engine wheel.

Brian landed on top and got in the first punch. Simmons no longer had a smirk on his face to wipe off. He shoved hard with both hands, and Brian's shoulder and hand hit the engine. Hard. He thrust the pain aside and threw himself at the murderer.

Lindsey stood ready with the defibrillator paddles. Simmons was scrambling for the gun.

"Not so fast." Brian jerked on the man's pants cuffs, skidding him across the cement. He kicked out, keeping Brian a leg length away, then rolled and twisted to his feet.

Brian quickly followed. The man's eyes were narrow slits; he used the back of his hand to remove the blood dripping from the smirky tilt to his mouth.

"You want a rematch? Come on, boy. I'll teach you a thing or two." Simmons gestured for Brian to come at him. Taunting.

Brian normally didn't respond to taunts. He normally turned the other cheek and walked away because he was the one who always got thrown into lockup. He looked around the dimly lit firehouse. A place where he should have been able to volunteer and save lives.

But he couldn't volunteer in his hometown, helping the people who should have been his friends.

Because of this man. This man's plan to systematically kill off Lindsey's family had destroyed too many things...too many people.

His fingers curled into fists, but his center was ready to do serious battle. Just because he didn't seek fights didn't mean he was a pacifist or didn't know how to fight. He did. He and his twin had fought so much, his mother had enrolled them in tae kwon do.

His fists relaxed, he steadied his breathing, found his calm and waited for Simmons to advance.

"You think you can beat me?" Simmons danced from side to side in his work boots.

Brian watched for the first kick and deflected it with one of his own. He turned and kicked backward, connecting with the center of Simmons's chest. He absorbed some of the momentum when he took a few steps back.

Brian followed with two punches to the abdomen and then received a right cross that he had not seen coming. They both used trained punches and blocks, sending each of them into walls and the truck. Each time Brian thought he was getting Simmons close enough to Lindsey to jump stop his heart, the older man would kick or roll or throw a punch that could loosen teeth.

Lindsey stood ready to blast Victor Simmons with a shock, hoping that she understood how to use the darn things. Braced against the wall, she'd loosened Brian's T-shirt so she could hold the paddles in her hands. She had to wait for the men to get close to her, unable to drag the machine away from the counter.

Brian was an excellent fighter. He could take a punch, but the way his body rippled was something to admire. If it weren't a life-and-death situation, she'd let him know how impressed she was. And she'd allow herself to be more excited about seeing his shirt off.

Each time the monster in black kicked or shoved or swung, Brian countered with a beautiful kick or punch of his own. She was so caught up in the actual fight, wanting Brian to knock this horrible person out for the count, that she almost forgot what she was holding.

Simmons crawled on his belly, trying to get to something. The gun. Should she drop the paddles and run to the other side of the garage for it? She couldn't run. Just balancing on her foot was too painful for words. Gripping the paddle with the hand of her torn shoulder was excruciating. She had to stay where she was and hope for the best.

The fight was slowing a bit, both men drawing longer breaths, both a little slower to get up. Brian threw a punch, pounding Simmons's inside thigh, and he gave a scream. Brian hit him time and time again. The psycho couldn't get his arms up to deflect or defend. Brian kept at him, backing him toward her. One last hard kick and Simmons went flying into the office door next to her.

"Are you okay?"

Brian winked at her. It was over.

Simmons lay on his back, crumpled and passed out.

"Get the gun. It's at the front of the engine by the door," she told him.

Brian turned to pick up the weapon. She turned to set hers down just as a bloodied hand grabbed her from behind. Simmons wrapped one paw around her chest. And held the knife to her throat, ready to slice her from ear to ear with one stroke. He used her body as a shield from the gun that Brian pointed in their direction.

"Put the gun down or you can say goodbye to her forever."

"Won't that mess up your accident plans, Victor?"

"I have contingencies." Simmons tugged on her neck a little. "I can still make this look as if you decided to kill her. That you abducted her and me and held us captive. Drop the gun."

Her eyes locked with Brian's. He looked as though he was apologizing. He couldn't do it. This devil couldn't win.

"He's not going to win." She didn't want Brian to surrender. He was the only hero in her life and she trusted him. She knew what she had to do.

"No!" Brian shouted.

Trusted that whatever happened, he'd save her.

Brian ran, the gun falling to his side.

"I trust you," she said, raising the paddles to Simmons' arms. She pushed the buttons that sent the electric shock jolting through both of their bodies.

Chapter 25

Lindsey jerked and the paddles fell from her hands. Brian wished everything happened in slow motion, but it didn't.

He erupted forward as soon as he saw the look in her eyes. She'd placed both paddles directly on Simmons, but didn't she know the electric charge would travel through her, too? She had. *I trust you.* Dear God, to bring Simmons down, she'd shocked them both.

Lindsey trusted that Brian would bring her back from having her heart stopped. She crumpled to the floor, the murderer falling on top of her. Brian ran to the paramedic case and half dragged, half kicked it near the defibrillator.

Not so gently, he rolled Simmons off the bravest woman he'd ever known. The only woman he'd ever loved or wanted to love. The murderer had no pulse.

Lindsey was facedown; there was a flutter, a chance. He'd told her he could keep her alive with a rig full of equipment. It was time to keep his promise.

The backboard was in place. He'd left it there, ready for Simmons. He skidded it next to Lindsey and gently turned her over to rest on it.

Training took over. He went through the steps that eight long years of practice had turned to muscle memory. Pulse. Breathing. Airway. Air bag. Monitor. AFib. Charge. Paddles. Jolt. Stop. Pray.

Pray harder, it's Lindsey.

Listen.

Give it a second. No more.

He was about to shock her heart another time when he detected a regular rhythm. Where was the phone? He searched the room perimeter. Nothing. He broke the window on the office door, grabbed the phone on the wall and dialed 911.

"Send emergency vehicles to Aubrey Fire Station. Police and ambulance."

"Please stay on the line, sir."

"Brian?" Lindsey called, her head twisting from side to side.

Brian dropped the phone, leaving the line open. He knelt between Lindsey and Simmons, attempting to block her view of the dead man. Taking her hand between his, he brought it to his lips, more grateful than he'd been since his dad's stroke that she was alive.

"I'm so…tired. Is he…?"

"Dead? Yes. You shouldn't talk. Just rest."

"Will they think we… That… I killed him?"

"He was a serial killer. We did what we had to do."

"You saved me." Her hand curved around his chin.

He caught it and kept it there, wanting to kiss her and tell her everything would be all right and she was perfect. But he didn't know if it would. Simmons was dead from the shock. Lindsey was still in danger.

"Shh, sweetie. I called for help. If I had the keys to this engine, I'd take you to the hospital myself."

"Selling Jeremy's house. Never step foot again. I want my beach. Don't you love beach?"

"I don't think there are too many horse ranches on the beach, hon."

"Nope. Not many boots…in sand. So sleepy."

"Lindsey, wake up, sweetheart. Stay with me." Brian patted her check and her blue, blue eyes opened, acknowledging him with a soft smile. "I hear the police, darlin'. Stay awake now, okay? Concentrate and promise me."

"I prom— Kiss me bye."

"Not bye."

He bent down and dropped his lips against her cool cheek. She turned her head, sealing their lips together. He wanted to devour her; the need hadn't gone away. If anything, it got stronger the more they went through. He straightened onto his knees again, hearing the squeal of tires on the pavement outside.

"Get away from her," Ronnie Dean shouted, pulling his handgun. "Cindy, I have two down," he spoke into his radio. "Confirm ambulance needed. Where the hell's the volunteer EMT?"

"Holy smokes, it's the fugitive, Brian Sloane," a second officer said, charging through the door. "What's he doing, trying to kill her?"

"Step back, Sloane."

The dialogue continued between the two officers

who had pulled the Sunday night speed trap duty. He ignored them. The most inexperienced. The youngest.

Lindsey's eyes closed. Her head fell slack.

"Lindsey? Come on, hon." He shook her chest. "Wake up." He grabbed her wrist, her pulse was erratic. "No. No. No! I am not going to lose you."

The monitor showed her heart was AFib again.

"I told you to get away from her," the guy he didn't know shouted.

"Ronnie, you guys can shoot me and let her die. Or you can let me do my job and try to save her life."

Ronnie nodded and stuck his hand out to stop the other officer.

"She's in AFib. I need to get a regular beat back. Clear." Brian shocked Lindsey's heart a third time.

"But you're not a doctor. Should we let him do that?"

"Do you know how to work that machine?" Ronnie asked the younger man. "Go outside and call Cindy. Check on the ETA of the ambulance."

Lindsey had a regular heartbeat. Brian dropped his head to his knee, more than a little emotional and not wanting to lose it in front of these guys.

Once the younger cop was gone, he knelt to feel for a pulse on Simmons. "He's dead."

"Yeah, I know."

"How long until your rescue unit shows up?"

Ronnie shrugged, "Who is she?"

"Lindsey Cook."

"She's wanted for questioning. You kidnapped her?"

"No. He did." Brian nodded to Simmons's body.

"How do I know you didn't kill him, too?"

His beautiful, brave woman did.

"You don't. But you'll be the next one lying here if you try to move me before help arrives for this woman."

The younger cop came back inside. "About five minutes on the ambulance. What should we do?"

Brian listened to Lindsey's heart, now beating in a normal rhythm. Her chest rose with normal breaths.

"We're going to watch. If anything looks wrong, we'll take him down," Ronnie ordered.

They stared at him and he stared at Lindsey, willing her to beat the odds and survive. She had to live. They were a good team. She thought so, right? He stroked her hand and saw where the plastic cuffs had bit into her wrists. He dressed the gouges, biting back the emotion. Using the back side of his hand to indiscreetly wipe his eyes.

Then he secured her shoulder and strapped her to the board for transport. He didn't want there to be any delay. It was a long way to Denton Regional.

The ambulance arrived, he gave them Lindsey's vitals and history, they loaded her and they were gone.

Brian didn't care what happened next. He was handcuffed and stuck inside a squad car while Ronnie argued with the Denton P.D. that had been patched through and wanted him transported ASAP.

Lindsey's care was out of his hands. If she forgave him for getting her captured by that monster, as she called him, he'd go anywhere and do anything she wanted.

Terror that she might die hit him. He couldn't hold back any longer. He dropped his head as low in the car as possible and let go. He kept the noise to some sniffs and a couple of deep breaths. If anyone had been watching him closely, they would have seen the tears of fright mixed in with the prayers.

Lindsey Cook wanted to go to the beach.

Brian Sloane would make sure it happened.

Just let her live.

Chapter 26

Brian was asleep—or should have been—on the couch in his home. Or what would be his home for about six more weeks. Until the bank took possession of his family's ranch.

He'd showered and was glad to be clean, ready to smell like horses again. Even if it was only for a couple more days. He scratched his morning stubble and scrubbed his face, ending up on the new scar on his forehead. He hadn't received it fighting one of the worst serial killers in Texas history, but it would always remind him of finding one.

Brought home by a patrol car, he'd been released from jail in the middle of the night with the apologies of the P.D. No media frenzy. No reporter to tell the world he was innocent. No longer newsworthy. No longer employed as a Fort Worth paramedic. And no longer with a reason to follow Lindsey around night and day.

Except one.

He smelled toast, bacon and coffee. Time to get the day started. Time to face the family and tell them his decision. He heard the discussion and stayed quietly on the couch so he could listen. While in jail, no one had bothered to tell him why Simmons had killed the Cooks.

"The news said he wrote everything down," his sister-in-law explained. "In the beginning, he wanted the Cook family mineral rights. He faked their sale, was discovered and began killing. When he got away with it, he killed again. It became an obsession. The authorities said he enjoyed it and considered it a challenge to outsmart the police, so he began killing prostitutes. They aren't releasing how many died until they notify all the families."

"That was one sick SOB," his dad said. "If he confessed and they had a blasted book about it, we should sue someone for keeping Brian in jail almost a week."

"There wasn't a paper manuscript, JW. Simmons dictated tapes and hid them in a safe. So it took the police longer to sort through it all," Alicia explained patiently. "We're not going to sue anybody. We're darn lucky they didn't press charges against John for helping his brother escape from the hospital."

"Come on, Dad," John said. "We're burning daylight. Gotta get this place in shape for the appraiser if that financing is going to come through in time."

Financing?

"John, Dad, wait a sec," he called from the couch,

looking long and hard at his boots. He'd miss them. His family and the boots, but he'd made a decision.

Alicia was drying her hands on a dish towel, John had just put his Navy SEAL ball cap on his head and his dad leaned lightly on the cane that was more for Mabel's peace of mind now than for real stability.

"What's up?" his brother asked, standing at his normal parade rest.

Brian leaned forward on his knees, tired when he shouldn't be after "resting" in jail for four days. "I need to say something, so don't interrupt. Got it?"

They all nodded their heads.

"First off, I'm sorry that I dragged you kicking and screaming into finding Lindsey and ultimately Simmons."

"Right, like we're going to be mad that you single-handedly stopped one of the worst if not *the* worst serial killer in history," Alicia said, putting the towel around her neck and leaning into John's side. "Right?"

"He said not to interrupt." John wasn't smiling, but he did drop his arm around his wife.

"We should apologize." His dad sat on the arm of his reading chair. "We could have been more supportive."

"That's not what this is about." He looked at his dad. "We've avoided talking about the ranch long enough. You're moving in with Mabel. Don't deny it, Dad. You practically have already. John and Alicia will have her properties to run. And I'm leaving. Well, there's no reason to refinance the ranch. I won't be here. I'm giving it up, heading to Florida with Lindsey. If she'll have me."

All three of them spoke at once. Irate, indignant, mad

and just plain hurt. Then he realized there weren't just three people yelling at him, there were four.

Lindsey's sweet voice rose above the rest and asked from the kitchen, "What's he saying? I promise he told me he wanted the ranch."

"He told me the same thing the night in the hospital," John threw out.

"What are you doing here, Lindsey?" He stood, pulled her to him from behind his brother and kissed her as though he hadn't touched her in a year. "You still feeling okay?"

"I'm great. Are you? Okay, I mean?" His family had gotten strangely quiet. "I think we're all a little stunned by your announcement. I thought you wanted to be a rancher?"

"It's not that I don't. I—" He looked at his father and brother. "Any way we could get some privacy?"

"We all live here, bro."

He grabbed his boots and Lindsey's hand and pulled her through his family, straight out the back door with no explanation. His brother's laughter didn't slow him down.

"Hey, cowboy. Take it easy, my ankle's still swollen."

Taking the gravel in his stocking feet wouldn't have put a hiccup in his pace, but Lindsey reminding him she'd been severely injured recently changed his mind. He swung the best thing in his life into his arms and proceeded straight to the barn, where he set her on some feed bags. Once inside, he shut and bolted the door.

"Wow, it's dark in here."

He sat and pulled his boots on, letting his eyes adjust, watching her shy away from the horse stall. She watched for critters that might be near her feet. What was he thinking? She hated this place. She wanted to live at the beach, not in an old house falling down around his ears. But he had to explain, had to tell her.

"Don't get comfortable. Follow me." He led the way to the hayloft and opened the east doors, sitting down and dropping his legs over the side. The sun was just peeking over the treetops of the oaks that lined the drive to their house.

"It sure is pretty here."

"I love watching the sunrise from up here. Some mornings, especially the first week Dad was home after his stroke, it was pretty much the only pleasure I got during the day. I love the smell of hay, working with my hands, the feeling of success when one of the mares foals."

"I'm not sure I know one end of a horse from another. And I'm hopeless where cats are concerned. They don't like me and hiss all the time."

"It means something to me that this place has been in my family for over a hundred years. I was looking forward to setting things right, getting it back on its feet."

"What's stopping you? Money? Because I think we have someone willing to refinance the place." She paced behind him while he tried to understand.

Did that mean she planned on staying here? He craned his neck to watch her as she told him her plans.

"You see, once my financial stuff is settled—like selling Jeremy's house—we can get a loan in our names. What's that look for? If it's not money, then what's making you leave?"

"You."

"Me?" She sat next to him, dangling her boots over the edge next to his.

"Those are Justins. And they're extremely pink."

"Aren't they great? If you'd told me they came in this color, we would have bought some the first day. I needed some stuff and couldn't go back to...you know..." She pressed her lips together and shrugged. "So Alicia and I went shopping."

"You bought boots?"

"Of course I did. If I'm going to live on a ranch, I need boots to walk around in the mud and other stuff. Don't I?"

"I don't think those are mud boots." He shook his head at her expression, thinking he was crazy. "Lindsey, you love the ocean. You said you wanted sand between your toes. I planned to move because you wanted to live on the beach."

"Brian Sloane, it's you that I've been looking for. I was looking for someone to fall in love with. Not a wave. Not a job. Not a lifestyle. Even though I'm scared to death of snakes and I don't think I'll ever learn which ones won't eat me. Don't laugh at me."

"Come here." He was laughing and smiling so much it hurt. He maneuvered them back into the loft and onto the hay. "Did you just propose to me?"

"I don't recall the words *will you marry me* coming from my lips."

Their greeting kiss had been in front of his family. Not this one. It was a reunion. He tugged her to mold their bodies together. There was no doubt how much he'd missed her. She gave as good as he did and after five minutes there was no doubt how much she'd missed him.

He sat her on an old apple crate that had been there since the time of his grandfather—but maintained by him as a thinking stool. His answer didn't take much pondering. He'd probably made up his mind about Lindsey before he'd ever met her.

"I think I will."

"Will what?" she asked, the sunshine creating a halo of light behind her.

"Now that you've asked politely, I'll marry you."

"Oh, you. Stop fooling around." She threw a handful of hay at him. "I love you, but I refuse to say yes before we have an official date."

"What did you say?"

"That I want a date first?"

"No, ma'am. You said you love me, and that's a real good thing, 'cause you're the only woman I've ever wanted to say this to."

He pulled her into his arms. Sunbeams were flooding the old hayloft, and her eyes were the perfect color of blue that matched the sky behind her.

"Uncle Brian," came a young singsong voice from the yard below.

"Yeah?"

"Pawpaw wants to know if you asked her yet. And said to tell you to hurry up 'cause we want pancakes."

"Skedaddle, baby girl." He plucked some straw from Lindsey's golden hair as his niece left the barn. "Living here's going to be an adventure every day."

"I believe it."

"I love your boots." He kissed one of the bruises on her cheek from their previous *adventure*.

"They say with the right pair of shoes, a girl can do anything." Lindsey dragged a finger across the pulse point in his throat. "If she's lucky, she might even catch

a handsome cowboy/paramedic turned detective/body-
guard."

"I'm done with all those jobs. I only have one now.
Loving you. That's it."

"I'll take it and love you right back."

* * * * *

She had hopes, high hopes. She wanted to hear him say
he'd taken one look at her and felt the same way she
had: here was someone he wanted to get to know better.
Someone attractive, appealing—even sexy.

But the moment passed. Then another. He studied the
darkness beyond their little pool of light. "You never
leave someone behind in battle. Never."

Not sexy. Kind of grim, actually.

"Were you in the military?" she asked.

"Yes. Were you?"

"No." But there was a compliment in there. It wasn't
sexy, but it was something. "No one's ever asked me that
before. What makes you think I might have served in the
military?"

He didn't answer her.

She wanted to see his smile again. She nudged him with her shoulder. "Come on, tell me. Was it my fabulous driving skills? Do you think I'd be good at driving a tank, or what?"

His smile returned briefly. "That wasn't your first time off-roading."

"I couldn't call myself a Texan if I'd never taken a truck off-road."

She wanted to touch him. She'd already stood in the warmth of his arms. Heck, he'd already had his hand on her rear end twice, even if both times had been during an escape.

Fortune favors the brave. Those had been the man's own words.

"You want to know why I thought you might be in the military?" She dared to reach up and touch the back of his neck, the clean skin above his collar. She let her fingers comb through the short hair at the back of his head. "It wasn't this haircut. It's short, but not as short as the soldiers from Fort Hood."

"I'm a civilian now. A regulation haircut would be too…unnecessary." He didn't shake her off or step away, but he didn't touch her in return, either, except with his gaze.

She let her hand slip over his shoulder lightly before falling away. "I'll tell you what gave it away. It was the way you ordered me to get back in the truck. Do they teach you to bark out orders in that tone of voice? It's scary as hell."

"It didn't work on you." He grumbled those words, which made her smile.

"I'm stubborn like that, and I already know it's not a good trait. I hear about it from my family all the time."

She pushed away from the door and turned to face him—which meant she stepped over his crossed ankles with one foot and stood in her minidress with her legs a little way apart, his boots between hers. The night air was cold on her inner thighs. "But I didn't bark out any orders like a military man, so what made you think I might have served? Come on, talk to me." She gestured toward the red and blue glow on the horizon. "We can't go anywhere, anyway. Was it my haircut?"

She was joking, of course, but her laughter faded at the intensity of his gaze. She couldn't look away, not even when he turned his attention from her eyes to her hair, somewhere near her temple. Her ear. Slowly, so slowly, his gaze followed the length of her hair as it lay on her shoulder, as it curved over her breast, as it disappeared in the open edge of his coat, near her hip.

She wanted him. He was leaning against his vehicle, arms crossed, ankles crossed, not moving a muscle, setting her on fire with a look.

"There's nothing military about your hair," he said quietly, and he looked back up to her eyes. "It was your head. You keep a cool head."

"A cool head." She breathed in cold air, willing herself to say something, to do something, although her thoughts weren't cool at all. "That's it?"

"That's not all that common." He pushed away from the door and stood before her, a little too close, and not nearly close enough. "You also didn't leave your ex and his friends behind, even though they didn't deserve your help."

Kiss me, kiss me.

But the man didn't move an inch closer. "They were lucky. If I hadn't wanted to dance with you so badly, I would have gotten you out of there before trouble started, and they wouldn't have had you around to bail them out."

Wait—what? To heck with her ex and the fight. "You wanted to dance with me?"

"The second that band played anything remotely resembling a slow song. I ignored the beginnings of that fight, because I wanted to see if the band would play something we could dance to. It's the only way to touch a woman you barely know without being too…"

"Handsy?" Dear God, she sounded breathless. She was breathless.

"That's the word."

He'd wanted to touch her from the start. This insane chemistry was the same for both of them.

He didn't reach for her now. Why didn't he reach for her?

"So dancing is an acceptable way to touch a woman you just met." She kept her voice low in the dark.

"Right."

"And we decided keeping someone warm when it's cold out is allowed."

"True." He didn't move.

"Graham." Emily put her palm on his chest and tilted her face up to his. "It's cold out."

Don't miss
How to Train a Cowboy *by Caro Carson,*
available now wherever
Harlequin® Special Edition books and ebooks are sold.

www.Harlequin.com

HARLEQUIN®

SPECIAL EDITION

Life, Love and Family

Save **$1.00**

on the purchase of ANY
Harlequin® Special Edition book.

Available whever books are sold,
including most bookstores, supermarkets,
drugstores and discount stores.

Save $1.00

on the purchase of any Harlequin® Special Edition book.

Coupon valid until September 30, 2018.
Redeemable at participating outlets in the U.S. and Canada only.
Limit one coupon per customer.

52615825

Canadian Retailers: Harlequin Enterprises Limited will pay the face value of this coupon plus 10.25¢ if submitted by customer for this product only. Any other use constitutes fraud. Coupon is nonassignable. Void if taxed, prohibited or restricted by law. Consumer must pay any government taxes. Void if copied. Inmar Promotional Services ("IPS") customers submit coupons and proof of sales to Harlequin Enterprises Limited, P.O. Box 31000, Scarborough, ON M1R 0E7, Canada. Non-IPS retailer—for reimbursement submit coupons and proof of sales directly to Harlequin Enterprises Limited, Retail Marketing Department, 22 Adelaide St. West, 40th Floor, Toronto, Ontario M5H 4E3, Canada.

U.S. Retailers: Harlequin Enterprises Limited will pay the face value of this coupon plus 8¢ if submitted by customer for this product only. Any other use constitutes fraud. Coupon is nonassignable. Void if taxed, prohibited or restricted by law. Consumer must pay any government taxes. Void if copied. For reimbursement submit coupons and proof of sales directly to Harlequin Enterprises, Ltd 482, NCH Marketing Services, P.O. Box 880001, El Paso, TX 88588-0001, U.S.A. Cash value 1/100 cents.

® and ™ are trademarks owned and used by the trademark owner and/or its licensee.

© 2018 Harlequin Enterprises Limited

HSEHOTRCOUP0718

 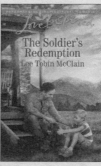
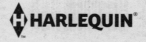

Looking for inspiration in tales
of hope, faith and heartfelt romance?

Check out **Love Inspired**® and
Love Inspired® **Suspense** books!

New books available every month!

CONNECT WITH US AT:

Harlequin.com/Community

Facebook.com/HarlequinBooks

Twitter.com/HarlequinBooks

Instagram.com/HarlequinBooks

Pinterest.com/HarlequinBooks

ReaderService.com

Love Inspired®

LIGENRE2018

Reward the book lover in you!

Earn points on your purchase of new Harlequin books from participating retailers.

Turn your points into **FREE BOOKS** of your choice!

Join for FREE today at
www.HarlequinMyRewards.com.

Harlequin My Rewards is a free program (no fees) without any commitments or obligations.

MYR18